VIRGIN PRINCESS'S MARRIAGE DEBT

PIPPA ROSCOE

DEMANDING HIS DESERT QUEEN

ANNIE WEST

MILLS & BOON

First Published in Great Britain 2019
by Mills & Boon, an imprint of HarperCollins*Publishers*
1 London Bridge Street, London, SE1 9GF

Virgin Princess's Marriage Debt © 2019 by Pippa Roscoe

Demanding His Desert Queen © 2019 by Annie West

ISBN: 978-0-263-27362-5

MIX
Paper from
responsible sources
FSC www.fsc.org FSC™ C007454

Printed and bound in Spain
by CPI, Barcelona

VIRGIN PRINCESS'S MARRIAGE DEBT

PIPPA ROSCOE

For Sharon Kendrick.
Without your amazing, encouraging, supportive advice I
would never have finished this book.
You are a true Modern queen!

PROLOGUE

THEO LOOKED AT his watch again. She was late. This wasn't the first time they'd snuck out of the impossibly expensive Swiss boarding school at night, but this time felt different. She'd said that she had a surprise for him and he couldn't for the life of him figure out what that might have been.

Knowing Sofia, it could be anything. She was like that. Impulsive, reckless, often secretive…and most definitely alluring. It had taken Theo a good long while to believe that she wasn't like the other kids at this school. This school that he hated.

He wasn't naïve. He knew attending a school this reputable was a thing he could not take for granted—even if at every single turn the other students tried to make him believe that he shouldn't be there. It hadn't taken him long to realise that he was not wanted, the poor illegitimate scholarship kid polluting their air. He almost shrugged a shoulder at the train of his thoughts. Why should here be any different to the way he had been brought up in Greece, with his mother's family?

The teachers were hardly any better than the students. If there was something to be blamed, it would be his fault. But they couldn't deny his grades. At seventeen he already had scholarship offers at some of the world's leading universities and there was nothing he'd do to jeopardise that. No, Theo Tersi was going to make damn sure that he never had to return to his mother's family vineyards in the Peloponnese. He would be a banker, something in finance. He wanted an office, like his mother's current employer who had paid for his education here. He would never scrabble around in the dust like his uncles and cousins—the ones who had taunted him since his birth. So, no. He wouldn't fight back against the bullies here. He couldn't. Not without risking everything he'd worked so hard for. Because he wanted more. For his mother, for himself. He wanted never to feel the sting of rejection and shame and hunger... And once he got out of this school, once he finished university, he would make sure that no one would taunt him again.

He looked again at his watch, the round white face gleaming in the moonlight. Where was she? Sofia was usually already waiting for him. He looked around. The night seemed almost unnaturally still, as if it were holding its breath, as if in expectation...

And he felt it too. That anticipation, the moment when he would see Sofia emerging from whatever shrub she was hiding behind. He still had to pinch himself sometimes. Never quite sure if he could really believe that someone like her would really be interested in someone like him. But tonight...he was going to tell her. Tell her that he loved her. That he wanted her to be with him when he left for university...that he wanted the life they had often talked about having in the last six months. Because somehow she'd worked her way through the anger and distrust he'd first met her with, she'd broken down the barriers all the taunts and cruel tricks the other students had thrown his way.

She had been the one bright thing in his days at school

over the last few months. For so long his life had simply been about him and his mother, doing whatever it took to get through the day. He'd hated how his mother was treated by her family...because of him, because of the father he'd never met, and never wanted to. The move from Greece to Switzerland had been a fresh start for them both—the opportunity at this school one almost unimaginable for a housekeeper and her son.

And no matter what people threw at him, Theo was determined to bide his time here, knowing that it would get him to where he wanted to be. But the moment he'd first seen Sofia...the way her oceanic blue eyes had sparkled with mischief, the way his heart had kicked and thrashed, as if for the first time, when her gaze collided with his he had found something more from life than just lessons and determination. And it had never stopped, that heart thumping. He felt that same way every single time he saw her.

She had this air about her, as if nothing bad could ever touch her. And it was addictive. He leant into it every chance he could get. But he worried about her, wanted to protect her from herself even. If the school prankster was caught pulling another stunt, the headmaster had been clear—they would be expelled. He doubted they'd ever guess it was the sweet, innocent-looking blonde angel she appeared to be. But he couldn't deny that it was exactly that strange, thrilling combination of innocence and recklessness that had first drawn him to her.

He wasn't quite sure what it was, but there was also a deep desperation within her. Some kind of urgency that called to him, to his feelings for her...his love. She hadn't said much about her family, dropping little breadcrumbs of information about a loving but strict home that stifled the freedom Sofia loved so much. It certainly didn't sound like something that he would run from. But there would be time to uncover the secrets she held. There would be the rest of their lives.

That he was another of her secrets, he hated… It came far too close to the way he thought his father must have felt in order to flee from their village the same night of his birth. As if there was something about Theo that was shameful or embarrassing somehow.

A noise in the bushes off to his left startled him, his heart racing, knowing that it wouldn't settle until he saw her.

'Tersi. I was told I'd find you here.'

Instead of Sofia's softly accented Iondorran tones, fear sliced through his high hopes as the voice of his headmaster cut into the night.

He didn't move. Not a muscle. His heart dropped, sickness and nausea an instant reaction to being caught doing something he shouldn't be doing. But greater than that was his concern for Sofia.

'What's going on?' Theo ventured to the man who had never liked him.

'What's going on is that I now have my prankster. Did you really think that I would allow my car, *my car*, to be put onto the roof of the sports hall and take no action?'

Theo was shaking his head. 'I don't know anything about that, sir, honestly.'

The grim look of determination on the older man's face told Theo that he wasn't believed. Not for a second. Panic began to set in then.

'Where's Sofia?'

'The princess has returned to Iondorra.'

'Princess? What are you talking about?' Theo demanded, any hesitation overruled by his confusion.

'She didn't tell you?'

'Tell me what? Sir, please—'

'Did you really think that a princess would be interested in…?'

The man must have seen the look on Theo's face, the one he knew had descended as quickly as the fury had whipped within his chest. If there was even a moment of pity, or hesitation from the headmaster, Theo didn't see it.

'Well, it's done. She's gone. And you, skulking around in the shadows waiting to see the effect of your handiwork, will regret the day you pulled this last prank.'

'Mr Templeton, I didn't do anything to your car,' Theo said, desperately trying to hold on to his temper.

'No? Then why is your school scarf wedged underneath the wheel arch of my Mini Cooper?'

'I have no—'

Horror hit Theo hard and fast. The last time he'd seen his scarf he had been looping it around Sofia's neck as she shivered in the cold winter's sun. Sofia had lied to him? She was a princess? It was impossible. But as Theo was marched back to the headmaster's office, his quick mind ran over the images that shifted like a kaleidoscope in his memory. Every interaction, every conversation, every kiss and his stomach turned. Each memory played to the sound of taunts he had never risen to. The cries and jibes of students belittling him for his humble beginnings—ones he had taken because this school had been his ticket out. His way to rise up, no matter what people said or did. But Sofia? She was the one who had wanted to keep their relationship a secret. She was the only one who had known where he would be that night. She was the one who had said she had a surprise for him. She was the one who had been pulling the pranks all this time, and had finally left his scarf at the site of the latest one. Had it all been a ruse? Had she spent the last six months priming him to be the patsy? The fall guy to take the blame for her pranks? Was that why he'd doubted her in the beginning, because somewhere deep down he had known it was all lies? Had she really been the cruellest of them all, to make him fall in love with her, when he should have known better?

He was going to be expelled. He was going to lose everything. Because of her.

CHAPTER ONE

Paris...ten years later

Princess Sofia de Loria of Iondorra looked out across the Parisian skyline as the sun began its slow summer descent over the rooftops and cobbled streets of Europe's reportedly most romantic city. The irony was not lost on her. Tonight she would meet the man she would spend the rest of her life with. Not that romance had anything to do with it. No, that was the domain of Angelique—the practical, determined matchmaker who had been employed for that express purpose.

The hint of jasmine that settled around the room of the luxurious hotel near the Sixth Arrondissement from some invisible air dispenser was nothing like the real thing and Sofia longed to return to her palace in Iondorra. Although she did appreciate the soft white and gold tones of the room and, casting a look to the king-sized bed, her heart lurching, she felt desperate to throw herself amongst the soft pillows and deep comfort offered by the impossibly thick duvet. She had been away too long, immersed in diplomatic duties unruffling more than a few feathers caused by her father's recent and increasing absence from the world's stage. More and more, she found that she just wanted to go home.

She pulled her gaze from the incredible view of the Jardin de Luxembourg and paced towards the larger seating area of the stunning suite. Only yesterday she had been in Prague, two days before that, it had been Istanbul. Her body moved oddly within the costume for that evening's masquerade ball—the full corset holding her back straight and pushing her breasts against the gentle arc of the low, sweeping neckline. She felt confined by it, not that it was an unfamiliar feeling to Sofia. The bustle of material behind her, falling into a wide golden train, made her feel as if she were pulling the weight of more than just her, and Sofia couldn't help but think that it somehow fitted that evening.

The masquerade ball being held to celebrate the birthday of one of Europe's minor royals had presented the perfect opportunity to meet her three would-be suitors without attracting the notice of the world's press, or the intrigue of the very royal and rich society that had been waiting with bated breath to see who the Widow Princess would marry next.

A sliver of pain twisted through her heart as she recalled the description favoured by the international press so much that it had almost become part of her title. Princess Sofia of Iondorra—the Widow Princess.

Every time it was mentioned it was accompanied by images of her in mourning, her pale skin harsh against the depth of the black clothes she had worn to honour her husband. Four years. Antoine had been gone for four years. The familiar sense of grief, softened only slightly over the years, edged around her heart. Theirs might not have been a love match in the truest sense, but Antoine had been her friend, her confidant. He had known about her father's illness and helped shield it from the world. He had supported her through their brief marriage as she adjusted to the reality that she would be queen much sooner than anyone had ever expected.

She missed his quiet support and understanding and once again felt the strange sense of bafflement that had met the news of his shockingly unexpected death at a charity car race. The footage of the six-car pile-up in Le Mans had shocked nations, but only devastated one. Because only Antoine's life had been lost.

But she could not afford to indulge in her grief. Not tonight. Antoine, more than anyone, would understand why she needed to remarry for the good of her country. Her father's illness had deepened in the last few months, and, whether she liked it or not, the council was right. If the news of his illness broke while she was still considered the Widow Princess, then the future of her country would be in serious jeopardy. With a fairly inexperienced prime minister forced into making difficult austerity measures, the monarchy was the only stability and security the people believed in. And the only way Iondorra would survive the impending announcement of her father's diagnosis was if they had some hope for the future—a fairy-tale marriage heralding the next generation of royals.

It hadn't been Antoine's fault that they'd not conceived during their four-year marriage. They had tried a few times, but even Sofia had been forced to admit that neither had been able to bring themselves to actually consummate their marriage. And she knew why. Only once had she experienced a chemistry, an attraction that had been at once all-consuming, that had seemed almost to threaten her very sanity. And it hadn't been with Antoine.

It hadn't taken long before her husband had started to look elsewhere for the pleasure that she simply could not offer him. He'd been so devastatingly discreet and quiet about it all. Every now and then he would disappear for a few days, and return with some impossibly expensive gift, offering it to her with eyes that could never meet her gaze. It hadn't angered her, torn her up inside the way it should have done. Instead, all she'd been able to feel was so very sad for the man she cared for like a friend, like a brother, to be trapped in the same cage she was caught within. Duty. A passionless marriage.

And here she was again, on the brink of yet another one. Wasn't the definition of madness doing the same thing over and over again, expecting a different result?

'Are you ready?' Angelique's voice came from somewhere behind her.

'For the royal equivalent of speed dating?' Sofia asked. 'Yes,' she said, answering her own question, all the while shaking her head to the contrary.

Angelique smiled, the movement softening her features into something more relatable than the fierce businesswoman persona she usually adopted.

'Are you sure this is what you want? We can always cancel, find some other way…'

'Are you trying to do yourself out of a commission? That doesn't seem very wise.'

Angelique cocked her head to one side, quite birdlike. 'My finances are perfectly secure, I assure you, Your Highness. And, as you have requested the utmost secrecy, then so would be my reputation. You *do* have a choice, Sofia.'

But they both knew that was a lie. Sofia looked to the window again, as if it were an exit route, as if she could fly to it and escape from what was about to happen. Because somehow, in some way, Sofia simply couldn't shake the feeling that, after tonight, her life would drastically change.

Yes, she'd have met and chosen the man she would

marry, but it felt bigger than that. It felt as if she were on a precipice but that she couldn't see the edge. And it made her angry. Angry for all the sacrifices she had already made, and the ones she could continue to make in the future. As if a summer thunderstorm had zapped her with a lightning strike, coursing white-hot heat through her veins. But where once she would have vented her anger, her fear, all this impossible-to-express energy, Sofia had to fight it. Princesses didn't get angry. They got married.

'Okay,' Angelique said finally as if, too, sensing there was no going back. 'So, would you like the motivational speech now, Your Highness?'

Sofia couldn't help but smile at the gentle humour in Angelique's tone. It felt like years since someone had laughed with her. It *had* been years.

'What would you like? *Braveheart*-style, Beyoncé *Run the World*, or something *à la* Churchill?'

Sofia let a small, sad laugh escape from her lips. 'I'll forgo the attempt at a Scottish accent, I think. I don't suppose you have anything just for me?' she asked, instantly hating the sense of vulnerability her words evoked.

'I do,' Angelique said, locking serious eyes with hers. 'You will be a great queen. You will care for Iondorra with as great a sense of purpose as any who have gone before you. You will rule her with love and duty and sacrifice, but all of that will ensure Iondorra's longevity amongst the world's greatest nations. And you will do it with a man at your side who will love, honour and protect you in a way that allows *you* to protect *your* country. You, Your Highness, are a force to be reckoned with and my wish for you is that you find a man worthy of that. These three suitors are perfect candidates. They understand your duty, your role in life, and are willing and able to support you in that. And now it is time.'

'To go to the ball, Fairy Godmother?'

'No, Sofia,' Angelique said gently. 'To remove Antoine's ring.'

Sofia's fingers flew to the wedding band around her fourth finger. It felt as sacrilegious to remove it, as much as it was easy for her to do so. Antoine would have understood. She placed the simple wedding band she had worn for eight years on the dressing table and felt a little bit of her past slip away from her grasp.

As Angelique left the room, Sofia returned her watchful gaze to the Parisian rooftops. For just a moment, she had fallen under the spell of the other woman's words, grateful for them, thankful. But that positive determination she had felt fizzing in her veins had disappeared with Angelique's departure. And for the first time in a while, she let the façade drop and allowed the feel of exhaustion to sweep over her. Her father's deterioration had increased in the last few months and propelled the need for the one thing she'd been putting off for several years. The cost of keeping her father's illness a secret had been a great one to pay, but one that she would do again and again. Because the people of Iondorra needed security.

She thought of her little European principality, cradled in between France, Switzerland and northern Italy. The country that she was to rule, protect as if it were her child. The country that, ever since she was seventeen and had been whisked away from her boarding school, she had been trained to protect, ruthlessly sculpted to become the perfect princess.

And then, as always following these moments of weakness, came the inner strength that saw her match even the strongest heads of state at the tables of European negotiations. She, and Iondorra, had no time for selfish, moping thoughts. She'd put those things aside a long time ago. Just as she'd put aside the thoughts of her own happy-ever-after.

Poor little princess, an inner voice mocked, sounding very much like that of a young man she'd long ago loved. A young man she'd been forced to leave behind, lie to, and a man she very much refused to think of now.

She glanced at the embossed invitation, smiling at how the gold detail of the lettering matched the soft golden yellows of the corseted Victorian-era dress she wore, the crinoline underskirt as heavy as a crown.

For so long she'd been cast as the Widow Princess, it had begun to feel as if she'd lost herself. Not that it mattered. The only thing of true importance was Iondorra. And attending the masquerade ball was just the next step towards the throne.

Each of the three men had been carefully vetted and would, in their own ways, be perfectly acceptable candidates for their role as husband. So there she was, in Paris, dressed up and ready to find the man she would spend the rest of her life with. And if she'd once thought she already had, then it didn't matter. Such fanciful daydreams were for others. Real princesses didn't have the luxury of Prince Charmings.

Theo Tersi scanned the expanse of the large Parisian ballroom, took a breath and instantly regretted it. Where he had expected to taste the hint of satisfaction at the thought of what tonight would bring, the only thing on his tongue was the cloying and competing scents of the perfume adorning the many women in the room. It was an assault on his olfactory system and he was half tempted to retreat and preserve that much-needed function. When he would think back to this moment in the months to come, he would wonder if it had been some kind of cosmic sign to turn back. To think again.

But right now, there was no turning back for Theo.

'All right, I'm here,' grouched the exiled Duke of Gaeten.

'You don't need to sound so pleased about it,' Theo said absently, still scanning the faces in the ballroom for the one that he wanted. No, *needed*. 'Surely the great Sebastian Rohan de Luen is not bored in the face of all this as yet untouched potential?'

'Hah,' his friend almost spat. 'You think me jaded?'

'No, as I said. Bored. You need someone to challenge you.'

'And you need to walk away from this madness before it gets us all into trouble.'

Theo turned and cast a look over his closest friend, the only person who had been there for him when his world came crashing down for the second time. They had been in the middle of a business meeting—Theo soliciting a deal that would see the wine from his vineyard served at Sebastian's Michelin-starred hotels scattered across the globe—when he had received the call from the hospital informing him of his mother's admittance and diagnosis. The bottom had literally dropped out of his world, and Sebastian? Had chartered a private plane to return him to Greece and, rather than simply letting that be the end of it, had contracted Theo's vineyard to his hotels. It had been the only thing that had saved Theo and his business from the wolves—but more importantly it had provided him with enough capital to pay for his mother's healthcare. Without that contract, he would have lost the vineyard, would have lost the roof over his and his mother's heads, and possibly would have lost his mother. And Theo had never forgotten it, and would never. Their relationship had quickly grown from business to brotherhood and, despite the awful foundation of its start, he wouldn't regret it. It had been his salvation in the years since.

But, throughout that dark time, Theo had only seen one face, one person to blame, one person who had lied to him, set him up to take full blame for her actions, and had singlehandedly ruined his life. Had it not been for her, he would have finished his education—would have attended one of the finest universities the world had to offer, and would have been able to provide his mother with more, with better. He would never have been in a position where he could have lost it all. And that fear, the fear of nearly losing his mother, had changed him, had transformed his DNA. Never again would he be the naïve youth he had once been. Never again would he be that *innocent*.

Sofia was the origin point of the change in the course of his life, one that had only exacerbated his mother's later illness. He hadn't been surprised when the doctor had explained that the stresses of the last few years had taken their toll on his mother's already weak heart. The shock of losing her job after his expulsion, the struggle of the following years… Had he not met Sofia, he would never have lost everything he'd held within his grasp—the opportunities, the chances he had been given to be and do better than either he or his mother could have ever expected. Naïve and foolish, he had believed every single one of Sofia's lies before she disappeared, making a mockery of all those words of love, of a future she would never give him—could never have been able to give—when he finally discovered the truth about her.

Oh, he had thought her to be so different to the cruel students of the international boarding school his mother's employer had sponsored him to attend, but at least they had owned their cruelty. No—Sofia's had been worse, because she had hidden her betrayal until the last moment, she had purposefully set him up to take the blame for her reckless actions and he had been expelled.

And the shame he'd felt when he realised he had lost it all? The anger that had coursed through his veins when he realised her words, her touches had been nothing more than a game to be played by a bored and spoilt princess? It had been nothing compared to the moment where his heart had shattered into a thousand pieces. The moment he'd seen the announcement of her engagement. To be betrayed by someone he had…he could no longer bring himself to say the word. He forced his thoughts fiercely away from reflections that would only see him lose his temper. And if anything was to be lost tonight, it couldn't be that.

'I spent years—*years*—watching and waiting to see if I would lose this…need for vengeance.' He had thrown himself into any willing woman he could find in an attempt to erase the memory of her. He hadn't managed to turn his tastes to the blonde hair that seemed dull and lifeless in comparison to the lustre his memories had endowed *her* with. Blue eyes seemed bland and insipid against the sparkle and shine of the strange combination of intelligence and recklessness that seemed unique only to her. Brunettes were the only way forward through those dark, hedonistic two years as he had tried and failed to satiate the wild, driving need for her…for revenge that had all but consumed him.

'Two years in which you developed a truly debauched reputation,' Sebastian said, cutting through his thoughts.

'You sound jealous.'

'I am. How on earth am I supposed to be the most

notorious playboy in Europe, if you are there competing for that same title?'

Theo couldn't help but smile.

'But,' Sebastian said, his mocking gaze growing serious, 'despite all that, my sister doesn't seem to have realised that she will never have your heart.'

'I don't have a heart to give, Sebastian,' he growled, 'but I will speak to Maria. I had hoped that it might dissipate with time, but—'

'I know you do not encourage it,' Sebastian said, slinging an arm around Theo's shoulders. 'Truly. But she is still very much…'

Clearly unable or unwilling to describe the extent of Maria's infatuation with Theo, Sebastian trailed off.

'It will be done. *Kindly*,' Theo assured him.

He liked Maria, but no matter how much he resisted her somewhat naïve attempts to pursue him, nor how many headlines proclaimed him to be just as debauched as her brother, she had not been put off. Yet. Depending on how tonight would go, it could be the final nail in the coffin of her yearning for him.

Apparently appeased, Sebastian replaced his mask and turned back to the party. Following his lead, Theo took a glass of the prosecco and bit back the curse that Europe's insistence that the masses should drink the alcohol like water had clearly infiltrated this Parisian ballroom too. Yes, he made his money with wine, but his tastes ran to whisky this evening, and right now he'd give someone else's kingdom for one.

Theo took in the glamorous couples, the range of costumes that were everything from the sublime to outrageous, but never ridiculous. The sheer extravagance and money in the room saw to that. His quick mind calculated the cost of such an event. The room hire, the staff, the overpriced and frankly unpalatable alcohol being served, all of it would fund a thousand small businesses well into the next year, a fact probably not even considered by the birthday girl's family.

After he'd spent the first few years of his adult life weighing up every single decision, every single purchase, his ability to price almost anything was ingrained. Deeply. From the moment he had returned to Greece with his mother after his expulsion from school, the shame he had brought to the family who had funded his education there, the termination of his mother's employment, and the return to the people who had rejected them both ever since his conception…he had never lost the taste of bitterness in his mouth, no matter how rich, sweet or satisfying the grape or wine he produced.

After initial notoriety as the young vintner shocking the international wine industry—and his mother's family—with the incredible popularity of his Greek blended wine, he had proved himself time and time again. And despite the almost constant criticism proclaiming his success as a flash in the pan—as if it hadn't taken blood, sweat, his mother's tears—even after eight years in the profession, he was still seen as the most upsetting thing to happen in the wine world since the invention of screwtop caps. That he'd dared to produce an award-winning blended wine rather than that of a pure grape somehow suited his own illegitimate status. That he persevered with blended wines seemed only to infuriate the old-school vintners who sniffed and huffed as he dominated the market, proclaiming him a young upstart. He didn't feel young. Especially as he cast a frowning glance around the fancy frippery of the masked ball in Paris. No. He just felt jaded.

None of these people would have given him the time

of day before he'd found his success, and Theo now returned the favour, ignoring the lascivious glances cast his way. Instead of firing his blood, they only turned him cold. If he was honest, not since he was seventeen had he felt the heat of passion truly stir. Desire? Yes. The arousal of attraction? Of course. But never need. Never passion. And he fiercely reminded himself that he liked it that way. Because the last time he had felt that had heralded the destruction of every hope and dream he and his mother had ever held.

And now he was on the brink of facing his demon, he had to remind himself that he was not a monster. That *he* was not as cruel as she had been. As if sensing his resolve, Sebastian turned to him with a raised eyebrow in query.

'I will give her one chance,' Theo said, forcing his eyes back to the ballroom, back to his prey. 'If she apologises for what she did, then I will walk away, no harm, no foul.' But if she didn't, then Sofia de Loria would rue the day she had crossed him and finally learn the consequences of her actions.

CHAPTER TWO

As Sofia stepped away from the second of the would-be suitors with a resigned smile, she realised that she was losing hope. Neither he nor the first were right and she couldn't help but feel that she was expecting the impossible. She was the worst Goldilocks ever. But as much as she didn't want to rush into another marriage, she didn't have a choice.

She hung back around the edges of the grand ballroom, thankful that she was hidden amongst the crowds of people watching the figures making their way round the dance floor. She had dismissed her personal assistant in order to speak to the suitors alone, and relished the opportunity for the closest thing to anonymity she'd experienced in almost ten years. The fine golden leaf-like swirls of her mask tickled at the edges of her hair, but she would take that minor discomfort for the concealment it offered. It swept upward, asymmetrically, to one side, and matched the colour of her dress perfectly.

Sofia bit back a laugh as she imagined for a moment that this would be how a wallflower, found between the pages of some historical romance, felt. Both terrified and hopeful of being plucked from obscurity to dance beneath the candlelit chandeliers by the handsome prince. But hers wasn't that kind of story. No, *she* was the royal and it seemed that the second sons, or cousins—like the two previous candidates who had seemed so fine on paper— had quite definitive ideas about *their* place within *her* royal office.

She had never wanted it. Not in truth. As a child, she had hardly been perfect princess material. Her parents had despaired and sent her to boarding school, tired of having to bribe the Iondorran press to silence yet another social faux pas on their daughter's behalf. For security reasons they had all agreed to keep her royal status a secret. But for Sofia it hadn't been about a desire for protection, it had been her last attempt for something normal, to be treated like anyone else. But ultimately that had backfired in the most spectacularly painful way.

She became aware of the feeling of someone watching her. As a princess, she was reluctantly familiar with the sensation, but this was different. This *felt* different. The hairs on her arms lifted beneath the unseen gaze, and her pulse picked up at her neck almost painfully. She couldn't shake the feeling that she was somehow being sought out...*hunted*.

She cast a glance around the room to see if she could identify the source. A sea of vivid masks and incredible costumes greeted her, and she caught herself in the unconscious protective movement she hated as her hand went to soothe the phantom sensitivity at her ribs caused by that awful night a year and a half ago.

She was surrounded by people, all engaged in conversations, bodies pressed closer together by the illicit nature given to the mass by the disguise of masks and costumes, but none seemed to be looking her way.

Discarding the feeling as foolish, much like her earlier impression that somehow her life was going to change irrevocably, she searched for Angelique, who had gone to locate her final suitor, but saw no sign of either of them. As the orchestra picked up the threads of a familiar waltz a feeling of nostalgia swept over her.

She could only hold out hope for this final suitor, because without him her country would be left vulnerable and she couldn't, wouldn't, allow that to happen.

It was not her father's fault that he'd been diagnosed with early-onset dementia. But she couldn't help but feel responsible that she hadn't been ready to assume royal duties earlier to prevent the extreme financial loss her country had experienced under his unstable reign. Feel embarrassed that she had been so carefree and reckless as to need two years of strong, mindful guardianship to ensure that she wouldn't bring further damage to Iondorra as every wilful, mindless frippery was ironed out of her character. Feel that sense of guilt that the necessary secrecy of her father's ill health had continued for so long...the silence almost as painful as the disease itself. For surely if she had been a better princess, a better ruler, they wouldn't have had to indulge in this secrecy?

She thought of her mother, tucked away in the privacy of the smaller holdings of the royal family in Iondorra, imprisoned with her husband and a handful of staff and medical professionals ready to manage and care for whatever latest outpouring of anger, frustration or confusion her father experienced almost daily now.

She knew she needed to accept the grief at the loss of a man who had once been a loving father and a fantastic ruler, but she just couldn't. She had grown to almost resent the days of coherence as much as the ones where all semblance of his sanity was lost. They were the ones that she hated most. When she saw her father once again as the man who had loved her, laughed with her, despite the strict requirements he needed her to adhere to. Of course, that was before the diagnosis and her sudden and shocking departure from the international boarding school. Ever since then her life had become one solely of duty.

A waiter paused by her side, offering her a glass of prosecco. She knew that she needed to keep a clear head for this evening, but she couldn't help but clasp the fine glass stem, relishing the cool liquid as it fizzed and bubbled on her tongue.

She was just about to leave the confines of the crowd around her when the hairs on her neck lifted once again and she felt enveloped by the warmth from a body close behind her. Shocked at the proximity of the unseen figure, she breathed in, ready to turn, when the musky, earthy scent of cologne hit her and held her still. It was unfamiliar amongst the sickly sweet, almost chemical fragrance of many of the men here. He waited, as if allowing her to become familiar with his presence, before sweeping around to stand in front of her and bowing long and low. As he straightened and held a hand out to her, she took in the way the white mask disguised his face and almost smiled as his head cocked to one side towards the dance area. The gesture seeming both inquisitive and vaguely arrogant at the same time. A challenge almost, as if daring her to refuse his request.

A feeling familiar, yet so distant as to almost be heartbreaking, rose in her chest. Defiance, recklessness and something more…something almost tantalising made her reach out, made her place her hand in his, even though no word had been spoken, even though the mask he wore concealed his identity. As his fingers closed over hers and he led her towards the dance area she felt a strange sense of vertigo, reminding her of the precipice she had imagined herself upon earlier that evening.

Her thoughts were sent scattering and fleeing as the

figure released her to bring her whirling around in such a way that she had to press her hand to the man's chest in order to prevent herself from crashing into him and losing her balance and breath in one move.

The warmth that greeted the palm of her hand through the thin shirt burned her, sending tingles and fire bursts across her skin and neck, raising a blush of sudden and shocking heat to her cheeks. But, as she went to pull back, his hand came down against hers, anchoring it in place. She stared at his fingers, unaccountably reluctant to see the face of her captor. The deep tan spoke of sunshine and heat, and her eyes snagged on the roughly calloused skin covering the powerful hand.

As the music began he pulled her hand away from his chest into the traditional hold for the waltz as warmth and something else, something almost dizzying, spun out from his hold at her back. The positioning was wrong—his hand too close to the base of her spine to be appropriate for strangers, almost possessive in a way that fired her blood and sent a thrill through her that settled horrifyingly low within her. But that was madness. Surely she couldn't be feeling the stirrings of desire for a complete stranger?

His hold was firm, commanding, and, God help her, she relished it, welcomed it, the need to give herself over to this one stolen moment, for someone else to take the weight of responsibility and duty that almost crippled her. Hidden by the disguise of her mask, she was convinced that this man had no idea who she was. He couldn't, because surely he wouldn't behave so daringly with a princess? And the freedom that thought offered sang in her veins. That just for this moment she could be something other than the Widow Princess. Simply Sofia—herself, a woman with nothing more on her mind than dancing with a handsome man. For despite the mask he wore, she could tell he *was* handsome. The breadth of him, the smoothness of his skin, the inherent confidence more appealing than any physique she could determine. Her heart kicked within her chest as the stranger guided her into the first steps of the waltz, and she raised her gaze, expecting to find him looking down at her intently.

But he wasn't.

She traced the angle of his neck with her eyes, the fine, straight cord powerful and determined, to a jaw that was stubbled in a way that almost wilfully challenged propriety. Treated only to his profile, she consumed every inch of what she could see, and her body reacted as if it had been starved of the sight of it. Which made no sense.

The turn of his head hid the bare section of the mask she recognised from a well-known musical, concealing much of what she could see. His eyes were focused on some distant point on the other side of the room and the heady scent of him filled her lungs as she breathed through the steps of the dance.

There was something almost cold about the way his head was turned away from her…as if, despite the intimacy of the hold, he was *forcing* himself to touch her. And suddenly she felt nauseous. As if her body had somehow tricked her, fooled her into thinking that… what? That her Prince Charming had finally come for her? As if sensing her sudden resistance, her attempt to flee before it had even registered in her mind, he tightened his embrace, all the while remaining turned away from her.

Realising the futility of escape, she used the time to observe the stranger. He was tall, at least six feet, if not more. His shoulders, though pressed back in a perfect frame for the waltz, somehow managed to crowd her in a way that made her, made *them*, feel isolated from the other couples on the dance floor. He led her almost expertly through the movements of the dance and her body's muscle memory bowed to his command. While her mind raced with outrage and confusion that she would be so ignored, so manhandled, her body soared at the unspoken dominance.

The stranger had yet to say a word to her and somehow that made this moment all the more surreal, as if they had mutually agreed that speaking would break this strange spell that he was weaving around her. She knew she should break it though, she knew she should be outraged, terrified even, but there was something… the breadth of him, the feel of his hand within hers…both strange and familiar.

She felt known by him, even if she did not know him. She began to count down the steps to the end of the dance, recognising the cadence and swell of the music as her pulse beat within her chest in time with the waltz, in time with him.

She didn't know what to expect when the dance came to an end. Would he finally speak? Would he look at her, or would he disappear as easily as he had swept her towards the dance floor? She both longed for and resisted the end to this moment and as he brought their steps to a close, bowed, deep and low, her curtsey only half what it should be, because she had yet to be able to take her gaze from finally seeing who this stranger was.

Only when their eyes met, a sob escaped her mouth as she caught the devastating brown orbs, dark against the pure white of the mask, and she was filled with a fury and anger that stole her breath. She actually felt the single lost heartbeat caused by the jolt of recognition.

Theo Tersi.

* * *

Theo had feared that he might not recognise her here amongst the disguises and outrageous costumes of such rich company. He had lost Sebastian to his own personal pursuits some half an hour before, and had been beginning to lose patience. It had to be tonight. It had to be now. Everything in him had been building to this moment for years. He would not let this chance pass.

In truth, it was his body that had recognised her first. The way his pulse unaccountably hitched in his chest, the way awareness had pulled from him an almost electric current that snapped and hissed across his skin. And when he finally did see her, clinging to the edges of the ballroom, he knew that he shouldn't have doubted himself. Even had he not gone to sleep each night for ten years with her face the last thing he saw, the lies and abused promises on her lips the last thing he heard, he would have known her in the dark surrounded by a thousand people. Because she shone like a beacon of pure golden light and he bitterly noted that it had nothing to do with her costume. She had looked like the stepdaughter in the Mother Holle story told to him by his mother in childhood—the one who passed beneath a waterfall of gold. Yet he knew better. She was the other sister—the one who should have been covered in tar.

He hadn't intended to lead her into the waltz, but the moment the idea struck, it wouldn't loosen its grip on his mind. He knew that she wouldn't recognise him, certainly not if he kept his head turned away from her. She probably hadn't given him a second thought since setting him up to take the fall for her pranks. Or maybe she had, laughing to herself long and hard at how she'd manipulated him, how she'd got him to do her bidding.

Holding her and not looking at her had been a sweet

torture. He'd wanted to bare his gaze to her, bore into her the feelings of anger, pain and betrayal… But when he had finally met her eyes, holding them captive with his own, he'd nearly cursed. Because it was he who consumed every emotion that flickered and sparked in her sapphire-blue eyes.

After all these years he'd thought himself immune to her. He'd thought the consequences of her actions would have made him impenetrable to the insatiable desire for her…but the way her body had melted into his, the flickering of her pulse beneath his hand, mocked him as his body had claimed her in the most primal of ways. Because no matter what had passed between them, his body still wanted her, still craved her touch.

Until the jolt of recognition from Sofia that he felt against his skin, the irrefutable horror that filled her gaze.

Now she knew him.

He was about to open his mouth, when her sudden, shocking departure slammed it shut. She had picked up her skirts and was racing away from the ballroom floor, disappearing into the crowd of people. But she would not get away that easily. He saw her at the wide French doors, open to the beckoning darkness of the gardens, and a smile curved the edges of his lips.

Theo Tersi drew out his mobile phone, and as he followed her out into the night he fired off a text to the man he had waiting on standby. If she failed to offer him the apology he so very much deserved, Sofia de Loria would regret the day she had ever thought to play him.

Plunged into the darkness of the Parisian night, he stalked amongst the manicured gardens, expecting to have to hunt much more than he did, and nearly crashed into her.

'What are you doing here?' Sofia demanded, appar-

ently satisfied that there were no longer people to over-
hear them as her raised voice was carried away on the
night air. Her outrage struck him low in the chest.

'Why? Not used to discovering an ill-bred bastard
amongst your high-society companions?'

'What?' He noticed her brow pucker in momentary
confusion. 'That has nothing to do with anything.'

'No? I'd have thought your security teams would have
vetted every single person here, check their DNA for their
blue-blood credentials.'

'Don't be such a snob.'

Now *he* was outraged. 'How dare you accuse me of
being a snob?'

'Just because it's reverse snobbery, it doesn't make it
any less prejudicial.'

'You're speaking nonsense.'

'Because I disagree with you? You never did—'

'Don't. Do not talk to me of what I did or did not do
in the past,' he spat as he lifted his mask away from his
face and cast it aside onto the thick emerald grass of the
gardens.

He watched her almost physically bite her tongue and
he used the moment to take her in. The Sofia he knew
had been breathtaking, but Sofia de Loria the Princess
was obscenely beautiful. Her cheeks had lost some of the
softness, striking cheekbones sculpting her face to perfection. The thick plaits of golden hair wrapped around
her head glowed silver in the starlight of the night sky.
A high brow made even more superior with the arch of
a perfect, rich, honeyed eyebrow peeking out from the
top of the mask, brilliant golden furls glinting in the
moonlight.

And, as always, crystal-blue eyes crackled and sparked
as she tried to repress the anger she clearly felt. An anger

he matched, if not exceeded. Oh, he'd had his share of beautiful women in the last two years, once he'd given himself permission to relish and enjoy the success that all his hard work had reaped. Once he'd lifted his self-imposed embargo on sensual pursuits. But no matter how many times he'd cursed her to hell and back, he'd never been able to deny Sofia's beauty.

But even in that he knew he lied to himself. It wasn't just a simple fact of her beauty. It was as if a chemical reaction had ignited within him, fizzing in his veins, urging him to reach out and touch her. Draw her to him and seek her mouth, her kiss…to feed the burning arousal he had really only ever felt with this woman. He wanted her, needed her, with every ounce of his being. But he fought it. He would *not* give in to the temptation she unconsciously offered.

Sofia felt her chest heave against the confines of the tight corset as her body struggled for an outlet for the anger and pure shock at Theo's appearance. Masked, he was impressive. Unmasked he was undeniable. Age had only honed what were already incredible features. Even in his youth he had stood heads above even the older students, and now she had to crane her neck to look up at his scowling gaze, his deep brown irises swirling like the richest espresso. His clenched jaw was dusted with a fine dark stubble as if, even in that, Theo rejected the same propriety that saw every other man there either clean-shaven or fully bearded. His straight nose created a sense of balance between the downward slashes of his cheekbones, and the night cast his proud jaw in deep shadows.

In obvious frustration he ran his hand through his thick hair and on any other man the result would have looked chaotic, but on Theo? It just made Sofia want to reach out and do the same. He was magnificent and for a second she imagined that she could reach for him, that she could draw him to her. Desire, thick and fast, rose up within her chest, even as she knew that she could not act upon it, should not feel it.

She tried not to flinch at the sound of apparent disgust as he finally turned that lethal focus of his to her, casting the entire length of her body in a glance that was anything but lazy, or accidental. No. There was purpose to this...to make her uncomfortable, and she hated that it was working.

'If you've had your fill and there's nothing else?' She refused to stand there before his assessment and be found wanting. She just couldn't. Not tonight. She still had to meet with Joachim, the third possible suitor, her last hope. She could not stand here caught between the past and her future—it was threatening to tear her apart.

Sofia turned to leave, but his hand snuck out and caught her at her wrist. His hold deceptively gentle. The delicate ring his fingers created around her skin thrummed with repressed tension. He tugged, and she almost fell against his chest and this time she just managed to stop her hand from leaning on his chest for...balance, she told herself. Balance.

With her hand still hovering mid-air between them, she risked a glance at his face. It was so close, angled down at her, lips that once she would have delighted in now cruelly sensual and taunting her with a knowing smile. But the anger in his eyes was easier to read than her own reaction, and she welcomed it, embraced it, used it to fuel her now.

'I'm here for an apology.'

'An apology?' Sofia didn't know how he'd caused her to revert to the stammering seventeen-year-old she'd once been. More than a decade of training, diplomacy, education and learning trade negotiations and she seemed only capable of two words around this man.

She knew she owed Theo an apology…more than that. An explanation at the very least, but before she could summon the words to her lips, he pressed on.

'You doubt it?'

'No, not at all, I—'

'Do you know what I regret most? That even as I waited the first hour for you, the second, hidden amongst that ridiculous shrubbery, I didn't even doubt you. It didn't even cross my mind that you wouldn't show. I waited, like a moon-eyed calf, half drunk on love for you. Even afterwards, when the headmaster came to find me, told me of the trick *you* pulled on his car, my first concern was for you, not for myself. My fear was that something had happened to you.'

She felt shame slash across her cheeks in a dark crimson blush, painful and stinging, as if he had slapped her with his hands rather than his words. And all the wishes, wonderings and dreams of what happened to him that night were painted in stark reality by his words.

'It didn't take me long to realise, though. Realise what you had done that night and in the weeks, months leading up to it. To realise that everything you had told me was lies, *Your Highness.*'

Secrets and lies had come back to haunt her and Sofia turned her head away, but his fingers, once again seemingly gentle, but determined, found her chin, and brought her back round to face him, to see the truth written in his eyes.

'Can you imagine what it was like to realise that I had fallen in love with a fabrication? That everything I'd felt was simply the by-product of the ruse of a bored, pampered princess with nothing more to do with her time than to move people around a chessboard of her own imagination? That I was expelled because of *your* actions?'

Shock reared through her, and she stepped back as if she could distance herself from what he was saying.

'I didn't—'

'You didn't know?' he demanded harshly, his fury palpable, shaking the very air between them. 'You didn't even know?' He cursed harshly. 'You all but ensured it when you left my scarf, *my* scarf, beneath the car. Tell me, did you even think of me when you ran back to your country playing the part of the perfect princess as I was kicked out of school? When I lost the scholarships to every single university I had gained entry to? When my mother was fired and we were forced to return to her family with little more than what we could carry? I thought of you, all the while knowing that everything we had lost, every struggle we experienced, was because of your lies!'

Sofia was struck dumb by the pain his words evoked, and the truth that lay within them. She hadn't known that he had been expelled, she hadn't even remembered that she'd been wearing his scarf when she pulled the prank with the car. Because that night, in between her plan to get revenge against the headmaster and meeting Theo, her parents had come to the school and revealed that her father had been diagnosed with early onset dementia. And in that moment, the bottom had fallen out of her world.

Every thought, hope and dream she'd ever held in her heart since falling in love with Theo had flashed through her mind, while she should have been focusing on the physical and mental sentence that had been handed to her father. That the entire time her parents had patiently tried to explain what that meant, what would happen, how she would have to ascend to the throne much sooner than anyone had ever planned for, all she had thought of was him. Theo. Standing there, waiting for her to come.

She had begged and pleaded with her parents to allow her to speak to Theo. To find him where he waited for her. To tell him what was happening. But her father had been uncompromising—no one could know of his diagnosis. No one. And then they had bundled her into a car, and then a private jet, and the whole time she had felt as if she had left her heart behind.

So, no. She hadn't thought of what had happened to him after that night, because she couldn't. She just couldn't allow herself to go there. Because every time she did, what little remained of her heart fractured and shattered just a little bit more.

But she couldn't explain that to Theo. Not now. Because her father's diagnosis still had the power to rock the already shaky foundations of her precious country. Because this? This moment between them wasn't about her or what she could say to justify what had happened that night. This was about him, and God help her, but she deserved every single word, every single feeling he expressed. She needed to honour that, because it was the only thing she would ever be able to give him.

'Tell me, Sofia, did you mean any of it? The pleas you made, the plans…the future you fabricated, all the while knowing it was impossible? Punctuating lies with kisses? Untruths with touches and caresses? When did you know that you would ruin me, Sofia? Before you first spoke to me, or when you realised how easily manipulated I would be?'

'That is enough,' Sofia commanded, digging through

the hurt to find some kind of strength to ward off the harshness of his words.

'Enough? I've barely even begun. *"Please take me away, Theo, I cannot return to Iondorra, Theo. Help me. Theo."'* The cruel mockery his voice made of her childhood words stung as much as the memory of her desperation to escape the confines of a royal life she had been forced to accept.

Theo knew that he had gone too far. He had said too much. Revealed too much of his own pain and heartbreak. And he hated himself for that. He saw the moment that his words hit home, the shimmer of unshed tears in her eyes more bright than any star that night. He cursed, the breeze carrying it away from them. He steeled himself against the innate sympathy welling within him, knowing better this time than to fall for her games.

'*Christós,* I didn't know you at all, did I?'

Suddenly the cord that had bound them in the past snapped, pinging away under the pressure of a decade of hurt and distance between them. And he watched, half fascinated as that royal mantle settled once more around her shoulders, leaving no trace of the young girl he had once loved. Instead, a fury stood before him, iron will steeling her spine and her body as if no soft movement had ever settled beneath her skin.

'You are right. You did not know me. You knew a child. A girl who was reckless, pulled pranks and gave no heed to the people or things about her. A pampered young woman, who knew nothing of real life, or consequences. I am sorry if that girl hurt you, caused you pain. Truly. But she is gone, living only in your memories and imagination.'

It wasn't enough. It wasn't nearly enough, her half

apology. Pain reared its ugly head. Not for the loss of her, he assured himself, but the years he endured after her. The years his mother endured. They did *not* live solely in his imagination. They were etched across his heart and hands as he had clawed his way to where he stood today.

'Now, if you don't mind—'

'Off to find your next husband?'

She stilled her entire body. It was unusual for her, because everything about her contained a restless energy, its sudden and shocking absence such a stark contrast, and for a moment he could have been forgiven for thinking she'd turned to stone.

'How do you...?'

He huffed out a cynical laugh. 'Still keeping your secrets and lies close to your chest? Well, this time I've made sure that I will not fall for either. Unlike whatever poor bastard you've chosen for your next target.'

'Target?' she sighed, a scoffing sound that grated on his ears. It was too similar to the dismissive gestures of people who had thought themselves better than him. 'You know nothing, Theo. Nothing of duty, of sacrifice. Nothing of what needs to be done as a royal.'

'You think your concerns above those of mine?' he demanded.

'Yes,' she said simply. 'Yes, I do. I have to.'

'You once begged to wear *my* ring,' he said, cursing the moment of weakness that allowed his inner thought to escape his lips. 'And instead you married that insipid—'

'Do not speak of him like that,' she commanded.

'Why not? I saw the pictures. Hell, the world saw the pictures of you together. You might as well have been siblings for all the connection you seemed to share. And after his death? You were the Widow Princess who never cried, for all you may try to profess your love for him.' If it had not been so dark, Theo might have seen how Sofia paled beneath the moonlight, might have seen how much his barb had hit home. 'Tell me, Sofia, did he ever make your pulse race, your body throb with desire? Did you ever crave his touch as you professed to crave mine?'

Theo caught the gasp that fell from Sofia's lips, proving the truth of his words and enflaming the sensual web weaving between them, as if he had conjured the very reaction from her body by his words.

Anger, frustration and desire burned heavily on the air between them, and his eyes caught the rise and fall of her perfect breasts against the curve of the corseted dress she wore. Their argument had drawn them closer together, and he could have sworn he felt the press of her chest against his through the mere inches of air that separated them, thickening his blood and his arousal instantly.

'Do you remember, Sofia? What is was like between us? Or were you faking everything?' he demanded. Because somewhere, deep down, he needed to know. He needed to know if it had all been lies. Before him, Sofia swayed, caught within the same tide of desire that he felt pulling at his entire being.

Her lips parted, shining slightly as if recently slicked with her tongue, and he was desperate to taste, to touch, to consume. He needed to know if this time, with all the knowledge he now had, he would be able to taste the lies on her tongue.

His mind roared against it, but his body closed the distance between them, unable to resist the feel of her, the siren's call she seemed to pull him in with. Surely his memory had exaggerated the way she had made him feel. Surely it could never have been that incredible.

He watched her closely, the way her eyes had widened as he'd moved closer, the way she too struggled with the thick, heavy want wrapping around them both. And he saw the moment she gave in to it. Gave in to the silent demand he hated his body for making.

He gave her the space of one breath, to turn, to flee, to refuse him. He gave himself that time, to turn back, to walk away. But when her pupils widened, that breath she took a sharp inhale, all but begging him to press the advantage, to make good on his unspoken promise, he was lost to the need pulsing in his chest. Lost to the insanity of what had been, what now was, between them.

'Tell me you don't want me, don't want my kiss. Tell me, Sofia, and I'll walk away. *Lie* to me again, Sofia,' he challenged.

'I can't,' she whispered, as if hating herself for the confession.

His arm swept around her small frame, drawing her to him and him into madness as his lips descended on hers with ten years of pent-up frustration, anger and a raging need that even the sweep of her tongue against his could not appease.

Passion and desire crackled in the air as they came together, her touch as bruising as his, the almost painful clash of lips, tongues, the merciful bite of teeth that brought clarity as much as it brought confusion.

He had thought himself lost, but a small part of him whispered instead that he'd been found. Found within her, the scent of her winding around him, pulling him even deeper into the kiss. It was everything he remembered and more. His pulse beat erratically in his ears, as if in warning, but it was drowned out by the gentle, almost pleading moans she made into his mouth. But whether Sofia was begging for more or less, he couldn't tell. And that was what made him pull away.

He wrenched himself back, shocked by the intensity

of what they had shared, Sofia, looking equally stunned, her mouth quickly covered by the back of her wrist, pressing their kiss to her lips or swiping it away, he couldn't tell. He needed to sever whatever hold this madness had on him and quickly.

'Now, there's the Sofia I remember.'

'You bastard,' she cried and ran from the gardens towards the safety of the ballroom.

And he knew that, for possibly the first time in any of her exchanges, she had spoken the truth. He was a bastard. Because even as he had lost himself to the kiss, lost himself to the chaotic emotions storming within his chest, his mind was moving at the speed of light.

Because now, it was too late for her. The moment Sofia had issued that half-mustered apology had sealed her fate as surely as the shutter on the camera of the paparazzo Theo had hired to capture the moment of her compromise.

He let loose a bitter laugh. He had hoped that an image of them in a heated argument would do damage enough, but a kiss? So much better for his plan of revenge.

Yes. Sofia de Loria would very much regret the day she had ever thought to play him the fool.

CHAPTER THREE

*Widow Princess Caught in Clinch with
Wine Playboy!*

*From Widow Princess to
Scandalous Princess in One Kiss!*

*Widow Princess Tames Bad Boy
of the Wine Industry!*

THE HEADLINES SCREAMED in Sofia's mind, punctuated by
exclamation marks that struck almost physical blows as
she threw down the collection of newspapers unceremoniously handed to her by the royal council earlier that
day. She peered through the window of the car and cast
a glance up and down one of Monaco's most famous
streets. The light illuminating the Plaza del Casino de
Mónaco caused the water feature in the centre to sparkle
in the night like a thousand diamonds.

And each and every glint scratched against her already
frayed nerves and temper.

It wasn't the fact that she had been captured in a
kiss with one of Europe's most notorious playboys, and
splashed across the front pages for the world to see. It
wasn't even the fact that the morning after the party,

Joachim—her third and last hope for a fiancé—had regrettably informed Angelique that he could no longer consider matrimony with Sofia.

It was the fact that Theo Tersi—notorious womaniser—had refused to comment. And he *always* commented. By neither confirming nor denying their speculative questions, he had served only to inflame the rabid press. The Iondorran privy council had further tied her hands and refused to allow a statement to be issued by the royal communications office in a desperate act of blind ignorance, wilfully hoping that it would all 'blow over'.

But she knew better. Because the sneaking suspicion that had begun the first moment she'd seen the awful photographs had grown into a living, breathing belief that Theo Tersi had somehow managed to orchestrate this whole disaster. The birthday party in Paris had been under a strict press embargo, the girl's family having sold the rights for images to *Paris Match*. Furthermore, the only photos surfacing from that night were of them—no other guests—despite the fact that Sofia was aware of at least three front-page headline-worthy incidents. In the last three weeks she had stopped wondering how and instead focused on the why.

She bit back a distinctly unladylike growl as she exited the dark diplomatic-plated sedan, remembering how she had held herself that night as her body trembled after their conversation, after their kiss, as it shook at how he had weakened her. For the hours following, her body left overly sensitised, she had found herself pressing her fingers to her mouth as if in denial or longing, she couldn't tell, and no matter how much she wished it the low, aching throb between her legs and in her chest had both shocked and terrified her. She had allowed herself that night to feel, to ache, to want. But in the morning when she had seen the headlines, something within her had turned to steel. Sofia dismissed the guards she usually travelled with. She did not want an audience for what was about to happen.

She cast a glance up and down the stunning architecture of the buildings gathered around Monaco's famous gambling district. She had never been anywhere like it. People filled the streets, couples holding hands, groups of men stalking the bars and cafes brimming with tourists and celebrities. Their excitement was infectious, but she resisted the instinct to relish in their levity, instead clinging to her incredulity that Theo would do something so…so…

Theo had resisted every single attempt she had made to contact him. Email, telephone, text message…she had dismissed the idea of carrier pigeon as ridiculous. In the last two days he had repeatedly posted images of himself on Twitter at some of the many casinos in Monaco, and finally, just an hour ago, she had located this club as his current place of residence, if the latest Victoria's Secret model to hit the headlines was to be believed.

Two blondes, two Doms and two Ts. Lol.

Lol. Honestly. Sofia had barely repressed the acidic taste of bile at the back of her throat the moment she saw the accompanying obligatory selfie of two beautiful blondes, two bottles of Dom Perignon and 'TT', aka Theo Tersi, grinning in the background as if he was purposefully taunting Sofia. Which he was.

Clearly less than two hundred and eighty characters were needed to explain the models' ecstasy, and the fact they had snared Theo's legendarily short attention span.

She knew that Theo wasn't naïve or stupid. He must have known that every single indecent headline following the publication of their kiss nearly three weeks ago now would take her down with him. She knew that this was an act of revenge, knew that in his mind she most definitely deserved it. And in a very small, very quiet part of her own mind, she feared that he might be right. But right or wrong had no place here. She needed to get him to issue a denial so that she could do whatever damage limitation was required and press forward with her hopes to find a forgiving fiancé.

Her heartbeat thrummed beneath the thin silk top and jeans she had chosen with the express purpose of blending in. Her aim was to get in, get him to agree and get out, without being spotted. In her youth, she had achieved much greater things under the radar. Surely this would be possible?

Her inner voice mocked her naivety, while her desperation drove her forward.

She reminded herself that no one would be looking for her here. It was the first time in nearly ten years that she'd been outside amongst people without the trappings of her royal status and she was slightly fascinated and slightly sad.

Sofia couldn't help but wonder what her life would have been like had her father not become ill. Yes, she still would have ascended to the throne, but could she have had some time? Time to explore a little fun, or even herself just a little…*more*? Would she have found some enjoyment in life in a way she could never do now? Not that she would ever have been able to fritter away money on a hand of cards, or tweet mindlessly using emojis and take selfies with any number of handsome men.

If her father hadn't come to find her that night, would

she have risked it all and found a way to be with Theo as she had often dreamed? No matter how hard she tried to imagine what would have happened had she met him behind the shrubs at their boarding school, rather than the headmaster who must have been sent by her father, she just couldn't. Was that because it could never have truly happened as she had once told herself? Or because she had spent years repressing those exact thoughts and desires for far too long? She could no longer say.

Still, the Theo that she fell in love with all those years ago was now long gone. There had been no trace of him in the eyes of the man who had mocked her so cruelly. Who had taunted her, teased her into furious, anger-filled words in the Parisian garden just three weeks ago. And if there had been traces of him only in the kiss he stole from her, she chose to ignore it.

The large security guard beside the entrance to the club gave her a cursory glance and allowed her to pass through the doors into the dark, cavernous chamber beyond. Music assaulted her ears, and she blinked against the chaotically strobing light throbbing in time with a baseline she felt buzz through her skin and bone to the soft inside of her.

She shouldn't be doing this. She should just let someone else confront Theo, but she knew—instinctively—that this was what he had wanted. As if he had planned everything down to the finest detail and only her presence would do.

Sofia brushed aside her concerns, her fears, and scanned the chaotic mass of people on the dance floor. No matter how hard she tried, she couldn't imagine Theo amongst the thriving group. No. He was far too voyeuristic for that. She remembered the feel of his gaze upon her skin at the Parisian ballroom. Remembered the feel of being hunted by a predator purposefully choosing when best to strike.

Her gaze finally took in the raised area of the club, an entire glass-fronted section roped off and guarded by another large, dark-suited man. She caught sight of the blonde model she recognised from the tweet, and, sure enough, Theo was sitting with one arm draped around her, the other draped around the thin shoulders of the other, the only difference in the scene being the additional upturned bottle of champagne beside the other two. Either the staff were very slow at tending to the tables in this club, or Theo was enjoying showing off his power and wealth. Sofia very much leaned towards the latter.

She made her way towards the large, suited man, and when she tried to pass he thrust out a meaty arm to block her. Shocked, she very nearly uttered the famously awful words, *Do you know who I am?*, but just managed to prevent herself. She was here incognito and she had not the first idea of how to get around the man. She had no experience in these situations, no idea what was required, as usually her security handled every single small thing… but she had dismissed them. Boarding school had been the last time she'd been allowed her freedom and since her return to Iondorra she hadn't exactly been out 'clubbing'.

Did she offer him money? she wondered, then belatedly realised she didn't have any. And even if she had, Sofia had no idea how much would have been appropriate. She could have given the man a year's salary, or not even enough to buy milk. Suddenly feeling completely out of her depth, she felt the sting of tears pressing against the backs of her eyelids and blamed Theo Tersi wholeheartedly. She had not cried once since the night of the debutante ball when she and her mother had spoken. When she had realised there truly was no other option but to assume the throne and marry her childhood friend, Antoine. But in the three weeks since Theo had stormed into her life and turned it upside down, she felt as if she were only a breath away from it at all times.

Suddenly he appeared at the top of the stairs behind the bouncer, towering over her like an avenging angel, and she hated the way that her pulse instantly kicked at the sight. She pushed away the thoughts of how she had reacted to the kiss that night, with all the wanton, suppressed desire of ten years of need and yearning that she had refused to acknowledge. The photographer had caught the exact moment that she had clung to him as if her life depended on it, and the memory brought a furious blush to her cheeks even now.

She took in the sight of Theo's broad shoulders filled out from youth with powerful masculinity, dark hair artfully messy—or at least she hoped it was by design and not the hands of either of the models he was currently parading about. She bit down on the thread of shocking jealousy unfurling in her chest, and replaced it with anger as Theo growled the phrase, 'Let her come.'

It sounded more like the taunt of a battle cry than permission to enter some private section of a club. He'd turned his back on her before she'd taken the first step, and by the time she'd reached the top of the stairs he was nestled in between the two women once again.

She stood before the three of them, separated by the depth of a table with half-filled glasses and empty champagne bottles.

'Can we talk?' she shouted over the loud music.

He placed a hand to his ear, and simply shrugged

in confusion as if the blasted man hadn't heard what she'd said.

'I said—' she shouted, only to realise that a sudden lull in the music had carried her voice far and wide over the private section of the club.

The two models snickered into their hands and Theo's smirk made her utterly convinced that he'd known that would happen.

'I said,' she tried again, 'can we talk?'

He waved a hand before her in a way more regal than any gesture she'd ever managed to achieve. He still had yet to say a word to her.

'In private?'

'Anything you have to say to me can be said here.'

Sofia wanted to snarl. She felt the deep yearning to be reckless, to act out, to do something so un-princess-like as to throw the remaining contents of the glass on the table all over his proud, defiant face. But ten years of suppressing that wild inner instinct won out. Even though she suspected he knew exactly what she wanted to do, what she would have done in the past. Unconsciously she rubbed at the old ache on her forearm, the other arm wrapping around the long since faded bruise against her ribs, while she chose and discarded what to say next.

'We have…business to discuss.'

'Sit,' he said, knowing full well the only place to sit was beside one of the two women he still had his arms around. And Sofia point-blankly refused to add to the collection of women he'd gathered about himself.

'I'll stand.'

He shrugged, once again as if it were her choice.

One of the girls leaned over and whispered in his ear, producing a high-pitched giggle from the other, and an amused grin and a nod of agreement from him as they both returned their attention to her, making it clear she was the subject of the private discussion.

It was becoming increasingly hard to hold on to the thin thread of her control. She locked her eyes on his, ignoring the two women either side of him, and waited. Because the one thing that no one had been able to remove from her in all her years of royal training was her stubbornness. So she watched and waited. She'd have stood there all night too, but he seemed to realise that, and finally dismissed the two women, who pouted and protested but ultimately removed themselves to a table further away. Not before casting her glances that Sofia was sure would have quelled lesser individuals. She had won that battle, but not the war. Not yet.

Theo called over a waitress and requested a chair for her, which was duly produced, and Sofia finally sat down opposite him.

'I see that you have dressed for the occasion,' Theo said as his gaze covered her once again from head to toe and back to her head again.

She raised an eyebrow and shrugged. 'When in the henhouse…'

'Are you calling me a hen?' he asked, full of mock-horror. 'Pecking and scratching around for any little titbit you'd throw my way? Oh, no. I assure you, Sofia, that is not how this is going to play out.'

'For goodness' sake, Theo. It's the cock in the henhouse. You're the…' A painful blush rose to her cheeks before she could finish the sentence.

'Oh, that's adorable, sweetheart.'

'Don't call me that,' she commanded.

Theo felt the thrill of satisfaction as he watched her crystal-blue eyes storm like a Mediterranean downpour. He'd never failed to find enjoyment in teasing her. But seeing her feathers ruffled, seeing her annoyed and angry, held a bittersweet taste this evening.

Good. He wanted her angry. He wanted her annoyed. He wanted her to feel every single thread of emotion that had wrapped around his heart the moment he'd re-alised just how artfully she'd played and betrayed him. Because it wasn't just him that her machinations had af-fected. That his mother had been caught up in the fallout was untenable. So when Sofia failed to issue the apol-ogy he knew he deserved, she had sealed her fate. The photographer he had hired had done well and been paid well for his services too. Securing front-page headlines throughout the world had been exactly what Theo had wanted, knowing that it would back her into a corner. Knowing that no other royal would want to go near her after being associated with his debauched reputation. He had ignored her for weeks, knowing that it would only infuriate her more. Until yesterday, when he had begun to leave little breadcrumbs on social media of where she might be able to find him. He wanted her on his turf, he wanted her on the back foot, *needed* her to be. This was only the second step towards his utter and complete revenge. She would know the sting of humiliation, she would know the deep slice of hurt and betrayal—feel-ings that were so familiar to him it was as if he had been born with them—and she would know, ultimately, that she had brought it on herself.

His gaze ate up the image before him. She was wear-ing clothes he'd never seen her in, certainly nothing that would ever grace the style magazines she was often lauded in. The tight grey denim riding low on her hips made his mouth water, and the silky white top tucked into them was nowhere near indecent, but as it moulded to her perfect breasts, topped by thin straps, he couldn't imagine that she was wearing a bra. He would have seen the evidence of it. The low heel of the suede nude-coloured heels gave her overall appearance a conservative contrast to the barely dressed women at the club, teetering on almost death-defying stilettos.

He had imagined her monstrous over the years, every heartache added to the list of crimes she had perpetrated against him and his mother. He had imagined her begging and pleading for forgiveness, but in reality he could not deny the effect she had on him and cursed his body's weakness for her. Even now, he had to lean forward to hide the evidence of his arousal, his desire for her. The one thing that had never gone away.

Her pupils dilated at his slow perusal, and the realisation that she too was as beholden to their mutual attraction was the only balm to his ego.

'Theo—'

'Princess Sofia de Loria of Iondorra…'

This time she scowled. More like the youthful woman he had once known, and it struck him in his chest. He slowly exhaled the shock, but took great pleasure as those about them started to produce their smartphones and snap pictures of the two of them—some not even bothering to be discreet. He would not be her dirty little secret. Not this time. This time, he would make it impossible for her to walk away from him.

'You must issue a denial,' she said finally, as she tried to ignore the flashes punctuating the beginning of their exchange.

'A denial of what, Your Highness? That we kissed? I believe that is quite undeniable at this point.'

'That we are in a relationship,' she hissed beneath her breath. 'I can't have the world thinking that…'

'Thinking that you are involved with an illegitimate Greek commoner?'

'I was going to say Greek millionaire playboy.'

'Please,' he scoffed. 'It's *billionaire* playboy to you.'

She artfully raised an eyebrow.

'You can look at my financials if you doubt it,' he replied, unable to keep the heady mixture of pride and arrogance from his voice. Everything he'd achieved, every grape, bottle, vineyard and investment, had been despite her machinations and through his own hard work. She could hardly claim the same.

'I'm not here to debate what names the press call *you*, I'm here to get you to put a stop to the ones they're calling *me*.'

He held back the smile that his lips itched to tease into. Instead, shaking his head and offering her a simple shoulder shrug, he said, '*Óchi*. No. I don't think so.'

'Why not?' she demanded incredulously.

'It doesn't suit my purposes to do so.'

'What do you want, Theo?' Suspicion darkened her eyes to a midnight-blue. A colour he remembered from his past, and he thrust the thought aside.

'I want,' he said, unfurling his large frame from the sofa beneath him, closing the distance between them in order to see the moment she realised that she was helpless, that she had no other choice... 'you to learn the consequences of your actions. I want you to learn that we mere mortals will not be as easily discarded as you seem to think.'

I want you to learn that you cannot destroy me and everything I hold dear and just walk away, he concluded silently.

'I want you to pay for the way you set me up—'

'Theo—'

He didn't even register her interruption as the wave of indignation and fury pounded in his veins, competing with the heavy base of the club's music.

'I want what you once promised me, what you once begged me for. I want you to make a truth from your lies. I want you to wear my ring.'

His eyes narrowed as Sofia failed to move a muscle, blink even. This mask that she wore, this impossibly regal poise, was different to the young woman he remembered. He had seen her desire to throw a glass of champagne over him earlier, a fit of female pique. But this? No, this was unacceptable. He didn't want poised. He wanted furious. He wanted her to feel what he felt.

'In fact,' he pressed on, now standing, towering above her, cocking his head to one side in a way that showed only disrespect, 'I don't just want you to agree. You see, your name is now entwined with mine. No one of royal pedigree would attach themselves to you in marriage, no matter how desperate they are. No one would want my seconds, my cast-offs. No one would ever choose you again. It doesn't matter how long you wait. Every time I cause a scandal—and trust me, *agápi mou*, I am more than willing to engage in as many I can find—every time I'm seen out with my next conquest, your name will be dragged down with me. Compared to whatever woman graces my bed, the speculation as to whether your poor, wounded little princess heart is breaking over my latest indiscretion will be on every single front page around the world.

'You should be happy, Sofia. You are now tied to me as securely—if not more so—than you used to pretend you wanted to be. So no, I don't want you to simply agree to be my wife. I want you to *beg*.'

Just like the way his mother had begged her employer

to reconsider. Like the way she had been forced to beg her own family to take them in once again. Just like he had been forced to beg to buy the first piece of neglected land that he'd wanted to develop for his own grapes from his mother's family. So that was what Sofia would have to do now.

'I want you to beg.'

The words cut through Sofia like fire and ice.

Surely he had to be joking. There was no way they could marry. Not with all this hurt and anger between them. Not with the events of the past between them.

But she only had to look at him, take in the determined gleam in his eyes, the slightly forward bent of his body, the tense muscles of a predator that had already struck, had already cornered its prey and was now only playing, toying with it, before the poor creature was completely devoured. She was that creature. And she hated it. Hated him.

Still, just like that prey, she sought a way out.

'What do you get out of this?'

'Do you not see how this works? My wine sales will go through the roof. I may even request a royal seal,' he said again with that infuriating shrug.

'You'd tie yourself to me in marriage for the rest of your life, just for sales?' she demanded incredulously.

'Princess, how is that any different than marrying for the good of your country?'

'But what about…' She trailed off.

'Love? Happy-ever-afters? I think we learned that lesson quite some time ago, don't you?'

She wanted to argue, to deny his words, to find some way of reasoning with him.

'You are blackmailing me? I have no choice in this whatsoever,' she said, panic rising from deep within her.

'Of course you have a choice. You can walk away, with your reputation in tatters and never see me again. Or we will marry. Give this little scandal a royal fairy-tale ending.'

Sofia knew that he meant it. Knew that he wouldn't let this go. Knew when she had fled the garden in Paris that she had taunted the lion in its cage.

'I'll need that answer now, Sofia.'

She bit back the curses, because there was definitely more than one ready to fall from her lips. There was too much to take in. He had set her up because he thought *she* had set him up? Was this really just some obscene marketing plan for his vineyard? The thoughts were crashing through her mind at lightning speed, but it was the realisation that he was right that came through loud and clear. There was no way that she would ever *not* be associated with him now. And she knew enough about him to take him at his word. He would make sure of it. No one would go near her now that she was linked with a debauched billionaire playboy. She had run out of time. Her father's recent deterioration had seen to that. The only way forward was the one he was offering. No, demanding. The one he had orchestrated and executed so perfectly.

She hated the smile that unfurled on his lips. The thrum of satisfaction she felt coming off him in waves that lapped her skin so very painfully. Sofia bit her tongue, as if her body was protesting the words that she was being forced to say.

'Theo Tersi, please. Pretty please, with a damn cherry on top. Will you marry me?'

CHAPTER FOUR

THEO DIDN'T KNOW what he'd expected, and, though it might have had to have been forced out of him with the threat of serious bodily harm, he was impressed.

The power and might of the Iondorran royal mechanisms was something to behold. Within a month of her agreement to his demand, a backstory to their sudden engagement had been constructed, non-disclosure agreements had been signed and an engagement party had been planned.

Only one hour ago, an airtight prenuptial agreement had been delivered to the suites assigned to him and his entourage in Iondorra's impressive castle.

Theo stood in the living area nestled within a turret, looking out through a slender window that displayed a view of the rolling green countryside and the mountains beyond, still snow-capped in the height of summer. He knew that from the other side of the palace could be seen Callier, Iondorra's capital city, almost Swiss in its cleanliness and gleaming, ordered precision. For a country that was primarily agricultural, Theo had been surprised to discover just how much the royal family had focused their energies on generating a strong capital, insisting on the development of a university to keep the next generation's interest, rather than seeing them look elsewhere for centres of learning and jobs.

He had done his research on Sofia long before their engagement—his private investigator having been working overtime for the past year in order to set this up. He'd begun the moment that he'd realised he could not let go. He'd often questioned what it must have taken to smooth out the rough, wayward edges of the reckless, almost wild girl he had once known. And he wondered, not for the first time, whether she missed that part of herself. The very part that had drawn him to her like a moth to a flame. Sofia's freedom, her carefree fire, had been too much for a boy who could never have afforded it for himself.

Maria was sat, bent over something small and silvery by the window seat at the opposite end of the room.

'What do you have there?' he asked, forcing himself to turn away from his thoughts.

She looked up and smiled, her dark hair falling in a cascade over one shoulder. 'It's a piece I created for the exhibition in a few days' time,' she replied, offering up the necklace that fell like a river of silver from her hands. 'You're…you're still coming?' she asked. The way she failed to contain the mixture of hope and hurt in her eyes reminded Theo that they really did need to have that talk.

'You are going to sign this?' Sebastian demanded from behind him.

Theo's attention was called back to Sebastian where he sat reading the prenuptial agreement.

'Theo, you cannot sign this.'

'Of course I can.'

'I mean, I expected a few subclauses from her, but really? Twenty million euros to be paid in the event of your infidelity, scandal, or… Is "tomfoolery" even a legal term?'

'I believe she is trying to put me off. But it won't work.'

'If you sign this, then you are a madman.'

'Perhaps. If I had any intention of actually going through with the wedding.'

Theo turned to find both Sebastian and his sister, Maria, staring up at him in confusion. He wished they could have seen what they looked like, frozen in a tableau of shock. He nearly laughed. He had momentarily forgotten that Maria was there too, but he knew that Sebastian would never have kept his charade from her.

'Theo, what are you doing?'

'I am doing what I had always intended to do,' he said, watching Sebastian with heavy-lidded eyes. 'I am going to ensure that Sofia knows what it feels like to wait. To stand there and wonder, and doubt. To feel the humiliation, to have it marked upon her indelibly. I want her to wait there in front of her wedding guests, her country, at the church alone. To realise that I am not there and that I am not coming. I want her to suffer the consequences of her actions, as my mother and I suffered.'

'So, you don't love her?' Maria's quiet voice cut through the silence of the room.

'I could never love that woman.' *Not again.*

'Have you really thought this through?' Sebastian enquired.

'Every day for ten years.'

'What happens afterwards?'

'I'll release a statement saying that I could not force her into a loveless marriage. The press will lap it up. I will be saving her from herself and a marriage that would have broken her. I'll come out a hero.'

'That is cynical, even for you, my friend.'

Cynical maybe, but necessary. It was time that Sofia de Loria learned that there were consequences to her actions.

* * *

It had been years since Sofia had seen the palace's ballroom draped in such finery and filled with so many people. Her father's deterioration had consigned much of her small family's lives to brief external visits, rarely allowing for the opening of the palace, for outward glances to turn inward upon them. Sofia thought that the last time the ballroom had looked like this might have been her fifteenth birthday, before she'd been sent to boarding school and met the man that had brought this down upon her.

This evening was costing the country money it barely had, but lord knew, everyone loved a royal wedding. It was an investment—for the future of her country. She had to see it as such or she'd curl into a ball in her room and never come out.

She resisted the urge to soothe her brow where the beginnings of a tension headache the size of the San Andreas fault line was gathering. She hated the fact that Theo had blackmailed her, hated that there was no confidant, no friend that she could turn to. Her entire life since leaving that school had been about training, learning the tools that she would need to put the country first. She'd had no time for friends, for people her own age. The last friend she'd thought she had was... Theo. With him, she'd been utterly herself.

It could have been so different, she thought. She'd once dreamed of it being different. The same man, yes. But this? No.

However, part of the future she was securing for her country required children. That thought sent sparks of fire and ice across her skin and down her spine. They hadn't yet discussed that. But she'd made sure to put it into the prenuptial agreement. She could be just as sneaky as he. She'd thought with some small pleasure at how shocked he might be to read the clause that required his contribution to IVF treatment. She had absolutely no intention of sharing her bed with him. And even as she'd had that thought, her inner voice cried *liar*. It brought to mind memories of their kiss…the way her body had sung, had clung to him as desire moved like wildfire through her veins, as her body and soul had yearned for more.

The sudden and shocking thoughts raised a painful blush to her overly heated cheeks, and, cutting off her thoughts, she glanced again at the clock, placing the practised smile on her features to satisfy the eager curiosity of various visiting dignitaries. Where the hell was Theo? Perhaps he *had* seen the clause in the agreement and had decided to punish her temerity.

But that thought was completely overridden by the sense of unease beginning to build. Her father was set to make a royal appearance for only a short allotted time. It was needed for publicity, to soothe potentially ruffled feathers on the Iondorran council for the inappropriateness of her chosen fiancé. Theo didn't need to know that at least two whole weeks had been spent in tense negotiations as she'd lied and cajoled her father's old cronies into accepting Theo. She had extolled his virtues, instead of parading his vices, argued the strength of a true love match, even as the lies had caught in her throat. Unconsciously she had repeated the same pleas she had once made to her father, ten years before as he had tried to extricate her from the boarding school.

She'd been surprised how readily they came to her lips, how easily the same fidelity, emotion, desperation had come to her aid. And the privy council had believed it in a way that her father never had.

And now, when she needed Theo by her side, he was

keeping her waiting, keeping her father waiting. His medication was working for the moment, but she knew better than most how quickly that could change. Once again, she absentmindedly rubbed her forearm, feeling the phantom ache where the accident—as she thought of it now—had fractured the bone there and bruised the ribs beneath. From across the room her mother had caught the unconscious action, and she sent her a reassuring look.

When she finally saw Theo at the top of the grand sixteenth-century staircase, her breath caught in her throat. In the back of her mind she was a little jealous—surely this was the princess's moment, to stand atop the staircase and be admired? But this was no fantasy, and Theo was certainly no prince. Yet admired? Yes. He was.

He stood in between Sebastian Rohan de Luen and a young woman so like him that she must have been his sister. Sofia caught the exiled duke's eye, his gaze held just the fraction of a moment, and she saw something more than speculation towards the woman who was to marry his friend…something foreboding.

Theo's powerful frame unfolded down the stairs into a jog, an *actual* jog, towards her. Sofia's head almost whipped around to search for the long-ago voice calling in her mind—*No running in the Grand Room, Sofia!*

He came towards her so fast, she had no time to react, the expression of joy across his features so shocking to her that she didn't prevent the hands that came to her cheeks and took her face in a warm caress as he placed his lips gently against hers. Instantly he enveloped her senses, the soft, earthy smell of him, the traces of electricity that sparkled beneath the pads of his fingertips against her skin, the heat of his lips and the way her body unconsciously rose to meet him…all gone as suddenly as it came.

'*Kardiá mou*, my tardiness in unforgivable,' he said against her mouth, loudly enough for all about her to hear. Sighs rose up about her from the women and indulgent smiles painted the faces of Iondorra's staunchest male dignitaries.

For a moment, the space of a heartbeat, Sofia had been fooled, had been transported back to a time when his kisses seemed to be her whole world. The way she wanted to sink into the pleasure, the comfort, the... Before her mind could finish the thought, she remembered. Remembered it all. The blackmail, the darkness behind his actions, the belief he held that she had set him up... and in a rash and defiant act, she nipped at his bottom lip with her teeth, quick and hard. He pulled back his head in surprise.

'Let me be the first to draw blood, then, Theo,' she hissed in a voice audible only to him.

'No, Sofia. You did that years ago,' he said darkly, his deft tongue sweeping at the thin trace of crimson on his lip, before a mask descended over his features and he turned to the gathering in the ballroom with a broad smile.

As Iondorra's leading figures lined up to pass on their congratulations to the happy couple Sofia and Theo continued their quiet lines of attack in under-the-breath sentences.

'I thought I was supposed to be the one who was fashionably late,' she whispered.

'Fashion doesn't have to be gender specific.'

'Your ego is impossible.' Sofia broke off to welcome the Minister of Trade and Industry. 'Eugene, lovely to see you.'

'Your Highness, felicitations.' She nodded her acceptance. As her father's trusted advisor trailed off and they waited for the next, Theo took up their conversation.

'It has serviced me well over the years.'

'It's not the only thing that serviced you,' she bit out darkly.

'Come, now, Sofia, jealousy doesn't suit you.' Before she could respond, he pressed on. 'You look ravishing as always,' he said, turning to take her in fully.

'That's what happens when the dress you wear to your engagement party is picked by the privy council after three rounds of rigorous polling.'

'You would have chosen something different?'

'Why?'

'I'd like to know what façade I'm going to get. At least if you had chosen your own it would allow me to draw some conclusion about you.'

'Why do you want to draw a conclusion about me? Surely I'm only here to increase your wine sales,' she hissed as she turned to meet the next guest. 'Lord Chancellor,' Sofia said as she extended a hand to meet the last and final man in the greeting line.

Introductions over and done, they both turned to face the large ballroom. As they stood side by side, it could have been forgiven to see them as the happy couple looking over their guests.

'Your governance is modelled on the British system.'

Sofia shrugged a nonchalant shoulder. 'It worked for them.'

Theo inclined his head in agreement.

Sofia drew a deep breath, reluctantly steeling herself. 'It's time to see the king.'

She felt rather than saw Theo sweep his gaze across the crowded room. 'He's talking to someone—let's have a drink.'

Sofia pressed down on her panic. Her father had been

here for fifteen minutes already and she didn't know how long he'd be able to continue before an episode began.

'Theo, please.' Whether it was the tone in her voice, or the fact her small hand had reached out to his, punctuating the request with a slight trace of desperation, she didn't know, but a low lean of his head gave his agreement.

Her mother met their approach with something like the same relief that Sofia felt. The moment this was done, protocol was met, her mother and father could return to the privacy of their suites.

'Your Majesty,' Sofia called to her father, instantly checking his eyes for signs of clarity or confusion, ready to whisk Theo away should the latter be the case. Her father took in the sight of her, assessment shining in his eyes. It gave nothing else away.

'Mother,' she said, pressing a kiss to each of her delicate cheeks.

'Father, may I present Theo Tersi,' she said, stepping slightly to the side, and suddenly overwhelmed with the fear that Theo would do or say something wrong.

'Your Majesty,' Theo said with a bow from his lean neck, drawing to his full height as each man assessed the other.

Her father cut her a glance, one that took her immediately back to ten years before. Anger, a slight trace of confusion, marred the older man's frowning brow. Sofia bit back a curse. They had waited too long.

'I told you,' he growled, 'that you could not...' He trailed off for just a moment, giving her the only opening she knew she'd get. She remembered those words, too, from that night all those years ago. Was that where her father was in his mind? She forced a smile to her face, hoping that if she and her mother could maintain the farce, they might just get through this.

'That I could not find a better man. I know, Papa.' Not waiting for any further act that might give away his deterioration, she pressed kisses to each of his cheeks. Surprise and brief happiness shone in her father's eyes, warming the cool place of sadness in her heart. 'He's perfect, Papa,' she said, turning to Theo, whose quick mind must have already picked up that something wasn't quite right. 'And makes me truly happy.' As she said the words, she felt the now familiar sting of tears pressing against her eyes.

She saw her mother squeeze her father's arm in a gesture both comforting and grounding.

'I'm glad that you found each other again. It's good. It's right,' he declared finally and the breath that had been held universally across the ballroom was exhaled by all the guests.

Theo bowed once again at the older man before they exchanged a strong handshake, Theo holding it for perhaps just a moment longer than required.

Released from duty, Sofia had turned, pulling Theo with her, when her father called her back.

She leaned towards her father to hear his whispered words.

'*En garde*, Sofia. *En garde.*'

She nodded, feeling his words more truthful than any she'd heard him speak in the last five years. For just a moment she felt that her father was back, with her, protecting her and caring for her. Until she heard his next whispered words.

'And watch out for the German parachutist. Do not speak to him!'

Without having to look at her mother, who was the only other person to hear the king's incoherent warning, she replied, 'I will, Papa. I will.'

* * *

Theo had imagined meeting Sofia's parents many times, under many different circumstances. Ten years ago, he had not thought for a second that she was a royal in disguise. Nothing of what she had told him about her family had indicated any such thing. As an only child, like him, she had spoken of finding ways to amuse herself, spending hours delving into imaginary worlds within books, or running through gardens and woods. He had picked through each and every one of her words since he'd discovered that she was a princess—but, as with all good lies, much of it must have been taken from some thread of the truth. But the exchange with her father was...not what he'd expected.

He hadn't missed the moment of panic shared by the two women, mother and daughter, at the way the king's words hadn't quite fitted the situation. And, though he hadn't heard the last exchange, Theo hadn't missed the raw vulnerability in Sofia's eyes when she had proclaimed her happiness and his perfection.

Were they worried that the older man would rile against his common birth? Was her father furious that she was to wed a commoner? Theo had met much discrimination over the years, for various different reasons. He knew what it looked like, felt like and tasted like. And the king? He was not happy.

But he'd said 'again'. He was glad they'd found each other *again*. Which seemed to indicate that he knew about their relationship in the past, which confused him. He'd been convinced that she had kept him her dirty little secret, but—

'Whisky? We will toast with champagne, but if you wanted...'

His dark look at her must have thrown her as her words

trailed off. Her eyes were overly bright, her words just a little too quick. What was going on? A slight noise behind him drew his gaze to see the retreating figures of the king and queen, discreetly spirited away through a side exit. And once again anger whipped through him.

'Your father isn't sticking around for the toast, then?' he couldn't help but bite out. Couldn't help but be transported back to a time when all he'd wondered was why his own father hadn't stuck around. Couldn't help but remember the way his family had treated his mother and himself because of it. Heat and hurt scorched him in an instant.

'No. He couldn't.' Before the growl could escape his lips, she pressed on. 'He's been...working hard and is tired.'

He was used to reflecting that every single word from her mouth was a lie, but this was different. There was the ring of truth in what she said, but there was also a shimmer of falsehood there too or, if not, then evasion distracting him from his reflections on the past.

The toast was given to them by a man he'd never seen before, but was probably a whole lot more appropriate than what Sebastian might have said to a room full of royals. He felt Maria's gaze on him throughout the evening, and not for the first time wondered whether if it might have been better to have let her believe the falsehood he was weaving through the night. She was young and impressionable and wholly overprotected by her brother.

Within an hour Theo was surprised to find himself on the verge of exhaustion. As a successful businessman and vintner, he was used to heading up million-dollar business meetings, but this constant diplomacy was tiring, yet Sofia showed no signs of fatigue, her fake smile—

for he knew it to be fake—was undimmed and as fresh as the first one she had offered.

'Little Sofia,' said an older man with shocking white hair and a broad purple sash spotted with medals and pins that proclaimed his importance. He felt Sofia bristle beside him at the patronising appellation. Unconsciously his protective instincts rose, and he drew to his full height.

'Theo Tersi,' he said, stretching out his hand to sever whatever connection had sprung between his fiancé and the older man.

'Georges de Fontagne.'

'Monsieur de Fontagne is the Minister of Agriculture,' Sofia said, apparently finally finding her voice.

'Sofia,' greeted the small, birdlike woman standing beside Georges, her diminutive stature only serving to magnify her husband's largess.

'Louisa,' Sofia replied with much more warmth.

When Louisa turned her smiling attention to him, Theo took her hand in his and raised it to his lips in such an old-fashioned move, he nearly surprised himself, satisfied to see that a small blush had risen to the older woman's cheeks as she smiled coyly.

'I wanted to offer my congratulations and beg that you satisfy my curiosity once and for all,' interrupted Georges. 'Please, do share the story of your rather *sudden* courtship.' His voice carried, as did the slight trace of cynicism heavy on his words. 'Do not tell me it was born of that horrifying trend of using matchmakers!'

The man's wife was looking thoroughly mortified at her husband's behaviour and Sofia, for the first time that evening, seemed shocked into silence. It was clear that the man knew something of Sofia's search in Paris six weeks before and was taunting her with it. It was untenable.

Theo might not have been born to this strata of society, but he knew in an instant that he had more manners in his little finger than this man did. It reminded him of the way that his mother's family had treated them, *before* he had turned the little dirt pile he and his mother had bought from her family into an award-winning vineyard. Before he had made enough money to buy out the remaining land his mother's family owned and shuffled them off to some distant part of Greece, only to be pulled out of their exile when he felt like it. Only his *giagiá* had taken pity on them, supported them through that first year and then afterwards when his mother became sick. Theo refused to acknowledge the perverse fact that he felt more than justified in seeking his own revenge, but would not counter an attack against Sofia from another quarter. And as such, all temptation to leave Sofia to stew in a mess of his making disappeared.

'We—' she started, but he squeezed her arm gently to stop her.

'*Agápi mou*, I have heard you tell this story before and your natural instinct towards modesty never does me justice. Allow me?' He watched her eyes widen just a fraction with surprise, and she nodded.

'I am sure that you will have heard something of my slightly *scandalous* reputation,' Theo confided ruefully to the couple. 'And I could not lie and say it is not deserved, as I had never thought to find a woman who could live up to the high standard set by my mother.'

From the corner of his eye, he saw Sofia struggle not to roll her eyes, and Louisa struggle not to sigh contentedly. His charm might not have been broadcast in the press, but it was no less potent a skill than his winemaking abilities and he was determined to use it now to its fullest.

'You see, years ago, when I was a young man, I fell deeply in love. I would have given everything for her, and in some ways did.' He felt Sofia flinch and could have sworn he heard the beat of her heart pick up in confusion as to where he was taking this fabricated story. 'But sadly it was not to be. So I hardened my heart, sure that I would never feel the same way again. And I was right.' He had predicted Louisa's brief gasp of shock, and had not been wrong as he'd imagined Georges' avaricious gaze ready for his next words. 'For when I met Sofia I realised that what I had thought was love was just a pale imitation.' Louisa melted, Georges scowled, and Sofia… he simply couldn't tell.

'From the first moment that I laid eyes on her I knew I was completely ruined…' He paused to see if even this would bring Sofia out of her perfect façade, and, though she paled just slightly, no outward sign of upset showed. 'Ruined for other women for ever,' he concluded. 'I knew that she was the woman that I wanted to spend the rest of my life with. You may dismiss that as pure fantasy. Or something based purely on her beauty. But it wasn't. Every word, movement, decision, enthralled. Her intelligence, her poise and, just as much, her playfulness. Did you know that Sofia has a naughty streak?'

'I remember as much from her childhood,' Georges said critically.

'Ah, but this is what makes Sofia so perfect, for while a country needs an iron-willed ruler, the people need fun and authenticity. And that is what really drew me to Sofia. This I knew in just a moment, but Sofia needed a little more time than I. Oh, she made me work for it, I assure you, Georges,' he said, leaning towards the obese man to intimate confidence, while his skin crawled. 'Over our first lunch together, I produced my finest wine…knowing that I had to seduce her senses as much as her mind and heart. It was a very special bottle of wine for me. There were only three made, from the very first grape of my vineyard in the Peloponnese. The first was for my mother, my child will have the third, but Sofia...she had the second.

'Unbeknownst to me, in the years before we had met, I had created the perfect blend of wine, solely in preparation for her. The playful notes of blueberry and bay leaves grounded in the rich, deep Greek soil were simply...*her*.'

Theo realised, as he had spoken, he had caught her gaze with his, the words casting a spell that had drawn the attention not just of the horrible Georges and his poor wife, but also that of the surrounding courtiers and dignitaries. A pin dropped to the floor could have been heard in the silence.

Sofia's face was upturned to his, only a few inches between them, shock and surprise evident in her eyes. He felt, as much as saw, her draw a deep breath, stealing the air from before him. In the silence everything disappeared. The room, the guests, the past...and he was seventeen all over again, looking at the young Sofia as her unpractised body begged him to take her lips. Need and desire encased them, separating them from the rest of the world. The stark sensuality of her calling to him across the years, the months, days and seconds.

He dipped his head, closing the distance between them, and drank from her lips, tasting all the flavours he had just described. The slight sting from where she had indelicately bitten him earlier making it so much more sweet.

Then she opened for him and he plunged into the soft warmth of her mouth, teasing them both with swift movements of his tongue, delving deep within her and relishing every moment.

The roaring in his ears shifted and morphed into the sound of a hundred hands clapping, and just as many voices cheering. He pulled back, suddenly shocked by his own actions mirrored in Sofia's gaze and kiss-bruised lips.

CHAPTER FIVE

'WHAT ON EARTH were you thinking?' Sofia demanded the moment she collected herself after *that kiss*, and the moment they were free of Georges and Louisa's attention.

'I was thinking that it would be the only thing that might wipe the insidious smirk from that obnoxious man's face.'

'You think *he* is obnoxious? Really?'

'I do.'

'He is an important man in the ministerial cabinet, Theo, I cannot afford—'

'The girl I once knew didn't give a flying fig for what she could or could not afford, Sofia. Tell me, where has she gone?' he asked, searching her face, 'for I cannot find a trace of her anywhere.'

'People change,' Sofia replied, turning away from his penetrating stare. Everyone changed. Her father, Theo, herself. No one was who they once were.

But not everything changed, her inner voice taunted her.

No. The way he had kissed her hadn't changed. The moment his lips had pressed against hers, first in that momentary initial greeting, and then later with *that kiss*, it had felt like…home. Some imaginary place in her mind when it had just been the two of them, all those years

ago, with no concerns other than how soon they could
see each other again. His body had called to hers in the
same way it had done all those years ago, and she hated
him for it. Because he was right. That girl was gone and
she could never come back. Not if she wanted to secure
a future for her country. They needed the royal woman
she had become, regal and poised. So she delved into the
inner strength she had forged from the loss of her hopes
and dreams and became that woman again.

She barely spared Theo another glance as she visited
with dignitaries, accepted their congratulations, agreed
to visit with various countries after the wedding—and if
her heart stuttered over that precise word or moment to
come, then she ignored it as she made plans for a future
she could no longer see.

Despite her attempts to relegate Theo to the sidelines,
he hovered almost constantly by her side, dishing out
the same charm he had drowned Louisa de Fontagne
in, showing a peculiar adroitness in conversation with
the various ministers and members of the privy council. And slowly she began to form an image of the man
to replace that of the boy she had known. One who had
skilfully nurtured an international wine conglomerate
from a small part of Greece, one who seemed to have
lost some of that inner sense of insecurity she had once
recognised as being similar to her own, a sense of not
quite being rich enough, or good enough…

'I must say, I'm impressed,' he said into the air just
above her head. For all the world they would look like a
couple very much in love as she tilted her face towards
his. Only he could read the confusion in her eyes. 'One
could be forgiven for thinking that this was an engagement party rather than an opportunity for you to net-
work. But so far I have seen you organise at least three

potential trade agreements with all the panache of a seasoned CEO.'

'Don't think I didn't miss the mention of your precious wine whilst you were talking to Georges. He was practically begging you for shares in your company once he realised that his wife, along with half the world, would seek out the magical wine blend that tasted *just like me*. It was a nice touch, by the way.'

'It was, wasn't it?' The pleasure was evident in his voice. 'You'll have to add it to the cover story your council made so hastily. Really, Sofia? You thought that the world would believe we had been introduced by a mutual friend? That's akin to saying we met on Tinder. But, as you know well, the best lies always have a hint of the truth.'

He waited until he had caught her gaze once more. 'Why did you not tell them we had met at school? Worried they would dig up my expulsion?' He wanted to look in her eyes as she answered his question. Wanted to see the truth she had somehow been able to hide from him. 'Or were you just worried about the world's press uncovering my low upbringing?'

'I never thought that of you, Theo. You were the only one who did,' she said in softly spoken words, and it was not an accusation, but he felt it as such.

Theo scoffed. 'You really have no idea, do you?' It took nothing to bring to mind a childhood that had felt like death by a thousand cuts, a thousand stares, snide comments and a fair few beatings when his mother wasn't looking. 'Up there, the little princess in the ivory tower.' He jerked his head up through the floors above the grand ballroom towards an unseen turret. 'Did you really not see the stares, or hear the words whispered by teachers and students alike? Do you really not know how the world *works*, Sofia? How the powerful turn on the weak in any attempt to guard their pedestal of superior wealth or position? Is it an accident of your birth, or wilful ignorance? I honestly can't tell any more. Because you were, are, many things, Sofia, but I didn't think that naïve was one of them.'

Her eyes turned the dark blue of an electrical storm. 'Naïve? You know nothing of what I have sacrificed—'

'What have you ever sacrificed, Sofia?'

You, the thought screamed silently in her mind. Anger rode her pulse to impossible speeds, her chest heaving against the low cut of her dress. An anger so much like desire—the fire in her blood quick to make the leap from one to the other. She felt the breadth of his shoulders expand beside her, and the way he stood proprietorially seemed to encase her, preventing her from seeing beyond the wall of the toned muscles of his chest, cutting her off from the room beyond. It was too much, the closeness of their bodies, the heat pulsating between them, the way her own body seemed to lean towards him as if wanting to pull rather than push him away.

'I didn't think so,' Theo said in the space of her silence. 'I look around the room, this party, this palace and see numbers. Because after I returned to Greece with my mother, it was all about numbers. The number of universities that retracted their scholarship offers after my expulsion. The number of family members that turned their backs on us, the single digit representing the one person willing to help. The number of euros begged and borrowed to buy that first plot of land, the number of times my mother and I went without food, the number of sleepless nights that wrecked us both as we plunged everything we had into that first grape harvest. The number of bottles we were first able to sell, after the number of failed attempts that preceded it. But do you know what doesn't have a number? How *hard* it was.'

She watched him with large, round eyes, and he imagined the pity there, surely. The way her eyes glinted with compassion just a remnant of what he wanted to see.

'I'm so sorry. Truly. I wish I could have helped.'

'Helped?' he demanded, the word almost getting stuck behind his outrage. 'I'm not talking about the work. I would do that every day for the rest of my life and still be happy. What was hard was the belief that *I* had done this to my mother. That *I* had brought this upon the one person in my life who had ever loved me. That, had I not fallen for your pretty lies, then I would have graduated at the top of my class, I would have attended one of the finest universities in the world with a scholarship. My future and my mother's would have not been filled with struggle and numbers of loss… I could have given her the world. For years I felt the weight of that on my shoulders. Until I realised that I was wrong. It wasn't my fault, it was yours. You laid a trail of pretty little lies like breadcrumbs for me to follow all the way to my destitution. And I believed those lies.

'How ironic that we survived the abandonment of my father, only to be cut down at the knees by a pampered princess. One that, no matter how exhausted I was, how many hours I worked in the dust, the mud, the earth, no matter how much I sweated, gained or lost…was the only thing I could think of each and every night. You.'

But his words had come out wrong. He felt the way they tasted on his tongue, heard the way they hit the air between them. He had meant it as a castigation, as an explanation or excuse for what he felt he had to do, all the things that Sofia didn't yet know of. But even to his own ears it had sounded more like a plea. A plea that he could not allow for, so he pressed on with the cruel taunt he knew would drive his desire for her away like no other.

'Until you married someone else.'

The last blow was too much for Sofia to bear. Each word, each statement filling in the blanks in her knowledge of him, changing and reforming what she had imagined for him in the years since that night ten years ago, had twisted the knife deeper in her breast. Until that final mention of Antoine. Her fingers reached for the comfort of the wedding band that was no longer there. Instead they scraped against the cold cut of the diamond that had been delivered to the palace two weeks before, the unfamiliar shape beneath the tips of her fingers cold and harsh. Another ring, worn from duty rather than desire or love.

She knew that she should tell him what had happened that night, knew that she should explain how she hadn't set him up to take the fall for her foolish actions, make him understand that she'd had no choice that night, or any since. Desperately she wanted to tell him that she had meant every word, every hope she'd ever shared with him, but what would it achieve? One part knew he'd not believe her and the other part knew she could not even if he might. The reason she had left that night was bound in secrecy and desperation, to protect her family from what was now only just around the corner. Did it really matter what he thought of her? Only to Sofia. It didn't change anything. Didn't change the fact she needed to be married, needed to no longer be the Widow Princess when the time came for her to assume the throne.

'I simply cannot fathom why you would have married a man who—'

'What, Theo? Wasn't you?' she demanded, cutting

into his sentence before he could cause even more pain by maligning Antoine. 'For all this talk of vengeance and needing to teach me the consequences of my actions— yes, I *was* paying attention in Paris—what is it really? That I dared to marry another man? Is your ego really that significant to you?'

His head reared back as if he'd been slapped and the thin shred of satisfaction at the sight made her feel both jubilant and petty at the same time.

'What would make you feel better, Theo? To hear that I didn't love him? Well, I did. He was a good, kind man who understood me, understood what I needed. Who also understood what my position meant in a way that you *never* will. I am truly sorry that you've faced such hardships, Theo. I am sorry that you feel responsible for them, I am also sorry that you believe that I caused that, that I did that to you. But if that's what you need to do, then so be it.

'And if you need to hear that Antoine and I didn't have the chemistry you seem to effortlessly taunt me with, then fine. We didn't. Does it please you to know that he took lovers? That it shamed him as much as me? Would that help? Do you need to know that each and every touch left me cold and more alone than I can possibly describe? Because the only person whose touch I had ever craved was you? The only person I had ever imagined sharing that part of myself with, was you? Would that ease your ego?'

Shame and misery sobbed in her chest, and tears that had formed without her knowledge or permission gathered behind the lids of her eyes, casting both Theo and the room about them in a blurry haze. She couldn't stand it any more, couldn't stand here knowing that he had drawn from her a secret that she had shared with no other.

So she fled her engagement party, turning her back on the gathered guests, picking up the skirts of her dress as she almost ran from the ballroom.

There were very few times in his life that Theo could remember being shocked into silence, and each and every one of them involved Sofia. But none of them had hit him with the power of a tsunami. Waves of something he did not want to put a name to crashed against him as he followed in her wake. He didn't care if he drew the curious glances of strangers as he left the ballroom with determined steps. He didn't care if they would have to come up with yet another story to define or excuse their actions and their engagement.

All he cared about was what Sofia had revealed to him, and if it made him want to beat his chest with pride and need, and ego, then so be it, even if it made him a bastard. His pulse raged and he felt the burn in his thighs as he took several steps at once towards her suite, feelings that he relished as he ate up the distance she had tried to put between them.

She had told him many lies in the past, but what she had said about her first husband, what she had said about *him*? That was most definitely the truth, and had somehow worked to lift the self-imposed barrier he had placed between them. Now, though, *now* there was no turning back.

Even as he stalked the palace hallways towards her room he felt the rush of desire, the swelling of arousal in his groin, the thickening of this band of want and need around his chest and throat. It might not have changed his plans for her, no. He would still have his revenge. But perhaps if he gave in to this insane desire burning between them, then he might finally be able to rid himself of the devastating hold she had over him. No, not him. His libido. He was a man of flesh and blood, and he would not deny either of them a taste of their basest desires.

He flexed his hand as it trembled ever so slightly in the space between him and the door to her rooms, and thrust it back by his side. Instead, he pushed the door open and kicked it shut behind him as he stepped over the threshold and drank in the sight of his prey.

She sat at the dressing table, staring off into the distance, looking as alone and isolated as she had claimed to be only moments earlier. Her golden hair, swept back into a chignon, glistened in the dimly lit room, matched only by the sparkle of the diamonds around her neck, dipping towards the V in her chest, and he stood half mesmerised by the sight of the rise and fall of her breasts, the only outward sign of her distress…

For the first time in years he felt an affinity with her, as he recognised that they were both in thrall to the spell of desire wrapping around them in great swathes of need.

'Stop.'

'Stop what?'

'This,' she said, gesturing between them. 'Whatever it is you're doing, just stop.'

'I would if I could, Princess, trust me.'

'You don't even like me,' she said, unable to help the smallness of her voice.

'I don't have to like you to want you,' he growled, the admittance rough on his voice. 'It's as if it's ingrained in me as much as my childhood lessons. When I should have been learning algebra, instead I learned the cosine of your skin, the angle of your chin, the circumference of your waist and the weight and feel of your breast. When I should have been learning French, instead I learned the language of the sighs of your pleasure, the rhythm and cadence of your pulse and your desire—'

'Stop,' she tried again, but failing to hide the pleading tone in her voice. And that plea called to him, taunting him, challenging him.

'No, Sofia. Because while I learned all these things, you seemed only to learn self-denial and how to lie.'

'And you are here to teach me my own body, Theo?' she asked, incredulity clear in her oceanic eyes.

He couldn't help the bitter laugh that left his lips. 'I would teach you how to demand the pleasure you so desperately plead for, beneath your cultured, perfect words. To unearth the truth of what your body craves beneath your mind's barriers. *Theé mou*, the Sofia I knew would have not hesitated.'

'I don't have to like you to want you.'

The words echoed in her mind. No, 'like' was too easy a word for what lay between them. He blamed her for every awful thing that had happened to him since that night ten years ago, and she blamed him for blackmailing her into this farce, for stealing her choice, even as he professed to give her a choice over this.

'I don't have to like you to want you.'

As if that one true acknowledgement had the power to unlock the cage she had just placed her inner self, her desires and wants into, need escaped as if his voice, his words were the key, twisting again and again within a lock so secure she had thought it never to be opened again.

'You want me?' Sofia said, with a voice raw with desire, turning to stand from the chair and stepping towards him. 'Take me,' she demanded.

He shook his head. Slowly. Not once taking his eyes from hers. 'Oh, no, Sofia. You're going to have to do better than that. You will not be passive in this, I won't allow you to hide behind excuses, proclaiming that I drove you to this. No. If *you* want *me*…then take *me*.'

The spell that had bound her from her wants and needs lifted, the challenge he laid at her feet rose into her accepting hands. Hands that tingled with the need to feel his bare skin beneath them.

Could she? Could she really do this? His words were a call to action, but her insecurities held her back. She wanted this. Wanted him with a need that shocked her, scared her even. But she had never done this before, certainly not with her husband… In truth she'd always dreamed of what it would be like with Theo. Fevered dreams, ones that had left her heated and wanting and unfulfilled.

She crossed the distance between them in shaking strides and when she stood before him, a hair's breadth between them, it was as if she didn't know where to start. She wanted it all. Years of hunger made her body stronger than her indecision. Her fingers trembled as they reached just beneath his perfect suit jacket to slip it from his shoulders, and leave it discarded by their feet.

They were on fire as they went to the silk tie around his neck and fed it through the loop that held it secure. She slid it from the collar of his shirt, focusing on the top button and fumbling slightly.

'Look at me,' he commanded. But she wasn't ready yet. She wasn't ready for him to see the desire and need and…innocence she felt shining from her skin, let alone her eyes. She wasn't ready for him to see the truth of her need for him, because if he did he would know. Know that she hadn't the faintest idea of what she was doing.

She slipped the button through its moorings, her thumb tracing a small pathway over hair-roughened skin, the heat from the contact spreading across the back of her hand, up her elbow and straight to her chest. Another button undone, and another tantalising glimpse of the hard planes of his chest…her hands awkward as they lifted the shirt tails from within the belt of his trousers.

Her fingers slid beneath the white cotton onto his deeply tanned abdomen, rippling beneath her touch, causing her to wonder at the evidence of the effect of her caress. His chin nudged her head to the side as he sought access to her neck. But she pulled away from the reach of his lips. He had told her to take him. So she would.

Unconsciously she arched against his chest like a cat, and when he nudged her thighs apart with his own she nearly cried out loud. The thick muscled thigh rubbing the soft silks of her skirt between her own legs was driving her senses wild. The low thrum that had started at her core now roared to life, pulsing with need for satiation, for his touch, for him.

She pushed him back against the wall, relishing her power, never having guessed that she would feel such a thing in this moment. Their bodies collided as his back pressed against the wall, her breasts aching for him.

She slid the shirt from his shoulders, broad and powerful from hard work and intense labour, and her hands swept behind him as he leant forward, allowing her nails to scratch at the thick, corded muscles, bunched with tension. His head rocked back as she did, a growl on his lips she desperately wanted to silence, because it heightened her own need and pleasure.

A pleasure she sought desperately from him as she learnt the adult body of a boy she had once desired, whilst punishing him by withholding a kiss…because if they kissed she might never find her way back. Instead of seeking his lips, she pressed hers against the suntanned skin of his chest, finding the spot beneath his ribs that caused him to suck in a lungful of air.

His hand came round to grasp her hip, and she brushed it away, refusing to let him share this moment of power she had only just discovered for herself. Within herself. The power that somehow he had given her to finally take what she'd wanted for so, so long.

Her tongue found his hard, flat nipple and flicked, the slight bucking of his body speaking only to the leash of control he was holding so strongly. She hated it, hated that he might have control over something that was almost totally overwhelming her.

Her hands went to his belt and drew the leather apart with a snap. The *hiss* as she undid the zip on his trousers was the only sound other than that of their pleasure, loud in the room.

His hands bunched the silk of her skirt at her thighs, pressing it against her skin as he drew the material higher and higher. Her hand went to his wrist, halting his progress, and a battle of wills ensued, finally drawing her eyes to him. He waited, tension evident in the dark blush against his exquisite cheekbones…waited for her permission to continue, and she marvelled at it. This game of power that was unspoken but clear in every movement, every sigh, every touch.

She released the hold she had on his wrist, and he lifted the skirts of her dress to her waist, one hand pinning the material, the other, pressed between her legs, paused, waiting, allowing the heat from his hand to soothe the ache caused by sheer need.

Sofia couldn't help a blush of embarrassment, as the evidence her desire had dampened the silken thong, and her body rippled as his thumb slid beneath the thin barrier to find her, wet and wanting.

Her head was flung back as the pad of his thumb found her clitoris and he stroked and stroked, ringing a pleasure so acute her legs began to shake. She had no idea that it could be like this, that somehow she had *denied* herself this all these years. She shifted as his hand turned, as his finger plunged into her, the strong, thick cords of his forearm almost holding her in place, holding her where he wanted and where she needed.

'Look at me,' he commanded, and this time she was unable to refuse. The deep brown of his eyes were drowned in pupils so large with desire she lost herself in the dark depths of them.

His lips crashed down upon hers, his tongue prying them open and plunging into her mouth as if he needed to consume her whole. As his tongue delved, so did his fingers, deeper and harder, bringing her to a point she didn't yet want to reach.

Her hands flew back to his trousers, pressing gently at the hard ridge of his arousal, even while her inner sense reeled in shock at her actions, and this time she felt the growl building in the back of his throat. Her fingers reached beneath the waistband of his underwear, desperate for the hot, silken skin covering a steel-like need. A string of Greek curses, too quick for her to decipher, littered the air.

'Bed,' he demanded against her lips.

'No.'

He prised open his eyes to take her in, the fierce look of need and want calling to him in a way he had never imagined, her eyes a shimmering turquoise he had never seen before.

'I need to be very clear on what you are saying no to, Sofia,' he said with a growl.

'The bed, I'm saying no to the bed.'

She glanced at it as if fearful…and perhaps it was not the bed itself but the intimacy it invited. And, while they might be tearing clothes instead of strips off each other, perhaps for her that kind of intimacy between them was not welcome.

'If there is anything else you need to say no to…' He had been called a lot of names in his life, some of which he'd earned, but one thing he would never do was force a woman against her will. There was a special circle in hell reserved for men like that.

He held his breath. It would be hard, but if she asked, he would walk away. Walk away and not look back. He watched as his tone settled about her and she realised the truth of his words.

'I'm saying yes, Theo.'

'You always were contrary,' he growled as he crushed his lips against hers, knowing that there would be no going back. No walking away. Not yet.

CHAPTER SIX

HE TOOK CONTROL as easily as she had given it away.

Peeling his back from the wall and walking her in his arms backwards towards the daybed, he spun them round and pulled her down with him as he lay back on the large expanse of what was probably an original Louis XVI chaise longue.

She still wore her dress, and he his trousers, but frankly he didn't care. The entire length of her body was pressed against his, and it welcomed the light pressure with a sigh.

He had meant what he said. He didn't have to like her to want her. But maybe, he prayed, if they finally gave in to the power of the sensuality that held them together, it would be over. It would sever its hold. Because no matter what woman had graced his bed until now, it had always been her. Sofia. It was she who had called to him in his most fevered of dreams. But the soft-as-silk skin beneath his touch, the heated flesh that seemed to warm even the coldest depths of him, was not a dream, nor a fantasy. She was here. In his arms. And he couldn't get enough.

He drew a knee upward to secure her, imprison her between his legs. The long length of his thigh encased her hip, and she pressed her hands down onto the seat beneath them, holding herself up on toned arms that were deceptively strong.

He didn't want her above him, he didn't like the way she looked down upon him, but the slender neck exposed by the upsweep of her hair called to him. He could resist no longer. His lips and teeth gently nipped at the exposed sweet flesh there, and he inhaled, deeply drinking her in, the soft blueberry and bay scent, heated by her skin, almost a mirror of the first wine he had produced. *Theos*, had he been consumed by her even then? The story he had woven for the obtuse minister came back to haunt him, as did his proclamation that the greatest lies held a kernel of truth.

But he didn't want to think of the past, nor the future, he only wanted to think of now. Her sigh brought him back to the present as easily as if she were a witch who had summoned him.

She placed a hand on his chest, his heart leaping there beneath it, as if it had finally found a missing piece of itself, and he itched to bat it away. Instead, he took her hand in his and pressed his lips against her palm, and even as his body cried out for quick release from this sensual prison he forced himself to stop and savour her as he would a wine. Surely only when he had identified each of the individual flavours, notes of what was unique to her, he would be satisfied, he would *know*.

He took each of her fingers, one by one, into his mouth, his tongue gently sucking on them, relishing the different sounds that fell from her lips as he did so. With one hand he traced the line of her delicate wrist, up to the elbow joint, around the firm muscles beneath her shoulder, and back up to her neck.

She rubbed against him, cradled in his hips, drawing an arousal so acute, so swift, it was almost painful. Once again the game of power was being played between them as she moved to take what she wanted.

He pulled her into his arms, and turned them so that her back was now against the chaise longue, and he was above her, surrounding her with his shoulders and body, and she knew it from the look that entered her heated aquamarine gaze. There was too much assessment there, too much calculation. He wanted her blind with pleasure, as blind as he was at risk of becoming.

He took her lips with his, pressing against the perfect pink plumpness, lathing it with his tongue, drawing moans of pleasure as he plunged into her hot, wet depths, knowing that they were both imagining his tongue somewhere else on her body.

He wanted skin against skin, he wanted to see the rosy, taut nipple he could feel pressing through the material that separated them. He wanted to taste it, tease it.

The dress was beautiful, but it was in the way. His hands ran down her sides, looking for a zip, something, anything to release her from the wrapping and get to the present of her body beneath. He groaned when he could not find anything.

'Theo?'

'The dress...it's...'

She groaned her own frustration. 'It needed nearly two people to get me into the damn thing.'

He looked down on her, for a moment their shared frustration a shared amusement.

'It will only need me to get you out of it,' he said, giving her one last assessing gaze before he took the bottom of the dress, found the side-seam and tore apart the fabric with his hands.

The squeal, almost guilty in its pleasure, that came from Sofia drew an impossible smile from his lips. A smile that died the moment he took in the body that he had been dying to see, touch, taste for nearly ten years.

She was incredible. Her chest bare to him completely, the perfect rounds of her breasts, full and almost tear-shaped against her torso, only her modesty covered by the thin scrap of lace that he had encountered between her legs. She tried to hide from him, her face turned aside as if she was embarrassed by her own skin. Her knees came together before him, as if she was protecting her-self from him. He couldn't help the words of praise that fell against her skin.

'Do not hide from me, Sofia. Not now,' he growled, hating how his voice almost broke under the power of his arousal, of his desire for her. His hands went to her knees, gently levering them apart to make room for him as he leaned over her, finally taking one of her nipples between his lips, lathing it and toying it into perfect hard submission.

Her back arched upwards, against his mouth, the al-most sob that fell from her lips the greatest satisfaction. He worked his mouth and lips lower, in open-mouthed kisses, leaving a damp trail that he knew the air would cool, sending shivers of arousal over her skin.

'Theo,' she begged and the sound of his name on her pleasure-filled voice nearly undid him.

'You want me here, Sofia? My touch, my tongue?' he demanded.

'You would make me beg?' Her voice broke.

'I would make you own it, own your pleasure, Sofia.'

Each time he said her name, her pupils dilated with pleasure. He almost couldn't say it enough. She nod-ded but it wasn't enough. He wanted to hear it, hear her wants, desires…*needs*.

For a moment they simply stared, the war of control ebbing and flowing between them like a tide, as he held himself back from what they both so desperately wanted. Until she said it, until she commanded it, until she gave in to it.

'Yes, Theo. I want—'

Her words were lost to a cry of pleasure as he pulled aside the thin, silken material between her legs, as he uncovered the heart of her with his tongue, as he lathed the length of her and returned again and again to the one place that drew the most exquisite sounds of tormented need from her.

Her hips bucked beneath his ministrations, and he placed a hand low on her abdomen to hold her in place for him, his thumb stroking the silken curls hiding her womanhood.

He took her to the brink of her pleasure again and again, refusing to let her fall. Because when she did, he wanted her to be there with him.

'Theo, please...'

He knew what she wanted, what *he* wanted, for the first time their needs the same.

He reached into the pocket of the trousers he still wore, finding the slim wallet and retrieving the foil packet it contained. He left her body only to discard the trousers, never once taking his eyes from her, as he placed the latex over himself.

'This is the last time I will ask, Sofia. If you have any doubts—'

This time it was she that cut off his words, reaching up to pull him down to her, her hot hand like an anchor at the base of his neck, her legs parting for him as if welcoming him home, her lips barely an inch away from his as she said, 'This is what I want, Theo. That is the last time you will ask me.'

Never had he seen her so regal, so commanding, so powerful in her focus, her intent, her need.

He slid into her, filling her slowly, shifting and…

And the moment he felt her tense, he stopped. Shock and surprise as much in him as it was in her. *Theos*, he hadn't even thought. Hadn't even imagined…

'Sofia—'

'Wait, please…just…'

His body was almost shaking, and he bit back the curse that lay on his tongue. As the implications of her innocence struck him, anger poured through him and he realised the true extent of the lies of her first marriage. She was a virgin and he had not known. And somewhere deep within him that made him both fiercely angry and deeply satisfied. But he held back, because he knew his fury would scare her. *Damn*, her naivety burned him, etching her name on his soul.

As her body relaxed into him, she moved her hips experimentally beneath him.

'Sofia,' he tried again, tried to warn her of what she had already lost.

'I knew what I was asking for, Theo.'

No, she hadn't known. But she would. Soon, she would know and for the first time he hated himself for the path he had set for them both.

She shifted once more against him, his body utterly at her mercy now. All thought fled and, coward that he was, he hid in his body's needs, in Sofia's wants, and finally released the hold he had on his control.

Gently, so gently, he withdrew from her, only to resume a torturously slow return. Subconsciously his body recognised the difference, the change from hurried intent to languorous pleasure, pleasure that was to be all hers.

Theo lost track of time in the sounds of her cries, needful and wanting, he knew only the ripple of her skin, the acres of smooth silk beneath his hands, the warm, luxuriously wet heat of her as he drew them towards the point of completion again and again.

Finally, at Sofia's desperate pleas, he took them into an abyss full of starlight and his last thought was that he was fundamentally changed for ever.

As the water poured over her skin, her heart still racing from what they had shared, still pounding before she'd even lifted her eyes to the scattered stars across the still night sky through the large windows of her room, she marvelled at the stretch of unfamiliar muscles across her body. Languid, but poised, as if already wanting Theo again.

She had meant what she'd said. She *had* known what she was asking for, asking of him. But she had not realised that it would make her feel... She shook her head in the shower, scattering drops of water from her hair. What did she feel? It was too much for words.

But there were words she did know. She knew that they needed to talk. Needed to confront the past...or as much of that night, ten years before, as she would be able to share. Because whether he'd wanted to or not, he *had* given her a moment of choice, of control. And as a result, it had become vital that she explain, vital that he knew that she hadn't had a choice when she'd left that night. That she hadn't purposefully set him up as he clearly believed. She couldn't tell him everything, the secret that locked her heart tight against the truth of her father's diagnosis, the secret that was to protect her country from instability and chaos, one so deep she wasn't sure she'd ever be able to reveal it. But she hoped that she could give him something...give him some sense of resolution about the past. Give him some truth amongst the one lie she still maintained.

She left the shower, wrapping herself in the large towel and retrieving a lightweight trouser suit, readily accepting any armour she could against the conversation that she knew would follow, any protection against Theo's impossibly penetrating gaze.

She dressed and went to sit beside the large windows, peering through the darkness to the elusive shadowscape of her beautiful country. The rolling hills she knew lay beneath the deep night, the mountains in the distance, and all the sleeping inhabitants of Iondorra in between. She heard him stir behind her, the sound of his roughened palm against the smooth silk of the chaise longue, consciously or unconsciously reaching for her, she wondered.

'We should talk.'

'Then I should have coffee.'

She gestured to a coffee machine in the corner of the living suite of her rooms. Soon, she heard the spluttering, juddering sound it made as it filled the air with the fragrant, almost bitter taste of coffee that instantly made her mouth water, and turned to find him standing there in his suit trousers and nothing else. She pushed down the distraction of the smooth planes of sun-darkened skin across his powerful torso. They needed to have this conversation. If there was any hope...

'If we're going to marry—'

'If?'

'*If* we're going to marry, then we need to clear the air. We... I need to tell you about that night.'

Nothing in him moved, not a muscle or a flicker of his eyes. Brooding and powerful. She'd always sensed that ability in him, latent, shimmering beneath the surface, but now? Now it had exploded in a technicolour aura that even the most obtuse would be able to identify. The alpha.

'Would you like to sit?' she said, gesturing to one of the two chairs framing yet another large set of windows.

'I'll stand.'

She nodded, returning her gaze to the panes of glass, but instead only seeing his reflection appearing behind her. Somehow she had always felt his presence, waiting, hovering over her shoulder.

'It may not surprise you to know that I was a wilful child. Stubborn and mischievous. My parents despaired of me. I managed to outwit at least three of the most professional nannies and au pairs Europe had to offer. Two were more than happy to sign non-disclosure agreements protecting their reputations as much as my family's. The last, instead, chose a change in her career path. I believe she is now working with horses.' She paused, taking a breath. Steeling herself against what she was to say. 'It's hard to explain what life was like growing up the only child to two parents whose first and last duty is to their country. Especially when one's own nature seems to run contrary to that sense of duty and self-sacrifice.

'When my parents agreed to enter me at the boarding school with my mother's maiden name, it was excused as being for my protection,' she said, with an absent laugh. 'It may have even been to protect the royal name, in case my wildness ruined that too.'

'In case?' Theo queried, as if the thought of her being anything other than the reckless, wayward teenager was impossible.

'But for me it was my *one* chance. Not to be seen as a royal, not to be the woman who would one day rule a country from beneath her father's long shadow, he the perfect king, and me the improper princess. In truth, we're quite minor royals in the grand scheme of Europe's nobility. It was surprisingly easy, especially given the infamy of many of the other students at the school.

'And at first it *was* easy. Creating the lies that kept my identity secret. They gave me protection from having to join many of the friendship groups my parents thought would help iron out my unsuitable behaviours. It allowed for me to be seen as *me*. And you were such a breath of fresh air to me, and I... I relished it. You didn't treat me as if I would break, or as if I was a disappointment, a failure. You just saw...me. You laughed with me, teased me and I couldn't get enough.

'Rather than bowing and bending to the rules of the school, I struggled against them, seeing it only as another form of constraint, another cage I would eventually swap with a crown.' Sofia took a deep sigh, sore and hurting for the child she had been. 'Much of my behaviour then was selfish and, yes, without thought for the consequences of my actions. I am sorry that I lied to you about who I was but... at the time it was my only comfort. The only light I felt within a bound and trapped existence.'

She watched as Theo shook his head against her words. 'You may excuse your lies as much as you want, but you knew what you were doing, *knew* that it was impossible for you to run away with me as you begged me to.'

She shrugged her shoulders helplessly. 'I think... I think that I believed the story I had told. I wanted so much to go with you, to run away from the school, from my responsibilities, from my future. The hours we spent talking about how it would be, where we would go, they had painted a future so firm in my mind that I...' She had thought she would die if she did not live it. 'Honestly, Theo—of all things, believe that what we shared was what was in my heart. I had no intention of making you take the fall for the prank on the headmaster's car. I had no intention of you being expelled.'

'Then what happened?' he demanded.

'I'd been furious with the headmaster. In design class, I and three others had been assigned a group project, but Anna—one of the group—had needed to return home and failed to pass on her part of the project and the remaining three of us were given detentions by the headmaster for not fulfilling the brief. It seems so petty now, but…then? It had seemed like a great injustice. So we hatched the prank to end all pranks. He loved his Mini Cooper. It was the most precious thing he owned, I think. We realised that if we could put two long planks up against the side of the sports hall, we could get the car onto the roof. Between us, the weight of the car wasn't too much, but the sharp edge of the wheel arch hurt, so I used your scarf to protect my hands and… I must have left it behind.

'I had arranged to meet you, to tell you about it. That was my surprise. I had…been showing off, I suppose. But an hour before I was supposed to meet you that night, there was a knock at my door. When I saw my parents standing there, I thought that they had discovered my part of the prank, I thought that they might have discovered my relationship with you. I was frightened then. For you, for me… So I was confused when…'

And now she began to pick and choose her words. She couldn't reveal her father's diagnosis. They were not yet married, the risk to the country still too great. Perhaps if somehow they managed to pull this marriage off then she could finally unburden herself of her secrets. But not yet. She had already prepared this speech, spent hours of each night in the last month, since he'd forced her hand, trying to work out the best possible threads to share, to unearth, to expose…

'They told me they had come to take me home. Iondorra was in a delicate state politically. There was a trend at the time for the smaller European countries to exchange royal rule for political governance, but our parliament was neither old nor strong enough to assume control. But there was enough talk within the parliament to force my father's hand and have me return in order to assume responsibilities much sooner than intended.'

He had still not moved, and she was still ensnared in his predatory gaze, as if his eyes were gently pressing against her words to find the truth of them.

'That night it was agreed that I would return to the palace, and begin learning what I would need.'

She had thought that at the very least she'd have two years before she would even have to start thinking of assuming royal duties. Two years in which maybe she could come to an understanding with her father...and if her father could just *meet* Theo—see what she saw in him—maybe she could somehow get him to recognise their marriage. Even now, her thoughts showed just how naïve she had truly been then.

In a rush she had told her parents about him. Explained that she was in love, begged and pleaded with them not to do this. Not to take her away from him. She remembered the way she had pulled on her father's lapels with white-knuckled hands, the way her mother had looked at her with both sympathy and pity.

But, as had been made painstakingly clear to her that night, she was their country's future and could no longer entertain a dalliance with 'that Greek', as her father had called him, her father's fear and frustration severing the softness of his affection for her and the freedom he had so often before encouraged.

'Could you not have come to me? Could you not have

explained? Could you not have told me so that when the headmaster discovered me I could defend myself? So that I could make him believe *my* innocence?' His words were quietly spoken, but nonetheless whip-quick and just as painful, and Sofia resisted her body's urge to flinch.

'No and no,' she said sadly, because in truth—she still could not. She knew that the excuses she had presented to him, while very much real, were not the whole story. And she counted on his anger as much as her hope for his understanding—because if he *was* angry he might not see the gaping holes in what she had told him.

'Would you make the same decision again?'

He almost wished he could recall the words the moment that they left his lips. But he knew he needed to hear her answer as much as he needed her to say them. If she said no, then he might try to find a way out of this, to extricate himself from his path of revenge. It was as if there was a tide between them, pushing one way and pulling another. He felt like a man drowning, knowing that one push of the ocean would take him to the depths, one pull could see him back to shore, to safety, to a future he could have only prayed for.

As if Sofia felt that same tide, that same sense of the precipice before them, she turned to him, finally facing him, drawing herself up to her full height, her chin angled up as if to meet an oncoming army.

'There was never a choice. For my country, for my duty, yes. I would do it again in a heartbeat.'

Had she known that was the moment she might have been able to save herself from what was to come, she might have answered differently, he thought. But she hadn't. Instead, she only confirmed the words he needed to hear.

He pressed away the excuses she had given him about

their time together, the slow erosion that had begun against the bedrock of his need for revenge. The image she had woven between them of a young woman trapped within a gilded cage of duty as she battled the natural, sprite-like instinct within her. Of a reckless young girl, ignorant of the consequences of her actions. His determination had begun to give...to loosen its grip around his plans and his feelings for her.

But Sofia's decisions that night had put into motion a chain of events that had led him and his mother to such pain... Had he stayed at the school, gone on to university, his mother would not have had had to work every back-breaking moment of those first five years alongside him, pouring their blood, sweat and tears into the very earth that eventually repaid them. But not without cost. His mother's heart attack could have been prevented. The bright, determined, loving woman he knew had been transformed into a vulnerable, weakened, pallid imitation of herself. And it had only been by nearly losing everything again that he'd been able to fund her treatment. But he could have done better. He could have taken his mother away from that hardship, from that life-or-death battle, had it not been for Sofia.

It took him a moment to realise that the buzzing wasn't just in his ears, but that of a mobile phone nestled on her dressing table.

'Do not answer it,' he commanded darkly. They were not done yet.

He watched her take in the number on the screen.

'I have to.' And for the first time after these ten years of absence he saw fear in her eyes and, speaking into the phone, she asked, 'What's wrong?'

CHAPTER SEVEN

HE HAD MADE Sofia wait while he quickly showered and changed. When she had insisted she needed to go *now* he had refused, firmly stating that five minutes would do no harm. And she hadn't been able to tell him why he was wrong. Bound by secrets she bitterly resented.

She had tried to walk out, but he had caught her arm and ordered her to take a breath. A breath? Even now she felt she hadn't inhaled once since hearing her mother's desperate pleas on the phone. He had dogged her steps as she had tried to leave without him, leaving muttered words like 'stubborn' and 'pig-headed' in their wake.

She scanned her mind for her father's routine. For something that would perhaps explain what could have happened to make her mother beg for her presence.

'You need to come here. Now. Please, Sofia.'

Panic was a feral thing, eating up the small, dark, cramped space of the limousine whisking her away to the small estate where her mother and father lived. Between her fear and Theo's brooding presence, she could barely move. It pressed in around her as she clutched the silk of the trouser suit at her thigh.

'I'll ask again—'

'And I'll say again, Theo, I cannot tell you what's going on. I don't even know.' And she hated the helplessness of her words and the truth in them. As the car drew up to the entrance to her parents' home, she commanded him to stay in the car.

And, for once, he must have seen the seriousness of the situation and listened.

Leaving him leaning against the limousine, the early morning sky barely touched by the light of the sun's rays, Sofia raced through the halls, the bodyguard who had ridden with the driver flanking her side.

One floor down from her parents' living quarters and she could already hear the muffled sounds of her father's anger. Her speed picked up, nearly causing her to stumble at the top of the marble stairs. She rushed through the heavy wooden doors, partly open as if ready for her arrival.

'Get your hands off me. Do you not know who I am?' her father demanded, his face red with anger and frustration.

'Of course they do, Frederick.' Her mother's gentle, soothing tone was doing nothing to calm her father's fury.

The sight of her father's frail old body being restrained by two men was almost enough to bring a cry to Sofia's lips. The skin on his arms loose, as if he were a puppy, still yet to grow into himself. Was this growing old? Sofia wondered. Reverting to a childlike state of tantrums, and folds of paper-thin skin?

'Sofia!' her father cried. 'Make them see. Make them see that they have to let me go. I need to speak to the council. The Prime Minister wants to raise the duty taxes on the…on the…' Becoming even more frustrated with his lack of memory, he growled, pushing and pulling against the two men restraining him.

Sofia didn't know where he was in his mind, but it wasn't now. The Prime Minister had greater things to deal with at the moment than raising duty taxes on anything, so it must have been some years ago.

'Papa, it's okay. We'll speak to him later. It's four o'clock in the morning, and he'll still be asleep. There's time, Papa.'

'No, there isn't,' he said, almost succeeding in throwing off one of the men. Sofia took a step back instinctively, hating the familiarity of the fear thrumming her pulse like a guitarist. Once again she rubbed at her forearm, at the place where a similar night had caused her father to accidentally fracture her arm and two ribs. She'd never forget the look of shock and confusion in her father's eyes as he'd utterly failed to grasp what he had done. It was a terrible thing to fear her own father.

'It's you, isn't it?' he demanded now, bringing her back to the present with a thump.

'What, Papa?'

'*You're* keeping me from him. You only want the throne for yourself. You've been…poisoning me. Whispering evil into my courtiers' ears. You want me gone.'

'Papa, that's not true,' Sofia said, gently, knowing that any trace of concern or upset only made him worse. Everything in her cried, *no*. Proclaimed that she had never wanted it. 'This country needs you. *I* need you.'

'You never needed me,' he growled. 'Running around the castle like some pixie. Desperate to run off with that Greek boy and turn your back on us all.'

The stark irony struck home for Sofia, but she tried instead to cling to the quickly changing direction of his chain of thought, so easy to flip between her wanting the throne and wanting to throw it away.

'We should have let you go to him. You will be the death of this country. You were never fit to rule,' he cried as one of the carers administered an anti-psychotic drug.

For them to be doing this now meant that they must have been struggling with him almost since he'd left the engagement party. Sofia knew they would have tried everything else.

'I know, Papa,' she couldn't help but admit as he somehow drew out her greatest fears. 'But I'm trying. I really am.'

As the two men assisting her father settled him gently back into a chair, her mother watched her with large, shimmering eyes.

'Sofia—'

'It's okay, Mama, I know. I know he doesn't mean it,' she lied as she turned away. Fear, sadness, loss, grief, it all pressed against her skin like little pin pricks, drawing blooms of invisible blood that left her feeling drained and exhausted.

Theo was watching the sun rise slowly over the forest surrounding the estate, the scent of pine and earth slowly unfurling from the ground in the gentle heat of the early morning. He relished that almost sappy resin taste and he tried to combine grape lineages in his mind in an attempt to distract himself from Sofia's revelation only an hour before.

He could tell that she had been giving him some truths. There was definitely something she was holding back, but…tiny tendrils of doubt about that night were corroding his fierce belief that she had purposefully set him up. They spread through his chest and tightened around his heart. Because just beneath that erosion was something deeper. Something darker and much more painful. Something that spoke of grief and the acrid taste of loss, one he remembered from years before meeting Sofia. This odd sense that he'd lived with almost all his

life…a barely audible whisper from an inner voice…
abandoned, again.

Usually Theo could go for months without thinking of
the man who had run from his mother, run from *him*. But
ever since he had set out on this path of revenge he had
always been a shadow at the periphery of Theo's vision,
hovering, waiting. He remembered thinking as a child
that it was only natural to think of his father and had half
convinced himself that when he became a man, when
he was eighteen, he'd somehow magically stop thinking
of him. And to a certain extent that had been true. But
only because of the damage limitation he'd been forced
into following Sofia's actions. But here, in Iondorra, a
place that—as far as Theo knew—his father had never
set foot, a phantom pain was tingling, burning back into
a life he thought he'd long snuffed out.

The creak of the large doorway at the top of the stone
steps to the estate cut through the early morning air, and
the moment he saw Sofia all thoughts fled his mind.

She looked…devastated. And it was horrible. Because
he recognised that look. It was the look a child wore, no
matter their age, when something truly awful was happening to a parent. He had seen it the moment he'd looked
in the mirror after his mother had been taken to hospital.

He went to take a step towards her but held himself
back. He wanted to take her in his arms, to hold her in the
way that no one had held him that day. But he couldn't.
Whether for her, or himself, he didn't know.

'Sofia?'

She descended the steps as if in a daze, her eyes unsee-
ing, a numbness almost vibrating from her. This woman
who had come alive in his arms, to his touch and his need
only hours ago, was now hollow and absent. She came
to stand before him, her head barely reaching his shoul-

ders, so that he had to bend almost, to try and catch her sightless gaze.

'Sofia…' Her name almost a plea on his lips.

'Take me away, Theo. Please.'

Her request rang out over the years from all that time ago, the one he so desperately wanted to forget. They were words he had thrown back at her outside the Parisian ballroom. As if realising it herself, only after it was too late to recall them, she flinched. And then trembled.

'Entáxei.' He nodded. 'Okay,' he repeated for her benefit. 'We will go.'

And then he finally gave in to his desire, and pulled her into an embrace.

He had spoken briefly to the chauffeur of the change in plans and, while settling Sofia into the back of the limousine, Theo started on the phone calls needed. He'd pulled up the contact details for Sofia's personal secretary, ordered her to pack a bag and get it to the airport, and cancelled all Sofia's appointments for a week. He'd messaged Seb to make his apologies to Maria, realising that he'd be unable to make the exhibition he'd assured her he'd attend the night before.

As the limousine ate up the miles of smooth tarmac, he began to doubt his decision. He had never taken a woman back to his winery, to the place where his mother still lived. He wondered what she would make of the young princess and hated that he had once had the same thought, under the same circumstances. Hated the fact that he would introduce Sofia to his mother as his fiancée, only to abandon her at the altar. But he would. He must. Because only then would she realise just how much damage she had caused. Just how much hurt…

But as the limousine passed the castle and carried on,

it failed to draw any kind of response from Sofia. The kind of numbness that she wore about her like a shield began to scare him. He remembered that feeling. That hopelessness that was so very easy to hide in. And he couldn't help the wish, the need, to protect her. To shelter her, even if it ran contrary to his own plans. She needed to get away. She needed to find herself again. And for the first time Theo began to doubt his plan for revenge.

Sofia opened her eyes and frowned in momentary confusion at the unfamiliar sights that met them. And then she remembered. Remembered the short flight on Theo's private jet, the drive to the exclusive marina, remembered the way that Theo had ushered her onto the small, but beautiful and most definitely luxurious, yacht and walked her straight into the cabin and ordered her to sleep.

Smooth mahogany surrounded her, and the gentle, rhythmic sway beneath her called her back to that blissful slumber. Sofia wanted nothing more than to bury herself in the comfortable bedding, but unease told her she couldn't. Instinct, memories, they all crashed about her mind and she felt…it all. The numbness that had settled about her had finally worn off, and everything in her hurt. Ached. Her heart for her father, her head for Theo, and her bones, a deep, low ache—that was for herself.

Untangling herself from the nest of sheets wrapped around her body, she sat up, swung her legs over the side of the bed and saw a bathroom off to the left. Peeling off clothes that felt days old, she turned on the shower, not even giving it time to warm up. The shocking cool jets of water hit her skin like a slap, bringing her round, before the water warmed and comforted like an embrace.

By the time she had emerged from the bathroom, a selection of clothes were laid out on the bed. Someone had been in here while she was in the shower. Unseen hands had placed the clothes on the bed she had only just left, an unseen body had been barely a foot from hers while she was naked in the shower, and instinctively she knew. Theo.

While everything in her wanted to scrabble into the clothes and rush to find him, demand that he take her back to Iondorra, she forced herself to stop. To slow the speeding of her thoughts.

Take me away, Theo. Please.

She had asked him for this. She blinked back the tears that pressed against the backs of her eyes. She wouldn't cry. She wouldn't break. But she needed this. She needed him. Perhaps, instead of rushing back to be the princess everyone wanted, she could steal this time away, just for herself. Before duty fell like a tolling bell against her, before there was no turning back.

Dressed in a soft white linen shirt and blue capri trousers, Sofia left the bedroom and followed the small galley to the stairs in front of her. The sun beckoned from where it slanted through the shadows and Sofia realised she had no idea what time it was.

Bare feet took the metal steps up to the deck of the boat, and when she emerged into the light she looked up at the stunning sloping arc of a brilliant white sail against a cloudless azure sky. The yacht was small—as in not one of the monstrosities that many rich Europeans preferred—but long and incredibly beautiful.

She would have stopped at the sight of the sea, stretching out on all sides as far as the eye could see, the magnificence of the aquamarine water melding with the sky at an invisible horizon. She would have stopped to relish the heat of the sun as it drenched her in a comforting warmth, finding even the darkest places of her heart and healing it beneath the touch of the rays. But nothing, *nothing* compared to the sight of Theo at the helm of the boat tall and proud as he directed the wheel with just the palms of his hands, his fingers outstretched, his movements smooth and his gaze on the horizon...until he turned that powerful gaze on her.

The sight of him took her breath away. His dark hair was wind-tousled, and a pair of sunglasses may have masked his eyes, but they did nothing to conceal the proud cheekbones and jut of his strong jaw, a jaw covered in a dark brush of stubble that just cried out to be touched. His white shirt, buttoned low, exposed a chest of defined muscle, dustings of dark swirls hidden then revealed as the linen was shaken by the wind. Dark navy linen trousers hung low on his lean hips, and Sofia bit back a curse or a plea to the gods, she honestly couldn't tell any more. This was not the man-child she had fallen for in her youth, this was something altogether different. Her eyes ate up the changes in his body, the muscles corded in his forearms, the glimpses of the trail of hair leading below the beltline of his trousers, the wide stance of his bare feet planting him securely on the wooden deck, looking for all the world as if he were its ruler.

All these things she had not taken in when they had come together...she had been blinded by passion then, and now? Now he simply stood there bearing the weight of her scrutiny, allowing her to take her fill. It was too much, and she used the excuse of the bright sun to shield her eyes, breaking the connection that had bound them together for a moment.

'There are sunglasses over there. As well as some deck shoes, and in the cooler bag some breakfast.'

He gestured to the bench just across the deck and she found everything he had described.

'You need to use the sunscreen too,' he said as he secured the wheel, and disappeared below deck. She sprayed herself liberally with the lotion and donned the pair of beautiful sunglasses. She was just reaching into the cooler bag for a pastry when the scent of fresh coffee mixed with the sea-salt air. She nearly groaned out loud.

'Still drink coffee like a lifeline?'

'Yes,' she smiled, the feeling on her lips foreign and strange after the last few weeks. 'Can't live without it,' she said, gratefully accepting the mug he offered her. She watched as the sea wind whipped away the steam before it could swirl and dance above the dark liquid. Waiting for it to cool before taking a sip, she turned back to the horizon. 'Where are we?'

'The Ionian Sea.'

'It's beautiful.'

He nodded. And for a moment she was glad that they shared this silence. That he allowed her to listen to the sounds of the waves crashing against the hull of the yacht as it glided through the water, the whip and crack of the sail as it strained against the wind. She knew he had questions, she could feel them emanating from him, but that he had not yet voiced them was a pleasant relief.

'You got your boat,' she said with a sad smile, remembering their youthful plans of some impossible future, the ones made at the Swiss boarding school.

'Eventually,' he said, the word marshalled as if he'd wanted to say more.

Theo resumed his position behind the wheel and she folded her feet beneath her on the bench and sipped at her coffee, savouring the strong hit of caffeine and the smooth, sweet taste of the honey he had added. He remembered. She feared that he remembered everything.

It had been so easy to embrace her anger for him when he was being demanding, blackmailing and ruthless. Even when he had played her body's desires against her, plucking strings between them she had long thought severed. But now? Now she could see glimpses of the youth she had fallen for. His kindness, his acceptance of her, unlike anything she had ever known before then, and not since. Not even with Antoine.

If he had forced her to explain, shouted and demanded, she would have retreated. But in this space he gave her she found herself unfurling, expanding within it in a way that was all about her. Not about duty, or trade negotiations, not about a ring she would wear, or a role she would play for her country, for her family.

She couldn't remember the last time she had found time for silence, for herself and her thoughts. Even as she considered it, she felt the rising panic, the fear that something might be happening and she wouldn't know about it. As much as she hated it, she started to look for her phone.

'Your people have instructions to call me if they need you. They have the number of the yacht's satellite phone. Your mobile wouldn't have signal out here anyway.'

'But the meeting with the Hungarian ambassador—'

'Has been rescheduled.'

'And the interview with the *New York Times*?'

'And with *Paris Match*, the Iondorran prime minister, and the Swiss consulate. Your assistant is nothing if not efficient.'

'Yes,' she said, smiling at the thought of the apparently ruthlessly organised Theo dealing with her imperious assistant.

Instead of panic at the thought of all these important events in her diary, she felt oddly relieved. For so long she had borne the brunt of her duties alone. For the first time it felt as if she had someone with her to share the load. Even if only to make the decision she would have known she had to make, but been incapable of making.

She caught sight of Theo's cocked head as he observed her. 'What?' she asked, feeling around her mouth and chin for flakes of the pastry that might have remained from her breakfast, oddly self-conscious under his scrutiny.

'You don't mind,' Theo stated.

'Mind what?'

'That I rearranged it all. I thought you would be hissing like a cat, threatening to throw me overboard and leave me behind in the sea as you hightailed it back to dry land and the nearest helicopter.'

'That's quite a long chain of thought you had there.'

'You were asleep for quite a while. I had enough time to imagine several possibilities.'

'There was definitely a time that tossing you overboard would have seemed like the right thing to do.' But her words reminded her that that was almost exactly what she had done ten years before. And just like that the dam was lifted on the all the questions and all the curiosity about him she had hidden beneath layers and years of denial about him. About them. 'Can I ask…how did you get here? Your own yacht, a billion-euro wine industry… how did you make it happen?'

It hurt him, scratched at a wound that he had buried deep, that she had never thought to find out what had happened to him after that night. That she had so easily discarded him, even as he had at first stalked the internet to find any trace of news of her, as if knowing what she was doing would make the hurt and betrayal any less… or worse in some masochistic way. He pushed back his bitter thoughts and focused on her question.

'When I returned to my mother, she was already packing our belongings. Moritz, my mother's employer, was understanding, but his wife…not so much. She was furious that I had squandered the opportunity they had so generously provided and was determined that we should not bring further shame to their family name.' He still remembered the woman screeching at him and his mother from the top of the stairs, the way all the servants in the house had gathered to watch and the way, despite all this, his mother had placed her arms around him as if to protect him. He remembered the last look Moritz had cast him before they had left. One of pity, not shame, but full sadness and disappointment. He had never wanted to see such a look ever again.

'We returned to my mother's family because there was nowhere else to go. And it started up almost immediately. The snide comments, the years of resentment. My father's abandonment of his pregnant lover had consigned my mother to a life of shame. And the expulsion from school? Just compounded it.'

He couldn't look at Sofia as he told her this. He didn't want to see her expression, to see the truth of her feelings, so instead he looked out to the horizon as he steered the yacht to some indefinable destination.

'My mother had saved some money. Not a huge amount, but some. Enough to buy some land from her family. They were happy to get rid of it, and us, to the small home nestled in its boundary. The land was hard, dry and difficult and not one of them had ever been able to grow a thing on it. Their small winery was failing and, though they did not welcome her, they welcomed my mother's money, every last, single cent of it.' He couldn't help the bitterness in his tone. He hated them for what they had done to his mother. 'They could just as easily have given it to us because it had never made them any money and they hadn't used it for years, almost two generations. Which, ironically, is why it was much easier for me to work with it.

'For the first six months, I simply cleared the land. Each day, each night, bit by bit.' It was as if the mind-numbing work had been the only thing that had kept him going in those first few months where he'd been so raw it felt as if his very heart was exposed to the elements. The pain, the ache of her betrayal, the humiliation that he'd been taken in by her lies. But now, after all that had happened between them, he began to recognise something else in his feelings... the heartbreak that she had turned her back on him. That she had left him. The jagged, wrenching pain that had made it almost difficult to breathe at times.

'My mother would help.' But only when she was feeling up to it, he now recognised. 'I hadn't realised how much knowledge I'd garnered from working in my mother's family's fields. The soil was good, having been left fallow for so long. I worked to ensure decent irrigation systems were in place to not undo all the work already achieved.

'Nikos, my neighbour, would watch from the seat in front of his home. He and my mother would sometimes share a coffee, and occasionally he'd call out suggestions. Mostly he was calling me several shades of a fool for doing it, but,' Theo said with a smile, 'it just made me more determined.

'Once the land was cleared, the night before I was to

start planting Nikos called me over for dinner. Of course, his idea of food was three-day-old, tough-as-a-boot rabbit stew, but the *raki* was good. And so was a bottle of wine he produced from his cellar.

'He explained that it was his own wine, from a small variety of grape that had been growing on his land for generations. He'd never told my mother's family because in his opinion they were money-grabbing, pious *malakes*—his words—something we both agreed on. We stayed up until about three in the morning that night, drinking the few bottles of wine he'd produced. The problem with his grape was that, while it was hardy, it was also harsh. But it had potential. I think we must have talked about the characteristics of the grape, the barrel, the age, with more detail than scientists discussing genetic testing.

'So the next day, instead of planting pure *malagousia*, I took a risk. Half the land was the *malagousia*, and the other half was Nikos's grape. He didn't know the lineage of it, and his grandfather had probably forgotten the name of it. To Nikos, it was just wine. To me, it was the perfect grape to blend.

'The first two years were terrible.' He huffed out a reluctant laugh. It covered the sheer hours of the day he had spent outside, tending to those damn vines. But he wouldn't have changed it for anything. Those years were ones spent with his mother. Eating together, working together, laughing… Before it was nearly cruelly ripped away from him and he realised the true cost of the land.

Could he really lay the blame of his mother's illness at Sofia's feet? Could he hold to the anger that had driven him over the years and once again the moment she had refused to make a different decision? One that might have prevented his mother from ever having to experience such a devastating attack on her health?

In the silence that had settled between them he re-alised that the wind had picked up and set about secur-ing the lines, considering whether or not he needed to bring down the sail.

'Did you ever think about giving up?'

'Every single hour of every single day,' he replied.

'But you didn't.'

'I wouldn't be standing here today if I had.'

'Do you...?' She paused and it drew his gaze to her. 'Do you ever wonder,' she pressed on, 'what would have happened if I had stayed? If perhaps...we could have had the life we'd hoped for?'

Whether he blamed her for what happened to his mother or not, Sofia had still not learned the conse-quences of her actions. Or she would never have asked that damn question.

'Never,' he bit out.

Her sigh was stolen by the wind, and he stalked the length of the deck, hoping that she would leave the con-versation alone. But his hopes were in vain.

'I do. I thought I hadn't, but... I was just lying to my-self. I did. Especially in those first few months. I'd wake up expecting to see you beside me, expecting to find my reality a dream, and my dream a reality.' The wistfulness in her voice cut him deep and he tried to ignore it, espe-cially as she stood and made her way towards the side of the yacht. 'But perhaps,' she pressed on, 'it wouldn't have worked. It was a childhood fantasy. We couldn't have lived off dreams and desire. Reality would have always been waiting around the corner.'

'We would have made it work,' he said despite him-self, finally looking back at her to find her standing at the side of the yacht, looking out at the sea.

'Really? The princess and...'

'The pauper,' he replied.

'You were never a pauper to me.'

'You were *always* a princess to me.'

The wind cracked the sail, lines creaking and groaning under the sway of the boat. The boom started to move, and terror raced through his veins. He shouted a warning to Sofia, but it was too late—she didn't hear him and, facing the sea, was ignorant of the oncoming danger. As the large wooden boom swung round with speed and weight he launched himself towards her, but was too far away. Sofia turned just in time to raise her hands to take the brunt of the hit, but not enough to avoid it. It caught her across the shoulder and thrust her into the sea.

CHAPTER EIGHT

THEO HATED HOSPITALS. He felt as if the sterile scent of
them carried on the air entered his bloodstream and
scratched at him from the inside out. He hadn't been
back to this one since he had mortgaged his life to the
hilt to fund his mother's operation, and he couldn't stop
pacing, desperate to escape its walls, but unable to leave.

Lyssandros, the doctor who had become his personal
physician of sorts, had kicked him out of Sofia's room for
his assessment. Fear. It was a feral, living thing within
him. Had he reached her in time? She hadn't been under
the water more than five seconds before he'd dived in to
reach her. He'd pulled her out, hauled her onto the deck and
secured her as quickly as possible, before he dropped the
sail and used the motor to get them back to land, breaking
every maritime speed law around the world. A helicopter
had met them at the marina, and staff had dealt with the
vessel as he and Sofia were brought to the hospital.

He'd fought with Lyssandros not to leave her side, and
even during the MRI scan he'd been in the small booth
with the older man, ignoring the quiet discussions and
assessments going on around him as he'd been unable to
take his eyes from Sofia's small frame.

She'd been in and out of consciousness, babbling
strange words that had scared him. She seemed to have

been having an argument with someone about not wanting to leave. It had taken him a few rounds of the repeated conversation to realise that she wasn't imagining herself on the yacht with him, but at some long-ago point in time as she begged and pleaded to stay. He'd been able to do nothing but soothe and promise her that he wouldn't make her leave, but he doubted Sofia had heard him.

A sound at the door to her private room alerted him, and he spun round to find Lyssandros saying something to a nurse and dismissing her. Finally the older man turned to him.

'She is going to be okay.'

Breath whooshed out of Theo's lungs, and he pinched the bridge of his nose as if it were the only thing holding him together. *Dóxa to Theó.*

'She has a concussion, unsurprisingly, so I want to keep her in overnight at least. Given her…status, it's possible that her people might want to move her—'

'They don't know about it yet.'

'Theo,' the doctor admonished. 'She's a princess, so her people, family, even her country, will want to know about this.'

'I'm not keeping it from them, but she needed this time away and—'

'Okay. It's your call, but if I'm asked—I had no idea who she was, other than your fiancée.'

'That's very ethical of you.'

Lyssandros smiled ruefully, though there was a hint of something in the other man's eyes that made Theo pause.

'What's wrong? You said she was okay,' Theo practically growled.

'She is, Theo. She is,' he said, placing a large hand on Theo's shoulder. 'But…look, I really shouldn't be saying anything, and I wouldn't…but it did give me some concern. It wouldn't have been picked up in a normal assessment, but you asked for every test under the sun, and I did them.' Lyssandros led Theo a little further away from the nurses' station of the private wing Sofia had been brought to.

'I don't know what happened, only Sofia will be able to tell you that, but I've noticed a few injuries that would seem…unusual for a…for someone of her status.'

Theo frowned. 'Injuries? She usually has the reflexes of a cat.' Or at least she had done when they were at school. She had to have had, to get the headmaster's car on top of the sports hall. Except when she was distracted, as she had been on the yacht.

'It looks to have happened about a year, maybe a year and a half, ago, from the healing patterns, but around that time she took what must have been a pretty hard hit.'

'A hit from what?'

Lyssandros shrugged. 'She had a fractured ulna—' he gestured to his forearm '—and several broken ribs. I only mention it because it's uncommon for an adult to fracture only one of the two bones in the forearm, unless they are defending themselves.'

'Could she have done it horse riding?' Theo queried, unable to quite understand how else it could have happened.

'I would have expected more damage, or less, depending.'

'You think it was a person. You think she was attacked.'

The older man nodded. 'As I said, it's only because of her status that I ask.'

Theo clamped his jaw on a million unasked questions, able to voice only one. 'May I?'

'Of course,' Lyssandros said, directing him to the door to Sofia's room.

* * *

Sofia's throat felt as if someone had poured sand down it, and she was half convinced that someone was trying to prise her head open with a jackhammer. When the door opened she managed to force her eyelids up enough to take in a figure wearing blue scrubs, and promptly closed them again. If she never saw another doctor again, it would be too soon. She wanted to go. Where, she wasn't sure. She didn't want to be back in Iondorra yet, and she wondered why Theo hadn't arrived to whisk her away. Had he left her? Had he finally decided that even his wine sales weren't worth this much hassle? The thought rocked her. Is this what he'd felt that night? Tears began to gather behind her closed eyes, but she wouldn't cry. Not in front of some stranger.

'Sofia…'

Her eyes flew open to find Theo coming to sit on the edge of the bed.

'Theo? What are you doing in scrubs?'

The rueful smile on his perfect lips did nothing to hide the fierce concern in his gaze. 'Lyssandros, the doctor, told me that I was getting his medical centre wet, so forced me to change into these,' he said, pulling distastefully at the blue material.

'Why were you wet?'

'Do you not remember? You fell into the sea, and I went in after you.'

'You did?'

'How else would you have got out?'

Sofia sighed. 'I'm surprised you didn't leave me in there,' she grumbled, frustrated with herself for not being able to put the pieces of what had happened together in her own mind. The doctor—Lyssandros—had explained that it was to be expected, and, as long as the confusion was only around the accident, he wasn't too concerned. All her tests had come back fine mostly. A bang to the head from the fall, a decent bruise to her shoulder from where the boom had caught her, but aside from that she'd been lucky.

'I was tempted. But the Greek government might frown at the manslaughter of a princess.'

'It would have been murder if you'd intentionally left me.'

'I'd have got away with it.'

A smile pulled at the corners of her mouth, just as a wave of exhaustion descended. 'When can I get out of here?'

'Tomorrow.'

'I hate hospitals. Can you sneak me out?'

'Lyssandros is as close as a friend, but even he's not taking risks with you.'

And neither am I. She felt his words, without him voicing them.

'I want to go,' she said, the words slightly slurred.

'I know. But you're safe here. I'm not going anywhere.'

Sofia tried to shake her head, but that hurt, and whatever she'd been about to say disappeared as she fell into the welcoming arms of sleep.

When she next woke, Sofia was thankful that the light didn't hurt her eyes any more, and she experimentally moved her head from side to side, relishing the fact that the jackhammer seemed to have given up.

She turned to find Theo in the chair beside her, his long legs thrust out in front of him, his head resting awkwardly on his fisted hand, elbow on the arm of the chair, and even in sleep the man looked incredible.

Long, midnight-coloured eyelashes dusted his cheeks, his dark hair tousled as if he'd spent the entire night thrusting his hands through it, and his jawline was now in serious risk of growing a half-decent beard. She kind of liked the look on him. It made him even more…just more.

When a nurse entered, Sofia thrust a finger to her lips, unwilling to wake him. The small, dark-haired woman smiled conspiratorially and came to her side to check the little monitor assessing her vitals.

'How are you feeling?' she whispered.

'Like I was struck off a yacht by a boom.'

She huffed out a small laugh. 'You should be able to go soon. I'll have the doctor sign your discharge papers.'

'Thank you. I can speak to the Iondorran consulate and arrange for payment if—'

'No need. That's all been taken care of.'

At Sofia's frown, the nurse gestured to Theo, still asleep, and Sofia nodded and sighed. Not only had he rescued her from the sea, but also paid for her care. He was hardly getting his money's worth out of this, was he? A thread of sadness began to wind through her. Was that all there was between them or could there ever be more? she wondered. For years she had consigned thoughts and memories of him to a locked box in her heart. But now? She wasn't so sure any more.

It took them about an hour to get out of the hospital, partly because Sofia had wanted to thank everyone who had treated her. She made a mental note to ensure there was a donation to the hospital for their generosity and discretion. She couldn't express how relieved she was that there were no reporters camped out on the steps, that no international incident had been accidentally created. She wasn't naïve enough to think that it was out of respect for her, and could plainly see the adoration for Theo in the faces of most of the medical staff. He seemed to be on first-name terms with half of them, and it went beyond simple patronage, which confused her a little. Surely he had not worked up such strong bonds just in the time of her overnight stay there?

She waited on the steps to the hospital as a man brought round a large black Jeep and handed Theo the keys.

He ushered her into the passenger seat and went round to the driver's side, and got in.

'You're driving yourself?'

'Why? Did you want to?' he said with a laugh.

It stung. She couldn't help it. 'I can't.'

'When you're feeling better—'

'I can't drive,' she said angrily. It had been a small fight with her father, certainly not one of their greatest, but it had hurt just as much. Somehow it had become a larger symbol of all the things she wasn't allowed to do as a princess-in-waiting. But more than that, it had signified the true end to her freedom.

'I suppose you don't need to know how to drive,' Theo said as he pulled out of the hospital car park.

'No. I suppose I don't,' she replied bitterly, and almost growled when she saw Theo suppress a laugh. 'It's not funny.'

'I'm not laughing at you, Princess. It's just that you're cute when…when you're angry.'

'I'm not cute either,' and even she couldn't help but let loose a small laugh at the ridiculousness of her own sulk. This. This was what she had missed most about him. The ease. The ease and friendship that had turned into distrust and resentment the moment they had met again in Paris. 'Where are we going?' she asked to turn the wayward direction of her thoughts.

'Home. *My* home.'

Theo directed the car with the same ease with which he had directed the boat. He had always loved travel, movement, something that appeased the restlessness he'd always seemed to feel back in Greece. The freedom he felt at being in charge of his own destiny, especially having spent years at the whim of the elements and the vineyard. He couldn't imagine not being able to control that, and wondered whether that was what had made Sofia so bitter. Not being able to choose when and where and how she wanted to go.

He frowned as he remembered the thread of a conversation from the night in Monaco.

'I have no choice in this whatsoever.'

Casting an eye over to where Sofia slept, he felt unease stir in his chest. He hadn't given her a choice. Not really, no matter what he had said to her. Every single moment of that night in Paris, and then Monaco, had been carefully orchestrated to ensure Sofia's ultimate humiliation. But now? Was that still what he wanted?

He changed lanes and came off the motorway as they began to make their way through the Peloponnese countryside, travelling along the southern part almost to the border with Messinia.

Cypress and olive trees skirted the mountains in the distance, scarred with jagged lines of white stone and brown scrub, and through the open window the scent of home filled the Jeep. Large stretches of mottled green land were occasionally interrupted by red-roofed towns and he welcomed the sight of them. Arcadia might not be the typical tourist destination popular with travellers from across the world, as Athens and the islands were, but that just made it even more precious to him.

It had been hard hit in recent years, especially with so many of the younger generation leaving for America, or other parts of Europe, but its people were surviving, hard work and determination making the most of this place that could be made. He was pleased that his vineyard had grown to such an extent that he now employed almost half of the nearby town. The estate he and his mother had dreamed of building one day was now able to offer luxurious stays in the vineyard, wedding packages and tours, and the seven-course wine-tasting menu at the Michelin-starred restaurant enticed guests from all over the world.

He pulled off into the road that led towards the gated estate, slowing until the electronic security system at the side entrance recognised the car's plate, just as Sofia stirred from her sleep.

The gates opened and he guided the car down the long drive, the smooth turns allowing him to observe Sofia's eyes growing wide as she took in the large, sweeping vineyard to the left.

'This is…magnificent,' she sighed and he couldn't help the swell of pride he felt deep in his chest.

'This is only a quarter of the vineyard. There is more to the back of the estate.'

'Where is…?' She trailed off as they rounded the last bend and the building before them rose up to greet them. 'Oh.'

He took in the sight of it as if with her eyes—eyes that had never before seen the estate. The large central building was almost monastic in design, built from reclaimed grey stone, and had sweeping archways that his mother had loved from the first sight of it. It provided the entrance as well as the large dining restaurant and access to the front half of the wine cellars below, the area that was available for guest tours.

The more modern annex off to the left provided views both front and back from large windows on three floors for each of the guest suites, all of the twenty rooms lavishly designed with en suite bathrooms big enough to house the first home he and his mother had shared on the land. One that was still tucked away at the back of the large property.

'Theo, this is incredible,' Sofia said as he pulled up to the staff car park to the side of the building. He could tell from the number of vehicles in the guest parking area that they were at low capacity. He cast his mind over the appointments and remembered that the estate was winding down before a wedding booking in just two days' time.

She was out of the car before he was.

He watched her spin in a slow circle, taking in the view of the estate. 'Do you want to freshen up? There's—'

'No!' She turned, laughing. 'I want to *see*. I've been in bed for twelve hours or more, sleeping in the car for the last three, and now I want to move. Please? Show me?'

And he wondered when he'd ever really been able to deny her anything.

'I would love nothing more. But I intend to do it in something other than a pair of scrubs,' he said, pulling at the scratchy material of the blue top. 'It will still be there after a shower and a change of clothes. I promise.'

Sofia had been surprised by the sheer magnificence of Theo's vineyard. Oh, she'd known that he had made money from his business, clearly enough to gain entry to the society of the masquerade ball in Paris. As she cast her mind back she remembered his taunt about his billionaire status and couldn't help but marvel at what he'd achieved.

The marble flooring in the entrance to the main building was beautiful and shot with veins of dark green and black. She had watched, fascinated, as Theo had nodded to his employees on Reception, paused to ask after the father of one of the young girls manning the desk. It gave Sofia time to explore the room. She marvelled at the wooden bench that stretched the entire length of the room. On top were squares of slate, wedging wine bottles in between, with handwritten names and descriptions in italicised chalk. Beneath were large oak barrels that added a touch of authenticity as well as artistic integrity to the main hall.

When she turned she found Theo watching her, as if waiting for some kind of censure or disapproval. She sent him a reassuring smile, and he whisked her away to the private wing.

He had deposited her and her bag retrieved from the boat in a room most definitely fit for a princess. The large canopied bed had been an indulgence she had never personally given into, but loved the moment she set her eyes on it. Rustic luxury. She was surrounded by it.

The bathroom was something completely other. One entire wall was lined in antique mirrors, in front of which was a free-standing cast-iron bath. To the left was a large window that looked out on to a stretch of vineyard behind the property. She hung back slightly, wondering if she would be seen, but realised that from this height and distance only the birds would be able to spy her.

In the corner was a glass-fronted shower, large enough for two people…in her mind, two people that looked very much like her and Theo. A blush rose to her cheeks as her wayward imagination ran wild…a heady mixture of memory and fantasy, desire and need aching within her. When they had come together after the engagement party, anger and resentment had dominated despite her aching desperation to feel him. She wondered if that would be so now? If perhaps to make love to Theo would be different…

She turned the shower on and stripped off the clothes that clung to her aching body. She had said that she wanted to see the vineyard but knew that Theo had been right. She allowed the hot jets of water to ease the aches from the last few hours, gently washing her hair, careful of reawakening the dull ache from the fall into the sea. Scrubbing away the remnants of the salt water, she felt fresh, new and oddly happy.

Happy. She considered it. When had she last felt it? A small part of her was so sad that she couldn't remember when it had been. She padded into the bedroom wrapped in a towel and searched through the bag of clothes that had been packed for her by her assistant back in Iondorra.

Her fingers brushed something lacy, and with something like horror and fascination she produced a silk negligee fit for a honeymoon. Doubting very much that Theo had requested such a thing, she realised that her assistant had only packed what Sofia might have wanted for a last-minute getaway with her fiancé.

Because he *was* her fiancé. No matter how or why it had happened, it was the case. And she would be marrying him. But what would that marriage look like now? The start of their engagement had been all anger and vengeance, but somehow over the last few days that had changed, and it had morphed into something that she hardly dared to hope for.

Placing the negligee on the bed, she dug into the bag and produced a pair of tan high-waisted linen palazzo pants and a cream silk vest. With her hair still wet, she wound it into a knot and secured it high on her head.

She buckled a pair of brown leather low-wedge sandals at her ankles and, snagging the sunglasses on her way out, left her room and returned to the reception area, safe in the knowledge that Theo would find her there when he was ready.

When Theo found her, Sofia was leaning against the large domed archway, her slender hips shown to perfection by the trousers encasing her narrow waist, one ankle crossed over the leg bearing her weight, and the wind blowing the loosely tucked-in silk top. It was such a sight it gave him pause. Pause for what he was about to do, because he knew that he couldn't continue on his path of revenge without first finding out what had happened to cause the fracture of her arm and damage done to her ribs. Without finally getting to the truth of her. The fierce streak of protectiveness that leapt to life in his chest at the mere thought of it shocked him with its intensity.

As if she sensed his presence, she turned, her face cast in a shaft of soft sunlight peering through the shadows of the cool reception, and her smile caught him low in his chest. He stalked towards her, fighting with his desire to haul her into his arms and kiss her. Kiss her in a way he hadn't since he was seventeen. Kiss her in the way he should have that night in Iondorra.

Shame filled him as he thought of how they had come together that night. As if they were combatants on a battlefield, rather than lovers on a bed of silk sheets and roses. As he reached her, she turned her face towards him as if waiting for that same kiss. But instead of doing what he so desperately wanted to do, of taking what he so desperately needed, he offered his arm and escorted her away from the reception and away from his wayward thoughts.

Theo was thankful that she made easy small talk as they walked towards the rows of vines that made up the vineyard. Questions of what types of grape, how long they took to grow, when he had first known that he wanted to develop wine… All things he had answered a million times and knew by heart. And, if she noticed that he was distracted, she was restrained enough not to mention it.

Finally, as they drew to the furthest point from the estate, he turned to her.

'What is it?' Sofia asked. 'You've had something on your mind for a while. Ask.'

As if it were that simple. As if she would not deny him anything.

'At the hospital, I asked Lyssandros to run every possible test he could think of. The thought…the possibility that you were hurt—'

'I'm fine, Theo. Truly. Look,' she said, shaking her head from side to side in a way that made him wince, even without the possibility of concussion. She laughed. The sound should have soothed him, but it didn't.

'Lyssandros is a very professional man, but he also has a huge heart. He was concerned by… He saw there were fractures, from a previous injury. Did someone hurt you?' he asked, his voice drawn and gravelly to his own ears. Watching her closely, he saw the way she paled, the way her cheeks lost their rosy glow, her eyes filled with shadows and she made to turn away. Before she could, his hand snuck out and gently grasped her chin, guiding it back to him, snaring her gaze with his.

'Please. Don't hide from me in this. I need to know.'

She pulled a breath into her lungs, but it seemed to get caught there, the slight stutter in her breathing enough to tell him that he really did need to know. As if unable to bear the weight of his gaze, she cut her eyes to the ground.

'Sofia, whatever it is…whoever it was… If it was your husband—'

'No!' she cried, cutting him off mid-sentence. 'No,' she said again, more gently, more softly. 'Antoine never raised a hand to me. Ever.' He watched her pause and take another deep breath. 'My father isn't well.'

It was not what he'd expected her to say, but he silenced his inner thoughts and allowed her to continue.

'He hasn't been for…some time. I…we, the palace, have been sworn to secrecy, for fear of it destabilising the future of Iondorra.'

'What is wrong with him?'

'He was diagnosed with early onset dementia.'

She started to move away from him then and in the space between them his suspicions began to grow, like roots from somewhere deep within him, reaching towards the light, towards the truth.

'When?'

'When what?'

'Don't play games with me, Sofia—when was he diagnosed?'

'Just before I was taken out of boarding school.'

A curse fell from his lips as he stared to rearrange the past to fit with what she was now telling him.

'The night that I was supposed to meet you, he and my mother came. At first, I thought they'd found out somehow. About you, about the pranks… But it was worse than that. They explained what the diagnosis meant, that in time he would begin to lose more and more of his memory, of himself. I couldn't see it. This man, this powerful, loving, larger-than-life ruler of an entire country…it wasn't possible. Or at least that is what I thought at the time.

'He was only fifty. There should have been years before I needed to assume the royal responsibilities I was so ready to reject. But there was no one else. I was going to have to wear the crown, I was going to have to learn to be the ruler of Iondorra, and I couldn't do that to you.'

'*To* me, or with me?' he demanded.

'Neither,' she said, shaking her head helplessly. 'We were children, Theo. You…you had your whole life ahead of you, to do what you wanted to do, to be who you wanted to be. And who you are now is incredible,' she said, her eyes large and bright in her eyes.

Theo shook his head against her words, against the thought that she had been right. All this time he'd blamed her, hated her…

'Why didn't you tell me this?' he demanded, pain and anger making his words harsh on the soft summer breeze.

'I couldn't. Don't you see? No one could know of my father's diagnosis. The risk to the country, to its finances and its people…it was just too great. So I was taken back to Iondorra, and spent the next few years cramming in as much of the knowledge of a would-be ruler in the shortest amount of time possible.

'It's not like in the movies, where a simple makeover is enough. My wayward recklessness needed to be ironed out of me at every turn. It took years learning the rules, etiquette, languages, diplomacy needed to ensure the success of the throne. All the while keeping this secret. One that ate away at me each day.

'Could you imagine what the world's press would do with a sniff of hereditary early-onset dementia in the Iondorran royal family? They are tough enough on debauchery, let alone something as devastating as a genetic disease.'

'You have been tested.' It was a statement rather than a question.

'Yes. I don't have it. The gene. Not that it means I

won't develop the same condition, but the chances are significantly less.'

'So the injuries you sustained…'

She looked up at him then, her eyes matching the blue depths of the sky, large enough for him to see the sorrow, the pain and the frustration.

'My father had a bad turn. He…we'd been managing his condition fairly well up until that point. But that night, he was…not the man I knew. He had been restless and demanded to see me. He wanted to know how I was managing a negotiation with the Hungarian consulate, but… that had been months before. The negotiation done and dusted. Only…he didn't seem to remember that. He became frustrated and angry, furious even. I tried to calm him, but he saw it somehow as an attack, and he…he was just defending himself,' she tried to explain. 'The horror in his eyes, the moment he realised what he'd done…the guilt, shame…all of it was—' she paused as if searching for the right words '—so awful.'

Theo tried to shake his thoughts into clarity, as if they were flakes within a snow globe, hoping that they'd settle into some kind of sense. But no matter how they ebbed and flowed, all he could think of was that he believed her. That he could see the pain and hardship she'd been through. But, worse than that, he'd begun to feel as if his anger and hatred towards her for what happened to him and his mother was masking something else. He felt as if he'd been hit by an avalanche of guilt and it was covering everything.

A huge, fat, tear-shaped raindrop thudded on the ground beside his feet. Then another, and another. In just seconds, the heavens had opened as if they were crying for them, for him, for a pain he couldn't yet express.

Sofia looked up at him, seemingly heedless of the

rain pouring down on her, and reached her hand to his hard jaw.

'I'm so sorry. I'm so, so sorry,' she said, her voice barely a whisper amongst the pounding of the rain on the earth beneath them.

And in that instant, he honestly didn't want to hear anything more. No words, no explanations, no apologies. He reached for her as his lips seized her with the same ferocity as that of the storm, drew her towards him as if she were the breath he needed to exist.

His tongue delved between soft, sweet lips and it wasn't enough. He wanted it all. Desire drenched him as surely as the rain as he felt her body mould against his own, the firm jut of her breasts against his chest, and he pulled her even closer, his thumb tracing down her slender neck to her ribcage, snagging on her hip and anchoring her to him.

She gave him everything he demanded, gave herself completely over to him, until she began to tremble, and in turn he finally felt the stinging cold of the summer storm. He broke the kiss, glancing towards the main building, which was too far away. He grasped her hand.

'Come with me,' he said, asked, possibly even pleaded in that moment, as he took them towards the summer house nestled on the boundary of the vineyard.

CHAPTER NINE

SOFIA COULDN'T STOP SHAKING, even as she took a second step and a third into the small beautiful wooden summer house. She knew it wasn't just because of the rain. She had never told anyone about her father. No one outside her mother, or her father's carers. She had put her trust in Theo. And it had been terrifying, but she wouldn't take it back. Not for a second.

She had seen him war with the truth of her words, with what it had meant for them all those years ago, and possibly even what it meant for them now. But she didn't want to think about her father, or Iondorra. No. Now she wanted to lose herself, or find herself, she couldn't say.

She turned to see Theo standing in the glass-fronted doorway, the fierce sky pouring rain down on the vineyard, casting everything else in dull grey, but Theo in full, bright glory. He looked like an avenging angel, dark hair even blacker than the night, his clothes drenched and clinging to the dips and hollows of his body as if he were a thing to be worshipped.

As he stalked towards her she fought the instinct to step back. She wouldn't hide from this any more, hide from her desire, she was now focused on him completely, the one man, the *only* man she'd ever wanted. The only

man who had seen her for who she truly was, before duty
had moulded her into something new. Something other.

They reached for each other at the same time, col-
liding in need and passion and want. She felt the beat
of her heart leap as his lips crashed against hers, as his
hands cradled her head, angling her in a position that felt
as much like surrender as it did defiance. He thrust his
tongue into her mouth, filling her, consuming her, and
she needed it. It was too much. She felt like laughing,
like crying, as if she simply didn't know which way was
up or down any more, all she knew was him.

Her hands flew to his shoulders, large, solid, bigger
than the breadth of her hands. Her nails dug into the
thin, wet material covering his body and she wanted to
feel skin, needed to. Her hands went to the buttons of
his shirt, but the tremors shaking her body made her actions too slow.

He released his hold on her, and she swayed from the
loss, the support, the anchor of his body. She watched as
he tore apart his shirt, buttons flying and scattering on
the wooden floor, marvelling at the smooth planes of his
chest, the soft whorls of damp hair clinging to a deeply
tanned torso. As he reached for her she gazed, fascinated
by the cords of muscles rippling from the movement,
and reached out a hand tentatively. She wanted to touch,
needed to, but…

He swept up her hand in his and placed it on his chest,
on his heart, and looked at her with such intensity she
could hardly bear the weight of it. She felt the beat of his
heart, powerful, strong and fast, raging in time with her
own. His skin was hot beneath her cool palms and she
shuddered, wanting to feel that heat wrapped around her,
fill her, warm the places of her that had been left cold

the moment she left him standing at the boarding school all those years ago.

It was then that she knew what it felt like to be in the eye of the storm—the moment of shocking quiet stillness while chaos raged around them. The moment that life as she knew it would change. She knew that he was giving her this. This moment to walk away. To stop. But she couldn't, wouldn't.

She reached for him then, raising to her tiptoes to reach that proud, utterly sensual mouth of his, desperate to feel it against her own. Her hands explored his rain-slicked skin, delighting in the feel of his strength, his power. His hands cupped her backside and he lifted her off her feet, her legs wrapping round his lean waist as if they'd always been meant to be there.

He backed up and sat them down on the large summer lounger, her knees anchoring against his hips, as he pulled at her silk top, freeing it from the waistband of her trousers, pulling it over her head and tossing it aside, snagging on the pins that held her hair in place and pulling it free as her long blonde hair hung down in thick, wet ropes about her shoulders. He stopped then and stared.

'You are so beautiful,' he said, placing open-mouthed kisses along her neck as she shivered under the feel of his tongue on her skin. His hands cupped her breasts, his thumbs brushing her nipples, stiff with pleasure, and Sofia's head fell back, relishing the feel of him, of what he was doing to her body, as he honoured her with his touch.

She gasped when he took her nipple into his mouth and sucked, teasing her with his tongue, his arm around her waist holding her in place against the onslaught of desire that threatened to overwhelm her.

Unconsciously she rocked against his lap, the hard ridge of his arousal at her core making her slick with need as much as the groan that fell from Theo's lips.

'You're killing me here,' he said, the words half huffed out on a laugh.

He pulled back, looking at her, his gaze taking its fill of her. He reached behind her, and began to unbuckle her sandals, first one, then the other. He took her foot in one hand and firmly pressed the entire length of the arch of each foot, sending delight and pleasure through her. He caressed her ankles beneath the wet linen of her trousers, encased her calf in powerful, calloused hands, rough against smooth, sensations overwhelming her. She moaned out loud and he cursed, wrapping one strong arm around her as he twisted them in an embrace and turned her back to the seat.

Her fingers fought against his to undo the button of her trousers, and, once done, he peeled them from her, slowly, languorously as if enjoying the unveiling as much as anything else. She couldn't find the words to describe him. He was glorious. Shirtless, his chest was magnificent, and she watched with the same delight as he kicked off his shoes and removed his trousers without taking his eyes from hers once. She almost shook her head against the impossibility of seeing him standing there naked, proud, and every inch her fantasy. She began to tremble again, not with cold, not from the elements, but from the sheer virility that was Theo, the magnetism, just him.

Theo stood naked before the most beautiful woman he'd ever seen. There she was, laid out before him like the last meal he'd ever taste, and he hovered on the brink of something indefinable, as if he didn't know where to start.

He wrapped a hand around her ankle and gently pulled

her so that she almost lay flat. He lifted her foot, pressed kisses against the delicate arch, the inside of her ankle, he made his way slowly, languorously along her calf, spreading her slightly to allow the space for his own body, as he trailed open-mouthed kisses over her thigh and upwards to the hollow at her hip. Her body quivered beneath his lips, and he dusted the gentle swell of her stomach with his tongue. He kissed over her ribcage, and bit back a smile as she twisted and bucked as if as overwrought by the pleasure they built between them as he was. He kissed between her perfect breasts as he moulded them with his hands, each kiss driving him closer to the brink of need and desperation. This wasn't the angry coupling from the other night, this was honour, and respect, and desire building pathways to his heart that he'd never imagined.

He wanted to give her the greatest pleasure, as if he could make up for the ills he had thought her guilty of, the ills he had almost wreaked upon her. Because he realised now that he could not go through with his plan… he could no longer leave her at the altar humiliated and abandoned. Because beneath the ache and sting of what he had felt for Sofia was something deeper, darker and something he did not yet want to face.

She reached for him, as if pulling him back to the present, pulling him back to her, and he was more than willing to take the comfort she offered, even as he realised that it should have been the other way round. After what she had told him, it should be him soothing her hurts.

Leaning on his forearm, he looked down at her, the damp golden ropes of her hair framing her face, the exquisite perfection of it, and the way her head cocked to one side elongated her neck made him yearn to devour her there, the pulse point, the connection to life, the flutter there speaking of her need for him.

Wide, round, azure-blue eyes stared up at him in complete trust, and part of him wanted to shy away from that gaze, from the hope and innocence within it. Instead he followed the trail of his hands with his eyes as his fingers traced the outline of her ribcage, the pad of his thumb dipping into the hollow at her hip, his hand delving beneath her, curving around her backside to pull her against him, their centres flush, their cores both throbbing with need, and he released her only to sweep his hand low across the gentle swell of her abdomen and between her legs to find the place that drove her wild with ecstasy.

His thumb caressed and played with her clitoris, the sounds of her need rising higher than the pounding of the rain against the wooden roof of the gazebo, ringing vibrations over his skin through to his very soul. This time he would not tease her, keeping her at the brink of an orgasm. No, he would drench her in as much pleasure as she could take, and then more.

He thrust into her with his fingers, feeling the walls of her body clench around them, again and again, all the while his body aching with need, an ache he felt he deserved to bear even though it was Sofia that cried out, Sofia's body that trembled beneath him, incomprehensible words begging and pleading falling from her perfect lips. He wanted to kiss them, to consume them with his own mouth, but he couldn't, wouldn't, stop watching how beautiful she was when she came apart in his arms.

It wasn't enough, not nearly enough. Sofia's body, still vibrating with the power of the orgasm Theo had pulled from her very soul, still wanted more. It wanted him and wouldn't be denied. Her hands reached for him, drawing him down upon her, and finally, as if they were puzzle pieces fitting together, she felt some kind of completion as he placed the tip of himself at her core, and as he thrust into her deeply she felt stripped bare, vulnerable and powerful at the same time, as if she had stolen something from him to bolster her own sense of self.

The thickness of him filled her completely, the smooth hardness within her she was afraid she was already addicted to. He reached beneath her, bringing their bodies to a place where he could drive into her with more power, more delicious friction, just more... And she gasped, the air almost lodging in her throat, her heart as they became joined at the deepest, closest part of themselves. Was this what she had turned away from all those years ago? This impossible to describe sense of rightness, sense of wholeness? It was the last thought she had as he drove her closer and closer to a second orgasm—and with no need for silence or discretion, with no need for secrecy she cried out her release into his mouth as his lips came down on hers with the same desperation, the same craving that she could no longer resist.

Walking back through the vineyards as the sun hung low in the sky, slashes of pink against the cornflower-blue creating a stunning sight, Sofia wondered at the warmth and safety she felt as Theo wound his arm around her waist, holding her to his side. Their clothes still damp from the rain storm that had caught them by surprise, she almost welcomed the rough feeling, knowing what pleasures it had led to. She knew that they would have to return to Iondorra tomorrow for the charity gala, which—even though only a week before their wedding—she wouldn't have cancelled for the world. Her role as patron for Gardes des Enfants d'Iondorra—a charity that supported child carers—had given her the first glimpse she'd had that her royal status could be a positive thing—

could help and support something both wider and yet smaller and more immediate than anything her 'duties' could effect.

But for the first time she was torn. Torn between her duty and wanting to stay here in this magical bubble where the outside world didn't exist and where she and Theo were finally feeling as one, feeling right, as if this was how it should have been all along.

She laughed out loud, then, when she felt the gentle vibrations at her side from the phone in Theo's pocket—both at the feeling, and the contradiction of her thoughts of it just being the two of them cut off from the rest of the world. But when Theo joined in her breath caught—she had forgotten what he had looked like when he smiled, when they laughed together, and the sight was...incredible, full of hope for the future and the pull of nostalgia from the past.

'Nai?' he said, still laughing as he answered the phone.

Trying not to feel a little stab of hurt when he pulled away from her to speak into his phone, she forced herself to tune out the conversation and turned her mind to tomorrow...to the future. With him? Married to Theo Tersi? After all that had happened to them years ago, and since?

Unconsciously she had walked forward, tracing her steps back towards the stunning hotel hidden amongst the rows and rows of grapevines that stretched as far as she could see. The little narrow lanes created between them were barely enough for one person to step along.

She felt Theo behind her, the heat of him, the awareness...

'That was my mother,' he announced, disconnecting the phone.

'Oh?' She'd hoped her word sounded nonchalant rather than...what, worried? Intrigued? How much did his mother know about what had happened between them? What on earth must she think of her?

'She has invited us for dinner this evening. If that's okay?'

Sofia pulled every one of her concerns beneath the well-worn mask she used almost daily for her royal duties. 'Of course that's okay. I would love to meet her,' she said genuinely, all the while hoping that Theo's mother didn't hate her quite as much as she hated herself for what she had done to Theo all those years ago.

Theo had never, ever introduced his mother to anyone he had been intimately involved with. He knew that she refused to read the articles written about him in the last two years, and only now did he realise how ashamed he felt of them. Ten years ago, he had intended to bring Sofia to his mother and…what? It was only now that he was beginning to realise that what Sofia had said on the boat was true. That what they had shared at school had been the stuff of fantasies and impossible dreams. Had she perhaps not been a princess it might have been different, but even then, Theo wasn't quite sure.

He almost laughed, bitterly, at the thinly fabricated future they had concocted in their minds. Even had she not been a princess, even with the scholarships, the reality was that he would have had to take one, maybe two jobs to pay for living expenses. He would have struggled just as much as he had in reality, but with her by his side. He would have spent hours, days away from her, and possibly in the end either resented that he wouldn't have been able to provide the life he had wanted for her, or, worse, her. And she? Would have been ruined by the hard life he would have taken them to. And he couldn't shake this feeling that perhaps what had happened was how it had been meant to be. That the very reason he'd been able to achieve such impossible success was the drive and determination that had fuelled him all these years. These thoughts struck a cruel blow as they reached the door to the small house on the border of his land.

He'd tried so many times to entice his mother to a grander home, an easier home perhaps on one floor, with cleaners, and staff even, but she had refused, loving the little home that they had first shared when he'd initially bought this land.

Before he could even raise his hand to the door, it swung open and he was instantly enveloped by his mother's small frame and a stream of adoring, loving Greek spoken so quickly, even he only picked up on half the words. Within seconds both he and Sofia were being practically dragged over the threshold, straight into the small kitchen full of smells that instantly made his mouth water, and heart lurch with memories of the past.

He looked at Sofia standing in his mother's kitchen—a smile one of her biggest and brightest as she stood there in a pretty summer's dress. She had told him, every inch the royal, that she refused to meet his mother in wet clothes, and they had returned to the rooms in the hotel to shower and change before coming here. But now—with no trace of any etiquette, no royal greeting on his mother's behalf, simply welcomed through the door and into the kitchen, Sofia seemed happier than she had in all the days he'd spent with her.

Aggeliki was tactile, even for a Greek mother, and he marvelled at how Sofia—usually protected by a dozen bodyguards from anything even close to physical contact—was taking all the touching and hugging. His mother was asking her about how she liked the vineyard, and he was about to translate, when Sofia, along with a surprising amount of gesturing, managed to explain that she liked it very much. In Greek. When had she learned Greek? he wondered. She was doing fairly well, but every now and then had to defer to him for the translation of a few words, and after he'd warned his mother to slow down they seemed to be able to understand much of what was said between them. Their evening became a strange mix of Greek, English and the occasional French, when even English wouldn't do.

They sat outside at a wooden table beneath a pergola almost buckling under the weight of the stunning bougainvillea they had planted when they had first bought the land. Aggeliki had lit citronella candles the moment she had seen Sofia's pale skin, knowing that the mosquitos would love nothing more than to feast on the perfect blood in her veins, and the lemony scent hung in the warm night air as they feasted on the numerous dishes Theo's mother had produced.

He watched his mother and Sofia, heads bent together almost conspiratorially, and realised that he could not go through with his plan for revenge. He had told Aggeliki that he was to be married, but had refused to sink so low in his mother's expectations as to admit the truth behind his actions. He couldn't help but feel a sense of rightness as he watched the two women together, forging a relationship in the way he'd once imagined ten years ago.

He hadn't missed the way that Sofia had been nervous about meeting his mother, but hadn't managed to reassure her that she didn't have to worry, that he'd never revealed the source of his shame. Because he'd been so consumed by the way the blame he'd laid at her feet—which had once been on such on solid ground—was now shifting.

Sofia sat back in her chair, more full of food than she

could ever remember being in her entire life. She had tried to help Theo's mother take the plates away, but she had shooed her with hand gestures, firmly keeping her in the seat, and Sofia had reluctantly stifled her manners.

For just a moment it was her and Theo, his brooding gaze on her, glimmering in the darkness—the thin shadows cast by the little citronella candles enough to create warmth but not quite illumination. Not that she needed it. She knew every millimetre of his face, his features etched in her heart for ever ten years before—she'd only had to let herself remember them. For one moment, barely the space of a heartbeat, there was peace between them. Peace and something she'd dare not put a name to. Because if she lost it again, she didn't think she'd survive.

Aggeliki returned to the table with even more food, this time the scent of sweetness hitting Sofia hard and making her mouth water.

She laughed, 'What is all this?'

'This is dessert!' Theo's mother proudly claimed as she put down the tray covered with enough sweet treats to feed an army. She also noticed on the tray a small plate with a number of pills and frowned as she watched Aggeliki take them with a mouthful of water in between each one. She raised a brow at Theo, who had yet to take his eyes from his mother, now swallowing down the last one, but Aggeliki must have caught the look.

'It's okay,' she said, rubbing warmth into Sofia's cold hand. 'It's nothing. I am fine,' she said with smiling reassurance, but it did nothing to ease the concern building in Sofia's chest.

'My mother…she had a heart attack and was treated and is now—as she says—better than ever.' Sofia didn't call him on the brief pause that spoke of his own concern, instead focusing on what she needed to know.

'When?'

Theo shrugged and shook his head. But she wouldn't let it go that easily.

'When did it happen?' she asked, purposefully gentling her tone.

'Five years ago,' he said, refusing to meet her gaze.

Something cold and hard twisted in her chest and ached for him, for his mother, for her own selfish actions. From what he had told her earlier in the vineyard, he'd barely won his first vintner's award. He may have had some success at that point, and she didn't know much about the Greek healthcare system, but knew enough. Enough that meant it would have nearly crippled them financially, especially with a fledgling business underway, not to mention the hard work and struggle that it must have taken to be torn between a sick parent and full-time duty. Yes. She knew enough about that to know what it must have cost him.

She searched her mind for the words that would explain how she felt, how truly sorry she was, but they wouldn't come. They didn't have to. Finally Theo met her gaze and she knew that what he saw in her eyes was enough. He nodded, as if he'd understood, all the while his mother explaining the different types of dessert she wanted Sofia to try. And, as full as she was, Sofia would take a bit of each and every one of them.

This time, when it came to clearing the table, she ignored Aggeliki and helped the woman back into the small kitchen with the empty plates and coffee cups from the end of their meal. She liked this small room, how homely it felt, how easy it was just to prepare a meal and eat—rather than the impersonal feeling of a meal served to her each and every night, alone in a dining room big enough to seat twenty. Usually she brought her

laptop, immersed herself in work to avoid the stark realisation that she was alone, that her mother and father
had retreated to another estate far away from the palace.
There was no laughter, as there had been this night, no
gentle teasing or recounting of family stories, or praise
of Theo's successes...and it hurt in a way she had never
allowed herself to feel before.

As she glanced around the beautiful little kitchen, her
eyes caught on an old black and white photo of Aggeliki
and a man standing beside each other, with easy smiles
and laughter in their eyes.

'Oh,' she gasped, moving towards it. 'This is such a
beautiful picture of you, Aggeliki. Is this Theo's father?'

It was as if the temperature in the room had dropped.

'No. It is Nikos. We don't speak of my father. Ever.'

The words were in English, and even though she didn't
think Aggeliki had translated them in her mind, Theo's
reaction couldn't have been more clear. Especially when
he retrieved his phone and left the kitchen.

She felt Aggeliki rub her arm softly and smile.

'It wasn't you,' she said in Greek. 'He doesn't...' She
shook her head sadly, as if trying to find the words. 'He
never got over it. The way his father left. I tried...to give
him everything, to be everything for him. But,' she said
with a shrug of her shoulder, 'he is a man. A man needs
a father. For a while in Switzerland...' Sofia didn't need
Aggeliki to fill in the gap—clearly her boss, the man
who had paid for Theo's education, had been a father
figure to him. 'But look at him now,' she said, calling
Sofia back to the present, to look at him through the window. 'And look at what you both have. It is a joy to me,
Sofia. *Efcharistó.*'

For the first time since they had arrived, Sofia began
to wish that she hadn't come. That she hadn't seen the

pain and the struggle that Theo had been through since he had been expelled from the boarding school. Because finally Theo had got his wish. She was learning about the consequences of her actions.

CHAPTER TEN

SOFIA LEANED BACK in the plush cream leather seats of Theo's private jet, hating the way that her stomach dipped and swayed with the plane. The single air stewardess made her way down the short aisle on very long legs and retrieved the empty glasses and plates from the table between her and Theo.

'Efcharistó,' she said, forcing a smile she didn't feel for the woman.

'You didn't tell me you could speak Greek,' he said, the curve of his lips a rueful smile.

'You didn't tell me that your mother had had a heart attack,' she replied, shocking them both. She hadn't meant to say the words. Hadn't meant to bring up the subject she had hardly forgotten for a moment from the night before. Hadn't meant for the smile on his lips to die away.

'No. I didn't.'

Several times, Sofia tried to let loose the words that clogged her throat and failed. But she couldn't leave it at that. She had to know.

'Is that…was that one of the consequences you felt I needed to learn?'

He studied her, half-lidded eyes masking a whole host of emotions she desperately wanted to see the truth of.

'It was not your fault.'

'That is not what I asked.'

'I don't hold you responsible for what happened to my mother, Sofia.'

'But *did* you?'

The silence that fell between them was enough of an answer that she thought he would not speak of it again. Instead, she turned to look out of the small round window as the sprawling emerald-green stretches of Iondorran land came into view. Her country. Her home. The decisions she'd made to protect them now illuminated under the cost of her actions.

'Neither of us has had it easy, Sofia. The decisions we felt forced to make, each for other people. But this?' he said, the gesture between them drawing her gaze back to his. 'You and me? Our marriage? This is a decision that we make now, for ourselves,' he said. And she wondered at the vehemence in his tone, wondered who he might have been trying to convince…her or himself. 'It is one that I want very much,' he added, and his words soothed some of the ache that had taken up residence in her heart as he reached for her hand and drew the cool skin against the warmth of his palm.

She felt the rough calluses on his skin, marvelled at the texture as they spoke more of the hard work Theo had done than he admitted to. She knew that the fact he no longer resented her for the past should be enough, but despite the admittance she could feel a hurt emanating from him. A deeper, harder one than before.

'Do you remember my first prank? Do you remember what caused it?'

'I didn't think you needed a cause, Sofia, I thought you enjoyed playing Puck.'

'You thought me *"shrewd and knavish"*?'

'I thought you many things back then, Sofia. But yes,

your first prank—on Benjamin Reneux, I remember. It was the first time that I saw you. Holding back tears of laughter as he howled in horror when he opened the door to his locker to find everything covered in honey—his blazer, his books, his homework. You looked at me, and all I could see was you. You shone, in the dim corridor beside the Great Hall.'

Sofia nodded. 'It was not the first time I had seen you though.' She smiled, a sad smile. 'I had seen how the others treated you. How *Benjamin* treated you. The names he called you, the way even the teachers expected you to cause trouble, to be the first to throw a punch—'

'Well, I usually was the first to throw a punch...'

'No. You always threw the *second* one. I watched. I saw.'

Theo looked away as if no longer wanting to take this trip down memory lane. Unconsciously he rubbed his chest, seemingly trying to soothe an age-old ache.

'I hated it. The way they behaved towards you.'

'It was hardly less than what I had already experienced at the hands of my cousins, or...'

'Or the people who should have cared for you most.'

'Sofia, I don't want—'

'Did you ever look for your father?'

This time her name was growled on his lips like a warning.

'Do you know why he left?'

'He left because he was weak, because he was a coward who ran away from his responsibilities.'

'You were not just a responsibility.'

'What do you want me to say? That it hurt to know that my father never wanted me? That he ruined my mother and her happiness? That I swore never to be like him, only to grow into a young man who caused her more pain?'

'Is that what you think? That you caused your mother pain? That is not—'

'You know nothing of this. And I will not speak of it again.'

The gala was being held at La Sereine, a Michelin-starred hotel sitting on the edge of Lac du Peridot. As Theo leaned against the balcony looking out at the stunning sight, he tried with all his might to focus on the two large mountains in the distance meeting just at the horizon of the stunning lake, a vista of every shade of green stretching out before it. Further upstream, he'd been told, was a small town nestled around the top of a giant waterfall, feeding the river that wound its way through Iondorra to Callier.

But despite all this glory, all he could see, all he could hear were the faces and taunts of his past. He'd been shocked by Sofia's revelation—that the pranks he had so loved about her once, and then vehemently hated, had been started in retaliation against the behaviour he had received. That, all the while he'd thought to be the one who'd noticed her first, she had been there, watching him without his knowledge, and had seen him without being seen.

Somehow he felt both stunned and cheated. Cheated as if suddenly Sofia was reframing everything he thought he knew.

Did you ever look for your father? Do you know why he left?

He hadn't been able to answer her. Because yes, he did know why his father had left. His cousins had enjoyed taunting him with it. Older by several years, they had relished and recounted with venomous glee the story of the words he had hurled at his mother.

The story that his father had run from his mother, from the village, the same night he had been born. That he had refused to be weighed down by a child. His cousins had called him *bástardos*—bastard—for almost his entire childhood. And every time his mother had been shunned, every time his mother had been tutted at, or stared at, in the village, he knew he was the cause of it. And then later, when he had been expelled, Theo had felt as if it was happening all over again. That he had thrust shame upon his loving mother who had tried so desperately to compensate for the absence of his father, for the lack of security in their lives. So he had done everything he could, since then, to make sure that she would never feel shame or want again.

A knock sounded against the door to the suites he'd been given within the hotel, pulling him from his thoughts. A knock that sounded more like the nail on a lid that he was banging down against the memories of his father, of his childhood.

He had just walked back inside from the balcony, when he let out a bark of surprised laughter, put down the glass of whisky and greeted his friend in a warm hug.

'Sebastian! What are you doing here, my friend?' he asked.

Sebastian's grin matched his own as he explained that Sofia had arranged for him and his sister, Maria, to be in attendance for this evening's gala and for them to stay in Iondorra with Theo until the wedding. Theo poured them both drinks and, before settling down into the luxurious sofa, Theo couldn't resist one more hug. He had needed this. Had Sofia known he would? Was that why she had gathered up his closest friend and brought Seb to him?

'What is this? You getting soft on me? All this talk of romance—'

Theo laughed again, shoving at Seb before sitting down.

'Do not fear. My tastes have never run in your direction.'

'Fear? I am perfectly happy with my masculinity to appreciate another's attraction to me, no matter who it comes from. I just happen to prefer the female form.'

Theo quirked an eyebrow. 'Anyone in particular?'

'God, no. There is only one thing that would ever tempt me into the state of holy matrimony.'

'Money?'

'Amnesia.'

'I'm sure there are many women out there who would willingly oblige a good bludgeoning to ensure such a thing.'

'True. Perhaps I should start wearing a helmet.'

'A bicycle helmet?'

'Well, I was thinking something more dramatic like a knight's armour, but I suppose your suggestion would do just as well and be a hell of a lot easier to get my hands on. How have you been?' Sebastian demanded, an assessing gaze raking over Theo's features. 'You look… different.'

Theo shook off the question with a shake of his head. Sebastian was almost as close to him as his own mother, but he was not ready to open the can of worms that he'd been brooding on. Though he knew he could do with his friend's counsel. 'Honestly? I'm not so sure. Things are… different to what I had thought them to be. Sofia had her own reasons for doing what she did that night, and I… I think I understand them now.' And as he spoke the words he realised the truth of them. Theo refused to betray her confidence, even to Sebastian. But he did understand her choices, did believe her when she had said that she was sorry, and fully believed that she really did understand the consequences of her actions. And he couldn't shake the feeling that perhaps it was those very choices that had brought them to this point. This moment, where he finally had everything he'd ever wanted within his grasp.

But throughout it all was this rising sense of guilt. Guilt at what he would have done to her. Guilt for having preached all this time about the consequences of actions, when he had given little thought to anything of the consequences of his revenge. A guilt that was at once so familiar and terrible that it threatened to overwhelm him. But he could change his path. He could avoid those consequences. He *would*. This time, he could only hope that he would be good enough.

'I am going to marry her,' he said with a finality that did little to ease the feelings in his chest.

'Really?' Sebastian asked, shocked. 'I thought you might change your mind, but I didn't think you would actually get married.'

Theo shrugged off the weight on his shoulders, and Sebastian could have been forgiven for thinking that it was in response to his question.

'But I suppose it is still good business,' Sebastian said into the quiet room.

'That it may be, but no. It's more than that. It's… All these years I have thought her cold and calculating, but that's not the truth of her.'

'You love her?' Sebastian queried.

Did he? He might have been able to forgive the transgressions he thought she'd been guilty of, but love? Was he even capable of such a thing? When he thought of how he'd felt, seeing her struck by the boat's boom, when he'd paced the hospital hallways, devastated by the mere thought of her hurt, when he'd seen her share the laughter with his mother only the night before…the way it had eased a years-long ache in his chest... When he'd finally seen Sofia and how she had grown into a woman far greater than he had ever imagined possible...his lips curved into a smile, and something almost impossible to contain bloomed in his chest.

It was a strange thing, filling him from the inside out, covering and swelling to fit the empty places of his heart... Wondrous was the only word he could use to describe how it felt. And if there were edges of darkness, of a deeper hurt, of a twisted guilt in his chest, he pushed them aside with the same ruthlessness that had driven him to Sofia's doorstep.

'Yes. I do.'

'That is a wonderful thing, my friend,' Seb replied genuinely. 'Now, though, you just have to break it to my sister,' he said. 'For I believe she had pinned her hopes on the fact that you were going to abandon your princess at the altar.'

La Sereine was one of Sofia's most favourite places in Iondorra—and she had often wanted to come with Antoine, but they had never managed to find the time. She knew that being here with Theo should make her feel guilty, but she couldn't manage it. She hoped, believed, that Antoine would understand. They might not have shared everything, but they had understood each other and the pressures of duty.

Though could Sofia still claim that this wedding, this marriage, was solely for duty? She expected to feel unease as she questioned herself, but instead, she felt the thrum of excitement, of...happiness. Theo had said that he chose to do this, that he wanted it. And she was desperate to take him at his word, because somehow in the last few weeks she had begun to fall deeply for the passionate man who had woken her from a slumber of duty and grief. Her heart ached for the man she knew still hurt deep within himself. The man who had yet to resolve the real hurt that beat in his heart.

But since that night in Paris he had coaxed out some inner sense of herself—the one she had left behind with Theo that night at the boarding school—and she felt strange and new, and mysteriously whole. She felt strong…in her love for him. Because wasn't that what had really changed? That finally after all these years she had allowed herself to feel that love for him? The love that had always been there, waiting for a chance to escape, to be given to him?

With only a week before the wedding, Sofia didn't think she had enough time to undo the pain of the past, but after the wedding? Would they not have a lifetime together? For her to show him how much he meant to her, and just what he had done for her. Was it enough, perhaps, for her to do the same for him?

A knock at the door to her suite pulled Sofia's gaze from the lake and mountains beyond.

'Enter,' she commanded, her voice soft in expectation of what was about to happen. A small woman with dark hair pushed in a clothing rack with three heavy garment bags hanging from the rail.

'Your Highness,' said Alexa—her dress designer—the address slightly unfamiliar to Sofia after just a few days away from Iondorra and the formal etiquette required by her status. 'From our conversation on the phone, and the description of what you require, I have brought the original design along with some alteration options, but also two other suggestions in case they become preferable.'

'Thank you, Alexa, and thank you again for making the trip out here.'

Alexa smiled. 'It is my pleasure, Your Highness. Lac du Peridot is always a welcome sight, and La Sereine is just as beautiful as I've always heard.' Sofia couldn't help but smile at the older woman's enthusiasm. 'Now, let's see what we're dealing with.'

Sofia untied the silk robe and slipped the sleeves from her shoulders to reveal the bruise that was still quite evident from where the yacht's boom had caught her. Alexa might not have winced, but Sofia didn't miss the concern in her eyes. Alexa had been dressing and designing for her ever since she left the boarding school. She tutted as she circled Sofia with an assessing gaze. Hmmed and humphed a few times, before nodding to herself.

'You are okay?'

Sofia nodded quickly, feeling like the little seventeen-year-old Alexa had first met before her debut ball. Unaccountably she was blinking back tears and struggled to find the cause of them. She felt as if she were in a sea of emotions, her love for Theo, her hopes for the future, her ache for the past. She wanted to look beautiful on her wedding day, and the thought that had begun to wind around her heart, the possibility that the Widow Princess had finally found her Prince Charming…was one she wanted to hold on to so desperately.

'I have just the thing,' Alexa said, and Sofia lost herself in the bustling actions of the last-minute alterations to the dress she had always wanted to wear…for him.

The gala was going well. Sofia had delivered the opening speech and the event had moved on to the auction part of the evening. Theo had been with her as she had met with a few of the child ambassadors for the charity—and she couldn't help but smile at his surprise at how well she knew them. This had been her first charity, and would always have a special place in her heart. As an adult, she'd struggled with the secrecy and care around her father, so she simply couldn't imagine how much worse it was for children.

He had barely left her side all evening. And it had been both wonderful and terrible. She hadn't realised just how alone she had felt without companionship, without someone by her side since Antoine had died. Her parents had retreated to their estate, and she felt as if she had been alone for so long. But having Theo beside her made her feel stronger, more capable. It made the weight of the responsibility on her shoulders so much lighter to bear.

The thought of having him beside her in the future made her feel more capable of the things she wanted to do for Iondorra. And for the first time, perhaps ever, she began to relish the idea of the changes, could feel the power and energy there, to do even the larger things she wanted to accomplish. Now she began to hope that they might actually weather the storm that would hit once her father's diagnosis was made public.

She cast a glance around the hotel's grand ballroom, but couldn't see where Theo was. But his absence failed to dim the thrill and excitement that had filled her when trying on the beautiful wedding dress, and suddenly the hopes for her future were almost too much for her to bear.

She looked around the room, once again, for a glimpse of the man she loved with all of her heart. She wanted to tell him. An urgency she couldn't explain began to wind within her chest. As if something, time perhaps, was running away from her.

Finally she caught sight of him on the veranda, speaking to a young woman with long dark hair that she recognised as Maria Rohan de Luen—Sebastian's young sister. They appeared to be arguing, which confused her, drawing her to the couple. The sliding floor-to-ceiling French windows were slightly open, the gauzy white curtains shifting in the breeze, doing very little to disguise their words.

'But you can't!' The hurt in Maria's voice slashed him. Theo truly hadn't realised the extent of her feelings.

'Maria, please.'

'No. You said…you said that you weren't going to go through with it. You said that you were doing it to teach her a lesson! She hurt you and you were going to leave her at the altar! You can't marry her, Theo!'

He searched his mind for explanations, something that would lessen the pain, but he didn't know what to say.

'Maria—'

His words were cut off the moment Maria's whole demeanour changed. Shocked and wide-eyed, she was no longer looking at him, but over his shoulder…and every single hair on his body lifted as if touched by the same electric lightning bolt that had struck Maria still.

Horror filled him before he'd even turned and he barely registered Maria's flight from the veranda wrapping around the ground floor of the hotel.

Sofia.

He'd never seen her look the way she did in that moment. All the lies and mistruths he'd imagined he'd seen in her features were nothing compared to the raw pain and shock vibrating from her now.

'What did she mean?'

'Sofia—'

'Is it true?' she demanded, her voice breaking over the words.

Sofia saw the moment that fear and panic truly entered him. It froze him as if he thought that should he move, should he speak, it would set into motion a chain of events he could not take back.

Finally he moved, his long legs pacing wide steps across the wooden veranda, each one feeling as if it took him further and further away from her, even as it closed the distance between them. She'd hoped, in some far corner of her heart, that Maria had lied, had misunderstood somehow. But she knew that hope was futile.

'Yes,' he said simply. And her whole world came crashing down. 'When I first met you again in Paris that night, I had a plan. I thought that I was being merciful, offering you a silent, unknown chance to apologise and release yourself of a path that would lead to your eventual humiliation. When you didn't, when you refused, I had the photographer find us in the garden— I even chose which photo he should use. And yes, when I forced your hand to agree to our engagement I knew that I wouldn't go through with the marriage. That on the day of our wedding you would be at the church filled with hundreds of guests and filmed by thousands…and I would leave you waiting as you once left me waiting.'

His voice had gained a power, a guttural tone that suggested he was almost trying to convince himself that he'd been right. That he'd been justified. Hearing the words on his lips sliced away the soft layers of her heart, until the knife struck stone.

Because that was what Sofia needed most now. A heart of stone. Because she *loved* this man. This man who would have hurt her, yes, but even worse hurt her country. The humiliation wouldn't have been hers alone to bear. It would have been theirs. And that devastated her. The one thing she had been raised and trained to do, to put her country first, and she had nearly failed even before the crown came to rest on her head.

'But I had changed my mind, Sofia. I didn't know... I didn't know about your father, about why you were forced to leave that day, about any of it. I didn't understand.'

Desperate pain filled her completely. Pain and anger, an anger that felt almost uncontainable. 'It wasn't for you to understand, Theo!' She wanted to lash out, to howl her hurt, but she couldn't. She wouldn't. Not here, with hundreds of people behind them. She had been ruthlessly trained to bear the weight of the crown and she would not betray them now by giving Theo the humiliation he had once so desperately wanted. 'But it *is* for me to protect my country and people from those who would do it harm, even those I love. *Especially* those I love. For years I have done so for my father. And now I'll do it for you.'

'But you don't have to. Sofia, I want to marry you. I want to be standing at the top of the aisle you walk down in five days' time. Sofia, I—'

'I think you've done enough, don't you? You will have what you wanted. I will break the engagement. My humiliation will still happen for you. It will just not quite be as public as you wished.'

Theo let loose a growl. 'That is not what I want. This doesn't have to happen.'

'You think I can trust you, after this?'

'Why not? I trusted you after you...' His bitter words trailed off.

'So you still have not forgiven me. Not really.'

'I *have*,' he growled again. 'But you're leaving me, again. Just like...'

'Him,' she said, completing his sentence. Speaking of the one man that Theo refused to name. 'Is that what this is really about? Your father, not me?' She didn't wait for an answer. 'Until you forgive, Theo, you can't truly love me. Not really.'

'How on earth am I supposed to forgive him? I don't even know where he is!' he shouted.

'Not him. *You.* All this time, this unworthiness…it's you, you can't forgive, not me or him. And I can't make up for that, I can't *be* that for you.'

'Don't you dare turn this back on me. I'm here, telling you that I love you and that I'm yours.'

'You were never mine, and you're still not,' she said, her voice barely even a whisper.

'And you're still afraid!' he accused.

'What?'

'Still afraid of letting yourself be loved for you and not *what* you are. So tell me. Who is it that really feels unworthy here? Why is it that you're so eager to fall at this first hurdle?'

'Hurdle? You're calling your plan to leave me at the altar a hurdle? The fact that you consider even doing that means you have no respect or regard for my people, my country! They *are* me and you would have left us all.'

'But I'm not! I'm not leaving you. You're the one who is walking away and if you don't see that then you're lying to yourself.'

She didn't want to hear it. Couldn't. Because deep within her heart, she knew that there was some semblance of truth to his words. But she had to. She had to leave him. Her country had to come first. Hadn't that been drilled into her as a child? As a young woman? By her parents, her father? There was no other choice here.

'I have to return to the party—'

'Let them wait!' he yelled, his voice so loud she felt it echo within her body. 'I'm trying to tell you that I love you.'

'And *I'm* trying to tell you that it doesn't matter.'

She turned to leave, but Theo blocked her path.

He crowded her, his shoulders, his body a barrier that wouldn't be breached. She pulled herself up short before she crashed into him, but he caught her elbow and stopped her fall.

'I love you, Sofia,' he said, the only notice he gave her before drawing her to him, flush against his body, and kissing her with more passion and pain than she was capable of bearing. The moment his lips met hers, the fury and anger driving him, driving her, softened, and his tongue swept into her mouth as if it had a right to be there, as if it belonged to her and not him, just like his heart. Everything in her roared for release, desperate to escape and join him in this passion play. Her heart soared as much as it fell, as she realised that this would be the last time she could kiss him, hold him, show him all the huge, complex, amazing but terrible things she felt in that instant.

Her hands flew to his head, fingers riffling through his hair, pulling him to her, as the tears escaped her eyes and rolled down her cheeks. The salty-sweet taste of them mingling with their kiss was the last thing she remembered, before pulling away from him and fleeing.

CHAPTER ELEVEN

SOFIA HADN'T STOPPED crying for two days. She hadn't left her room in Iondorra's palace, she hadn't met with the council to help create the statement that would stop the wedding in three days' time, and even her sleep was broken by huge sobs that racked her body and tears that fell down her cheeks.

From the moment she had left Theo in the hotel by the lake it had felt as if her world had shattered, and somewhere deep down she knew that she deserved it. There were things she needed to do, but her mind couldn't hold on to them. It was as if her thoughts were being filtered, all else dropping away, to leave only grief and sorrow. If she had expected numbness, a deep, quiet agony to blanket over her heart, it had not happened.

Instead she felt raw, the constant dull ache of her broken heart her only companion.

'I'm trying to tell you that I love you... You're the one who is walking away...you're lying to yourself.'

Theo's words punctuated each breath, each thought. Because he was right. Once again, she had his heart. He loved her and she was walking away—only this time, she really was aware of what that meant. He had proclaimed to want to teach her the consequences of her actions... and now? She fully understood them.

She had been so sure in herself, so sure that she was right, putting her country first before a man who would have ruined it. Who preached consequences and gave no thought to the ones his own actions would have caused.

But beneath the words that ran around her head on a loop were the ones she didn't want to inspect. Didn't want to listen to, or believe. The ones that proclaimed her to be afraid of being loved for who she was and not *what* she was. As if the two things could be separated so easily.

This morning she had had marginally more success than the day before. She had made it to the bathroom and forced herself into the shower. Standing before the large mirror, she wiped away the steam and condensation from the cool, slick surface and stared at herself.

Her eyes, red-rimmed from the crying and a startling blue, stared back in accusation. *Coward.*

Sofia shook her head against her inner voice. No, she mentally replied. Broken-hearted.

She reached for the thick towelling robe and cinched it tight around her waist. All she wanted to do was go back to bed and pretend that the world didn't exist. She could have another day, surely. Because ten years ago, she hadn't been allowed even a minute, leaving the school and being thrust immediately into hours of lessons, measured, poked and prodded into the right dresses, as she kissed goodbye that moment out of time she'd had with Theo, kissed goodbye the young woman who had found fun and enjoyment and…love.

And four years ago, when Antoine had died, the world's press had documented her tearless grief—the loss of a man so precious to her… And for a moment she hated Theo. Hated him for showing her the truth of her relationship with Antoine—her friendship. Yes, she had loved him, but his loss had not had this devastating effect on her and somehow it made her feel as if she were betraying both men all over again.

Re-entering the suite of her rooms, she stifled a cry of shock with the back of her hand when she saw her mother standing beside the large window, looking out at the view. Shock turned into fear with lightning speed.

'Father, is he—?'

'He is fine, Sofia. He is not the one I'm worried about right now.'

Sofia's emotions seesawed, and guilt stirred in her breast. Was she so starved of love that her mother's concern—the simple fact that Sofia was being put first—made something shift in her heart? Guilt, hurt and love all mixed together in the headiest of potions, and for the first time that Sofia could remember in years she ran to her mother's arms and cried.

After what felt like hours, her mother released her and led her to the window seat.

'What are you doing here?'

'One of the staff was concerned when you refused to eat anything yesterday.'

Sofia wanted to hide, wanted to stay wrapped in her mother's arms, but knew that she could not. Slowly, haltingly, the words tumbled out. Of what had happened to Theo since she had left that night, of how he had orchestrated their engagement, but her words grew stronger as Sofia told her mother of how they had talked of the past, of the secrets she had entrusted to him, of the love she felt for him, and finally what had happened the night of the gala.

Her mother was quiet for a long while.

'Did you… Is it that you thought you couldn't have both?'

'After I left the boarding school, everything became about doing what was right for Iondorra and…'

'You didn't feel that you could have something for yourself?'

'I didn't know *how* to have both,' Sofia replied helplessly. 'It had, has, always been him. And I couldn't do that to him. I couldn't do what…'

'What was done to you.'

Sofia could hear the hurt in her mother's voice, the sheen of tears in the older woman's eyes almost too much to bear. She knew her words would hurt her mother. Knew that her mother would understand in an instant, that they had moved away from talking of Theo, and towards herself.

'Oh, my love,' her mother said, shaking her head. 'I'm so sorry that you felt that way. I… *We*…' Her words were interrupted by the shaking of her mother's head as she struggled to find the words that Sofia half feared. 'We never wanted you to feel that way. We love you dearly. And I am truly sorry that you ever felt as if you had no choice about your role.'

'I had to change so much about who I was, Mama. So much. But being with Theo again reminded me of who I once had been. And I missed that. I missed who I was.'

'And he helps you find that person you once were?'

'But it doesn't matter,' Sofia said, shrugging helplessly. 'His actions would have hurt Iondorra.'

'But they didn't, my love. And I am so happy that he brought something of you back to you. Because I have seen that smile…the one I thought lost ten years ago. I have seen what you are with him, the night of your engagement, and what you could be, in my heart's greatest hope.'

Her mother drew her into her arms again and this time

Sofia let go. Let go her fears, her resentments, the part of her she thought lost, found and lost again.

'Sofia, the crown, the country, it is important. But it is not worth the sacrifice of your heart. Theo,' she sighed, a small smile curving at the corner of her mouth, 'is clearly a man who made certain choices, and although that was his plan, did you believe him when he said he no longer wanted to abandon you? Did you believe the love he said to feel for you?'

'I don't know if I can trust him, Mama.'

'Trust him with what?'

Sofia frowned, unsure of what her mother was getting at. Seeing her daughter's confusion, she pressed on. 'Trust him not to make mistakes? Sweetheart, we all make mistakes, all the time. Just look at me and your father. Do you trust him to love you and be there for you? Do you trust him with your heart?'

'But how can I trust him with Iondorra?'

'Oh, Sofia. My one wish for you is not that you have someone who puts the country first, but who puts *you* first.'

For so long, everything had been about Iondorra. Leaving school, her first marriage, even the way she had planned her second marriage. The thought that it was even possible for someone to put her first, for her to allow that... Horror and hope mixed within the chambers of her heart, rushing out through her veins and around her body, setting it on fire with adrenaline.

Could she do such a thing? Could she really give herself over to that sense of trust...of love?

For two hours after her mother had left, with promises to return more often, to make more time for the two of them, Sofia stared at her phone.

Her heart knew what she wanted to do, and Sofia waited for her mind to catch up.

She dialled his number, her heart fluttering wildly, and was almost thankful when it went to the answering machine.

'Theo, I… There is so much we need to say to each other. But more importantly, I want you to know that I love you. I really do. And if you do love me, if you can forgive me the way we parted, then I will see you at the church in three days' time. Because I want nothing more than to become your wife. I want nothing more than to stand by your side for the world to see. I want nothing more than to show the world how much I love you and want to spend the rest of my life telling you that, each and every day. If you don't come, then I understand and will not hold it against you. I will issue a statement that takes full responsibility for the end of our engagement. But no matter what, please, please know that I love you.'

Theo sat on the stairs of his mother's decking, looking out at his vineyards from the veranda. He fished the phone out from his trouser pocket and threw it behind him, and leant his elbows on his thighs. It had been two days since he'd returned to Greece from Iondorra and he hadn't slept a wink. The early morning rays from the sun heated the rain-soaked earth, covering the ground in an unworldly mist, swirling in the still morning air.

For two days he had thought of little else than Sofia, of what she had said to him, of how she had accused him of being unable and unwilling to forgive, not her, not his father, but himself. The guilt that had settled about him that night had been slowly revealed as the layers of hurt and shock from their argument had dissipated. It was as if Sofia's words had picked at an invisible thread, wound tight around his heart—as if she had tugged on it, showing him proof that it existed, that it had bound his young heart and the muscle had grown around that binding... And he could no longer ignore it.

He had tried to lose himself in estate business, but that had failed and finally his feet had brought him to his mother's door. And although she woke early, five o'clock in the morning was perhaps a little much to be banging on her door and seeking...what? Answers? Advice? Forgiveness?

The smell of coffee hit his nose long before he detected the sound of his mother moving about in the house, and before he could get up from the wooden decking, his mother opened the door and wordlessly handed him a cup of the strong, fresh Greek coffee that he loved so much.

She went to sit beside him on the steps, and he rose in protest but she shooed him back down.

'I am not so old that I cannot sit on the steps with my son and look at the amazing things he has done. I do it even when you're not here, Theo. It is my favourite place in the world.'

Theo felt a heaviness within him. The weight of all the unanswered questions, of the guilt and anger and pain, resting on top of his already tightly bound heart... he thought he might actually break under the weight of it.

'I did something unforgivable, *mitéra*,' he said.

His mother humphed. 'There is very little in this world that is unforgivable, *yié mou*.'

He swept a hand over his face, scrubbing away the exhaustion and doubts and all the things that worked to stop his words in his throat, and opened his heart to his mother.

'I had this plan. This...act of revenge I wanted to take against Sofia for leaving me all those years ago.

I blamed her for…everything. And all this time, it was me. I thought it was her fault, what happened to me at school, the expulsion, having to come back here… But those decisions and choices were mine—yet I would have humiliated her in front of the world.'

For a moment, his mother seemed to consider his words.

'But you did not.'

'Yet I would have.'

She smiled at him in the way only a mother could. 'But you did *not*.'

'The outcome will be the same. The cancelled wedding will ruin her.'

Aggeliki rocked her head from side to side as if to say maybe, maybe not, and he knew that there was only one thing to make her realise the truth of what he was feeling.

'I would have left her, just like my father left you.'

Aggeliki sighed and blew the deep breath over her coffee before sipping at the thick dark liquid. 'Theo, your father…he… I have not really spoken of him, because you never seemed to want to, or be ready to, hear of him. He was—' she let loose a little laugh '—charming—a little like his son. Very handsome—a lot like his son. But insincere and careless—*nothing* like his son.'

'Do you regret it?' *Do you regret me?*

'*Agápi mou,* no. I gave him my heart, and he gave me you. And I would do the same again and again, because you are my joy. He may have been my sadness, but *you*? You are my happiness and more precious to me than anything in the world.'

'If I hadn't been expelled I could have gone to university, and we wouldn't have had to struggle, we wouldn't have nearly lost everything when you became ill, we could have…'

'Could, would, should? Theo, you seem to think that it all would have been so easy for you had you not loved Sofia back then. But look at what you have now. Look at what you've achieved. It is impossible to say what might have happened if you had not been expelled, but it is undoubtable what *did* happen, and what you have now.'

'But we wouldn't have had to come back here. You wouldn't have had to feel beholden to your family, the cruelty and prejudice you experienced… And then with the vineyard… The hours, days, weeks, *years* of hard work—'

'I wouldn't change a thing. Life is not meant to be easy, Theo. Easy is…nothing,' she said, throwing her hands up as if throwing around air. 'Meaningless. It is the hard work that makes it all the more precious and wondrous. It is the difficult times, the sacrifices that make the joy all the more valuable, the *love*. And every sacrifice you *think* I've made? I would do it again and again, because I love you.'

'But Sofia is right. I would have brought humiliation not just to her but her country.'

'But you did not,' his mother repeated with much more emphasis than before.

'All this time, all I have thought about is myself, the vengeance I wanted, the debt *I* felt *she* owed.'

'Theo, from what I saw of Sofia, of the truly brave and powerful woman I met, she carries that burden herself. And will always carry that burden. But it is for *her* to do. You? You are the only one who can help her. The Sofia that you fell in love with ten years ago, and the Sofia that is the woman she has become. Yes, she may have to think of her country first…but you? You get to think of her first.'

He felt his mother's words deep within his chest. He

felt her acceptance of his sins, his mistakes, ease some of the guilt in his heart. Soothe the way towards his own forgiveness for himself. Not for his attempt at revenge, but something deeper. But was it enough?

Theo stood and rolled his shoulders, flexing the ache from his muscles before placing a kiss on his mother's cheek.

'I need some time to think.'

Aggeliki nodded in response.

'Maybe I'll go and see Sebastian for a few days, but I'll be back. Soon, I promise. I love you,' he said, placing one last kiss on Aggeliki's forehead before walking back to the estate through the miles of vineyards between the two buildings.

Within minutes he was too far from his mother's house to hear his phone vibrate with an incoming call, and within hours the phone's battery had died, long before Theo returned to retrieve Sofia's voicemail.

What on earth had she been thinking?

As Sofia stood tucked behind the door at the back of a church packed full of nearly eight hundred of the world's leading figures, she couldn't stop the tremors that had taken over her body. Was this how Theo had felt that night ten years ago? Hopeful that she would arrive and fearful that she wouldn't?

She cast a quick glance to where her assistant was peering through a small sliver of space in the doorway, watching for Theo's arrival at the wedding that Sofia had never cancelled. The scared look in the young woman's eyes enough to tell her that Theo was still not there.

She had sent her father back to sit with her mother, after kind, coherent words of love had eased an age-old ache, but not this fresh one. And this time she had not batted her father's words away, but really listened, taken them to her heart and held them to her as if something astounding and precious.

She tried to take a breath, but the tightly corseted white satin dress just didn't expand enough to allow for it. Her hold on the exquisite garland of flowers, peonies and thistles, had become looser and looser as time had worn on, and they now hung from her listless arms at her side. The smile she had worn with determination hours before was rapidly losing its brilliance as Sofia now became convinced that he wasn't coming.

The ache in her heart was devastating, but she refused to cower beneath the pain. If this was his decision, then she would bear it. Her country would bear her mistakes too. But they would survive. This wedding, this marriage, it had been for her. The one thing she had selfishly wanted all those years ago, and again now. But she knew that no matter what the future held, all she needed to do was put one foot in front of the other. And if that was down an aisle to tell her guests that the wedding was off, then she would do so.

She couldn't blame Theo. She understood the pain she had caused, and the hurt he felt not only from her actions, but also from his father's. Forgiveness was already there, in her heart, because she understood him, and loved him. Even if she never got to utter the words to him in person.

She gave a final nod to her assistant, who disappeared to instruct the organist not to play the wedding march as she opened the door and began to make her way down the aisle.

The unsettled and deeply curious guests all turned to watch her as she took her first step, her second and a third. Already aware that something was off, in the silence, Sofia's heart sounded in her ears like a drum.

She willed away the tears that threatened to fall. She did not want to share them with these people. She would hold them to her in the darkest of nights, but not let them fall here, beneath the streams of sunlight falling through the stained-glass windows.

As she reached the top of the aisle where the priest stood, but the groom did not, she turned. Her mother's sad smile, encouraging and understanding, was full of love and that was all Sofia needed.

She took a breath, ready with the words she had prepared just in case...

The sound of the large wooden door being pulled open with a force that screeched across its hinges cut through the silence and there, cast in shadow amongst the brilliant rays of sunshine, was Theo Tersi.

The open promise of love shining bright in his eyes was what she'd longed to see and a sob of joy escaped her, the smile no longer forced, but came to her lips without hesitation. He took proud, deep and quick steps towards her, perhaps a little unceremoniously, closing the gap between them in moments, pulling her close and into a passionate kiss full of love and joy, much to the twittering giggles from the church's many guests.

'I'm sorry I'm late,' he said in between delicate presses of his lips to hers.

'I thought you might not come.'

'I will *always* come for you.' He whispered the vow into her ear and her heart.

Theo pulled her close to him, her heart beating against his, through the layers of clothing and skin. Only then did he allow himself to breathe. He had returned to his mother's house only the day before, and listened to the message Sofia had left on his voicemail and left almost immediately, breaking every speed-limit law in two countries to get to his future bride.

The wild beating of his heart, caused from his desperate run to the church, showed no signs of slowing. And he knew that nothing would prevent it other than the words of love he longed to hear from Sofia in person.

For the second time that day the church's doors were thrown open and Sebastian launched himself through the doors, to find the entire church staring at him. With a half laugh, half gasp, he bent double, his hands on his knees, dragging in giant lungful's of air into his chest, causing even more laughter amongst the guests than the kiss Theo had shared with Sofia.

'We would have been here sooner, but it seems there is a no-fly zone over the church and we had to leave the helicopter about a mile away.'

'*Two* miles,' groaned Sebastian as he came to join them at the top of the aisle.

As the priest called for silence and calm, drew the guests to their role of witnesses to the marriage between Sofia and Theo, neither the bride nor groom paid heed to the ceremony, lost to each other and the love that shimmered between them. But before the priest began the vows, Sofia interrupted him.

'I have my own vows,' she whispered to the priest. 'If that is okay?' He gestured for her to continue.

Sofia took Theo's hand in hers.

'Theo, when we first met, you didn't know my title, you didn't know me as a princess, you simply knew me. You loved that person and gave her a happiness, joy and love that she had never known before. I lost a little of myself when I—' she nodded, holding back the tears '—when I left you that day ten years ago. A piece that I never thought I would get back. But in the last few weeks you uncovered that lost part of me, you showed me that I could be and have both parts of the life I so desperately wanted. And that piece was you. You were the first man I ever loved, and will be the last and only man I want by my side, whatever comes next. I want to share my joys, my heartaches and my future with you, every day.

'There are promises that I could make, some that I could struggle to keep, but the only important one is that, although I might be Queen one day, and although I will wear the crown and must think of my country first…it is our love that I will *put* first, because *that* is what gives me the strength to be Queen, to be me to the best of my ability. My love for you. My heart has, and always will be, yours.'

And as she spoke the words of her heart, Theo felt a rightness settle about his shoulders. And for the first time in so many years he finally felt whole, just as she had described.

'Sofia, you know better than most how hard the past ten years have been for me. I used to wish it had been another way. An easier way. But a very wise woman recently told me that nothing in life that is meaningful is easy. And now I wouldn't take each and every one of those hard days back for the world. Because they led me to you.

'I don't have fancy words to describe my love for you. I have only the truth in my heart, that lets me know that you are, and always have been, the only woman I would give everything for. The hard days and the good. Because you have always seen me, the truth of me, and loved me in spite of my flaws, in spite of my actions and in spite of the consequences. And I promise you here today, with *eight hundred* witnesses—' Theo paused, letting the gentle laughter of the congregation flow over the outpouring of love he felt for Sofia in his heart, before he continued '—I promise to love you, to hold you to me when things are not easy, to hold you to me when you need strength and when I do, and to hold you when we need nothing more than each other. Because you are my strength, my love and my heart.'

The truth of his words settled into the tears that pressed against his eyelids, and barely had the words left the priest's mouth declaring that he could finally, *finally*, kiss his wife, he poured his heart and soul into the kiss that would seal their marriage.

That evening, Sofia and Theo danced their first dance as man and wife to 'At Last' in front of the guests gathered for the evening's reception. The words of the song wound around their hearts as the cheers and joy of the entire room welled up around them. That night they made love, so heartfelt and poignant it felt like a dream, and it was the night they conceived their first child. Through the years to come, there would be tears of joy at the birth of their daughter, and later their son. There would be sleepless nights as Iondorra weathered the difficult revelation of Sofia's father's dementia, but there were early nights when as a family they came together to share their love. There would be tears of grief and sadness as their parents passed, but throughout it all they held each other close, whispering words of love and comfort that settled the beating of their hearts each and every single day they would share together.

* * * * *

DEMANDING HIS
DESERT QUEEN

ANNIE WEST

For Marianne Knip,
the first of my German readers I was lucky enough to meet.
Marianne, thank you for your continuing friendship.
Your warmth and your enthusiasm for my stories
are precious to me.
*Ich hoffe, wir begleiten weiterhin gemeinsam viele
Liebespaare auf ihren Weg ins Glück.*

CHAPTER ONE

'THE ANSWER IS NO.'

Karim's voice was harsher than usual, sharp rather than simply firm. The Assaran envoy's suggestion had stunned him. It seemed, despite his actions five years ago, he was still a part of Middle Eastern politics.

Karim stared through the window at the panorama of sapphire lake, verdant foothills and Swiss mountains, yet felt none of the calm the view was supposed to inspire. He spun around, ignoring the quickened beat of his pulse and the clench of his gut.

'But, Your Highness...'

Karim stiffened at the words. 'I no longer use a royal title.'

He watched the envoy absorb that.

'Sir, at least take time to consider. You haven't yet heard the Royal Council's reasoning.'

It was an enormous honour to be asked to take the Assaran throne. Especially since Karim wasn't Assaran. He came from the neighbouring kingdom of Za'daq, where his brother now ruled.

Karim wouldn't accept the Assaran crown. Yet he wondered why the Council was looking beyond its borders for a new sheikh. What about the heir? He knew the recently deceased ruler of Assara had left behind a wife and son.

When Karim realised the direction of his thoughts he

sliced them off. But not quickly enough to dispel the sour tang on his tongue.

'Please, sir.'

The man looked distressed. Karim knew his visitor would be blamed for failing in his mission. If it was discovered he'd been ejected by Karim in mere minutes...

Stifling a sigh, he gestured to the lounge. 'Take a seat. You might as well be comfortable.'

The presidential suite of this exclusive hotel might be comfortable, but sadly it hadn't proved exclusive enough to prevent this unwanted diplomatic delegation. As the hotel's new owner, Karim would change that.

'Thank you, sir.'

Even so, he waited till Karim had taken a seat facing him. Deference towards royalty was ingrained in the man. Even royals who'd renounced their regal claim.

For a mad moment Karim considered revealing the truth and ending this farce. But he'd vowed not to. His brother Ashraf had enough to deal with, imprinting his own stamp on Za'daq. He didn't need full-blown family scandal as well.

Their father had believed Ashraf, the younger brother, was the result of an affair between their mother and the man she'd later run off with. It had only been as the old Sheikh lay dying that they'd discovered Ashraf was legitimate.

Instead Karim, the firstborn, the one groomed from infancy to take the throne, was the cuckoo in the nest.

When, soon after, the old Sheikh had died, Karim had renounced the Za'daqi throne in favour of his brother. No one but the brothers knew the scandalous reason for his decision.

'The Council has given this its deepest consideration since the tragic death of our Sheikh.'

Karim nodded. The Assaran King's death had come out of the blue. 'But surely there's an heir?'

If the envoy noticed Karim's voice had turned to gravel, he didn't show it.

'Yes, but he's far too young to take up the reins of government. If the boy were older…a teenager, perhaps…a regent might be appointed to rule in his stead and help guide him. Given his extreme youth, the Council has decided unanimously that it's better for the country to find a new sheikh.'

'Thus disinheriting the child?' Karim had never met the boy. Intended never to meet him. Yet he felt for the child. His own brother would have been denied his true birthright if disapproving old men had had their way.

'Our constitution is different from yours in Za'daq, sir. In Assara what we propose is quite legitimate. The crown is passed from adult male to adult male.'

Karim nodded. This wasn't his battle to fight. He was only hearing the envoy out so the man could tell his masters he'd done his best.

'Surely there are suitable leaders in Assara? You don't need to go outside your country.'

Especially to a man who'd already turned his back on one sheikhdom.

The envoy pursed his lips, clearly taking time to choose his words. 'I need hardly say, sir, that the Council's deliberations are in strictest confidence.'

'Naturally.' Karim nodded. 'You have my assurance that nothing you say will leave this room.'

It would have been easier to end the meeting and send the man away. But Karim's curiosity was roused. He'd spent years building his investment business in lieu of ruling a country. But some things hadn't died—such as his interest in state affairs.

'Though the Sheikhs of Assara have been from the same family for over a hundred and fifty years, other significant families claim the right to offer a candidate in times where the inheritance is…complicated. Several names have been put forward. The one with the best claim is Hassan Shakroun.'

The visitor paused and Karim knew why. Shakroun was a bully whose idea of negotiation was bluster and intimidation. He was interested in personal aggrandisement and expanding his wealth, not in his nation. No wonder the Assarans were scoping other options for a king.

'I see you know the name.'

'We've met.' Once had been enough.

'Frankly, sir—' The man swallowed, then ploughed on. 'The Council is of the opinion that it's not bloodlines that should determine our next leader so much as personal attributes.'

Karim swallowed a wry smile. They certainly wouldn't get royal bloodlines from him, even if his mother *was* from a powerful family. His real father, as far as he could tell, came from humble stock.

'You're after someone who will do the bidding of the Council?'

It had been the same in Za'daq. Many councillors had been close friends of the previous Sheikh and, influenced by the old man's disdain for Ashraf, had made his succession difficult. Things were better now, but for a while many had sought to bring Karim back and install him on the throne. Which was one of the reasons he'd refused to return to visit his homeland, except for Ashraf's wedding. The other being that he knew it was better to cut all ties rather than pine for what might have been.

'Not at all, sir.' The envoy interrupted his thoughts. 'The Council wants a strong leader capable of taking responsibility. A man who knows diplomacy and statecraft. A man who'll be respected by other rulers in the region. If that man is from outside Assara, then it will short-circuit internal squabbling between rival families with an interest in the throne.'

So he was to be the outsider who united the unsuccessful parties? The Assaran Council had a high opinion of his capabilities, if they believed him able to walk in, calm any fractious rivals and make a success of the role.

Once Karim would have been pleased at such proof of respect from a neighbouring government. He must have impressed them in his years helping his father rule Za'daq, trying to persuade the old man into modernisation.

But that had been then. This was now.

He couldn't accept the offer. Even if the Assarans did want him on merit rather than because of a royal pedigree. He'd built a new life. A life that hadn't been laid out for him because of his supposed lineage.

For thirty years he'd followed a narrow, straight path, putting work first, shouldering responsibility for others. He had been dutiful and decent, a hardworking, honourable prince.

Till his life had crumpled like tissue paper in an iron fist.

For a moment an image swam before him of wide brown eyes. Of a cupid's bow mouth. Of smashed hopes.

His breath hissed between his teeth as he banished the memory.

Karim was responsible for no one now but himself. That was exactly the way he wanted it. He knew the burden of being royal. He had no intention of putting on that yoke again.

'Please pass my compliments and thanks to your Royal Council. I'm deeply honoured that they should consider me for such a noble position.' He paused, watching his guest stiffen. 'However, my answer is still no.'

Safiyah stood in front of the mirror in her suite and tried to still the panic rising from her belly to her throat. She wiped her hands down her thighs, hating that they trembled.

It didn't matter what she wore. Yet she'd tried on every outfit she'd brought to Switzerland, finding fault with each one till all that had been left was this. A western-style dress, beautiful, in a heavy fabric that looked almost black. Until she moved. Then the light caught it and it glowed like deep crimson fire.

She bit her lip, suppressing a bitter laugh. Black and crimson. The colours of mourning and sacrifice. How apt. She'd done her share of both.

Safiyah shook her head, refusing to wallow in self-pity. She was far luckier than most. She had her health, a comfortable home and more money than she needed. Above all she had Tarek.

Life had taught her to set her shoulders and keep going, no matter what problems she encountered. To make the best of things and focus on others, not herself.

That was why she was here. To save someone precious.

To save a whole nation if her fears were right.

She swung away, but stopped before the balcony and the spectacular view of lake and mountains. This was her first trip out of the Middle East and she felt like a country bumpkin, gawping at everything. Well, not everything. She knew about luxury, about limousines and discreet security guards. But those mountains! And the green that was so incredibly green! She'd seen photos, of course, but this was different. Even the air through the open window tasted unique, ripe with moisture and growing things.

In other circumstances she'd put on jeans and flat shoes and find a way to slip out of the hotel, away from the bodyguards. She'd stroll through the public gardens, take her time staring into the glittering shop windows, then go to the lake and sit there, soaking up the scenery.

But circumstances weren't different. Circumstances were difficult. Possibly dangerous, if the fears that kept her awake at night proved right and Hassan Shakroun took the throne.

Not surprising that her heart knocked against her ribs like a hammer on stone. Too much hung on this visit. Failure wasn't an option.

Safiyah's hand rose to her breastbone, her fingers touching the base of her throat as if to ease the riotous beat of her heart and the acid searing the back of her mouth.

It's fine to be nervous. That will keep you grounded so you don't get distracted by anything else.

Anything else being *him*—the man she'd travelled here to see. Even so, she'd hoped against hope it wouldn't be necessary. That things would be sorted without her involvement. She'd been appalled to learn nothing had been agreed. That she had to see him after all.

Just thinking of him made her insides clutch as if someone had wrapped a rope around her middle and yanked it mercilessly. Her blood pumped so fast it rushed in her ears.

That's good. The adrenalin will keep you alert. Give you courage.

Safiyah took a deep breath and smoothed her hands once more down her skirt. They were clammy, and her knees shook. But her dress covered her knees, and there'd be no handshake, so no one would know how nervous she was.

No matter what happened, she vowed one thing. She would not reveal weakness to this man.

Not after what he'd done to her before.

Ignoring the cold fingers dancing down her spine, Safiyah swung around and headed for the door.

'Her Highness, the Sheikha of Assara.'

The butler announced her in a slow, impressive tone that helped steady her jittering nerves.

This she could do. For years she'd compartmentalised, leaving the real her—Safiyah—behind and donning the persona expected of a queen, gracious and unruffled.

She lifted her chin, pinned on a calm expression that hid her inner turmoil and stepped into the suite's vast sitting room.

A few steps in and she paused, blinking against the light pouring in from the wall of windows. The butler bowed again and left, closing the door behind him with a quiet snick. It was only then that she made out a tall figure, motionless in the shadow just past the windows.

Even looking into the light, even unable to make out his features against the glare, she'd have known him. That rangy height, the sense of leashed energy. That indefinable shimmer in the air.

Her pulse quickened and her ribcage squeezed her labouring lungs. Fortunately she was old enough and experienced enough to know that this was her body's response to the pressure of her situation. It had nothing to do with feelings she'd once harboured.

'This is…unexpected, *Your Highness*.' His voice was whiplash-sharp as he used her title.

Good. She didn't want him trying his charm on her. Once bitten, twice shy. The thought steadied her nerves and stiffened her knees.

'Is it, Karim?'

Deliberately she used his first name. He might prefer to pretend they were strangers but she refused to rewrite the past to soothe his conscience. If he thought to intimidate, he'd discover she wouldn't yield meekly to a mere hint of displeasure. She'd had years to toughen up since they'd last met.

'I'd assumed, as the hotel owner, you'd be informed of royal guests.'

She stepped further into the room, onto a thick-pile carpet that would have taken a team of master weavers years to produce.

'Ah, but I'm here to conduct important business, not entertain passing acquaintances.'

As if she and her business were by definition unimportant. As if they had been mere acquaintances.

Safiyah had never been more grateful for those hard-learned lessons in self-control as his words ripped through to the small, vulnerable spot deep inside. To the tiny part of her that was still Safiyah, the eager innocent who'd once believed in destiny and happy endings.

Pain bloomed as if from a stabbing dagger. She breathed slowly and rode the hurt, forcing it down. 'My apologies for interrupting your…important business.' Pointedly she raised her eyebrows and glanced about the luxuriously furnished sitting room, as if expecting to see a conference table or a bevy of secretaries.

The voice inside told her not to rile him. She was supposed to persuade, even cajole him. But Safiyah refused to let him think he could brush her off.

'To what do I owe this…pleasure?'

There it was again, that emphasis that made it clear she was uninvited in his private space. Wounded pride made her want to lash out, but she reined in the impulse. She owed it to Tarek to stay calm.

'I need to talk with you.'

'About?'

Even now he didn't move closer. As if he preferred her to be at a disadvantage, unable to see him clearly while she stood in the full light from the windows.

She'd thought better of him.

'May I sit?' Did she imagine that tall body stiffened? She took her time moving to a cluster of chairs around a fireplace, then paused, waiting for an invitation.

'Please.'

Safiyah sank gracefully onto a seat and was glad of it, because when he moved into the light something inside her slipped undone.

Karim was the same, and yet more. The years had given his features a stark edge that accentuated his potent good looks. Once he'd been handsome. Now there was a gravity, an added depth that turned his slanted cheekbones, high-bridged nose and surprisingly sensual mouth into a face that arrested the breath in her lungs.

That black-as-night hair was shorter than before, close-cropped to his skull. That, too, reinforced the startling power of those masculine features. Then there were his eyes, dark moss-green, so intense she feared he saw beneath her façade of calm.

His clothes, dark trousers and a jacket, clearly made to measure, reinforced his aura of command. The snowy shirt emphasised the gold tone of his skin and she had to force herself not to stare at the space where the open top couple of buttons revealed a sliver of flesh.

Her breath snagged and a trickle of something she hadn't felt in years unfurled inside. Heat seared her cheeks. She didn't want to feel it. Would give anything *not* to feel it.

For a frantic moment Safiyah thought of surging to her feet and leaving. Anything rather than face the discomfiting stir of response deep in her feminine core.

This couldn't be happening! For so long she'd told herself her reaction to him all those years ago had been the product of girlish fantasy.

'My condolences on your recent loss.'

Karim's words leached the fiery blush from her face and doused the insidious sizzle of awareness. Shame enveloped her, leaving her hollow and surprisingly weak.

How could she respond like that to the mere sight of Karim when she'd buried her husband just weeks ago?

Abbas might not have been perfect. He might have been cold and demanding. But she owed his memory respect. He'd been her *husband*.

Safiyah looked at her clenched hands, white-knuckled in her lap. Slowly she unknotted them, spreading stiff fingers and composing them in a practised attitude of ease.

She lifted her head to find Karim sitting opposite her, long legs stretched out in a relaxed attitude. Yet his eyes told another story. Their gaze was sharp as a bird of prey's.

'Thank you.'

She said no more. None of the platitudes she'd hidden behind for the past few weeks would protect her from the guilt she harboured within. A guilt she feared Karim, with his unnerving perceptiveness, might somehow guess. Guilt because after the first shock of discovering she was a widow, and learning that Abbas hadn't suffered, she'd felt relief.

Not because she'd wanted her husband dead. Instead it was the relief of a wild animal held in captivity and suddenly given a glimpse of freedom. No matter how hard she tried, she hadn't yet managed to quell that undercurrent of excitement at the idea of taking control of her own life— hers and Tarek's. Of being simply…happy.

But it was too early to dream of freedom. Time enough to do that when she knew Tarek was safe.

'I'm waiting to hear the reason for your visit.'

Safiyah had imagined herself capable of handling most things life threw at her. She was stunned to discover Karim's brusque tone had the power to hurt.

She blinked, reminding herself that to hurt she would have to care about him, and she'd stopped caring long ago. She'd meant nothing to him. All the time he'd pretended to be interested in her he'd had other plans. Plans she hadn't understood and which hadn't included her. At best she'd been a smokescreen, at worst an amusement.

Safiyah lifted her chin and looked him full in the face, determined to get this over as soon as possible.

'I want you to take the Assaran crown.'

CHAPTER TWO

'YOU *WANT* ME to become your Sheikh?'

Karim's brow knitted. Before today he'd have said not much had the power to surprise him.

How wrong he'd been.

He'd assumed only self-interest would have budged Safiyah from the Assaran royal palace at such a time. He'd imagined she'd come here to dissuade him from accepting the sheikhdom.

Surely having him as her King would be the last thing she'd want? Shouldn't she be looking for ways to preserve the crown for her son?

'Yes. That's exactly what I want.'

Karim stared at the poised, beautiful woman before him. The whole day had been surreal, but seeing Safiyah again was the most extraordinary part of it.

The moment she'd walked into the room Karim's blood had thickened, his pulse growing ponderous. As if his body, even his brain, worked in slow motion.

He wasn't surprised that the shy young woman he'd known had disappeared. He'd long since realised her doe-eyed glances and quiet ardour had been ploys to snare his interest. The real Safiyah had been more calculating and pragmatic than he'd given her credit for.

Yet the change in her was remarkable. The way she'd sashayed into the room as if she owned it. The way she'd all but demanded he play by the rules and offer her a seat, as if they were polite strangers, or perhaps old friends about to enjoy a cosy chat.

But then life as an honoured and adored queen would give any woman confidence.

To Karim's chagrin, it wasn't merely her manner that got under his skin. Had her hourglass figure been that stunning when he'd known her? In the old days she'd worn muted colours and loosely fitting clothes, presumably to assure him that she was the 'nice' girl his father had assured him she was. The complete antithesis to the sultry sirens his brother had so scandalously bedded.

Safiyah's dress today might cover her from neck to shin, but the gleam of the fabric encasing those generous curves and tiny waist made it utterly provocative. Even the soft, sibilant *shush* of sound it made when she crossed her legs was suggestive.

Then there was her face. Arresting rather than beautiful. Pure skin, far paler than his. Eyes that looked too big as she stared back at him, as if hanging on his every word. Dark, sleek hair with the tiniest, intriguing hint of auburn. Lips that he'd once—

'Why do you want me to take the throne? Why not fight for your son's right to it?'

'Tarek is too young. Even if the Council could be persuaded to appoint a regent for him, I can't imagine many men would willingly take the role of ruler and then meekly hand it over after fifteen years.'

A man of honour would.

Karim didn't bother voicing the thought.

'Why not leave the decision to the Royal Council? Why interfere? Are you so eager to choose your next husband?'

Safiyah's breath hissed between pearly teeth and her creamy skin turned parchment-pale.

Satisfaction stirred as he saw his jibe hit the mark. For

he hated how she made him feel. She dredged up emotions he'd told himself were dead and buried. He felt them scrape up his gullet, across his skin. The searing hurt and disbelief, the sense of worthlessness and shock as his life had been turned inside out in one short night. At that crisis in his life her faithlessness had burned like acid—the final insult to a man who'd lost everything.

Nevertheless, as Karim watched the convulsive movement of her throat and the sudden appearance of a dimple in her cheek, his satisfaction bled away. Years ago she'd had a habit of biting her cheek when nervous. But Karim doubted nerves had anything to do with Safiyah's response now. Maybe she was trying to garner sympathy.

Yet he felt ashamed. He'd never been so petty as to take satisfaction in another's distress, even if it was feigned. He was better than that.

He opened his mouth to speak, but she beat him to it.

'I'm *not*...' she paused after the word, her chin tilting up as she caught his eye '...looking for a new husband.'

Her voice was low, the words barely above a whisper, yet he heard steel behind them.

Because she'd loved Abbas so deeply?

Karim found himself torn between hoping it was true and wanting to protest that she'd never loved her husband. Because just months before her marriage to the Assaran King she'd supposedly loved Karim.

He gritted his teeth, discomfited by the way feelings undermined his thought processes. He'd been taught to think clearly, to disengage his emotions, not to feel too much. His response to Safiyah's presence was out of character for a man renowned for his even temper, his consideration of others and careful thinking.

'That's not how things are done in Assara,' she added. 'The new Sheikh will be named by the Royal Council.

There is no requirement for him to marry his predecessor's widow.'

Was it his imagination, or had she shivered at the idea? She couldn't have made her disdain more obvious.

Which was tantamount to a lance, piercing Karim's pride. Once she'd welcomed his attentions. But then he'd been first in line to a royal throne of his own. The eldest son of a family proud of its noble lineage.

'What will happen to you when the new Sheikh is crowned?'

'To me?' Her eyes widened, as if she was surprised he'd even ask. 'Tarek and I will leave the palace and live elsewhere.'

Tarek. Her son.

He'd imagined once that she'd give him a son…

Karim slammed a barrier down on such sentimental thoughts. He didn't know what was wrong with him today. It was as if the feelings he'd put away years before hadn't gone away at all, but had festered, waiting to surge up and slap him down when he least expected it.

Deliberately he did what he did best—focused on the problem at hand, ready to find a solution.

'So if you have no personal interest in the next Sheikh, why come all the way here to see me? The Assaran envoy saw me a couple of hours ago. Couldn't you trust him to do the job he was chosen for?'

Karim knew something of Assaran politics. He couldn't believe the previous Sheikh had allowed his wife to play any significant role in matters of state. Whichever way he examined it, Safiyah's behaviour was odd.

'I didn't want to get involved.' Again her voice was low. 'But I felt duty-bound to come, just in case…' She shook her head and looked at a point near his ear. 'The Council is very eager to convince you. It was agreed that I should add my arguments if necessary.'

'And what arguments might those be?'

Karim kept his eyes fixed on her face. He wasn't tacky enough to stare at all the female bounty encased in rustling silk. But perhaps she'd guessed that he was wondering what persuasions she'd try. Colour streaked her cheekbones and her breasts lifted high on a suddenly indrawn breath.

'Assara needs you—'

'In case you haven't noticed, I'm not into a life of public service any more. I work for myself now.'

Her mouth settled in a line that spoke of determination. Had he ever seen her look like that? His memory of Safiyah at twenty-two was that she'd been gentle and eager to go along with whatever he suggested.

But that had been almost five years ago. He couldn't be expected to remember everything about her clearly, even if it felt like he did.

'I could talk about the wealth and honour that will be yours if you take the throne…'

She paused, but he didn't respond. Karim had his own money. He also knew that being Sheikh meant a lifetime of duty and responsibility. Riches and the glamour of a royal title didn't sway him.

Safiyah inclined her head, as if his non-response confirmed what she'd expected. 'Most important of all, you'd make a fine leader. You have the qualities Assara needs. You're honest, fair and hardworking. The political elite respect you. Plus you're interested in the wellbeing of the people. Everyone says it was you who began to make Za'daq better for those who weren't born rich.'

Karim felt his eyebrows climb. He was tempted to think she was trying to flatter him into accepting the position. Except there was nothing toadying about her demeanour.

'The nobles trust you. The people trust you.'

He shook his head. 'That was a long time ago.'

'Your qualities and experience will stand you in good

stead no matter how long it's been. And it's only been a few years.'

Years since he'd left his homeland and turned his back on everything he'd known. He was only now beginning to feel that he'd settled into his new life.

Safiyah leaned forward, and he felt for the first time since she'd arrived that she wasn't conscious of her body language. Earlier she'd seemed very self-aware. Now she was too caught up in their discussion to be guarded. He read animation in her brown eyes and knew, whatever her real reason for being here, that she meant what she said.

Karim canted closer, drawn to her in spite of himself.

'It's what you were born to do and you'd excel at it.'

Abruptly Karim sank back in his seat. Her words had unravelled the spell she'd woven. The moment of connection broke, shattered by a wave of revulsion.

'It doesn't matter what I was *born* to do.' His nostrils flared as he swallowed rising acid. 'I've renounced all that.'

Because he wasn't the man the world thought him. He was the bastard son of an unfaithful queen and her shadowy lover.

'Of course it matters!' Her clasped hands trembled as if with the force of her emotion. 'Assara desperately needs a ruler who can keep the country together—especially now, when rival clans are stirring dissension and jealousy. Each wants their own man on the throne.'

Karim shrugged. 'Why should I bother? One of them will be elected and the others will have to put up with it. Maybe there'll be unrest for a bit, but it will die down.'

'You don't see…'

She paused and looked down at her hands. Karim saw a tiny cleft appear in her cheek and then vanish. She was biting the inside of her mouth again. Absurdly, the sight moved him.

'What aren't you saying, Safiyah?'

It was the first time he'd spoken her name aloud in years. Her chin jerked up and for a moment her gaze clung to his. But he wasn't foolish enough to be beguiled by that haunted look.

See? Already it was gone, replaced by a smooth, composed mask.

'You're the best man for the role, Karim—far better than any of the other contenders. You'd make a real difference in Assara. The country needs a strong, honest leader who'll work for *all* his people.'

Karim digested that. Was she implying that her dead husband hadn't been a good ruler? The idea intrigued him. Or was she just referring to unrest now?

To his annoyance her expression gave little away. The Safiyah he'd once known, or thought he'd known, had been far easier to read. Even more annoying was the fact his interest was aroused by the idea of doing something intrinsically worthwhile. Something more meaningful than merely building his own wealth.

Karim frowned. How had Safiyah guessed such an appeal would tempt him?

He enjoyed the challenge of expanding his business interests. The cut and thrust of negotiation, of locating opportunities ripe for development and capitalising on them. That took skill, dedication and a fine sense of timing. Yet was it as satisfying as the work he'd been trained to do— using his skills to rule a nation?

The thought of Safiyah knowing him so well—better, it seemed, than he knew himself—infuriated him. This was the woman who'd spurned him when she discovered the secret taint of his illegitimacy. He'd believed in her, yet she'd turned her back on him without even the pretence of regret, much less a farewell. It galled him that anything she said could make him doubt even for a second his chosen course.

What was wrong with concentrating on his own life, his

own needs? Let others devote themselves to public service. He'd done his bit. Assara wasn't even his country.

Karim leaned back in his seat, raising his eyebrows. 'But I'm not a contender. I have already made that clear.'

He almost stood then, signifying the interview was over. But something prevented him. Something not at all fine or statesmanlike. An impulse grounded in the hurt he'd felt when she'd abandoned him.

'Unless…'

Satisfaction rose as she leaned closer, avid to hear more, her lush, cherry-red lips parted.

Karim had a sudden disconcerting memory of those lips pressed against his. They'd been devoid of lipstick and petal-soft. Her ardent, slightly clumsy kiss had enchanted and worried him. For, much as he'd wanted her, he had known he shouldn't seduce an innocent, even if they were on the verge of marriage. Especially an innocent who, with her father, was a guest in the royal palace.

Safiyah had been all the things Karim hadn't even known he wanted in a wife: generous, bright, shyly engaging and incredibly sexy. She'd been the reason he'd finally decided to give in to his father's demand that he marry.

'Unless?' Her voice was like honey.

'Unless there was more to the deal…an inducement.'

He leaned forward, and for a moment the space between them was negligible. He was close enough to see the tiny amber flecks in her brown eyes, to reacquaint himself with the creamy perfection of her skin and inhale a teasing drift of scent. A delicate floral perfume, with a warm, enticing undertone, that was unique to Safiyah.

That hint of fragrance hit him like a body-blow, sweeping him back to a time when he'd had everything. He'd been a prince, secure in his position, his place in the world and his family. He'd enjoyed his work, helping his father run Za'daq. He hadn't even regretted giving up his sexual freedom because Safiyah had turned the prospect of marriage from a duty to a pleasure.

'What sort of inducement?' Her voice was steady but her eyes were wary.

Karim told himself to leave it. To walk away. He had no intention of taking this further.

Then he heard his own voice saying, 'Marriage.'

He couldn't mean it.

He wasn't talking about marriage to *her*. Yet a strange shivery feeling rippled down her spine and curled into her belly like large fingers digging deep. Her skin prickled all over and heat eddied in disturbing places.

'I'm sure that will be no problem.' She forced a smile. 'You'll have your pick of eligible women.'

And Karim didn't need a crown or wealth to attract them. He was handsome, urbane and, she knew to her cost, charming. He could coax the birds from the trees if he set his mind to it. No wonder she, so unworldly and inexperienced at twenty-two, had been taken in, thinking his attentions meant something special.

'I don't need to pick when there's one obvious choice.'

His crystalline gaze locked on hers and his voice deepened to a baritone note she felt vibrate through her bones.

'The Queen of Assara.'

His words were clear. Safiyah heard them, and yet she told herself Karim had said something else. He couldn't really mean—

'*You*, Safiyah.'

'Me?' Her voice rose to a wobbly high note.

Once she'd believed he wanted to marry her, that he cared for her. Her father had been sure too. And so had Karim's father. He'd permitted her and her father to stay at the Za'daqi palace even while, as they'd discovered later, he was in the final stages of terminal illness.

But when a family emergency had dragged her and her father back to Assara everything had fallen apart. Karim hadn't farewelled them. Nor had he responded to the note she'd left him. A note she'd written and rewritten. There'd been no attempt to contact her since. Just…nothing. Not a single word. When she'd tried to contact him at the palace she'd been fobbed off.

Then had come the news that Karim's father had died. To everyone's amazement Karim had renounced the throne and left Za'daq. Even then she'd waited, refusing to believe he'd really abandoned her. Days had turned into weeks. Weeks to months. And still no word. And over those months her faith in him had shrivelled and turned into hurt, disbelief and finally anger.

Even at the last moment, when she'd been cornered in a situation she'd never wanted, a small, irrepressible part of her had hoped he'd step in and stop—

'Safiyah?'

She blinked and looked into that dark gaze. Once those eyes had glowed warm and she'd read affection there. Now they gave nothing away. The coldness emanating from him chilled her to the core.

'You want to marry *me*?' Finally she managed to control her vocal cords. The words emerged husky but even.

'Want…?' Forehead crinkling, he tilted his head as if musing on the idea. But the eyes pinioning hers held nothing like desire or pleasure. His expression was calculating.

That was what gave Safiyah the strength to sit up, spine stiff, eyebrows raised, as if his answer was only of mild interest. As if his patent lack of interest in her as a potential wife, a woman and a lover, didn't hurt.

She would *not* let him guess the terrible pain his indifference stirred. Everything inside her shrivelled. Bizarre that, even after his rejection years before, part of her had obstinately clung to the idea that he'd cared.

'You're right. No sensible man would *want* to marry a woman who ran out on him like a thief in the night.'

She gaped at the way he'd twisted the past. How dared he? Hearing the devastating news of her sister's attempted suicide, of *course* Safiyah and her father had gone to her immediately. Her father had made their apologies for the sudden departure, referring to a family emergency. Safiyah had assumed she'd have a chance to explain to Karim personally later.

Except he'd refused to take her calls. He'd led her on to believe he cared, then dumped her, and now he was pretending she'd been the one at fault!

'Now, look here! I—'

'Not that it matters now. The past is dead, not worth discussing.' He sliced the air with a decisive chopping motion, his expression cold. 'As for wanting marriage now… Perhaps *need* is a better word.' He opened those wide shoulders and spread his hands in a fatalistic gesture.

'I can't see your logic.'

Safiyah's voice was clipped, that of a woman ostensibly in control. She wouldn't demean herself by rehashing the past. He was right. It was over. She should count herself lucky she'd discovered Karim's true nature when she had. He hadn't been the paragon she'd believed.

'There's no reason for us to marry.'

'You don't think so?' He shook his head. 'I disagree. Despite what your law says, even the most optimistic supporter couldn't expect me to take the throne of Assara without a ripple. I'm a foreigner, an unknown quantity. You've said yourself that there are political undercurrents and rivalry in the country's ruling elite. To overcome those an incoming ruler would need to show a strong link to Assara and to the throne.'

He paused, watching her reaction. Now, with a sink-ing heart, Safiyah understood where he was going. And it made a horrible sort of sense.

'What better way of showing my respect for Assara and cultivating a sense of continuity than to marry the current Queen?'

Except said Queen would do just about anything to avoid another marriage. Particularly marriage to *this* man. Call it pride, call it self-preservation, but she'd be mad to agree.

'I disagree. With the Council's backing a newcomer, especially one with your qualities and experience, would be able to establish himself.' He was far, far better than the other alternatives.

Karim steepled his fingertips beneath his chin as if considering. But his response came so quickly she knew he'd immediately discounted her words.

'Besides, if I married you…'

Was it her imagination or did his voice slow on the words?

'Your son wouldn't be disinherited. That would satisfy any elements concerned at him being replaced by a foreigner. It would ensure the long-term continuity of the current dynasty.'

Safiyah sat in stunned silence, thinking through the implications of his words. 'You mean Tarek would be your heir? You'd adopt him?' The idea stunned her.

Emotion flickered across Karim's unreadable expression. 'I'm not a man who'd happily rip away someone's birthright, no matter what the constitution allows.'

There was something in his tone of voice, a peculiar resonance, that piqued her curiosity. Safiyah sensed there was more to his words than there seemed. But what?

She was on the verge of probing, till she read his body language. His hard-set jaw and flared nostrils revealed a man holding in strong emotion. Now wasn't the time to pursue this—not if she wanted him to take the throne.

Which was why she didn't instantly refuse. She needed time to persuade him.

'Are you saying if I agree to marry you…' she paused, fighting to keep her voice even '…you'd take the crown?'

His gaze sharpened. She felt it like an abrasive scrape across her flesh. The grooves bracketing those firm lips deepened, as if hinting at a smile, yet there was no softening in that austere, powerful face.

'I'm saying that if you agree to marry me I'll *consider* changing my mind about accepting the sheikhdom.'

Well, that put her in her place. Safiyah felt the air whoosh from her lungs, her chest crumpling with the force of that outward breath. Even if she agreed to marriage, it might not be enough to persuade him.

She'd never thought herself a particularly proud woman, but she hated that Karim had the power, still, to deflate her. To make her feel she was of no consequence. That incensed her.

For years she'd fought to maintain her self-respect and sense of worth, married to a man who adhered to the traditional view that a wife was merely an extension of her husband's will. Particularly a wife who'd been exalted by marrying a royal sheikh.

Fury surged at Karim's off-hand attitude. How dared he on the one hand ask her to marry him and on the other make it clear that even such a sacrifice on her part might not be enough to sway him?

Not that he'd *asked* her to marry him. He'd put it out there like some clause in a business contract.

Safiyah felt hot blood creep up her throat and into her cheeks. She wanted to let rip. To tell him he was an arrogant jerk, despite his royal blood. Her marriage had taught her that royals were no more perfect than anyone else. If anything, their ability to command not only great wealth, but the obedience of everyone around them, could amplify their character flaws.

But she didn't have the luxury of plain speaking. This wasn't about her. It was about Tarek's future, his safety. As well as the future of their country.

'What do you say, Safiyah? Is your country's wellbeing enough to tempt you into marriage again?' He sat back, relaxed in his chair, as if he didn't care one way or the other.

'There's something else.'

She'd hoped to persuade Karim without telling him of her fears, knowing he might well dismiss them since she had no proof. But what proof could she have till it was too late? The idea curdled her stomach.

'Another important reason for you to accept the throne. Hassan Shakroun—'

Karim cut her off. 'No more! I've already heard everything I need from the official envoy.'

As if *she*, the Queen of Assara, had no insight to offer! Perhaps he believed as Abbas had—that women weren't suited for politics. Or perhaps he was simply impatient that she hadn't leapt at the chance to marry him.

Safiyah was convinced Tarek would be in danger if Shakroun took the throne. She'd never liked the man, but the things she'd learned recently made her blood freeze at the idea of him in the palace. He wouldn't leave a potential rival sheikh with royal blood alive, even if that rival was a mere toddler.

Her throat closed, making her voice husky. 'But you must listen—'

'No.'

Karim didn't raise his voice, but that decisive tone stopped her.

'No more arguments. I don't *have* to listen to anything. You came to me, not the other way around.'

His words stilled her instinctive protest.

'I'm not inclined to accept the throne, but I'll consider it more thoroughly *if* you're willing to marry.'

Safiyah drew a deep breath, frantically searching for a semblance of calm. She couldn't believe the direction this conversation had taken. What had begun simply had become a nightmare.

She was about to ignore his warning and spill out her fears, but the stern lines of his expression stopped her. Karim didn't look like Abbas, but she recognised the pugnacious attitude of a man who'd made up his mind. Not just any man, but one raised to expect unquestioning obedience.

She'd learned with her husband that defiance of his pronouncements, even in the most trivial, unintended way, only made him less likely to listen. Safiyah couldn't afford to have Karim reject the crown.

Carefully she chose her words. 'I need time to consider too.'

Karim raised one supercilious eyebrow, obviously questioning the fact that she hadn't instantly leapt at the chance to marry him.

Except the thought of being tied in marriage to any man, especially Karim, sent a flurry of nervous dread through her.

'*You* need time?'

His tone made it clear he thought it inexplicable. He was right. Any other woman, she was sure, would jump at the chance to marry him.

'It seems we both do.' She held his gaze, refusing to look away. She might be reeling with shock inside, but she refused to betray the fact.

'Very well. We'll meet tomorrow at nine. A lot rides on your answer, Safiyah.'

CHAPTER THREE

'I LIKE IT,' Ashraf said over the phone. 'Accepting the Assaran crown is a perfect solution.'

Karim frowned at his brother's words as he wiped the sweat from his torso. The morning's visits had left him unsettled, and he'd sought to find calm through a workout in the gym, only to be interrupted by Ashraf's call.

'Solution? I don't see that there's a problem to be solved from your perspective—and especially not from mine.'

Yet, if not a problem, Karim sensed there was *something*. He and Ashraf had spoken at the weekend. It was unlike his brother to call again so soon. Unless something important had arisen. They didn't live in each other's pockets, but there was a genuine bond between them, all the more remarkable given the fact they'd been kept apart as much as possible by their father.

The old man had been prejudiced against Ashraf, believing him to be another man's son. He'd neglected the younger boy, fixing all his focus and energy on the elder. Not because he'd cared for Karim—the old tartar had been incapable of love—but because, as the eldest, he was the one to be moulded into a future sheikh.

If it hadn't been so personally painful Karim would have laughed when the truth had been revealed, that the Sheikh had picked the wrong heir. That Ashraf was the true son and Karim the bastard.

'I've no need of a throne, Ashraf. You know that.'

There was a growl in his voice. A morning besieged—first by the envoy from the Assaran Royal Council, and then by the only woman he'd ever seriously thought of marrying—had impaired his mood. The idea that Safiyah believed he still cared enough about her to be coaxed into doing her bidding set his teeth on edge. It would take more than an hour in the gym to ease the anger cramping his belly.

Karim stared through the huge windows, streaming with rain, towards the mountains, now shrouded in cloud. He usually found peace in a long ride. But he had no horses here. And even if he had, he wouldn't have subjected any poor beast to a hard ride in this weather just to shift his bad mood.

'Of course you don't need a throne.' Ashraf's tone was matter-of-fact. 'You've taken to being an independent businessman like a duck to water. Not to mention having the freedom to enjoy lovers without raising expectations that you're looking for a royal life partner.'

Karim's frown deepened. Did his brother miss his old life? Ashraf and Tori had been blissfully wrapped up in each other when he'd seen them last, but... 'What's wrong? Are you pining for your days as a carefree bachelor?'

Ashraf's laugh reassured him. 'Not a bit. I've never been happier.' He paused, his voice dropping to a more serious note. 'Except I'd rather you were here more often.'

It was a familiar argument, but Karim was adamant about not returning to Za'daq long-term. His brother was a fine leader, yet there were still a few powerful men who chafed at the idea of being ruled by a younger son.

His brother sighed at the other end of the line. 'Sorry. I promised myself I wouldn't mention it.'

'Why don't you just get to the point?'

The point being the outlandish suggestion that he,

Karim, should take the Assaran throne. Interestingly, the proposal hadn't been news to Ashraf. Nor did he think it outlandish.

'You rang to persuade me. Why?'

'Pure self-interest.' Ashraf's answer came instantly. 'Life will be much easier and better for our country if there's a stable government in Assara.'

Karim didn't dispute his logic. The two countries shared a border, and what affected one ended up affecting the other.

'If Shakroun becomes Sheikh there'll be stability.' Karim didn't like the man, but that was irrelevant. 'He's strong and he'll hang on to power.'

'That's what I'm afraid of,' his brother murmured.

'What?' Surely Ashraf wouldn't advocate civil unrest.

'You've been away a long time. Certain things have come to light that put a different slant on Shakroun and his activities.'

'I haven't heard anything.'

Despite removing himself from the Middle East, Karim followed press reports from the region. He'd told himself more than once that his interest in matters he'd left behind was a mistake, but though he'd cut so many ties he couldn't conquer his innate interest. He'd been bred to it, after all, had spent a lifetime living and breathing regional politics.

'We're not talking about anything known publicly. But a number of investigations are bearing fruit. Remember that people-smuggling ring that worked out of both countries?'

'How could I forget?'

Za'daq was a peaceable country, but years before the borderland between the two nations had been lawless, controlled by a ruthless criminal called Qadri. Qadri had unofficially run the region through violence and intimidation. One of his most profitable ventures had been people-smuggling from Za'daq into Assara and then to more distant markets. Tori, before she'd become Ashraf's wife, had been kidnapped for the trade, and Qadri had attempted to execute Ashraf himself.

'We don't have enough quite yet to prove it in a court of law, but we know Qadri's partner in the flesh trade was Hassan Shakroun.'

'I see…' The surprising thing was that Karim wasn't surprised. Not that he'd guessed Shakroun was a criminal. He'd just thought him deeply unpleasant and far too fixated on his own prestige and power. 'How sure are you?'

'I'm sure. The evidence is clear. But it will take time till the police are ready to press charges. Since Qadri's death Shakroun has taken over some of his criminal enterprises. They're trying to get an iron-clad case against him on a number of fronts. It's tough getting evidence, because Shakroun gets others to do his dirty work and witnesses are thin on the ground. A couple of people who stirred up trouble for him met with unfortunate "accidents".'

Karim felt an icy prickle across his rapidly cooling flesh. He grabbed a sweatshirt and pulled it one-handed over his head, then shoved his arms through the sleeves.

'That's one of the reasons the Council is searching for someone else to become Sheikh.'

Now it made so much more sense. Did Safiyah know?

Immediately he dragged his thoughts back. Safiyah wasn't the issue. He refused to be swayed by her. Yet the thought of her with her small child in the Assaran palace and Shakroun moving in made his stomach curdle.

'It's also why they're eager for an outsider,' Ashraf added. 'If they choose from within the country Shakroun is the obvious choice. He's from an influential family, and on the face of it would make a better leader than the other contenders. But with you they'd get someone they know and respect, who has a track record of ruling during those years when our father was ill.'

Karim let the words wash over him, ignoring Ashraf's reference to the man who'd raised him as his father. His thoughts were already moving on.

'How many know about this?'

'Very few. It's too early to accuse him publicly—not until the evidence is watertight. But if he becomes Sheikh…'

Karim could imagine. A criminal thug with almost absolute power. It didn't bear thinking about.

He ploughed his hand through his damp hair. 'It's still a matter for the Assarans.'

'And they want *you*, Karim.'

Karim's mouth flattened. His nostrils flared as he dragged in a deep breath. 'I've got a life here.'

He watched the stream of rain down the windows and another chill encompassed him. It didn't matter how long he spent in Europe and North America. He still missed the wide open skies of his homeland. The brilliant, harsh sun, and even the arid heartland where only the hardiest survived.

'I've got a business to run,' he added.

Ashraf didn't respond.

'I'm a private citizen now. I've had my fill of being royal. From the moment I could walk I was moulded into a prince, crammed full of lessons on public responsibility and politics. Now I'm living for myself.'

Not that he expected sympathy.

Finally his brother spoke. 'So you're telling me you'll just turn your back on the situation? Because you're having such a good time answering to no one but yourself?' He didn't hide his scepticism.

'Damn it, Ashraf! Do I look like a hero?'

His brother's voice held no laughter when he answered. 'I always thought so, bro.'

Karim flinched, feeling the twelve-month age difference

between them like a weight on his shoulders. Some hero! He hadn't been able to protect his own brother.

Karim had been a serious, responsible child, his world hemmed in by constant demands that he learn, achieve, excel, work harder and longer. Even so, he'd devoted himself to finding ingenious ways to keep the old Sheikh's attention off his younger brother. When he hadn't succeeded—when the old man had focused his hate on the boy he'd believed a bastard—Ashraf had been bullied and beaten. Karim hadn't been able to protect him all the time.

Ashraf had never blamed him for not looking after him better, but the twist of guilt in Karim's belly was something he'd always carry.

'You don't have to be a hero to become Sheikh,' Ashraf continued, as if he hadn't just shaken Karim to the core. 'Shakroun would have no qualms about taking the throne and there's nothing heroic about *him*. He'd enjoy the perks of the position.'

The words hauled Karim's thoughts out of the past and straight back to Assara. To the idea of Safiyah at the mercy of a man like Shakroun. Hassan Shakroun wouldn't be slow to recognise that tying himself to the previous Sheikh's beautiful widow would cement his position. Karim might not care for Safiyah any more but the thought of her with a thug like Shakroun...

Karim cursed under his breath, long and low. His brother, having made his point, merely said goodbye and left him with his thoughts.

Instinct warned Karim to keep a wide berth from Assara and its troubles. Yet his sense of responsibility nagged. It wasn't helped by the realisation, crystallised during the meeting with Safiyah, that his new life wasn't as fulfilling as he'd like. Yes, he had an aptitude for business and making money. Yes, he enjoyed the freedom to choose for himself, without pondering the impact of his decisions on

millions of others. And Ashraf was right: it was far easier enjoying a discreet affair without the encumbrance of
royalty.

But Karim had spent his life developing the skills to ad-
minister a nation. He'd had a few years of taking on more
responsibility when the old Sheikh's health had faded. He'd
thrived on it. It had been his vocation. Which was why he'd
been so devastated when he'd had to step away. Ashraf had
told him to stay as Sheikh but Karim hadn't been able to do
it. His brother had already been robbed of so much. Karim
had refused to take what was rightfully his.

The idea of making a real difference in Assara, doing
what he was trained for and what he enjoyed, tempted him.
He could do a lot for the place and its people. Assara was a
fine country, but it was behind Za'daq in many ways. He'd
enjoy the challenge.

Yet behind all those considerations was the thought of
Safiyah. Of what would happen to her and her son if Shakroun became Sheikh.

Karim paced the private gym from end to end. Safiyah
was nothing to him—no more important than any other Assaran citizen. He should be able to contemplate her without
any stirring of emotion.

He grimaced. Emotion had lured him into playing out
that scene with her earlier. He'd drawn out the interview
with talk of marriage purely so he could watch her squirm.
It had been a low act. Karim was ashamed of stooping to it.
He couldn't recall ever deliberately lying before. But he'd
lied blatantly today. To salve his pride. And because he
hated the fact that Safiyah could make him feel anything
when she felt nothing. To her he was, as he'd always been,
a means to an end.

But his talk of marriage had backfired mightily.
Because now he couldn't get it out of his head.
Karim was intrigued by her. He kept circling back to the

idea of Safiyah as his lover. Maybe because although they'd once been on the verge of betrothal, they'd never shared more than a few kisses. The night she'd agreed to come to him had been the night his world had been blown apart.

That had to be the reason he felt so unsettled. Safiyah was unfinished business.

Lust speared him, dark and urgent, as he remembered her in the crimson dress that had clung like a lover's hands. The delicate pendant she'd worn, with a single glowing red stone, had drawn his eyes to the pale perfection of her throat. He'd wanted to bury his face where her pulse beat too fast and find out if she was still as sensitive there as he remembered. Or if that too had been a hoax. Like the way she'd pretended to fall for him.

He knew he should walk away.

Safiyah tested his limits more than any woman he'd met. He didn't want to spend his life with a woman he couldn't trust or respect. Even to satisfy his lust.

But what if he did walk away? If he let Shakroun take the throne?

Karim would be in part responsible for what that thug did to Assara. And what he might do to Safiyah and her boy.

Karim stopped pacing and stared at the tall figure reflected in the mirror on the far side of the room. He saw hands clenched into fists, tendons standing taut, a body tensed for action.

He'd been raised to put the welfare of a nation before his own. That conditioning was hard to break.

Surely *that* was what made him hesitate.

He had a major decision to make and it would *not* hinge on Safiyah.

Karim forked his hand through his hair, scraping his fingers along his scalp. The trouble was, the more he thought about it, the more he realised marriage to the Assaran Queen was the best way to ensure he was accepted as Sheikh.

If he chose to take the role.

If he could bring himself to marry the woman who'd once spurned him.

'He's *fine*, Safiyah. Truly. It was just a runny nose and he's okay now. He's bright as anything and he's been playing with the puppies.'

The phone to her ear, Safiyah rolled onto her back on the wide bed, imagining Tarek with a tumble of puppies. He'd be in his element. He loved animals, but Abbas had always said a palace was no place for pets.

'You brought them to the palace on purpose, didn't you, Rana? You're hoping we'll keep one.'

Not that she minded. These last few years she'd missed being around dogs and horses. There was something soothing about their unquestioning love.

'Guilty as charged.'

Her sister's chuckle made Safiyah smile. It was such a carefree sound, and one she still cherished. Rana was happy and settled now—such a tremendous change from a few years ago.

'But you know how hard it can be to find homes for a litter. Especially since they're not pure-bred. What's *one* little puppy…?'

Safiyah laughed at Rana's exaggerated tone of innocence. 'Probably a lot of trouble until it's house-trained and learns not to chew everything in sight. But you're right. A dog would be good company for Tarek.'

Not that her son showed any sign of missing Abbas. He'd rarely seen his father more than once a week, and then only for short periods, usually in the throne room or the royal study.

Those meetings had been formal affairs. Abbas hadn't

been one to cuddle his son, or play games. He'd said that was how royal heirs were raised. They weren't supposed to cling to their parents. And besides, as Sheikh he'd had other things to keep him busy. He'd assured Safiyah that when Tarek was old enough he'd take him in hand and teach him what he needed to know to rule Assara.

That was never going to happen now.

Tarek would grow up without knowing his father.

Nor would he become Sheikh.

A pang of fear pierced her chest. Would her son be allowed to grow up in safety? What would happen if Karim didn't take the crown? He'd looked anything but happy about the idea. But if he didn't and Hassan Shakroun became Sheikh—

'Safiyah? Are you still there?'

'Sorry, Rana. I got distracted.'

'Things didn't go well?'

'I'm sure it will work out just fine.' Safiyah was so used to putting a positive spin on things, protecting her sister as much as possible, that the words emerged automatically.

'Reading between the lines, it doesn't sound like it.' Rana paused, then, 'You *can* talk to me, you know, Safiyah. I'm not as fragile as I used to be.'

'I know that.'

These days Rana seemed a different person entirely from the severely depressed young woman she'd once been. It was habit rather than need that fed Safiyah's protectiveness, yet old ways died hard.

'But there's no news yet—nothing to share.'

Other than the fact Karim had asked her to be his wife.

No, not asked. Demanded. Made it a condition of him even considering accepting the sheikhdom.

She couldn't share that fact. Not till she'd worked out what answer she was going to give.

Marrying Karim seemed impossible. Especially as

there'd been not even a hint of warmth when he spoke of it. Instead he'd looked so cold, so brooding...

She *couldn't* say yes. The very thought of accepting another marriage of convenience when she'd just escaped one sent shivers scudding down her spine.

Naturally they were shivers of distaste. They couldn't be anything else.

But if she said no what would happen to Tarek? She'd do whatever it took to see him safe. Of course she would. Yet surely there was some other way. Surely marriage wasn't essential.

'Well, if you need to talk I'm just here.'

It struck Safiyah how far Rana had come from the troubled girl she'd been. 'Thank you, Rana. I'm so lucky to have you.' Especially as a few short years ago Safiyah had almost lost her. 'To be honest, I—'

A knock on the door interrupted her. 'Sorry, there's someone here. I'll just see who it is.'

Safiyah swung her bare feet off the bed, retying the belt of her long robe. She glanced at the time. Nine o'clock. Too late for a casual visitor, even if she'd known anyone else in Switzerland. And the special envoy who'd accompanied her from Assara would never dream of simply turning up at her door. He'd ring first.

'That's fine. I need to go anyway.'

In the background Safiyah heard yapping. She grinned as she crossed the bedroom and entered the suite's sitting room, flicking on a lamp as she went.

'Okay. Give Tarek a hug and kiss from me and tell him I'll be home soon.'

'I will. And good luck!'

More yapping, this time more frenzied, and Rana hung up.

Safiyah reached the entrance of her suite and peered through the peephole. Her vision was obscured by a large fist, raised to knock. When it lowered she was looking at a broad chest, straight shoulders and the dark gold flesh of a masculine neck and jaw.

Karim!

Safiyah's pulse catapulted against her ribs, taking up a rackety, uneven beat. They'd agreed to meet tomorrow morning. Not tonight. She wasn't prepared.

She glanced down at the silk robe of deep rose-pink. It covered her to her ankles, but abruptly Safiyah became aware that beneath it she wore nothing but an equally thin nightgown.

That hand rose to knock again, and she knew she had no choice but to answer.

She cracked the door open, keeping out of view behind it as much as possible.

'Karim. This is a surprise.' Despite her efforts her voice sounded husky, betraying her lack of calm.

'Safiyah.' He nodded and stepped forward, clearly expecting her to admit him.

She held the door firmly, not budging. 'It's late. I'm afraid it's not convenient to talk now.' Not when she was barefoot and wearing next to nothing. 'Can this wait till the morning?'

By then she'd have some idea of what she was going to say. Hopefully. Plus she'd be dressed. Definitely. Dressed in something that didn't make her feel appallingly feminine and vulnerable just standing close to Karim.

Was she entertaining a lover? The idea flashed into his brain, splintering thoughts of sheikhdoms and politics.

Her cheeks were pink and her hair was a messy dark cloud drifting over her shoulders, as if she'd just climbed out of bed. Her eyes shone like gems and he saw the pulse jitter at the base of her throat, drawing attention both to her elegant neck and her agitation.

Karim's pulse revved as he propped the door open with his shoulder. He heard no noise in the room behind her but that meant nothing.

'I'm afraid this can't wait.'

Wide eyes looked up at him. Still she didn't move. He watched her swallow, the movement convulsive. Karim felt a stab of hunger. He fought the urge to stroke that pale skin and discover if it was as soft as he remembered.

Such weakness only fired his annoyance. Bad enough that his every attempt to think logically about this situation and his future kept swinging back to thoughts of Safiyah. Karim chafed at his unwanted weakness for this woman.

'Surely tomorrow—'

'Not tomorrow. Now.' He bent his head, bringing it closer to hers. 'If I walk away now, Safiyah, don't expect me ever to walk into Assara.'

He didn't mention the sheikhdom. Even in this quiet corridor he was cautious with his words, but she understood. He saw the colour fade from her cheeks and she stepped back, allowing him to enter.

One quick, comprehensive survey revealed that she wore silk and lace. Her robe clung to an hourglass figure that would make any man stare. Especially when she swung round after shutting the door and her full breasts wobbled with the movement, clearly unrestrained by a bra. That wobble shot a dart of pure lust to his tightening groin.

Karim guessed her robe had been put on quickly. It was belted, but gaped open over a low décolletage, over creamy, fragrant flesh and more pink silk. Even the colour of the silk was flagrantly feminine.

A flicker of long-buried memory stirred...of his mother's private courtyard, filled with the heady scent of damask roses, their petals a deep, velvety pink. It had been an oasis of femininity in his father's austere palace. And it had been razed to bare earth when the old man had discovered her sons, at four and three respectively, were pining for her after she'd run off with her lover and had secretly sought solace in her garden.

But memories of the past faded as he took in Safiyah, looking lush and sensual. Outrageously inviting. Especially with that cloud of dark hair spilling around her shoulders, the ends curling around her breasts.

Had some lover been fondling those breasts? Was that why her hard nipples thrust against the silk?

Heat drenched Karim as he flexed his hands and made himself turn from temptation. He strode into the sitting room, giving it a cursory survey before following the light into her bedroom. The bed was still neatly made, but a pile of pillows was propped up on one side. She'd been sitting there alone.

The knowledge smacked him in the chest, stealing both his air and his sense of indignation.

'What are you doing?'

Her voice came from just behind him. It sounded husky, and something drew tight in his groin.

'Nice suite.' He turned and gave her a bland look. 'I hadn't seen it before.' With luck she'd think that as the hotel's new owner he was simply curious about the accommodation.

He walked back into the sitting room and heard the bedroom door snick shut behind him.

Wise woman.

'What is it that can't wait?'

Karim swung round to find her closer than he'd expected. She'd adjusted her robe so barely a sliver of flesh showed beneath the collarbone and she was busily knotting the belt cinching her waist. As if a layer of silk could conceal her seductive body.

'Things are moving quickly.'

That was one thing his deliberations and a second discussion with the Assaran envoy had made clear. If he was going to accept the crown he needed to act fast—before Shakroun got wind of the attempt to bring in an outsider. The man could stir all sorts of trouble.

'I need your answer now.'

'Oh.' She frowned. 'My answer.'

Safiyah looked distracted. As if her mind were elsewhere, rather than on the honour he'd done her by suggesting marriage so she could retain her royal status.

Karim gritted his teeth, fury rising. She acted as if his suggestion they marry was trivial. Not enough to hold her interest when she had more important things on her mind. And this after the insult of her desertion five years before. It was more than his pride could bear.

Something ground through him like desert boulders scraping together, the friction sparking an anger he'd harnessed for so long.

Karim had spent a lifetime being reasonable, honourable, and above all rational. He'd been trained never to act rashly. To weigh his options and consider the implications not only for himself but for others.

Not tonight.

Tonight another man inhabited his skin. A man driven by instincts he'd repressed for years.

'What is it, Safiyah?' He took two paces, stopping only when she had to hike her chin high to hold his eyes. 'You've got something else on your mind? Is it this?'

He cupped one hand around the back of her head, anchoring his fingers in that lush, silky hair.

No protest came. His other arm wrapped around her waist, tugging her close. He had a moment of heady anticipation as her soft form fell against him, her eyes growing huge and dark as pansies.

Then his mouth settled on hers and the years were stripped away.

CHAPTER FOUR

SAFIYAH CLUNG TIGHT, her fingers embedded in the hard biceps that held her to Karim's powerful frame. It was so unexpected she had no time to gather her thoughts. No time to do anything but bend before the force of sensations and emotions that made her sway like a sapling in a strong wind, her body arching back over his steely arm.

To her shame it wasn't outrage that overwhelmed her. It was shocked delight.

Because she'd never been kissed like this.

Never felt like this.

Not even in those heady days when Karim had courted her, for then he'd been considerate and careful not to push her into a compromising position. She'd been innocent and he'd respected that.

Even when she'd married she hadn't felt like this.

Especially when she'd married. She'd felt no passion for Abbas. No desire except the desire to do her duty. And Abbas, though he'd enjoyed her body, hadn't expected anything from her other than acquiescence.

Which made the fire licking her veins unprecedented. Totally new.

Safiyah shivered—not with cold, but with a roaring, instantaneous heat that ignited deep inside and showered through her like sparks from a bonfire, spreading incendiary trails to every part of her body.

This was passion.

This was desire.

It was like the yearning she'd once felt for Karim, multiplied a thousandfold. Like the difference between the heat of a match and the scorch of a lightning strike.

Her mouth opened, accommodating the plunging sweep of his tongue, relearning Karim's darkly addictive taste. It was a flavour she'd made herself forget when she'd told herself to stop pining for the mirage of true love. When she'd given herself in a dutiful arranged marriage.

Because to hold on to those broken dreams would only have destroyed her.

Now, with a force that shook her to the core, Safiyah felt them flood back, in a deluge of sensation to a body starved of affection, much less delight.

Once Safiyah had yearned for Karim with all her virgin heart. Now, time, experience and loss had transformed her once innocent desire into something fierce and elemental. Something utterly unstoppable.

Instead of submitting meekly, or turning away, Safiyah leaned into his hard frame. It felt as natural as smiling. As necessary as breathing.

Her tongue slid the length of his, exploring, tasting, enjoying the rich essence of sandalwood and virile male that filled her senses. She revelled in the feel of his taut frame solid against hers and rose onto her toes to press closer.

A shudder passed through him and his hands tightened possessively, as if her response unleashed something in him that he'd kept locked away. He leaned in, forcing her head back, deepening the kiss, and she went willingly, exulting in the breathtaking intensity of the moment.

Past and future were blotted out. The present consumed her. Her need for this, for him. Nothing else mattered except assuaging that.

Karim's arm slid down her back, his palm curving over

her backside, lifting her towards the drenching heat of his muscled frame. Excitement tore through her, a fierce exhilaration as she read the tension of a man on the brink of losing himself.

Then, with an abruptness that left her swaying, he released her.

Blinking, Safiyah watched him step back. Saw his mouth lengthen in a grimace. Saw him shrug those broad shoulders and straighten his jacket as if brushing off the imprint of her clawing hands. Then he shoved both fists in his pockets and lifted one eyebrow in an expression of cool enquiry.

Flustered, Safiyah felt her heart smash against her ribs, her breasts rising and falling too fast as she tried, unsuccessfully, to get her breathing back to normal.

Her robe had come undone and she knew without looking that her nipples were hard, needy points against the thin fabric of her nightdress. Worse, between her legs was a spill of dampness. Restlessness filled her, and the need to climb up that big body and rub herself against him, chasing the fulfilment that no-holds-barred kiss had promised.

Instead she stood stock-still, feet planted. Mechanically her hands grabbed the sides of her robe and tied it tight. Because, despite the thwarted desire churning through her, Safiyah read the chill in those green eyes surveying her like an insect on a pin. Her skin turned to gooseflesh and the fine hairs at her nape stood on end.

Karim wasn't even breathing heavily. He looked as calm and remote as a stone effigy. And as welcoming.

Looking into those austere features, Safiyah felt all that lush heat dissipate. Instead of his deliciousness she tasted the ashes of passion. She might have been swept away by forces she couldn't control but Karim hadn't.

'Well, that little experiment was instructive.' His voice came from a great distance, like low thunder rolling across the wide Assaran plain. 'It's as well to test these things in advance, isn't it?'

'Test what?' Her voice was husky, but reassuringly even. She'd had years of practice at perfecting a façade that hid her feelings.

Those powerful shoulders shrugged nonchalantly. 'Our physical compatibility.' He paused, his gaze capturing hers as he continued with conscious deliberation, 'Or lack of it.'

Deep, deep inside, in that place where she'd once locked her secret hopes and cravings, something crumpled and withered. There was an instant of shearing pain, like a knife-jab to the abdomen. Then it morphed into an unremitting ache that filled her from scalp to toe.

He'd kissed her like that as an *experiment*?

Safiyah wanted to scream and howl. To pummel that granite-hard chest with her fists. But that would achieve nothing except further embarrassment.

A new kind of fire bloomed within her and seared her cheeks. *Shame.* Shame that she'd responded to this man who now surveyed her with such detachment. Shame that she'd ever been attracted to him.

Swallowing the tangled knot of emotion clogging her throat was almost impossible. Finally she managed, though it physically hurt.

Pain was good, Safiyah assured herself. Pain would make it easier to strip away the final fragments of feeling she'd harboured for Karim.

She'd repressed her feelings for years, told herself she couldn't possibly still want this man who'd rejected her. Whose abandonment had devastated her and branded her with a bone-deep disdain for him and his callous ways.

Yet once in his arms, once his mouth had met hers, she'd responded with an ardour that had been nothing short of embarrassing.

Even now part of her protested. He *had* responded. He'd

wanted to follow that kiss to its natural conclusion just as she had.

Then her brain began to work. People pretended all the time. Hadn't she pretended enthusiasm for Abbas in her bed even when she'd far rather have slept alone? Just because Karim's kiss had been passionate, it didn't mean he'd felt anything but curiosity.

The inequality of their experience told against her. She'd only kissed two men in her life: Karim and her husband. And no kiss before today had awakened such a powerful response in her. Whereas Karim had had women following him, sighing over him and trying to capture his interest for years. No doubt he'd kissed hundreds of women and could feign sexual interest.

He wasn't interested now.

Safiyah's mouth firmed. '*If* I were to marry you…' her words dripped acid '…it wouldn't be for the pleasure of your company.'

Let him read what he liked into her response. She refused to admit anything. After all, she could claim that, like him, she'd been experimenting, searching but not finding a spark between them.

Except she'd never been a liar. The knowledge of her complete submission to Karim's demanding kiss devastated her. She wanted to turn tail and hide.

'Then why *would* you agree to marry me?'

It was a timely reminder, and it stiffened her wobbly knees. She met Karim's stare head-on. 'For my country and my son. I'm afraid of what might happen to both if Shakroun becomes Sheikh.'

Slowly he nodded. 'I understand. I've been hearing more about him this evening.'

Relief made her shoulders sag. Karim sounded like a man who'd changed his mind. If he took the throne Tarek would be safe.

'But what I've heard only reinforces what I said earlier. He's from a powerful clan. If I became Sheikh I'd need to do everything I could to shore up local support. Like marry you.'

Karim's deep voice and narrowed eyes held nothing soft. His needle-sharp scrutiny grazed her skin and her pride. Safiyah might have let him make a fool of her years ago, and again just now, but no more. Enough was enough.

'*If* I were to marry you...' How the thought appalled. But Safiyah would sacrifice her freedom ten times over for her son's life. 'I'd expect you to take your pleasure outside the marriage bed.' She almost choked on the word 'bed', but forced herself to carry on as if unfazed by that kiss. 'Discreetly, of course.'

'Would you, indeed?' Something dark flashed in Karim's eyes. 'And where would you...take *your* pleasure?'

Safiyah stood as tall as she could, lengthening her neck and calling on all the lessons in dignity she'd learned in the past few years. 'That needn't concern you. Rest assured I won't cause any scandals.'

Because sex with Abbas hadn't left her with a burning desire for more. And the one man who'd had the power to wake her libido was staring at her now as if she were something he'd picked up on the sole of his shoe.

Safiyah blocked the jumble of hurt and indignation writhing within, shoving it away with all the other hurts and disappointments she couldn't afford to think about. Instead she concentrated on playing the part of Queen, as her dead husband had taught her. And instead of her usual composure, she aimed for a touch of Abbas's condescension. Presumably it worked, for Karim's dark eyebrows climbed high.

'And if I want pleasure *within* the marriage bed?'

The silky words drew her up short, made her pulse accelerate wildly.

Karim wanted sex with her?

Or was he just trying to make her squirm?

Her hair brushed her cheeks as she shook her head. 'No.'

'Because you don't want me, Safiyah? Or because you're scared you want me too much?'

'Your ego is monumental, Karim.' Adrenaline shot through her and her jaw tilted imperiously.

He merely shrugged. 'I call it as I see it. From where I stand I suspect you're not as uninterested as you say. But I would never force myself on an unwilling woman.'

Safiyah exhaled slowly, trying to banish that panicky feeling. 'I have your word on that?'

'You do.' He paused to let her absorb the words. 'No sex unless you want it, Safiyah. Does that satisfy you?'

She surveyed him carefully. Surely this was just macho male posturing because she'd said she didn't want him. Karim would soon find some ravishing mistress to keep him occupied.

He might be the man who'd dumped her, but she believed him too proud to break his word. Clearly the Council thought the same. And when it boiled down to it what real choice did she have? She needed to save Tarek.

Finally she nodded. 'Yes.'

'You actually trust my word?' His cool tone and the jut of his jaw spoke of haughty male pride.

'Yes.'

Still his frown lingered.

'After all, I'd be entrusting you with my son's wellbeing.'

Saying it aloud sent a shiver rippling down her spine. Not because Karim would hurt them, but at the idea of tying herself once more to a man who saw her as a mere convenience. But she'd survived that once. She could again.

Safiyah returned his stare with one of her own, trying not to catalogue those spare, attractive features she'd once daydreamed about. She reminded herself that he was arrogant and unfeeling, a man who'd toyed with her.

What had happened to the man she'd fallen for at twenty-two? Had she been completely misled by his charm and apparent kindness? What had made him cold and bitter? The same mysterious thing that had driven him to give up his throne?

It didn't matter. She wasn't about to pry into his past or his character, beyond the fact that he would do the right thing. When it came to his honour, and his work for his people, Karim's record was strong. The Royal Council wouldn't have made its offer if there were doubts. It had deliberated carefully before approaching Karim, investigating not only his years in Za'daq but his recent activities.

Nevertheless…

'If you become Sheikh, what about my son, Tarek? Are you serious about adopting him?'

Karim inclined his head. 'I told you before—I'm not the man to steal your son's birthright. He'll still be in line to become Sheikh eventually.'

It seemed too good to be true. If anyone else had said it Safiyah would have doubted they meant it. But Karim had already walked away from one throne. It was still on the tip of her tongue to ask what had prompted that action, but she kept silent. That didn't matter now. As he'd said earlier, the past was best left alone. All that mattered was Tarek's safety and Assara's.

She clasped her hands at her waist and stood silent, watching him. He couldn't have made it clearer that he saw marriage to her as a necessity, not a pleasure. And she should be used to being viewed as a political expedient.

Yet still it hurt!

Abbas had married her because it had suited him to build an alliance with her clan, so when the time had come for him to marry he'd turned his eyes to her family. At first he'd been interested in her clever younger sister, studying at university in the capital. When that hadn't been possible he'd made do with Safiyah.

To accept a second marriage of convenience, to another man who had no feelings for her, was a terrible thing. So terrible Safiyah wanted to smash something. To tell Karim in scathing detail what he could do with his marriage plans.

But she loved her son too much. She'd do anything to keep him safe. Her happiness meant nothing against that. And as for the dreams she'd once harboured of finding love...

Safiyah shuddered and rubbed her hands up her arms. As a twenty-seven-year-old widow she'd be a fool to believe in romance.

'What are you thinking?'

Karim hadn't come closer, yet his voice curled around her. She stiffened and moved to the window, needing distance from his looming presence. She looked out at the sprinkle of lights in the darkness, where the town bled down the slope towards the lake.

'What if you have children? Wouldn't you want them to inherit? I can't believe you'd put your own flesh and blood second to someone else's.'

Safiyah spun around to find him watching her, his expression intense yet impenetrable. Before she could puzzle over it he spoke.

'Don't worry, Safiyah, I won't foist any bastard children on you.'

His tone cut like a blade and his brow wrinkled into a scowl, making her wonder at the depth of his anger. For anger there was, vibrating through the thickening atmosphere.

Safiyah tried to fathom it. Even when she'd told him he could forget about sharing her bed she hadn't sensed fury like this.

Then, as abruptly as it had surfaced, it disappeared.

'So, you agree to marry me?'

He still didn't approach. Didn't attempt to woo her with soft words or tender caresses.

Safiyah told herself she was grateful.

'I…' The words stuck in her throat. Duty, maternal love, patriotism—all demanded she say yes. Yet it was a struggle to conquer the selfish part of her that wanted something for herself. Finally she nodded. 'Yes. If you take the throne, I'll marry you.'

She hadn't expected a display of strong emotion, but she'd expected *something* to show he appreciated her sacrifice. Even a flicker in that stern expression.

She got nothing.

'Good. We'll travel to Assara tomorrow.'

Karim kept his tone brisk, masking the momentary flash of emotion that struck out of nowhere and lodged like a nail between his ribs.

He inhaled, drawing on a lifetime's training in dismissing inconvenient feelings. He didn't *do* sentiment.

'Tomorrow?'

Her eyes rounded. Almost as if she didn't want this. Didn't want *him*.

'I'll accept the Council's offer in person. Now I've decided there's no time to be lost. There's no point giving Shakroun any opportunity to build more support.'

It would be a long, tough road ahead, establishing himself as Sheikh in a foreign country. Karim was under no illusions about that. But excitement burgeoned at the prospect. It was the work he'd been bred to, the work he'd missed even if he hadn't allowed himself to admit it.

And nor was it just the work he looked forward to.

He watched Safiyah watching him and kept his face studiously blank. It wouldn't do to let her guess that one of the benefits in acting quickly was to secure her.

Purely for political reasons, of course.

Yet Safiyah unsettled him more than she should. Thoughts of her had interfered with his decision-making and he'd kept following her around the room as if his body refused to follow the dictates of his brain. Baser impulses ruled—impulses driven by the organ between his legs and the urgent need to claim what he'd once so desired.

That *had* to be the reason for his current fixation. He'd once been prepared to offer Safiyah everything—his name, his loyalty, his wealth. Now he had the opportunity to claim what he'd been denied.

Relief dribbled through him. It was good to have a sane explanation for this urgent attraction.

A powerful throb of anticipation pulsed through him. That kiss, brief as it had been, had proved the attraction was there, stronger than ever.

'What are you thinking?'

She repeated his own question, her eyes narrowed and her chin lifted, as if she'd read the direction of his thoughts and didn't like it. That surprised Karim. He'd long ago learned to hide his thoughts.

'Just thinking about my priorities when we get to Assara.' He paused. 'I'll instruct my lawyers to draw up the adoption papers with the marriage contract.'

'Really? I hadn't expected that so soon. Thank you.'

For the first time since they'd met again Safiyah actually approached him. The tight line of her beautiful mouth had softened and her eyes glowed. If Karim had needed any proof that she was motivated by love of her child, here it was.

He watched the slow smile spread across her face and felt a curious niggle inside. What would it be like to have someone—Safiyah, for example—look at him that way.

Not because he was doing something for the one she loved, but because she cared for *him*?

Blood rushed in Karim's ears as he stiffened and pulled back. Such fanciful thoughts were totally foreign. He was a grown man. He didn't need anyone to care for him. It was just curiosity about the loving bond between mother and child. Something he'd never experienced.

As a child he'd convinced himself that his mother loved him. He had fragmentary memories of being held in soft arms and sung to. Of playing with her in that rose-scented courtyard.

But those memories were wishful thinking. If his mother had loved either of her children she wouldn't have deserted them—left them to the mercies of the man who'd raised them. The man he'd thought of as his father had been irascible, impatient, and never satisfied, no matter how hard Karim had tried to live up to his impossible standards.

'Karim? What is it?' Safiyah had lifted her hand as if to touch his arm.

A white-hot blast of longing seared him. Unlooked-for. Unwanted. Because hankering after such things made him weak. He'd almost fallen for that trap once before with Safiyah. But he'd learned his lesson.

'Nothing. Nothing at all.'

He let his mouth turn up in a slow smile. The sort of smile he knew melted a woman's resolve. Safiyah blinked. Twice. Her lips parted and he saw her pulse pound in her throat.

'On the contrary. Everything is perfect.'

CHAPTER FIVE

KARIM LEFT HIS meeting in the Assaran palace torn between satisfaction and frustration. The interminable deliberation over legalities was complete. Agreement had been reached on all the important issues—including the provisions for Tarek and Safiyah.

And if some of the Assaran officials had been surprised that he, the incoming Sheikh, was the one ensuring the little Prince lost nothing as a result of Karim's accession, they'd quickly hidden it.

As for the red tape…

His homeland of Za'daq had its fair share, but Assara outdid it. They'd spent hours longer than necessary on minutiae. But Karim hadn't hurried them. Time enough to streamline processes after he became Sheikh.

But now, after hours hemmed in by nervous officials and nit-picking lawyers, he needed air.

He turned away from the palace's offices, past the broad corridor leading to the state rooms, and headed down towards the main courtyard where he guessed the stables were.

Emerging outside, Karim glanced at the lowering sun dropping towards the distant border with Za'daq. Purple mountains fringed the horizon and even here, on the coast, he registered the unmistakable scent of the desert.

His nostrils twitched and he inhaled deeply, though he

knew he was imagining that elusive scent. The desert was half a day's journey away. Yet the very air seemed familiar here, as it hadn't in Europe and North America. He felt more at home in Assara than he had in years there.

Karim smiled as he sauntered across the yard to the stables. In the couple of days since he'd agreed to come here his certainty had increased. He'd made the right decision.

But his smile faded as he registered the stable's echoing silence. The doors were shut and there was no sign of activity except in a far corner, where part of the stables had been turned into garages. There, a driver was busy polishing a limousine.

'The stables?' he said, when questioned. 'I'm sorry, sir, but they're empty. No one has worked there in years. Not since the last Sheikh's father's time.'

'There are no horses at all?'

Karim couldn't believe it. Assara was known for its pure-bred horses. Surely the Sheikh would have the finest mounts? Plus, Safiyah had virtually been born in the saddle. Riding was a major part of her life.

He remembered the first time he'd seen her. She'd been on horseback, and her fluid grace on that prancing grey, her lithe agility and the way she and the horse had moved as one had snagged his admiration. The sight had momentarily made him forget the reason he was visiting her father's stud farm, the horse he wanted to buy.

'Where does the Sheikha keep *her* horses?'

'The Sheikha, sir? I don't know of her riding or about any horses.'

Karim stared. Safiyah? Not riding? It was impossible. Once there'd been talk of her possible selection for the national equestrian team. He recalled thinking she'd never looked more alive than on horseback. Except when she was in his arms.

The memory curled heat through his belly, increasing his edginess.

Thanking the driver, he turned and entered the palace, heading for the royal suites. It was time he visited Safiyah anyway. The past couple of days had been taken up with meetings and he'd barely seen her.

Five minutes later he was admitted into her apartments. His curiosity rose as he entered. This was the first room he'd seen in the palace that looked both beautiful and comfortable rather than grandiose. The sort of place he could imagine relaxing after a long day. He liked it.

'If you'd like to make yourself comfortable, sir?' The maid gestured to a long sofa. 'I'll tell the Sheikha you're here.' She bobbed a curtsey and headed not further into the apartment, as he'd expected, but through the open doors into a green courtyard.

Instead of taking a seat Karim followed her, emerging into a lush garden full of flowering plants. Pink, white and red blossoms caught his eye. Fragrance filled the air and the swathe of grass curving amongst the shrubs was a deep emerald.

He paused, taking in the vibrancy of the place, so unlike the courtyards elsewhere in the palace, which were all symmetry and formal elegance. This was inviting, but casual, almost mysterious with its thick plantings and meandering paths.

The sound of laughter drew him forward. There was the maid, moving towards someone half hidden from view. Beyond her, on the grass, was a tumble of movement that resolved itself into a floppy-eared pup and a small boy. Giggles filled the air and an excited yapping.

Karim stepped forward and discovered the half-hidden figure was Safiyah, seated on the grass.

His gaze was riveted to his bride-to-be. In Switzerland he'd seen her cool and reserved, then later satisfyingly breathless in his arms. He'd seen her mutinous and imperious. But he hadn't seen her like this—relaxed and happy, with laughter curving her red lips.

For a moment something shimmered like golden motes in the late-afternoon light. A mirage of the past, when they'd enjoyed each other's company, gradually getting to know one another. Safiyah had laughed then, the sound sweet as honey and open as sunshine. Her laughter, her eager enjoyment of life, had been precious to someone like him, brought up by a man who had been at best dour, at worst irate, and always dissatisfied.

'Karim.'

Her eyes widened and the light fled from her expression. Stupid to mind that the sight of him dulled her brightness. It wasn't as if he wanted to share her laughter. He wasn't here for levity.

Safiyah said something and the maid moved towards the boy as if to scoop him up.

'No. Don't take him away.' Karim turned to Safiyah. 'Don't cut short his playtime because of me.'

It was time for him to meet the boy. Karim had agreed to be a father to him. The idea still elicited a confusing mixture of feelings and he'd berated himself more than once for acting as if on a whim where Tarek was concerned.

But it was no whim. The thought of the little Prince at the mercy of a ruthless man like Shakroun had struck a chord with Karim. He'd had to act. Nor could he rip the child's birthright away. Just as he hadn't been able to take the crown of Za'daq over Ashraf, though he'd been brought up solely for that purpose.

Besides, Karim knew what it was like growing up with the burden of royalty. The child needed a role model—one who understood that there was more to life than court protocol and politics. Karim would be that mentor.

An inner voice whispered that he hadn't been such a

good mentor to his younger brother…hadn't been able to protect him from his father's ire or bring much joy into his world. He vowed to do a better job with Tarek.

Safiyah rose in one graceful movement. Her long dress of deep amethyst slid with a whisper around that delectable body and Karim cursed his hyper-awareness of her. It had been like that since they'd arrived in Assara. No, since that kiss in Switzerland, that had left him fighting to mask his urgent arousal.

Karim drew a slow breath and forced himself to admit the truth. He'd been attuned to her from the moment she'd turned up in his hotel suite. She still had the power to unsettle him.

Safiyah murmured something to the maid, who melted back down the path.

'How kind of you to visit.'

Safiyah clasped her hands at her waist and inclined her head—the gracious Queen greeting a visitor. Except this visitor was the man who was about to save her country and her son. And he was going to become far more to her than a polite stranger, no matter how hard she pretended indifference.

Satisfaction banished his jab of annoyance at her condescension. Soon there'd be no pretence of them being strangers.

'The pleasure is all mine.'

He let his voice deepen caressingly. Her eyes rounded and he smothered a smile. Oh, yes. He was looking forward to a much closer relationship with Safiyah. Her attempts to keep him at a distance only fired his anticipation.

'I thought I'd take a ride, but discovered the stables empty.'

'My husband wasn't a rider.'

Karim watched her refold her hands, one over the other. Her mouth flattened, disguising those lush lips. Curiosity stirred. His nape prickled with the certainty that he'd hit on a subject she didn't want to discuss. Which made Karim determined to discover why.

Was her reaction a response to him or to the mention of her dead husband?

'But you are.'

He wasn't sure why he pressed the point, except that it was sensible to know the woman he was about to marry.

She lifted her shoulders but the gesture was too stiff to be called a shrug. 'I was.'

Karim lifted one eyebrow questioningly.

'I don't ride any more.'

The words were clipped and cool, but he sensed something beneath them. Something that wasn't as calm as the image she projected.

He waited, letting the silence draw out. Concern niggled. Had she had a bad fall? Had she been seriously injured? It would take a lot to keep the woman he'd once known away from her beloved horses.

Finally, with a tiny exhalation that sounded like a huff of exasperation, she spoke. 'Abbas didn't ride and he preferred that I didn't either.'

'Why?'

Karim shoved his hands in his pockets and rocked back on his feet, reinforcing the fact that he had plenty of time. Especially as he sensed Safiyah was reluctant to explain.

Equestrian prowess was a traditional part of a warrior's skills. It was unusual to find a ruler who didn't ride—especially as Assarans were proud of their fabled reputation as horsemen. The country was world-renowned for the horses it bred in the wide fertile valley along its northern border.

Safiyah darted a glance at the little boy and the puppy, now playing a lolloping game of chase. Was she checking they were okay or whether her son was listening?

'When I got pregnant I was advised not to ride. To keep the baby safe.'

Karim nodded. That he understood. But that had been years ago. There was more to this tale.

'And after the birth?'

A wry smile curved her lips. 'Only someone who hasn't gone through childbirth would ask that.'

It was tempting to be side-tracked by that smile, but Karim knew a diversion when he heard it. 'Not immediately, but in the years since your son was born. Why haven't you ridden?' A crazy idea surfaced. 'Did he forbid it?'

Karim knew by the sudden widening of her eyes that he was right. Sheikh Abbas had forbidden his wife to ride. But why?

Safiyah lifted her chin. There was no trace of her smile as she surveyed him with regal hauteur. That was something she'd learned only recently. The woman he'd known had been as fresh and unaffected as they came. Or, he amended, had given that impression…

'If it was known that I rode regularly I'd be expected to ride during royal processions and official gatherings. That was what royals have always done in the past. But…'

'But then you'd show up your husband if you were on horseback and he wasn't?'

A flush climbed her slender throat and she looked away. As if *she* were the one with an embarrassing secret.

'What happened? Did he have a bad fall? Is that what made him afraid to ride?'

The colour had seeped across her cheekbones now. 'It's not important. Abbas was beginning to modernise Assara. He saw no point in clinging to tradition. Travelling by car is quicker and more convenient.'

The words sounded like something she'd learned by heart. No doubt they'd been her husband's.

Karim felt something gnaw at his belly. Dislike.

He'd carefully not allowed himself to dwell on thoughts of Safiyah with her husband. He'd spent enough fruitless hours in the past, fuming over the way she'd dumped him so unceremoniously and then given herself to another bridegroom a mere five months later.

At the time the idea of Safiyah with another man, in his bed, giving him what she'd denied Karim, had been a special sort of poison in his blood.

But now his animosity was directed at Abbas.

Particularly as the possibility now arose that her defence of the dead man might be driven by love.

It hadn't occurred to Karim that Safiyah had *loved* her husband. There'd been no outward sign of it. On the contrary, her response to *him* had told him she didn't carry a torch for Abbas. No, ambition had been behind her first marriage, not love.

'Tradition matters if the people still value it.'

He read the flicker in her expression and knew that to many in Assara seeing their Sheikh on horseback *was* still important.

'And it matters that he stopped you from doing something you love just to save himself embarrassment.'

It was the action of a coward. But Karim kept the thought to himself. He was, after all, talking to the man's widow.

Something dark and bitter curled through his belly. He ignored the sensation, shifting his stance.

Safiyah curved her mouth into a smile that didn't reach her eyes. 'Well, you'll be able to fill the stables if you wish.' Before he could respond she looked at her watch. 'It's getting late. Time for Tarek to go to bed. If you'll excuse me…?'

'Introduce me—' Karim stopped, wondering. Did four-year-olds *do* introductions, or should he just get down on his haunches and say hello?

For the first time since he'd agreed to come here and take

on the kingdom he felt unsure of himself. He ignored his uncertainty and crossed the grass to where the child and dog lay, panting, after their game. The kid registered his presence, looking up, then up again, till a pair of brown eyes met his. Brown flecked with honey, just like his mother's.

Why that should affect Karim he didn't know, but he registered a thump in the vicinity of his ribs as that little face with those wide eyes turned to his.

'Tarek, I want you to meet…' Safiyah paused. Was she wondering how to describe him? Not father…not Sheikh yet.

'Hello. My name is Karim. I've come to live at the palace.'

The boy scrambled to his feet and, after swiping his dirty hands on the back of his shorts, stood straight and extended one hand. 'Hello. I'm Tarek ibn Abbas of Assara. It's a pleasure to meet you.'

Karim closed his palm around the tiny hand and gave it a gentle shake. He stared into the small, serious face regarding him so intently, as if looking for signs of disapproval.

With an audible whoosh of sound in his ears Karim found himself back in time, learning from a courtier the precise grades of greeting and which was suitable for royalty, for members of court, foreign dignitaries and ordinary citizens. He must have been about Tarek's age and he'd mastered the lesson quickly, since the alternative—disappointing his irritable father—hadn't been an option.

'The pleasure is mine, Prince Tarek.' Karim inclined his head over the boy's hand before releasing it.

The child nodded in acknowledgement but his eyes were already flicking back to the puppy chewing at his shoe. Tarek might be a prince but he was above all a little boy. And in that instant Karim was swamped by a determination to achieve at least one thing. To allow Tarek to have a childhood despite being royal.

Something Karim had never had.

He'd grown up with no time for idle play or cuddles. Instead there'd been constricting rules and a strict regimen devised to ensure he became a miniature copy of his father.

Seeing the yearning look on the boy's face as his royal training battled his inclination for fun, Karim smiled and squatted down. 'He's a fine-looking dog.'

In fact the boisterous pup was anything but beautiful. It had the long, silky tail and soft ears of a hunting dog but those short legs and nuggety body belonged to some other breed entirely.

Karim recalled the pure-bred hounds his father had kept, whose pedigree was as important as any other quality. Karim felt a surge of empathy with the mongrel pup and reached out to pat it—only to have it gnaw experimentally on his fingers.

'He likes you!' The last of Prince Tarek's gravity disintegrated as he threw himself down on the ground with his pet. 'He doesn't mean to hurt you,' he added earnestly. 'He bites people he likes.'

'I know. It's what puppies do.'

Karim was rewarded with a wide smile and responded with a grin.

'Do *you* have a dog?' the boy enquired.

Karim shook his head. 'I'm afraid not.'

'You could play with us if you like.'

He was surprised to find himself moved by the child's generosity. How long since he'd done something as simple as play with a dog? Or talk to a child?

'I'd like that, thank you.' He scratched the dog's spotted belly. 'What's his name?'

'Blackie. I picked it.'

Karim nodded. 'You picked well. Is he yours?'

'Yes. But he doesn't sleep with me.' The boy pouted, using rounded cheeks and outthrust lip to full advantage as his gaze slid reproachfully towards his mother. 'He *should* sleep in my bed. So I can look after him if he gets lonely in the night. Don't you think?'

Karim sensed Safiyah standing behind him, yet she said nothing. Was she waiting to see how he responded?

'Dogs need space, just like people do. I'm sure Blackie has a cosy bed of his own.'

'He certainly does,' Safiyah chimed in. 'Just down the hall. He sleeps so well that Tarek has to wake him up to play sometimes. Now, it's time to say goodnight. Tarek and Blackie need to go to bed.'

Karim watched the little boy struggle with the urge to argue. But eventually he got to his feet.

His eyes were on the same level as Karim's as he said, 'I like you. Come and play again.' Then, with a flickering look at his mother he smiled and added, 'Please.'

Tarek's mixture of royal imperiousness and friendliness appealed. Far more than the cautious, almost obsequious approaches Karim usually got from those eager to impress.

'I'd like that. Thank you,' Karim said again. He returned the smile with one of his own.

He'd enjoy spending time with little Tarek. For one thing, it would be a pleasant change. For as long as he could recall he'd been unable to trust that the people who tried to get close to him did so out of affection instead of for personal gain.

Safiyah bent to scoop the tired pup into her arms and take Tarek by the hand. Karim felt that all too familiar clench in his groin as her dress pulled over ripe curves.

Once she'd played up to him because she'd believed he could make her a queen. Now she'd come to him because she needed his protection.

Always because she wanted something from him.

Not because she wanted *him*.

It was a timely reminder. One he wouldn't forget.

But that didn't mean he couldn't enjoy the benefits of having Safiyah as his wife.

Suddenly the tedium and frustrations of the afternoon's long meeting disintegrated. Karim found himself looking forward to embracing his new life.

The vast, circular audience chamber was filled to the brim. Guests even outnumbered the stars of pure gold that decorated the domed ceiling of midnight-blue. The crush of people made Safiyah glad she was on the raised royal dais. Yet her heart still pounded as if she'd had to fight her way through the throng.

As of a few minutes ago, Karim had become Assara's ruler.

Thinking about it made her light-headed—with relief, she told herself, not nerves. Yet she kept her eyes on the crowd, not on the man further along the dais.

She had a perfect view of their faces, the VIPs of Assara, as they took turns to swear fealty to their new Sheikh. There were politicians, clan elders and powerful businessmen. Even the other men who'd hoped to be Sheikh.

Safiyah watched, her breath stalling, as the person before Karim bowed and backed away. Next in line was Hassan Shakroun. Shakroun's lips twisted unpleasantly, but that wasn't unusual. The man rarely looked content.

To her immense relief, when Karim had been proclaimed Sheikh there'd been no protest. Karim's swift acceptance of the crown meant Shakroun had had no time to act against him.

Now Shakroun moved forward and bowed perfunctorily, then backed away.

Safiyah sighed in relief. She'd done right. Shakroun had no reason now to harm Tarek. He was safe. It was Karim who had the power to make or break Tarek's future.

Despite his assurances, it was impossible not to wonder what sort of ruler he'd make, and what sort of father.

What sort of husband?

A jitter of nerves shot through her, churning her stomach. She breathed out slowly, forcing her heartbeat to slow.

As soon as the coronation ceremony was over their marriage would take place, and then Karim's formal adoption of Tarek.

What she'd give for her sister to be here. But, following tradition, there were no females in the room. Except her. Karim had made an exception to past practice by inviting her to attend the ceremony that would make him Sheikh.

Reluctantly she looked again at the centre of the dais. There, surrounded by the leaders of the Council, stood Karim, regal in pure white trimmed with gold. Even the *agal* encircling his headscarf was gold, a symbol of his new status.

He stood a head taller than the older men around him. Confident and commanding. His strong profile was proud, betraying no hint of doubt or weakness.

Tarek would grow up as the adopted son of the Sheikh. And she... She was destined to become once again wife of a sheikh.

Another breath, snatched into lungs that didn't seem to work.

Even the knowledge that this would be a marriage in name only couldn't ease the hammer-beat of her heart or the uneasy feeling that she'd acted against her better judgement.

Her second marriage of convenience. Her second marriage without love or real caring.

Safiyah pressed her palm to her abdomen as pain sheared through her. She'd learned to live with Abbas's indifference. Theirs hadn't been a close relationship, and in some ways there'd been relief in the fact they hadn't spent much time together.

Surely this new marriage would be similar. Karim's distaste had been clear after that kiss in Switzerland. *She'd* been the one swept away. He'd been as unmoved as one of those looming Swiss mountains. Her cheeks flamed at the memory.

And yet, this marriage *wouldn't* be like her one to Abbas. Then she'd been so miserable and lost that even going through the motions of marriage had been just one more burden. Dazed with grief over her father and her broken heart, nothing had mattered but doing her duty.

Now there was nothing to cushion her from the reality of her actions.

Her gaze returned to the arrogantly masculine profile of the new Sheikh. A riot of emotions roiled through her.

This marriage was going to be far worse than her first. She was marrying not a stranger, but the one man she'd ever loved. The man she'd yearned for with all her youthful heart.

She didn't love him any more. The very idea chilled her. Because doing so would make her impossibly vulnerable. But she'd cared for him once and felt sickened by the idea of living a pale imitation of the life she'd once hoped for.

Yet it was worse even than that. For though she didn't love him, and he was indifferent to her, Safiyah still wanted Karim as a woman wanted a man.

She desired him.

How was she to survive this marriage? Ignoring his indifference and the women he'd take into his bed? She didn't—

Suddenly the old men around the Sheikh shuffled back and that bronzed, handsome face turned. Safiyah felt the impact of that stare. It seemed as if his gaze bored straight past her blushing cheeks, past the sumptuous gown and jewels, deep into her aching heart.

The illusion strengthened when his eyes narrowed and

his nostrils flared, as if he sensed her doubts and the urge to flee which she had only just mastered.

But Safiyah was strong. Or she could pretend to be—even if she felt weak-kneed and terrified.

She lifted her chin and held that keen gaze like a queen.

CHAPTER SIX

'SAFIYAH.' KARIM FOUND himself crossing the dais to stand before her instead of simply summoning her with a gesture.

He heard the murmur of voices as people noted his action, and he didn't care. The previous Sheikhs of Assara might have moved for no one, but Karim would rule in his own way. He'd wanted to go to her from the moment she'd paced decorously into the room, like some exquisite medieval illumination come to life.

She glowed in jewel tones, her long dress of gold brocade revealing amber and red depths when she moved. The tiara of old gold and rubies turned the sensual woman he knew into a regal beauty. The matching chandelier earrings drew attention to the delicate line of her slender neck. Her air of shuttered stillness made him want to muss her hair with his hands as he tasted those luscious lips again and brought her to frenzied, rapturous life.

Drawing back from her passionate kiss, pretending to be unmoved by it, had been appallingly difficult. Fortunately pride and his once-bruised ego had come to the rescue.

'Your Majesty.'

She sank into a curtsey so low that the shimmering gown rippled across the floor around her like a molten lake. Head bent, she stayed there, awaiting his pleasure. But despite the profound gesture of obeisance there was an indefinable air of challenge about her.

This woman kept her own counsel and tried to maintain her distance. When he'd spent a little time with her and Tarek he'd been even more aware of the wall she'd built around herself.

He reached down and touched her hand, felt her flinch, and then, as he slid his hand around her wrist, the quick flutter of her pulse.

'You may rise.'

She did, but even so kept her eyes downcast. Anyone observing would see a beautiful queen, modestly showing respect for her new Sheikh. But Karim was close enough to read the swift rise and fall of her breasts and see the tiny tremors that ran through her.

Not so indifferent, my fine beauty, no matter how you try to hide it.

'You look magnificent.' His voice deepened in appreciation.

She lifted her eyes then. The velvety brown looked darker than usual, without the gold highlights he used to admire. They looked soul-deep and…worried? Despite his impatience, the idea disturbed him. What had she to worry about now he'd come to her rescue?

He told himself not to be taken in.

His feelings for her were too confused.

Once he'd been well on the way to being enchanted by Safiyah. He'd believed her gentle, honest and sweet. Then he'd wanted to hate her for deserting him.

Since meeting her again he'd experienced a mixture of distrust, anger, lust and a surprising protectiveness. Whatever else, she'd proved herself courageous when danger threatened her son. Or was she just grasping, scheming to retain her privileged position?

But marriage had been *his* idea, not hers.

He didn't trust her, didn't want to like her, and yet his hunger for her was tempered by reluctant admiration. It took guts for her to face him again, to consent to marry him and carry it off with such panache.

He lifted her hand and kissed it. A whisper of a kiss, yet he felt the resonance of her shock in his own body.

Want. Need. Hunger.

Soon they'd be assuaged.

'Come…' He smiled down at her, not bothering to hide his satisfaction. 'It's time for our wedding.'

Safiyah closed the door to her apartments behind her and sagged back, grateful for the solid wood supporting her spine. She felt drained. The ceremony hadn't taken long, but the celebrations had lasted hours. And that was just the first day. Tomorrow the celebrations continued—and the day after that.

Yet it wasn't the hours in heavy brocade and jewels, performing her royal duties, that had exhausted her. It was stress. The knowledge that she was now Karim's *wife*!

A sob rose and she stifled it, pushing away from the door, making herself walk into her rooms though every limb felt shaky.

It was a paper marriage. It didn't mean anything except that Tarek was safe. And that she'd have to keep on playing the public role of adoring, compliant spouse of a man who didn't give a damn about her.

Again that tangle of emotions rose, almost choking her. She swallowed, blinked back the heat glazing her eyes, and kept walking.

Usually her maid would be there, but Safiyah had known she wouldn't be able to face anyone and had dismissed her for the night. Now she half wished she hadn't. Just unpinning the tiara would take ages. But better to wrestle with it and her overwrought emotions alone.

At least she had practice in doing that. It seemed a lifetime ago that she'd had anyone she could lean on emotionally. Not since her mother had died when Safiyah was in her teens. She'd loved her father, but he'd never fully recovered from the loss of his wife. And her little sister had spent years battling her own demons of anxiety and depression, so Safiyah had supported her rather than the other way around.

As for Abbas…despite their physical intimacy there'd never been any question of sharing her feelings with him. He hadn't been interested. And life at the palace had isolated her from her friends.

She swung around, caught sight of herself in a mirror, all gold and jewels, and grimaced, feeling ashamed. She had so much. She had no right to feel sorry for herself.

Nevertheless, she turned on the music her sister had given her for her last birthday—a compilation of gentle tunes harmonised with wild birdsong and even the occasional sound of water falling. Rana said it helped to relax her and Safiyah had found the same.

She switched on a couple more lamps so the room felt cosy, unhooking the heavy earrings with a sigh of relief and placing them on the waiting tray in her dressing room. Her bangles followed—ornate, old, and incredibly precious heirloom pieces.

With each piece she imagined a little more of the weight lifting from her shoulders.

She lifted her hands to the tiara, turning towards the full-length mirror that took up one wall of the dressing space.

'Would you like help with that?'

The voice, smoky and low, rolled out of the shadows behind her.

Safiyah froze, elbows up, staring at the figure that had stepped into her line of vision in the mirror. Her pulse rocketed and the remnants of distress she'd been battling coalesced into a churning, burning nugget of fire in her abdomen.

Karim looked good—better than good. The traditional robes suited him, accentuating his height, the breadth of his chest and the purity of his strong bone structure that made his stern face so appallingly attractive. He'd discarded his headscarf and for some reason the sight of his close-cropped black hair after the formality of their wedding celebration seemed too…intimate.

As did the fact he was in her private rooms!

'Karim!'

Safiyah swung round, her arms falling to her sides. How long had she held them up? Her hands prickled with pins and needles. Her nape too, and then her whole spine as she met those hooded eyes. His stare was intense, skewering her to the spot and totally at odds with his relaxed stance. He leaned with one shoulder propped against the doorjamb.

Safiyah swallowed, then swiped her dry mouth with her tongue. Karim didn't move a muscle, but she sensed a change in him. The air crackled. The tingling along her backbone drove inwards, filling her belly with a fluttering as if a thousand giant moths flapped there, frantically trying to reach the glowing moon that hung in the night sky.

'What are you doing here, Karim?' Finally she collected herself enough to clasp her hands at her waist to conceal the way they trembled.

'I've come to see you, obviously.' He straightened and crossed towards her, making the room claustrophobically close. 'Turn around.'

'Sorry?' Safiyah gaped up at the face that now hovered far too close.

His expression gave nothing away. 'Turn around so I can help with the pins.'

'I don't need any help.'

Too late. He'd lifted his hands and she found herself encircled by the drape of snowy white fabric, deliciously scented with sandalwood and hot male. *Very* hot male.

Her cheeks flushed and something disturbing rippled through her.

Desire. Memory. The recollection of how she'd lost herself in his kiss.

He plucked at a pin, twisted another. 'Shh…don't fidget. Let me finish this, then we can talk.'

Relief cascaded through her. He wanted to talk. Probably about tomorrow's festivities. She was letting her unguarded responses get the better of her.

When they talked, the first item on her agenda would be to make it clear he couldn't stroll into her rooms whenever he felt like it. But she'd rather make her point when they were out in the sitting room. Having him in this very private space was too unsettling.

Safiyah drew a slow breath and nodded, wincing when his hold on the tiara stopped it moving with her.

'Sorry.'

Her eyes were on a level with his collarbone and she watched, bemused, the play of muscles in his throat. How could something so ordinary look…sexy?

'Wait. I'll turn.' Anything to give her breathing space.

But when she turned she was confronted with a mirror image of him looming behind her, his shoulders too wide, too masculine. Especially when the dance of his fingers in her hair felt like a deliberate caress.

He was surprisingly deft, making her wonder what experience he'd had in unpinning women's hair. Safiyah had no doubt he'd undressed plenty of women in his time. But, to her shock, she discovered having Karim undo her hair felt almost as intimate in its own way as sex had felt with Abbas.

She blinked, stunned at the idea, and found herself looking into a stare that sent fiery shivers trailing to a point deep inside her. That elusive place where, just once or twice, as

Abbas had taken his pleasure with her, there'd been a hint that she too might discover something more—

'There.'

Did she imagine Karim's voice was huskier? He lifted the tiara off with one hand, and Safiyah was about to thank him when he ploughed his fingers through her hair, dragging it down to her shoulders.

His eyes held hers in the mirror as he used his hand like a comb, spreading her hair around her shoulders. Each stroke was a slow, delicious assault on her senses.

Safiyah felt the stiffness ease from her neck and spine... detected an urge to lean into that stroking touch. Horrified, she stepped forward—so fast that her hair snagged on the ancient gold ring that had been placed on his finger at his investiture today. Her head was yanked back, but she welcomed the pain because it broke the spell.

'Sorry.'

He frowned and worked his hand free, during which time she took the tiara from his other hand. Then she moved away, replacing it in the velvet-lined box with the earrings and bangles.

Snapping the lid closed, she spun round. 'Shall we?'

She didn't wait for a response but preceded him out of the dressing room and back to the bedroom. She was on her way towards her sitting room when his words stopped her.

'Here's fine.'

'Here?'

She swung around. Karim stood midway between the dressing room door and the bed. There were no seats in the room apart from a long cushioned sofa.

'We'll be more comfortable in the sitting room.'

'Oh, I doubt that, Safiyah.'

That deliberate tone sent a shot of adrenalin through her already tense body.

Suddenly, as if a curtain had been yanked back, Karim's

expression was no longer impenetrable. She read a glitter in those eyes that was shockingly familiar. Safiyah recognised the look of a man with sex on his mind. She almost fancied she saw the flicker of flames in Karim's dark eyes. The tendons at the base of his neck stood proud, and though he made no move towards her there was a waiting stillness in his tall frame that unnerved her.

Involuntarily, Safiyah backed up a step. To keep him from reaching for her or to stop herself doing something foolish?

In that second of realisation she was torn between dismay and the need to throw herself into Karim's embrace and let him do whatever he wanted.

Because *she* wanted. She'd been on a knife-edge of frustrated desire since that kiss in Switzerland and she despised herself for it.

'No!' She felt her eyes widen as he frowned. 'We're not doing *that*.'

'*That?*' he murmured. 'How coy you are.'

His mouth curled at the corners as if he were amused. Damn him. As if he knew she didn't even want to think about sex with him, much less say it out loud. As if he knew how desperately she fought the desire to do more than talk about it.

Safiyah stiffened her spine. She might not have Karim's no doubt vast experience. But that didn't make her a fool or a push-over.

Her chin hiked up. 'You seem to forget this marriage is for political reasons.'

'So? That doesn't mean we can't enjoy the personal benefits.'

The word 'personal' was a rough burr that rubbed across her skin, making the fine hairs on her arms stand erect.

'Can you honestly tell me you don't want me?'

His words sucked the air from her lungs as she realised

he'd read her secret. Of course he had. He'd had to peel her off him to end that kiss in his hotel suite. The memory mocked her.

Karim crossed his arms over his chest. The gesture emphasised both his powerful frame and that annoying air of arrogance. And, to her consternation, his sheer, unadulterated sex appeal.

She tried to concentrate on his arrogance. Even Abbas at his most regal had never irritated her with just a look. Karim did it with merely a raised eyebrow and the knowing gleam in eyes that looked smoky with intent.

Their marriage wasn't about them as individuals, but he saw no reason to deny himself a little sexual diversion with his new spouse. She was here, he was bored, or he wanted to celebrate, or maybe he just wanted to amuse himself at her expense. In Switzerland he hadn't bothered to hide his disdain.

She planted her hands on her hips and paced a step nearer as hurt, fury and frustration coalesced. 'I'm not a convenience, here for your pleasure, Karim. We established before we married that I won't share my bed with you.'

The lingering hint of a smile on that long mouth stiffened. He shook his head, taking his own step forward so they stood almost toe to toe and she had to tilt her neck to look down her nose at him.

Safiyah knew better than to back away. He'd take advantage of any show of weakness. So she was close enough to read what looked like conflicting emotions as he spoke.

'Believe me, there's nothing *convenient* about this, Safiyah. As for what you said before we married…' he spread his hands wide '…you're allowed to change your mind.'

'You don't really want sex with me, Karim. You're just here to score a point. To amuse yourself. It's a power thing, isn't it?'

He was just reinforcing the fact that *he* was the one in

this marriage who had the power, not her. He might have been kind to Tarek but with her he was ruthless.

'You're not even attracted to me. You made that clear the day you came to my hotel suite.' She refused to let her voice wobble as she recalled his dismissal.

'I did?' His mouth lifted at one side, but it didn't quell the impact of that hungry stare.

The air thickened and her breaths grew shallow as she fought to tug in enough oxygen. Her insides clenched and she pressed her thighs tight together, trying to counteract the bloom of heat at her centre. How could she feel furious and aroused at the same time?

'Don't play games, Karim. You said it was an experiment that proved you weren't interested.'

'An experiment, yes. But the results were obvious. Like a match to bone-dry kindling. If I hadn't stepped away when I did we'd have had sex on the sofa.'

Safiyah was so stunned she couldn't find her voice. She went hot, then cold, as her brain produced an all too vivid image of them naked on that sofa. Those long arms holding her close, that muscular body cradled between her thighs...

A shiver ripped through her and his eyes turned darker when he saw it.

Suddenly Safiyah knew she was in real danger—not from Karim but from herself. How easy it would be to give in and say yes, despite her pride and the way he'd treated her.

'It didn't occur to you that I was experimenting too? That maybe you misread my curiosity for something more?' It was an outright untruth, but it was all she could think of to rebut him. 'If you think I pined for you for years you're wrong. I didn't.'

That, at least, was true. She hadn't let herself pine. She'd tried to excise what she felt for him—like amputating a limb, cutting herself off from emotion. It had been the only way to survive. Lingering on what might have been would have destroyed her as depression had almost destroyed her sister. For five years Safiyah had been emotionally self-contained, her only close relationships with Rana and Tarek.

'Of course you didn't pine for me. You had another prince to snare.'

The sneer in his tone was like a slap. As if she'd deliberately set out to lure either him or Abbas into marriage! But before she could snap out a rebuttal he leaned forward, invading her space, filling her senses with the tang of hot male skin, with pheromones that made her all but salivate with longing.

'You wanted me in Switzerland, Safiyah. We both know it.'

The words ground through her, making her shiver. 'And you want me now. Every time we get close I read it in your eyes, in your body.'

His gaze dropped to her aching breasts as if he could see the hard nipples thrusting towards him even through the heavy patterned fabric.

Safiyah shook her head. The thick hair he'd undone slipped around her shoulders. She wished it could conceal her totally. She wanted to hide where he couldn't find her. Where she wouldn't have to face the truth about herself. That she wanted Karim as she'd never wanted any other man. Still.

'You're imagining things, Karim.' She paused and swallowed hard. 'I don't want you.'

His steady stare should have unnerved her, but she refused to look away. She'd done what she had to in order to save her son. Now she'd do what she must to save her sanity. Sex with Karim would be the worst possible idea.

Yet when he took that last tiny step that brought him flush against her, his feet straddling hers, it wasn't disgust that made her breath hitch. They were both fully clothed, yet everywhere they touched—her breasts against his torso, her thighs against his—fire ignited.

'Prove it.'

The words were warm air on her superheated flesh.

'Kiss me and walk away.'

Safiyah's gasp only succeeded in pressing her breasts against him.

'I don't need to prove anything.' Holding that moss-green stare grew harder by the second. In her peripheral vision she saw that firm mouth, like a magnet dragging her gaze.

'One kiss and I'll leave—*if* you want me to.'

'Of course I do. I want…' Her words died as a warm palm cupped her cheek, long fingers channelling through her hair, creating sensations so delicious that despite everything her eyelids grew heavy.

His other hand didn't grab at her, didn't force her close. Instead it settled light as a leaf on her shoulder, then slowly slid down the outside of her arm, and down…down to her hand where her fingers trembled.

He'd promised no coercion and he kept his promise. But the compulsion welling within her to give in to him was almost overwhelming. Safiyah stifled a sob at the strain of withstanding this torture.

He captured her wrist with a surprising gentleness. It was as if he cast a spell that kept her rooted to the spot, breathless. Even when he raised her hand and she felt the press of his lips to her palm, the hot, lavish swipe of his tongue setting off swirling sparks inside her, his compelling gaze and her enthralled brain kept her where she was.

He planted her palm against his cheek. She felt the hot silk of his flesh and the tiniest hint of roughness along his jaw, where by morning he'd need to shave. Under his guidance her hand moved up to his hairline, and of their own volition her fingers channelled through the plush luxury of his hair.

So many sensations to absorb. Not least of which was the fascinating play of light…or was it darkness?… in Karim's eyes in response to her touch.

Safiyah's breath hissed as everything in her tightened. She had to move away, break this illusion of intimacy. Her brain told her that he was toying with her, but it felt so…

'We both want, Safiyah. And it will be good between us, I promise.' Again there was that curve of his mouth on one side, as if the flesh there were drawn too tight. 'Better than good. It will be—'

'Mama! Mama!'

A door banged and a woman's voice came from the next room. Then, before Safiyah could do more than turn her head, a small whirlwind shot through the door and landed against her legs.

'Tarek! What is it?'

She scooped him up and he clung, wrapping his arms and legs around her. He felt hot, and his face was damp as he burrowed against her. Automatically she murmured soothing words, clasping him tight.

'I'm sorry, madam—' Just inside the doorway the nanny jolted to a halt so suddenly she swayed. Her expression grew horrified as she took in Karim's presence and she sank into a deep curtsey. 'Your Majesty. My apologies, I didn't know—'

'No need for apologies,' Karim said. 'Clearly it's an emergency.'

'Just a nightmare, sir. I could have managed, but madam said—'

'You did right,' Safiyah assured her, rubbing a gentle hand over Tarek's skinny back and taking a few steps across to the bed, so she could sit down, holding her son close. 'I gave instructions to bring Tarek here if he needed me.'

It had been liberating, giving that order. When Abbas had been alive he'd demanded the nanny deal with any night-time upset without Safiyah, lest they were interrupted on a night he'd decided to visit his wife's bed.

'It is just a nightmare, isn't it?' Safiyah put her hand to Tarek's forehead as she rocked him in her arms. 'Not a temperature?'

The nanny rose, nodding. 'Just a bad dream, madam, but he kept calling for you.'

'Then he's in the right place now.'

It was Karim who spoke, drawing Safiyah's gaze. He didn't look as if he'd just been interrupted seducing his wife. She saw no impatience or annoyance. In fact he smiled as he told the nanny she could leave.

If it had been Abbas there'd have been cold fury and harsh words. Not because he'd been evil, but because he'd believed he was entitled to have his own way. That the world was ordered to suit *him*. He hadn't been deliberately cruel, but nor had he been sympathetic or used to considering others.

Safiyah looked from the departing maid to Karim, wondering how it was that this man, who'd also been raised to be supreme ruler, could react so differently. Where was the man who'd been so cold and distant in Switzerland?

Rueful eyes met hers and she felt again that pulse of awareness. It hadn't gone. His plans had merely been deferred. The realisation stirred excitement in her belly.

'How is he?'

'Calmer.' Tarek wasn't trembling now, though he still buried his head against her. Soon he'd be ready to talk. 'I'll keep him with me…settle him here.'

She waited for a protest from Karim but there was none. He walked to the bed and placed a large hand on her son's shoulder.

'Everything's going to be all right, Tarek. Your mother and I will make sure of it.'

To Safiyah's surprise Tarek lifted his head, sniffing, and nodded at Karim. Her husband smiled at the boy, then moved away.

'I'll leave you two to rest. Get a good night's sleep. It's going to be a big day tomorrow.'

Karim slanted her a look that made her toes curl. Then he drew a breath that made that impressive chest swell.

'You've had a lot to deal with, Safiyah. We'll discuss this later, when you've had time to adjust. After the wedding. But make no mistake: this is unfinished business.'

Then he turned on his heel and left, closing the door quietly behind him, just as if he hadn't turned her world inside out.

Already Tarek's eyes were closing. It seemed he didn't want to talk, just needed the comfort of a cuddle. Safiyah began singing a soft lullaby, but as she watched her son's eyes close and felt him relax she thought about what Karim had said.

There were two more full days of wedding celebrations. Two more days till Karim expected her to surrender to him. What was she going to do about that?

CHAPTER SEVEN

SAFIYAH EMERGED FROM the bathroom the next morning wrapped in her favourite robe. It was old, but it had been the last gift her mother had given her. The cotton was thin now, but the colour reminded her of the rare pale blue crocuses that grew in the mountains near where she'd grown up.

She hadn't worn it for ages because Abbas had expected her to dress in only the best. But he wasn't here to disapprove now, and in this last week especially Safiyah had found comfort in the memory of her mother.

Life had been turned upside down again and she was reeling from the impact. She hadn't been prepared for the tumult that was Karim's effect on her. She didn't want to trust him, kept remembering how badly he'd hurt her, yet at other times he seemed considerate, even kind. Like last night, when he'd put Tarek's needs before his own desire. It wasn't what she'd come to expect from men…from a husband. Karim confused her and made her feel things she didn't want.

Briskly, she rubbed her hands up and down her arms, banishing that little judder of residual awareness. She smiled at her waiting maid, then stopped abruptly.

'What's that?'

Her gaze fixed on the clothes spread out on the bed. She'd requested her long dress in shades of ochre and

amber. Instead the fabric on the bed was an arresting dark
lilac, embroidered with gleaming purple and lilac beads.

'Isn't it beautiful? The Sheikh has requested you wear this.'

Safiyah crossed to the bed, leaning down to stroke the
fabric. The silk tunic was feather-light, the embroidery exquisite. It would be comfortable as she stood in the open
air beside her new husband to receive the greetings of their
people. The sunlight would glimmer off the rich decoration
with each movement, subtly reinforcing her royal status as
consort to the Sheikh.

'Are those trousers?'

Sure enough there was a pair of lightweight, loose-fit-
ting trousers to wear beneath the long tunic. The style was
often worn by women in the rural areas of her country, but
Abbas had preferred her to wear dresses.

'They are, madam, and I've checked. They're exactly
your size.' Her maid slid a sideways glance to her. 'Someone has been very busy making this for you.'

But why? Safiyah was quite capable of choosing her
own clothes for royal events, and Karim didn't seem the
sort to micromanage such details. But then, this second
day of the joint coronation and wedding celebrations was
an important one, during which they'd meet the people who
had flocked to the capital from every province. Perhaps he
was concerned about making the right impression. Wearing clothes that were a nod to the rural traditions of his new
people wouldn't hurt.

'Very well.' She shrugged out of her robe.

But as the silk garments settled on her, drifting over
her skin like a desert zephyr, Safiyah couldn't help but remember Karim's caress last night. He'd said things would
be good, better than good, when she came to him.

If she came to him.

She hadn't agreed.

Yet.

* * *

Safiyah stepped out of the palace and into the main court-yard, only to hesitate on the threshold. There, instead of a gleaming entourage of black limousines, was a bustle she'd never seen within the royal precinct. The scene was alive with movement, the jingle of metal on metal and the clop of hoofs on cobblestones. The rich tang of horse and leather filled her nostrils and something within her lifted like a bird taking flight.

The place was full of riders. Two standard-bearers carrying the turquoise and white flag of Assara were mounted at the head of the line. Behind them, on snorting sidestepping horses, were elders and clan leaders—a who's who of Assara, all looking confident and fiercely proud.

Safiyah thought of Karim's words when he'd learned that Abbas had ditched the equestrian gatherings so loved by his people. It was clever of him to reinstate them, for clearly this was what he'd planned.

'Safiyah.'

As if conjured by her thoughts, there he was, striding towards her, magnificent in pale trousers, boots and a cloak the colour of the desert sands. He had a horseman's thighs, flexing powerfully with each step. The fact she'd noticed sent a tremor through her.

Her stomach dived. How was she supposed to resist him when her body betrayed her this way? Her galloping heart-beat told its own story.

'Karim.'

She saw the gleam of anticipation in his eyes. Clearly he was looking forward to this. Yesterday he'd been solemn and proud, as befitted a newly made monarch. Today his eyes danced.

'You look magnificent.'

His smile was a slow spread of pleasure across his face

that did crazy things to her insides. He took her hand, lifted it and stepped back, as if to get a better view.

For one mad moment she felt that glow of anticipation was for her. Then sense reasserted itself.

Karim had more important things on his mind than the wife he'd married for purely political reasons. Like establishing his mark on the country. Making an impression not only on the great and the good, but on the ordinary people. Which was why he planned to ride out on horseback, as the Sheikhs of Assara had done for centuries.

'That's why you sent the trousers.' Belatedly it dawned on her. 'You want me to ride with you.'

As if on cue a groom led forward two horses. A magnificent grey for Karim and a chestnut mare with liquid dark eyes for her. Safiyah saw the creature and was torn between love at first sight and disappointment that all Karim's excitement was for the success of his plan.

It had been madness to imagine he was pleased to see *her*, personally. She was his convenient wife. Not good enough to marry for her own sake—he'd made that painfully clear years before—but useful to win the people's acceptance.

Safiyah slipped her hand from Karim's, ignoring the twitch of his dark eyebrows at the movement. 'You could have warned me.'

'Warned you?'

'That I'd be riding.' Clearly she wasn't important enough to be informed of his plans. She felt as if she was the last to know. This procession had clearly taken a lot of preparation.

Karim stepped closer, blocking out the stable hand waiting at a discreet distance. 'I thought you'd enjoy the surprise.'

Safiyah's eyes widened. He'd thought about what she'd *enjoy*? She shook her head. This equestrian parade was a PR exercise. Not to please her.

Yet the fact he'd bothered to consider how she'd feel about it was unexpected. Disturbing. She wasn't used to that. What did it mean?

'You don't believe me?' His eyebrows lifted and his chin too, in an expression of hauteur.

'I'm just surprised.' And bewildered.

His expression softened a little. 'Pleasantly so?'

Silent, she nodded.

'Good.'

For a moment Safiyah thought he'd say more. Instead Karim swept her once again with his gaze and it was all she could do not to blush like a virgin. For there was something about his expression that made her think not of the show he was putting on for the populace, but of how he'd stared at her last night. As if he'd wanted to devour her on the spot.

The hubbub died away till all she could hear was the quick pulse of her blood in her ears.

'Mama!'

She swung around as a small figure emerged in the doorway from the palace. Tarek, wearing his finest clothes, hurtled into her arms. Safiyah caught and lifted him, hiding her surprise.

'Did you come to see all the excitement, sweetie?'

He nodded and clung to her.

'He's come to take part in today's festivities,' Karim said. 'I want the people to see that he hasn't been shunted aside.'

That made sense to Safiyah. And it was in Tarek's own interests. It was a clever move that would help both Karim and her son. But, again, she hadn't been consulted.

Although had she really expected that Karim might discuss his plans with her when Abbas never had? Once more she could only obey and play the role demanded of her. It was stupid to feel disappointed that nothing had changed.

'What is it, Safiyah? You look troubled.'

Karim's low voice reminded her how dangerous he was, how much he saw. For she was wearing what she thought of as her 'royal' face. A mask she'd perfected over the years to hide her feelings. It disturbed her to think Karim could see past it.

She shifted Tarek higher. Her son was looking wide-eyed at the horses.

'He's never even seen a horse close up before. He can't ride. It's too much to expect him to be in this procession. It's far too dangerous.'

She refused to let Karim put her boy in danger for the sake of appearances, even if his word *was* law. She'd spent years being seen and not heard, but when it came to Tarek's wellbeing she refused to submit meekly any more.

For a long moment her new husband considered her. When he spoke his words were for her alone. 'You don't think much of me, do you, Safiyah?'

His eyes flashed annoyance. Yet for some reason she wondered if that anger hid something else.

Before she could respond another figure emerged from the palace.

'Rana!' Safiyah couldn't believe her eyes. Her sister… here? Her heart squeezed and her eyes prickled. She opened her mouth to say something but no words emerged.

Safiyah looked up at Karim, who was surveying her from under lowered brows, his crossed arms making him looking particularly unapproachable. As if the man who'd stirred her blood with that one appraising look just moments ago had never been.

Yet he, surely, was the man responsible for her sister's presence. Gratitude and a sudden flood of happiness quenched her indignation.

'Your Majesty.' Rana sank into a deep curtsey and Safiyah watched, stupefied, as Karim took her sister's hand and raised her, bestowing upon her a smile that was all charm.

'It's a pleasure to meet you, Rana. I'm glad you could come to support your sister and your nephew today.'

Safiyah looked from her sister to Karim. What was going on? Assaran royal weddings did *not* include female witnesses, even if the bride had no living male relatives. Safiyah had been the only woman at yesterday's ceremony. Nor were female members of the bride's family invited to the royal events in the days that followed. Safiyah had got through the interminable festivities of her first marriage unsupported except for the maid who'd attended her when she retired to her room.

Before she could ask for an explanation a harassed-looking steward came forward and murmured something to Karim, drawing him away.

'Surprise!' Rana kissed Safiyah on the cheek and Tarek on the forehead, her gentle smile lighting her face. 'Your husband invited me to the capital for the next two days.' Rana dropped her voice. 'You didn't tell me he was so nice. So thoughtful.' She paused, chewing her lip. 'I did wonder if you really wanted this marriage. It's happened so quickly.'

Safiyah could only be grateful that Rana didn't know about the history between her and Karim. Then she'd *really* have her doubts.

'I definitely wanted it, Rana.'

Her sister nodded. 'For Tarek's sake. But...' she paused '...maybe for your own too?'

Safiyah swallowed hard and managed a noncommittal smile. Now wasn't the time for explanations. Karim had already proved himself capable of protecting his new position and his new son. That was all that mattered. His attention to detail today was all geared towards shoring up public approval. Even down to having the Prince accompanied by his aunt instead of a nanny.

Karim was presenting the picture of a united, stable family to the nation.

What other reason could he have for making these arrangements?

'It's wonderful to see you, Rana.' Safiyah leaned in and cuddled her sister with one arm while holding Tarek on her hip. An upsurge of emotions blindsided her, catching at her throat.

She wasn't used to having someone by her side. Strange, too, to realise how much she needed that support. The last days had been a rollercoaster of emotional shocks.

Tarek wriggled in her hold. 'Down, Mama. I want to see the horses.'

'He's a chip off the old block,' Rana said. 'Once he gets a taste for riding you won't be able to keep him away from the stables. Just like you and me.'

Warmth swelled in Safiyah's chest at her sister's smile. They'd both ridden as soon as they could walk, like their father before them.

'Later, Tarek. If you're a good boy you can pat one of the horses later.' For now Karim was striding back towards them and the last of the riders were swinging up onto their mounts. 'It's time for you to go with Auntie Rana.'

But Tarek wasn't placated. He was going to argue. His bottom lip protruded.

'Here. Let me.'

Long arms reached for her boy. Karim's hands brushed against her as he took her son.

She didn't know what stunned her more. The ripple of sensation where Karim's hard hands had touched her arms and, fleetingly, the side of her breast. Or the sight of him holding Tarek. The way a father would.

Safiyah frowned. She couldn't recall the last time Abbas had held his son. For an official photo, most probably.

Karim caught the disapproving scrunch of Safiyah's forehead and turned away, anger flaring.

What was wrong with the woman? Didn't she trust him enough even to hold her precious son?

She trusted him enough to marry him, yet now she was fighting a rearguard action to keep a distance between them.

Karim had taken time to consider how to make these intense days of celebration easier for her. He'd gone out of his way to bring her sister here, and to involve Tarek in the event to shore up the legitimacy of his future claim. He'd even organised that whisper-soft concoction of a riding outfit that made Safiyah look even more beautiful and impossibly seductive.

Had he received any thanks? Only from her sister. From Safiyah—nothing at all. Not even a smile.

So much for gratitude.

But Karim shouldn't have expected gratitude. The woman had abandoned him when she'd discovered the truth of his birth. She only accepted him now because he could salvage her royal position and protect her child.

Wrenching his thoughts away from Safiyah in beaded silk, he focused on the child in his arms. Tarek stared up at him with big brown eyes, his bottom lip quivering.

Maybe Karim shouldn't have swooped in and grabbed the child, but it seemed better to head off a tantrum than have the boy yowling through the parade.

'You want to meet a horse, Tarek?' He smiled encouragingly at the child and felt inordinately pleased when he received a grave nod. 'I'll hold you up high so you can pat one. Would you like that?'

He read the boy's excitement and for a second was

wrenched back to those rare moments in his childhood when he'd managed to steal time out with his little brother. Ashraf's eyes had glowed in just that way.

Karim walked up to the groom holding the reins of his mount and Safiyah's.

Automatically he turned towards the mare, as the smaller and more docile. But Tarek shook his head. 'This one.' He looked up at the dancing grey stallion.

Karim shrugged. The boy had pluck, that was for sure, if this really was the first time he'd got close to a horse. He'd have thought a beginner would be drawn to the mare, standing sedately. But Karim would keep him safe.

'This is Zephyr,' he murmured, and the grey flicked his ears forward, then huffed out a breath through flared nostrils.

Tarek giggled as the horse's warm breath brushed his face and hands. The horse's head reared back and Karim spoke to it in an undertone, reassuring it as he reached up to scratch near its ear.

'You can't be scared of Tarek, surely now? A big strong fellow like you?'

Again Tarek giggled, suddenly lunging forward in Karim's hold, trying to reach the horse.

'Not like that.' Karim hauled the child back. 'Give Zephyr a chance to know you. You have to sit quietly so as not to scare him. Put out your hand like this and let him sniff you.'

'It tickles!'

But to his credit the boy didn't squirm, even when Zephyr, with a sideways look at Karim, pretended to nibble the little Prince's sleeve.

The child gasped at the wet stain. Worried brown eyes met Karim's and once more he was reminded of his kid brother, this time after he'd been summoned before their disapproving father.

'I'm not supposed to get dirty. Papa says—'

'I know, but the rules have changed,' Karim said quickly, ignoring a moment's discomfort.

The child's dead father was beginning to remind him too much of the ever-demanding Sheikh who'd raised him. Karim recalled constant childhood lectures on his appearance, his manners, his attitude and even the way he walked. And that had been before the old man had got started on his studies.

'Don't worry, Tarek. It will dry quickly and no one will notice.' He paused. 'Do you want to know a secret?'

Solemnly the boy nodded.

'It's more important to be happy than to be clean.' Deliberately he looked furtively over his shoulder and pressed his finger to his lips. 'But don't tell anyone I said that. It's a royal secret.'

Tarek giggled, and Karim felt the strangest flutter in response. Even knowing it was the right thing to do, Karim had had qualms about adopting the boy. His experience of kids was limited. He was still learning how to interact with his little nephew on his rare visits to Za'daq. But Karim was determined to do right by Tarek—which meant taking time to build a relationship with the boy.

Finally Zephyr consented to be introduced, bending his head gracefully so the child could rub his palm over the grey's long nose.

'He smells funny.'

'Not *funny*,' Karim amended, watching, bemused, as the most highly strung horse in the city consented to the child's rough pats. Clearly the little Prince had his mother's knack with animals. 'That's how horses smell.'

'I like it.'

Tarek beamed up at him and Karim was surprised at how much he was enjoying the child's pleasure.

Karim caught movement in his peripheral vision and saw the steward scowling at his watch.

'Okay, Tarek. It's time for you to go with your aunt.'

The boy nodded enthusiastically and it was the work of a moment to settle him in the car next to Rana. When Karim turned back towards the waiting horses it was to find Safiyah watching him, her expression serious.

What now? Was she going to complain about him holding her son? She'd have to get used to it. Tarek was officially *his* son now too.

The idea elicited a welter of unfamiliar emotions.

'Ready, Safiyah?' He made to walk past her, heading to where their mounts stood.

'Yes, I…'

Her words trailed off and Karim paused. It was unlike Safiyah to hold back. She said what she thought—particularly when she disapproved. He was sick of her disapproval.

Repressing a sigh, he turned. 'What is it? It's time we started.'

Their route was to take a circuitous route through the city. It would be at least an hour before they arrived at the open-air venue where the celebrations would commence.

Her eyes met his, then swung away. Yet in that instant Karim was surprised to discover not anger but uncertainty. He took in her heightened colour and the dimple in her cheek and realised she was gnawing the inside of her mouth.

She moved closer, her hand hovering for a moment over his before dropping away. His flesh tingled as if from her touch.

'Thank you, Karim. You were so good with Tarek. Not stern or disapproving.' She smiled tentatively. 'It's more than I expected and I appreciate it.'

It was on the tip of his tongue to say of course she should expect people to treat her boy well. Except he recalled what

Tarek had said about his father. And how much he sounded like the man who'd raised Karim. Sometimes common courtesy and kindness to children weren't the norm.

Had that coloured Safiyah's view of Karim? The thought snagged in his brain. Maybe that explained some of the anomalies he'd noted in her behaviour.

It also made him wonder about her relationship with her first husband...

'I told you. I aim to do my best for the boy.'

If his tone was gruff she didn't seem to notice. She nodded, but didn't move. Harnesses jangled nearby yet still Karim waited, knowing there was more.

'I wanted to thank you, too, for bringing Rana here.' The words spilled out in a breathless rush. 'It was the most wonderful surprise. I...' She paused and looked down at her hands, clasped tight before her. 'I can't tell you how much it means to me to have her here.'

Safiyah lifted her head and her gaze met his. Karim experienced that familiar sizzle, but this time her curious expression—a mix of joy and nerves—didn't just ignite the accustomed flare of sexual anticipation. It made some unidentified weight in his chest turn over. The sensation was so definite, so unique, it held him mute.

For a long moment—too long—Karim felt the deep-seated glow of wellbeing he'd known only once in his life. In the days when he'd believed Safiyah to be a sweet, adoring innocent. But, despite her pretty speech of thanks, those days were dead. It was important he remembered that.

He nodded briskly and turned towards the groom, gesturing for him to bring the horses. They'd delayed longer than planned. It was time to ride out.

Suddenly Karim was itching to be gone, to be busy with his new work, his new people. Not second-guessing Safiyah's motives or his own feelings. He didn't have time for feelings—not personal ones. He wasn't here for old times' sake. He was here to rule a nation.

Yet when another groom approached, to help Safiyah into the saddle, Karim shook his head and offered his own clasped hands for her foot, tossing her up into the saddle. It was hardly an intimate caress. Just a fleeting touch of leather on skin. Yet the air between them shimmered and thickened as she looked down from the saddle and those velvet eyes met his. They'd darkened now, all trace of gold highlights disappearing. Her gaze felt intimate and full of promise.

Was it genuine or fake?

Marrying Abbas's widow and adopting his child had never been a straightforward proposition. Yet he hadn't realised how difficult it would be. For, despite years of experience in distancing himself from entanglements, this felt…personal. And complicated.

Karim had walked into a throne but also into a family. Into a place full of feelings and shadowy hints of past relationships that still affected Safiyah and Tarek today.

Suddenly the work of ruling Assara seemed easy compared with playing happy families.

Yet there was one aspect of family life Karim looked forward to with searing anticipation.

Bedding his wife.

CHAPTER EIGHT

'THANK YOU.' SAFIYAH nodded to the maid who was turning down the bed. 'That's all for tonight.'

With a curtsey the woman left. Instantly Safiyah put down her hairbrush and shot to her feet. She was too restless to sit.

Each passing day had fed the awful mix of anticipation and dismay that had taken root inside her. The three days of public celebrations had passed in a whirl of colour, faces and good wishes. At the end of it, almost swaying with exhaustion and nerves, Safiyah had prepared herself for a showdown with Karim.

He'd said he'd come to her when the wedding was over. To claim his marital rights. As if she were his possession, to do with as he wished.

Inevitably the idea had stirred anger. Yet if she were totally honest it wasn't just anger brewing in her belly.

But Karim hadn't come to her room on the final night of the celebrations.

Nor had he in the ten days that had passed since the end of the festivities.

Ten days!

Each night she'd prepared to face him and each night he'd failed to show.

He'd clearly changed his mind about his demand that

she sleep with him. Or maybe he hadn't been serious at all—had just wanted to watch her squirm.

What had she done to make him despise her so much?

Safiyah felt her thoughts tracking down that well-worn trail, but she refused to head there again. Instead she crossed the room, hauling off her robe and nightgown as she went, tossing them onto the bed. Seconds later she'd pulled on trousers and a shirt. Socks and boots.

She'd had enough of being cooped up with her thoughts. Her sister had gone home after the wedding and Safiyah, always careful not to burden Rana, had smiled and sent her off rather than beg her to stay. How she wished she had someone to talk to now.

What she needed was to get out. At least here in the summer palace, just beyond the outskirts of the capital, she had the means to do just that. For her lovely chestnut mare, a wedding gift from Karim, was stabled downstairs.

To anyone who cared to enquire, the Sheikh and Sheikha had begun their delayed honeymoon today. The small, secluded summer palace was close enough to the city for Karim to be on hand should anything significant need his attention, but the location between two idyllic beaches was totally private—perfect for newlyweds.

If the newlyweds had been at all interested in each other!

She hadn't seen Karim since they'd arrived. He'd headed straight to his office, trailed by a couple of secretaries, leaving Safiyah, Tarek and his nanny to settle into their rooms.

With a huff of annoyance Safiyah decided she'd rather be with her horse than stewing over whether Karim would deign to visit her. For ten days she'd been torn between anticipation—wanting to cut through this unbearable tension that ratcheted ever tighter—and dismay that finally she would give in to what she could only think of as her weakness for her necessary husband.

Twenty minutes later she was astride her mare as they

picked their way down the path to a long, white sand beach that shimmered in the early-evening light. Once clear of the palace and the protests of the groom, who had been dismayed that she chose to ride alone and bareback, Safiyah drew in a deep breath. The scent of the sea mingled with the comforting aroma of horse, lightening her spirits.

After all, there were worse things than a husband who didn't want sex and left her completely alone.

Safiyah shuddered, remembering the avid way Hassan Shakroun had eaten her up with his gaze in the days following Abbas's death. The idea of his fleshy paws on her body was almost as horrible as the thought of Tarek's safety being in his control.

Marriage to Karim had been the only sensible option. Tarek was protected and she... Well, she'd survived one loveless marriage and she could do it again. She'd happily live without sex. A marriage on paper only was what she'd stipulated. She should be glad Karim didn't want more.

Safiyah squashed the inner voice that said perhaps there was more to sex than she'd experienced with Abbas. Perhaps with another, more considerate lover, there might even be pleasure.

'Come on, Lamia,' Safiyah whispered to her mount. 'Let's go for a run.'

They were halfway down the beach when the sound of thunder reached her. It rolled along the sand behind her. Safiyah looked up but the sky was filled with bright stars, no sign of clouds. Besides, this noise kept going—a rumbling that didn't stop.

Pulling back on the reins, Safiyah looked over her shoulder. Instantly she tensed. Galloping towards her was a tall figure on a grey horse. An unmistakable horse and an unmistakable man.

Karim.

Together they looked like a centaur—as if Karim were

part of the big animal. Their movements were controlled, perfectly synchronised and beautiful. Yet the urgency of their sprint down the beach snared Safiyah's breath.

A frisson of excitement laced with anxiety raced up her spine to grab at her nape and throat.

There was nothing to fear from Karim. Only from herself and the yearning he ignited in her. Yet she couldn't shake her atavistic response. The instinct to flee was overwhelming. She was desperate to get away from this man she hadn't been able to escape even in her thoughts. He crowded her, confronted her, made her feel things she didn't want to feel. Even after ten days of waiting for him to come to her she found she wasn't ready to face her weakness for him.

Safiyah turned and urged her horse faster, first to a canter and then, as the thunder of hoofbeats closed in, to a gallop. The mare leapt forward and Safiyah leaned low, feeling her hair stream behind her as they raced away, exultation firing her blood.

But they weren't fast enough. Even over the sound of Lamia's hooves and her own heartbeat Safiyah heard the grey close in. Each stride narrowed the gap.

Her breath was snatched in choppy gasps. Her pulse was out of control. Still she sped on, desperate to escape her pursuer and all he represented. The man who threatened her not with violence, but because he'd awoken a need inside her that wouldn't let her rest.

He'd stolen her peace.

She had to get away. To preserve her sanity and the last of her self-respect.

Eyes fixed on the end of the beach, and the narrow ribbon of track that rose from up to the next headland, she wasn't aware of how close he was till a dark shadow blocked the silver of the sea and the thunder was upon her, filling her ears and drumming in her chest.

Even then Safiyah wouldn't give in. If she could get up on to the headland track before him—

It wasn't to be. One long arm snaked out and grabbed her bridle, then they were slowing, her mare easing her pace to match that of the stallion.

Safiyah's heart hammered. Her flesh prickled all over as the fight-or-flight response still racketed through her.

Finally they came to a halt in the shadow of the headland. Safiyah's blood pumped too fast and her breath was laboured. Each sense was heightened. The mingled scents of horse, sea salt and hot male flesh were piquant in her nostrils. The brush of Karim's leg against hers unleashed a storm of prickling response.

She stared at the sinewy strength of Karim's hand and wrist, clamped like steel on her reins. The silence, broken only by the rough breathing of the horses, grew louder.

'What the hell did you think you were doing?' The words sliced like a whip. Karim's eyes glittered diamond-hard even in the gloom.

Safiyah sat straighter, refusing to be intimidated. 'Going for a ride. Alone.' Was he going to take issue with that? After the thrill of being allowed to ride again for the first time in years, it was too much.

'You were heading straight for the rocks.' He sounded as if he was speaking through gritted teeth.

'You think I couldn't see them?' She shook her head, too annoyed to be quelled by the warning jut of his arrogant jaw. 'I was about to take the track up the headland.'

Karim's grip tightened on the reins and her horse sidled, pushing Safiyah closer to the big, glowering form beside her.

'Not at that speed. You'd break your neck.'

Safiyah glanced towards the pale track. This time the route didn't look quite so easy. Yet she refused to explain the urgent impulse to escape at any cost. She knew it would only reveal the fear she'd vowed to hide from Karim. That if she wasn't careful he'd overwhelm her and all her hard-won lessons in self-sufficiency.

She'd learned to cut herself off from the thousand hurts of a casually uncaring husband. She couldn't afford to lose that ability now when she most needed it.

'I'm more than capable of deciding where I ride. I don't need you dictating to me.'

A sound like a low growl emanated from Karim's throat, making the hairs on the back of her neck stand up. She'd never heard anything so feral. Karim had always been the epitome of urbanity, always in control.

'Do you have a death wish? What about Tarek? How would he cope if you broke your neck up there?'

Red flashed behind her eyes. 'Don't you bring Tarek into this!'

How dared he accuse her of being an irresponsible mother? Her mouth stretched into a grimace and her belly hollowed as she thought of the sacrifice she'd made for her son. Giving up her freedom for his sake by yoking herself to a man who disliked her.

Fulminating, Safiyah released the reins and vaulted from her horse.

'Where do you think you're going?'

Safiyah set her jaw and stalked away. Let him work it out for himself.

She'd only taken half a dozen steps when a hard hand captured her wrist, turning her to face him. He towered above her, imposing and, though she hated to admit it, magnificent.

'Don't turn your back on me, Safiyah.'

His voice was soft but ice-cold. It sent a shiver scudding across her skin. Even Abbas at his most imperious hadn't affected her like this.

Karim's hold was unbreakable. She'd look ridiculous

trying to yank her hand free. Instead she chose defiance cloaked in a façade of obedience.

She sank to a low curtsey, head bowed. 'Of course, *Your Majesty*. How remiss of me to forget royal etiquette.'

She heard a huff of exasperation and for a second his hand tightened around hers. Then, abruptly, she was free.

'Don't play with me, Safiyah. It won't work.'

She rose, but found Karim had stepped right into her space. They stood toe to toe, her neck arching so she could look him in the eye. She couldn't fully decipher his expression but saw enough to know she'd pushed him dangerously far.

Good. It was time someone punctured that ego.

'I'll get the horses.'

She made to move but he caught her upper arms. His clasp wasn't tight but for some reason Safiyah couldn't break away.

'Leave them. They won't go anywhere.' He paused. 'Why did you run, Safiyah? You knew it was me.'

She shrugged. 'I wanted a gallop.'

'Don't lie.' Gone was the icy contempt. In its place was a piercing intensity that probed deep.

'I'm not—'

'Was it because of this?'

Before she had time to register Karim's intention he hauled her up onto her toes. His head swooped low and his mouth crashed onto hers. Safiyah felt pressure, tasted impatience and hurt pride.

His anger fuelled hers, made it easier to withstand him. Even so, her body quaked with rampant need from being pressed up against his hard frame.

She just had to hang on a little longer, till he grew tired of this and pushed her away. He was angry. He didn't really want her.

Except even as she thought it everything changed.

Those hands wrapped over her arms turned seductive as they slid around her back. One slipped up into her loose hair, tangling there possessively and cradling her skull as he bent her back. His other hand skimmed her hip bone, then moved to cup her bottom. His fingers tightened as he pulled her up against a ridge of aroused flesh so blatantly virile that she gasped.

That gasp was her mistake. It gave Karim access to her mouth, where he delved deep, evoking shuddery thrills of excitement.

Safiyah told herself she shouldn't want this. Shouldn't want *him*. Not the dark coffee taste of him, not his sea and sandalwood scent, not that honed body. And especially not the tight, spiralling feeling low inside as he pressed against her, his erection a blatant male demand.

Yet there was no escape. Because already her fingers clenched into the soft cotton at his shoulders, digging into taut muscle so she felt the bone beneath. Safiyah tried to make herself let go, but her body acted on instincts that had nothing to do with self-preservation.

Karim murmured something against her lips that might have been her name. She couldn't hear it, just felt it as a vibration in her mouth. Then he kissed her harder, and she clung to him as everything spun away in an explosion of sensual delight.

When she could think again it was to find his hand sliding under her shirt to close over her breast. Her knees wobbled as, instead of a hard, crushing hold, she felt his touch gentle. Her breath hissed out as one finger traced narrowing circles around her silk-covered breast till he reached a nipple pouting with need.

Safiyah trembled at the pleasure of Karim's touch. Even the way he moulded her breast in his hand seemed designed to please her as much as him. The rush of moist heat between her legs surprised her. How could she feel like this when she didn't want him?

But you do, Safiyah. You've wanted him for weeks. For years.

It was the knowledge she'd tried to avoid. But denial was impossible as she shook in his arms. Only the support of his embrace held her upright.

As if reading her thoughts Karim broke the kiss, in the same movement scooping her up into his arms. There was something shocking about being held that way, reliant totally on him, curled against that broad, powerful chest as he strode towards the inky shadows beneath the cliffs.

Her eyes widened as she realised the most shocking part was how much she revelled in it. How the coiling twist of heat between her legs grew to a pulsing, urgent throb.

Safiyah caught a glimpse of their horses grazing at the edge of the beach. Then the world tilted as Karim lowered her to cool sand. He knelt above her, the star-quilted sky behind his head, his shadowed face unreadable.

For a second the idea infiltrated that she should stop this. She'd come here to get away from Karim. But only for a second. This…whatever this was…was unstoppable, like the surge of the tide or the rise of the moon.

Karim's knees were astride her thighs, his heat warming her through her trousers as deft fingers worked the buttons of her shirt undone. Safiyah reached for his shirt, flicking those buttons free with an ease borne of urgency. She was working her way down when he pulled her shirt wide and sank back, imprisoning her legs with his weight.

His eyes glinted like starlight, and he had the stark look of a man about to lose control, his flesh pulled tight over bone.

In one quick, ripping movement he tore his shirt free of his trousers and shrugged it off, leaving her in possession of a view that blew her mind.

She'd felt the solid muscle beneath his shirt, seen the way his wide shoulders and broad chest tapered down towards a narrow waist. But the naked reality stunned her.

Safiyah's throat dried. Karim was built like an ancient sculpture of idealised male athleticism. Dark skin and a dusting of even darker hair covered a muscled torso that drew her like iron to a magnet. Her hands lifted, pale against his bronzed flesh, to settle, fingers splayed, across satiny heat. Intrigued, she let them rove higher, over pectorals weighted with muscle and fuzz that tickled her palm.

Karim's ribs expanded into her palms as he snatched in air. In the soft darkness all she could hear was ragged breathing and the pulse of her blood, louder even than the shush of the waves.

Safiyah let her hands slide down across all that searing heat. She reached his belt, her knuckles grazing his flat belly and the tiny line of hair that disappeared into his trousers. Muscles tautened at the brush of her fingers, the tiny movement incredibly erotic.

'You want me.'

It wasn't a question. How could it be when he could read the need in her touch, in her quickened breathing, in the way she ate him up with her gaze? Yet she felt compelled to reply as he waited for the admission.

He'd challenged her to admit what she'd tried to hide, even from herself.

She swallowed, feeling that, despite their wedding vows last week, this was the real moment of truth between them. The moment of consent. With no witnesses but the vast sea and impervious stars. Where even in the shadows she could no longer hide.

'I want you, Karim.' She watched the quick rise of his chest on another mighty breath as if her words brought relief from pent-up pain. 'And you want me, don't you?'

His teeth gleamed in a smile that looked more like an expression of pain than pleasure.

'Of course.'

He took her hand and dragged it low, pressing it to his trousers. Her hand firmed on his erection and his eyelids lowered, his breath hissing as he pushed forward into her palm, his hand still cupping hers around him.

Heat suffused Safiyah. The sight of Karim half naked, questing after her touch with his head arched back in pleasure, was the most arousing thing she'd ever seen. The pulse between her legs quickened and she squirmed against his solid thighs. The sensations were simultaneously delicious and terrible. She'd wanted him for so long, even as she'd told herself she didn't.

The depth of her desire frightened her with its unfamiliarity. And that gave her the strength to drag her hand away.

Karim made as if to grab her hand, then stopped.

'You didn't come to me.' Her voice was a harsh rasp of fury and hurt as she struggled for breath. 'Ten. Whole. Days. You ignored me.'

How could she be sure he wasn't still playing some cruel game? Making her want, despite her better judgement?

Karim shook his head like a swimmer surfacing, trying to clear water from his eyes. 'You hold that against me?'

Suddenly Safiyah knew this was a bad idea. She lay half naked with a man who'd toyed with her before. Yet here she was, baring if not her soul her desires.

She tried to shift him, but those strong horseman's thighs held her in place.

'I'm sorry.'

Karim's apology froze her in place. Or maybe it was the way he trailed his index finger from her navel over her ribs till he reached her bra. Her nipples pebbled and she couldn't prevent the arch of her back, thrusting her breasts higher. He pressed his thumbs against her nipples and Safiyah gasped as pleasure shot straight to her core.

'I wanted to be with you,' he murmured, his voice low as he bent over her, his breath hot on the bare upper slopes of her breasts. 'But I couldn't. There was too much work to ensure key people were loyal to me, not Shakroun.'

He squeezed her breasts through the lacy bra and everything inside her turned molten.

'I worked day and night to make sure he couldn't mount a challenge.'

His words blurred under the force of her restless hunger but still he spoke.

'To ensure you and Tarek were safe.'

A mighty tremor racked Safiyah from head to toe. Whether from the idea of Karim—of anyone—putting her and her son first, or from the erotic intensity of his touch, she didn't know. But her indignation bled out like water through sand.

Karim reached behind her. Then her bra was undone and he pushed it high. She felt his thighs tighten around her hips. He bent, one hand closing around her bare breast while his mouth locked onto the other. No feather-light caress this time. Karim drew her nipple hard into his mouth and fire shot from her breast to her womb, spilling liquid sparks in a torrent through her blood. His hand kneaded her other breast and she bucked against his constraining legs, trying to shuffle her own legs wider.

Safiyah had never known such urgency, such need. Doubt was forgotten as her fingers dug like talons into his hips. She wanted him to move so she could spread her legs, wanted him to stay where he was and ease the hollow feeling inside her.

He moved, lifting his head and his hand from her body, and Safiyah bit back a cry of loss. Everything in her throbbed, aching for more. She'd felt a weak shadow of something like this in the past, but never so intense.

She was still absorbing that when Karim tugged her boots and socks off, tossing them aside. Then his hands were on the zip of her trousers, wrenching it undone and hauling the fabric down.

Safiyah lifted her hips, helping him drag her trousers and underwear down over her thighs, past her knees, then off. Cool air brushed her skin as she wrestled off her shirt and bra.

But when she'd finished, eager to help Karim undress, he hadn't started. Instead he knelt above her, his gaze like hot treacle, sliding over her bare body.

'You're beautiful.' His voice was hoarse, his hands possessive as they skimmed her trembling flesh.

Safiyah caught his wrists, holding them still as she met his eyes. 'You're slow. Take your clothes off.'

Never had she spoken so. Never had she made sexual demands. But something had altered within her.

Maybe it was that uninhibited race down the beach, unleashing a woman more elemental, less cautious than the one she'd learned to be. Maybe it was the fact that with Karim, for this moment at least, she felt able to admit to desire rather than just submit to another's wishes.

She felt strong as never before, even while his stance, as he loomed over her, was a reminder of his greater physical strength.

Karim laughed, the sound ripe and rich. Then he shifted off her. But instead of stripping his trousers off he moved lower, his hands spreading her bare legs. 'I like a woman who knows her mind.'

Then, before her stunned eyes, he sank onto the sand, his hands on her upper thighs, his dark head between her legs.

Safiyah felt a slow, slick caress that trailed fire. And then another caress, in a way no one had ever touched her before, and she shuddered, a deep groan lifting up from the base of her ribs to lock in her throat.

She shook all over, torn between shocked rejection and utter delight. Her hands locked in that dark hair, clawed at his scalp. She was going to push him away, because what he was doing made her feel undone in a way she'd never known. It scared her and aroused her and demanded too much of her.

She was about to—

The third caress—slower, harder, more deliberate—turned into something new. Safiyah opened her mouth to demand he stop when something slammed into her and she lost her voice, herself, lost everything in a searing, sparking, exquisitely perfect moment of rapture.

Not a moment but an eternity. It went on and on, rolling through her taut, trembling, burning body. It went beyond acute delight to a soul-deep conflagration that catapulted her into the stars.

Karim gathered her close in his arms as she shuddered and gasped and clung. He'd expected passion, known there'd be pleasure, but this…

He stopped trying to catalogue why this was different and merely held her. Finally Safiyah softened in his embrace and turned into him, nuzzling at his collarbone.

He was smiling in anticipation of entering that satisfaction-softened body when he registered wetness on his skin. He pulled back just enough to look down at her face. She watched him with stunned eyes. Silvery streaks tracked her cheeks.

He frowned. 'Safiyah? You're crying.' He'd had the occasional emotional lover, but the sight of Safiyah weeping unknotted something in his belly.

'Am I?' She raised a hand and wiped her cheeks. 'I'm

sorry. I just never—' She bit her bottom lip, as if to stop the words tumbling out.

'You never what?'

He waited, but her gaze slid away. He fancied he saw a blush rise in her cheeks, except surely in this light that was impossible. As was the notion her words had planted in his brain. It couldn't be. Could it…?

'Are you saying you've never had an orgasm?'

His voice rose in disbelief and he saw her face shutter. As if he'd accused her of something bad. It confounded him.

'Safiyah, talk to me.'

Five minutes ago it hadn't been conversation he'd wanted. As it was, his groin felt so hard he feared one wrong move might make him spill before he even got his trousers off. Yet he needed answers.

'It's nothing.'

Her mouth curved up in a smile that didn't fit.

Quickly she reached for his belt, starting to unbuckle it. 'I know what you want.'

Yet she didn't sound eager any more. She sounded… dutiful.

Incredibly, Karim felt his hand close on hers, stopping her when she would have pulled the belt undone. She was shaking, fine tremors rippling beneath the skin. The aftermath of her climax or something else?

'What I want is an answer.'

His voice emerged harsh. He felt her flinch and guilt eddied. Curiosity, too, about her relationship with Abbas. For years he hadn't let himself dwell on that. Now he was consumed by the need to know.

'But you haven't even—'

'I can wait.' He couldn't believe he was saying this when desire still rode him so painfully. 'Tell me, Safiyah.'

'It's nothing. I'm just a little…overwhelmed.'

'Because you've never climaxed before?'

The idea battered at him, making it difficult to think. It didn't change anything. So what if Safiyah hadn't found sexual satisfaction with her husband? So what if her eagerness to satisfy him suggested her experience had been about giving rather than receiving pleasure?

But it did matter.

Karim didn't understand why, but it did. He gathered her in and held her close till the last tremors subsided, even though it was torture in his aroused state. When she was warm and pliant in his arms he released her and moved away.

'Where are you going?'

She sounded shocked. As shocked as he felt.

'To get your clothes. We're going back to the palace.' He grimaced, his gait stiff and uncomfortable with his erection.

'Don't you want me?'

Her voice was a whisper, and when he turned she was sitting with her arms wrapped around her knees. Her pale flesh glimmered seductively and it took everything he had not to drop to his knees and continue what they'd begun.

'Of course I want you.' He drew a deep breath, strengthening his resolve. 'But when I take you, Safiyah, I want the first time to be in a comfortable bed—not hot and hard in the sand and over in two seconds.'

Which sounded good in theory, yet Karim wasn't sure how he was going to make it last—bed or no bed.

Why, precisely, the location suddenly mattered, he wasn't sure. Except he suspected Safiyah hadn't been an equal partner in sex before.

Karim didn't want her sharing his bed out of duty. He wanted her as she'd been moments before, full of passion and delight. She deserved more than a quick coupling on the beach.

He wanted to make their first time together special.

Karim refused to dwell on what that meant.

CHAPTER NINE

SAFIYAH LISTENED TO the sound of the shower in the next room and slumped down to sit on the end of the bed. Karim had spoken barely a word on the ride back to the summer palace, or after they'd left the stables for their bedroom.

Their bedroom.

Instead of horrifying her, those words settled in her mind like a comforting blanket. Because she'd given up hiding from the truth. She wanted her new husband and she looked forward to being with him. Even though she knew from previous experience that the actual sex act would be less than satisfying, she still wanted him.

Because he'd been the first man to give her an orgasm?

Her lips curved at the memory.

That would be an easy explanation. But Safiyah refused to settle for anything less than the truth.

She'd never stopped wanting Karim, even after he'd treated her so callously.

Throughout her first marriage she'd compartmentalised, putting her feelings for Karim away in a box marked 'Ancient History', devoting herself to her husband. But now there was nothing holding back those old feelings and they were stronger than ever.

She shifted, trying to ease the ache between her legs—so inexplicable given that stunning climax. Beneath her clothes she felt the abrasive scratch of sand. What she wanted—apart from Karim—was a wash, but he'd stalked straight to the bathroom and she, out of training and habit, was content to wait on her husband's wishes.

Except Safiyah *wasn't* content. She felt edgy and uncomfortable. She wanted a wash and she wanted Karim.

His words kept replaying in her head. He wanted her in a comfortable bed where he could take his time. He didn't want sex to be hot and hard and over in two seconds.

She knew about sex that was over almost before it had begun, and she was accustomed to the listless sense that she'd missed out on something just beyond her reach. Now she knew what she'd missed and she wanted more. How would it feel to reach that pinnacle of bliss with Karim moving inside her?

Safiyah shivered and wrapped her arms around herself, trying to hold in the breathless excitement. An image rose in her head of herself following Karim into the bathroom, stripping off her crumpled sticky clothes and joining him in the shower. Her skin drew tight and her palms dampened as she remembered how good he looked without his shirt.

How would he look totally naked?

Once more she shifted. But nothing could ease that restless ache. Except Karim.

Abbas would have been horrified at her making a sexual advance. He'd always taken the initiative. Not that she'd ever wanted to.

But then he'd never caressed her with his mouth the way Karim had. Never made her fly in ecstasy and never, for that matter, pulled back without taking his own pleasure. Seeing Karim do that tonight had stunned her, making her question what she knew about him.

For years she'd believed him callous, even cruel. Yet he'd adopted her son, made Tarek his heir. There'd been acts of kindness enough to make her think this forced marriage wouldn't be all bad.

Safiyah thought of Karim's very obvious erection as he'd gathered the horses and helped her up, of his grimace as he'd mounted and turned his horse towards the palace. She thought of his ebony head buried in the V between her thighs and the extraordinary experience he'd bestowed upon her.

Karim was a conundrum. But one thing was obvious—he didn't follow Abbas's rules. Whatever rules they followed in this marriage were for her and Karim to decide.

The realisation made her feel suddenly strong.

Toeing off her shoes, Safiyah rose and marched, heart hammering, to the bathroom door. She opened it and slipped in. There was no steam to obscure her husband's naked body. He stood, palms flat on the tiled wall, head bowed beneath the sluicing water that trailed down over wide shoulders and a tapering body to firm, round buttocks and long, muscled legs.

Ignoring the doubts pecking at her determination, Safiyah stripped off her clothes, shivering as the fabric scraped across her hyper-aware flesh. Nervousness almost stopped her, but determination won out. She padded across to the shower, opened the glass door and stepped in.

An arctic chill enveloped her and she yelped as the water sprayed her.

'Safiyah?'

Stunned eyes met hers as she recoiled from the cold water. But when she tried to retreat she found her way barred by one long arm. The other reached for the taps. Seconds later the water turned warm.

'What are you doing here?'

'What are *you* doing standing under cold water?'

One black eyebrow crooked. 'Why do men usually take cold showers?'

Involuntarily she looked down. The cold water had done

its job. He was no longer rampantly erect. But, she realised with a rush of heat, Karim still looked well endowed.

The restless feeling between her legs intensified and she shifted her weight—only to brush up against that brawny arm stretched between her and the exit, reminding her abruptly of her own nakedness.

Her brows knitted. She didn't understand him. 'You don't want sex, then?'

Her stomach plunged. It was like when they'd courted. She'd believed then that Karim cared for her, might even love her. She'd daily expected him to propose. Instead, when she and her father had been called away because Rana had needed them desperately, Karim hadn't even bothered to say goodbye. She'd gone from happiness and breathless expectation to disbelief and hurt in the blink of an eye.

Safiyah reached for the door.

This time he didn't just bar her way—he took her shoulders and turned her to face him. 'Of course I want you. Didn't I tell you so?'

Her heart gave a little shimmy when he said he wanted *her*, not merely sex. Oh, she had it bad. But she couldn't find the energy to worry about that now.

His gaze dropped to her bare breasts and Safiyah saw the spark of masculine appreciation in that look. A pulse ticked at his temple and suddenly she *felt* his stare. His eyes met hers and her breath snagged. Such intensity, all focused on her.

'Then why don't you do something about it?'

His laugh was like a crack of thunder, sharp and short. 'Because I want to make it good for you, not explode the minute I touch you.'

That was the second time he'd said that. She couldn't decide if she felt flattered or frustrated.

'You've already made it good for me.'

Better than she'd ever experienced, though she didn't

say that. It was bad enough that he'd guessed her relative inexperience. She refused to act as if this was a big deal.

Safiyah reached for him, her eyes rounding as she discovered him already growing hard.

Karim's smile was a tight twist of the lips, then he leaned in and whispered, 'There's more to come.'

But instead of turning off the water and opening the shower door Karim crowded her back against the tiled wall. He was all heat and slick muscle and she trembled at the feel of skin sliding against skin, heat against heat. Excitement spiked a fizz of effervescence in her blood.

The flesh in her hand was heavy now, soft skin over rearing steel, his erection larger than she'd expected.

As if reading the scurry of sudden anxiety along her spine Karim stilled, then pulled back so he was no longer pinning her to the wall. 'We'll go back to the bedroom and take things slow.'

He reached out an arm to switch off the taps, but Safiyah wrapped her fingers around his wrist. 'No.' Those remarkable eyes met hers, ripe with question. 'I don't want to wait.'

To reinforce her words she pulled one of his hands towards her, planting it over her breast. Instantly his fingers moulded to her with exquisite pressure and the flesh in her hand swelled as Karim stepped closer and his erection slid against her.

Safiyah bit her cheek against the sudden wash of delight. 'Don't.'

Karim's other hand brushed her cheek, her mouth, pressing her bottom lip till she opened her mouth and tasted him with her tongue.

'Witch!'

Those green eyes seemed to eat her up. A hairy thigh, solid with muscle, insinuated itself between her legs. And a moment later she felt his touch in that most intimate place.

Safiyah's gaze clung to his as he deftly stroked her, evoking a response that made her hand tighten around him.

'You like that, don't you, Safiyah? And you liked it when I kissed you there too. Didn't you?'

She swallowed, trying to find her voice and failing. Instead she nodded, wondering how much longer she could stay on her feet when each deliberate slide of his fingers made her feel weak and trembling.

She loved what he was doing but she didn't want to be weak. She wanted to participate. So she took him in both hands, cupping and stroking, delighted when his eyelids lowered, turning his eyes to gleaming slits.

His nostrils flared and his strong features looked stark and tight. He groaned. 'So much for taking it slow.' Swiftly he moved her hands away, placing them on his shoulders and then lifting her up off the floor. 'Hook your legs over my hips.'

The words emerged as a terse order, but Safiyah read his juddering pulse and the convulsive movement of his throat as he swallowed. Karim was at the edge of his control, just as she'd been on the beach. The thought thrilled her and she complied, wrapping herself around those tight hips, clinging to his wide shoulders.

But there was no time for triumph. Instead she bit back a gasp as he brought them together in one slow, deliberate thrust.

Safiyah's eyes were snared on his and she couldn't look away. She fancied she saw his darken as a second thrust unlocked something deep within her and sensations rushed through her. This felt unfamiliar and a little scary—especially as she was pinned high against his tall frame, not even supporting herself. Yet at the same time she exulted in it when she moved to meet him and felt a shudder rip through him.

'Yes,' he whispered through gritted teeth. 'Like that.'

His big hands held her hips, helping her angle herself to meet him. Instead of feeling used, Safiyah felt powerful. She'd chosen this. Nor was it solely about Karim's pleasure. She craved this with every cell in her body. And, impossibly, the flames she'd felt on the beach were flickering again deep inside her.

Those flames skyrocketed when Karim palmed her belly and pressed his thumb down on that sensitive bud between her legs. Safiyah jerked as lightning sheared through her.

Karim grinned, the picture of male smugness.

She responded by tightening her muscles around him.

His grin solidified and his powerful thrusts turned jerky.

Safiyah saw the bunch of his muscles, the tendons standing proud in his neck and his eyes glazing.

But this wasn't a contest. Nor was it duty. This was what she'd craved for so long. This was Karim and her together, connected in a way that felt almost too profound to be just sex.

Then all thinking stopped as Karim changed the angle of his thrusts. For a moment everything stilled. A second later she was flung into a cataclysm that melded delight and something much more far-reaching.

Safiyah heard a deep shout, felt the hard pump within her and fell into ecstasy, holding Karim tight as he gathered her in.

They lay sprawled sideways across the bed. The pillows had long since disappeared, but no matter. Karim felt as if it would take a tsunami to make him move.

He lay on his back, his bones melting into the mattress, his body limp with satiation. With a supreme effort he slid his hand through the spill of Safiyah's hair, lying like a silken cloud across his chest and shoulder. Predictably, even that simple caress stirred an eagerness for more.

She lay draped over him—a lush, erotic blanket. If he'd

had more energy he'd have devoted himself to exploring that delectable body again. He'd been fascinated by her reactions, a mix of wholehearted responsiveness and shyness. But after a night devoted to carnal pleasure, giving in again and again to the urge for just one more taste of his bride, he'd have to wait to summon some strength.

That didn't stop his mind from working. On the contrary, it was busier than ever, trying to make sense of tonight's events with something that in another man might have come close to panic.

But Karim never panicked. He assessed, reviewed, and determined the logical course of action. It was what he'd been trained to do.

Right now logic wasn't helping.

Sex with Safiyah was phenomenal. Urgent and explosive, yet deeply satisfying. Terribly addictive. The more they shared, the more they wanted.

Karim had been taken aback by the demands of his libido, as if after years of denial he was making up for lost time. As if sex with Safiyah was more real, more satisfying, than with any other lover. Even when they did no more than lie together, body to body, sharing the occasional gentle caress, it felt *different* from previous experiences.

The notion was unsettling. Karim had expected their first night together to be memorable. He'd waited long enough for it, having never quite managed to excise her from his memory. But this was so much more than he'd anticipated.

He thought back over his actions.

The way he'd denied himself instant gratification on the beach because he'd decided on a whim that their first time needed to be memorable. It had been memorable, all right. Harder and hotter and more intense than anything he could recall, with Safiyah's lush breasts jouncing up and down against him, her welcoming body wrapped so tight around him he'd detonated with the force of a rocket.

The way he'd spent so much time denying his own pleasure in order to bring her to climax again and again, despite her pleas and her pouting demands that he take her fully. And his desperation whenever he'd relented and joined her.

He'd taken his fill but he'd done far more. It was as if he'd tried to imprint himself on her consciousness, to make her associate ecstasy with him and only him. As if he'd wanted to obliterate any memory of her first husband.

Was he jealous of a dead man?

Of course not—especially since he'd learned that Abbas hadn't had the sense or generosity to please his wife in bed. The idea of him using Safiyah for his own satisfaction but giving none in return twisted like a drill boring through Karim's gut. He hadn't liked the man but now he despised him.

Yet that didn't explain the other riddle. Why it was that with Safiyah sex seemed more than just an expression of lust and physical pleasure.

He frowned into the darkness, telling himself there was a reasonable explanation. Release after the stress of recent weeks, perhaps?

Safiyah shifted as if to roll away and he stopped her. 'Stay.'

'You're awake?'

'Barely.'

She chuckled, the sound rich and appealing, but it was the way he felt the vibration of her laugh through his body, his hunger to hear more, that threatened to undo him.

Why, he didn't know. Except suddenly there came the certainty that this sense of closeness, of emotional intimacy, was dangerous.

Through the night physical desire had been transformed into the illusion of something more profound. Something akin to what he'd felt when he'd first known Safiyah. When she'd had the power to hurt him—and not just his pride, he finally admitted, but something buried even deeper.

That wouldn't do. No matter how spectacular the sex, Karim needed to remember who he'd married and why. He couldn't allow himself to be lured into thinking this was more than sexual attraction.

'Tell me about Abbas.'

Safiyah stiffened and he heard her indrawn breath. Then she rolled away to lie on her back. Though he'd decided to establish some distance, Karim had to make a conscious effort not to haul her back into his arms.

'Why?'

'Why not?' He turned towards her, pillowing his head on one bent arm.

'You really want to do this *now*?'

He couldn't read her features but the discordant note in her voice sounded defensive.

'Your first marriage is hardly a secret.' He kept his voice even, though it still rankled that she'd gone straight from him to Abbas.

That last night, when she and her father had stayed at the Za'daqi palace, she'd agreed to meet Karim secretly. She'd been his for the taking, though no marriage contract had been drawn up.

Except Ashraf had found him in the secluded garden instead, breaking the news of the medical results that had proved he wasn't the Sheikh's son.

The shocking revelation had pushed everything, even Safiyah, from Karim's head. It hadn't been till later that he'd realised she must have come to their rendezvous and overheard their conversation. After learning he was illegitimate, she'd dumped him for Abbas.

Now she scrabbled for a sheet, dragging it up to cover

herself. 'There's nothing much to tell.' Her voice was brisk. 'He wanted to marry into my clan.'

'Go on.' Was it masochism that made him want to hear more?

'Rana, my sister, caught his eye first. She was studying in the capital and she was…is…intelligent and pretty.'

Her words struck Karim. It sounded almost as if Safiyah believed her sister outshone her.

'But then she got sick. Marriage wasn't possible. And so—'

'And so you jumped at the chance to marry a king?'

For a second she didn't answer. Then, tucking the sheet close around her, she rolled to face him. They were less than an arm's length apart, yet it seemed like more. Even in the darkness he felt the chill in her stare.

'When I was in Za'daq you weren't the only one whose father was unwell. My father had received a terminal diagnosis, though he didn't tell me straight away. He knew he'd be dead within months.'

Karim frowned. He'd never have guessed. Safiyah's father had looked so hale and hearty.

'He was old-fashioned in some ways, and desperate to get Rana and me "safely settled", as he called it, before he died. When Rana got sick…' another pause, '…all his hopes rested on me. He wanted me to marry well—not just for myself, but so Rana would be cared for while she recovered.'

Karim thought of the woman he'd met during the wedding. If she'd been seriously ill it didn't show now.

'So it was all your father's doing?'

On learning of Karim's illegitimacy her father would have pushed her towards another man. But if Safiyah had loved Karim she'd have stuck with him. She wouldn't have let herself be driven into another man's bed. The fact she'd done just that still stuck in his gullet.

'My father suggested it. Abbas agreed and I…consented.'

Karim cursed the darkness that prevented him reading Safiyah. Something in her voice intrigued him. Despite his residual anger he felt reluctant admiration that she'd admitted it had been her choice.

He breathed deep. Time to let this rest. Yet…

'It was a happy marriage?'

Safiyah scanned the dark form before her, trying and failing to read his expression.

A happy marriage?

She almost laughed. She'd believed once that she'd have just that—with Karim, of all people. The absurdity of those dreams tasted like ash on her tongue.

She'd been all but forced into marriage. Technically, she could have said no. But with her father fading before her eyes and both of them worried about Rana, Abbas's offer had been a *fait accompli*. Karim had turned his back on her. Her father's health had been spiralling down as worry increased and they'd struggled to find the care Rana needed after her breakdown.

Abbas had taken care of everything. He'd got Rana immediate entry to an exclusive clinic renowned for its excellence. A clinic which usually had a long waiting list. Safiyah had been so grateful, and in the circumstances what reason could she have given for rejecting him?

'It was a good marriage,' she said finally.

If by *good* she meant that it had conformed to expectations.

Publicly, Abbas had honoured her. Yet otherwise he'd had little to do with her except when he'd wanted sex or needed a hostess. He'd helped her support her sister, and in his own way had been pleased with his son—if disturbingly distant. And if he had been too autocratic for her taste and hadn't loved her—well, he'd been the King and she'd never expected love. She'd done her best to play her royal role.

'A good marriage? Not a happy one?' Karim leaned close, as if intent on her answer.

Safiyah stiffened. Despite the joy Karim had brought her tonight, she didn't have the emotional resources to deal with an autopsy on her first marriage. She'd survived it and that was what mattered. Dredging up the details would only reinforce the fact that, despite tonight's sexual satisfaction, she'd given herself in another loveless marriage.

She swallowed hard, forcing down the metallic taste of despair. Could she really go through this again? Especially when this was a hundred times worse because part of her kept hoping for some sign that Karim cared for her. Even though she *knew* that was impossible.

'That's enough, Karim. I don't ask you about your past. I don't delve into your secrets.'

In the gloom she saw him stiffen as if she'd struck him. Because she'd answered back or because he had secrets he wouldn't share? She was too weary and upset to ask.

'You'll have to forgive my curiosity.' But his voice held no apology. Instead it cut like honed steel. 'I thought it would be useful to know more about you since we've undertaken to spend our lives together.'

He sounded anything but thrilled about that! He made it sound like a prison sentence.

Gone was the passionate lover. Gone the tenderness that had wound itself around her foolish, unthinking heart and made her begin to believe that miracles might be possible.

Karim's haughty tone reminded her exactly why they'd married.

Pragmatism, not love.

Never love.

Safiyah choked back the sob that thickened her voice. Perhaps she was vulnerable after tonight's unprecedented experiences, but suddenly the idea of spending her whole future in a marriage where she'd have to pretend not to crave what she could never have was too much.

'Don't bother about that,' she said. 'A successful royal marriage doesn't require you to know me or I you. In fact, it will work best if we meet as polite strangers.'

She gathered the sheet tight around her and rolled away. 'I'm going to sleep now. I've got a headache.'

CHAPTER TEN

POLITE STRANGERS.

Karim grimaced. The idea was ludicrous, but that was exactly what they were. Even after seven nights away from the capital on their supposed honeymoon.

He swore and shoved his chair back from the desk, swamped by the discontent that hounded him whenever he tried and failed to break through Safiyah's reserve.

Or when he tried to determine why doing that was so important to him.

Every morning and for a couple of hours in the evening Karim worked, grappling with the multitude of matters requiring the new Sheikh's attention. Each day he breakfasted with Tarek and Safiyah, and they spent the afternoons together as a family. For Karim was determined to establish a good relationship with his new son. Not for Tarek a life in which the only male role model was a man he hated spending time with.

To Karim's surprise the boy had accepted him. Not only that but, given the chance, Tarek dogged Karim's footsteps as if fascinated by him.

Or just previously starved of male attention?

The picture Karim had built of Abbas was of a man with little time for his wife or son. A man caught up in the business of ruling, or perhaps a man too wrapped up in himself to care about anyone else.

That possibility stirred indignation in Karim's breast.

His own dysfunctional family had made him impatient with those who didn't appreciate the value of what they had. Which was why he was determined to make this work—for all of them.

Yet between Karim and Safiyah there yawned a void. Safiyah held herself aloof. Each day it was like conversing at a formal banquet with a foreign ambassador—all charm on the surface but with neither letting their guard down.

He'd never met a woman so adept at avoiding discussions about herself. Whenever he pressed for more she lifted her eyebrows as if surprised and deftly changed the subject.

If she'd fobbed him off with trivialities it wouldn't have worked, but Safiyah was a fount of knowledge on Assaran politics. Her shrewd observations on key individuals, on brewing issues and provincial power-plays were informative and incredibly useful to a man shouldering the burden of ruling a new country.

The only time she let her guard slip was in bed. Or in the shower. Or during their midnight swims. Or wherever else they had sex. Then she was a siren who drove him wild with her responsiveness and, increasingly, her demands.

Sometimes he felt as if he was really connecting to the vibrant woman hiding behind the mask of conformable queen and wife. He glimpsed something in her velvety eyes that hinted she was there—the woman he'd once believed her to be. But then, after sex, the barriers came up like steel barricades. Shutting him out.

Karim wasn't emotionally needy. He hadn't been since he was a child and his mother had abandoned him to the mercy of a tyrant. He'd made himself self-sufficient in every way. So it wasn't for his own sake that he wanted to break down the wall between him and Safiyah. It was so they could create a sound footing for a future together, to bring up Tarek and any future children.

His groin tightened and his pulse skipped faster at the idea of fathering Safiyah's children. He'd been semi-aroused all morning, despite the hours dealing with budget papers and plans for law reform. The sea breeze through the window reminded him of their race down the beach that first night here—that fever of need as he'd stripped Safiyah and given her a first taste of rapture.

Karim closed his eyes as a shudder ran through him. Hunger and longing. And regret. Because after the triumphant sex and that incredible sense of closeness she'd said coldly that it was best if they were strangers.

It was what he'd visualised when he'd first imagined this marriage. Keeping her at a distance, using her to secure his standing in this new country and for personal pleasure—not least the satisfaction of having at his mercy the woman who'd spurned him.

But from the start he'd wanted more.

Frowning, Karim shut down his computer and stood, rolling his shoulders.

He'd erred in pushing her for details about Abbas that night in bed. They'd both been exhausted after a sexual marathon that had left them off balance. Yet Karim had been driven by an urgency to establish control over circumstances that had suddenly seemed more complex and fraught than he'd anticipated.

He'd expected great sex, given the constant shimmer of attraction between them. Yet he hadn't expected to *feel* so much when he finally bedded Safiyah. It had been as if the years had peeled away and he still believed she was the one woman for him. As if her happiness was important to him.

His glance strayed to the brilliant blue sky outside the window. It was their last afternoon at the small summer palace. His plans for today would surely help him break down Safiyah's defences.

* * *

'A picnic lunch?'

Safiyah met Karim's glinting eyes. His brows slanted up at her surprise, giving him a saturnine appearance that was both goading and sexy.

It was appalling the way such a little thing made her knees weaken and her insides liquefy. At breakfast today she'd been reduced to wordless yearning just by the crook of Karim's mouth in the hint of a smile.

That half-smile had reminded her of last night, when Karim had teased her mercilessly with his mouth and hands till she'd begged for him to take her. Last night there'd been something in his expression, too. Something she couldn't name and didn't want to, for she feared she'd make a fool of herself, imagining tender emotions when he had none.

She was his convenient bride. Nothing more.

'Yes, a picnic. It's all arranged.'

He made it sound like a typical royal event, with retainers on hand to serve them. She didn't particularly enjoy formality, but if it meant less time alone with Karim that was a good thing. Because it got harder by the day not to be seduced by his charm.

'I'm sure Tarek will like that.'

'Oh, I know he will.'

Was Karim laughing at her? That gleam in those dark eyes—

'He was thrilled when I told him. Ah, here he is.'

Safiyah turned to see Tarek running from his room, not in his usual shorts and T-shirt, but in the trousers and boots he wore for visiting the stables.

'Mama, Mama, we have a surprise for you.'

He stopped beside Karim and looked up at the tall man. Then, to Safiyah's surprise, her son lifted his small hand and Karim's long fingers enfolded it.

A pang pierced her lungs. Could she be jealous of the burgeoning closeness between the two? That would make her pathetic. It was good for Tarek that Karim made time for him and seemed to enjoy his company. Her son had bloomed since coming here, becoming more and more the carefree little boy she'd seen in snatches since Abbas's repressive influence had gone.

'A surprise? How lovely.'

Her boy nodded gravely, then frowned. 'But you need other shoes. For safety.'

He looked up to Karim, who nodded. 'That's right. We don't wear sandals around horses.'

'Horses?'

That explained Tarek's beaming smile. So they were having a picnic in the stables? Despite her attempts to distance herself a little from Karim, she couldn't help smiling at the idea. Tarek was fascinated by horses and she'd promised to teach him to ride.

'That sounds like fun. I'll be right back.'

But when she went to the stables there was no picnic laid out. Instead she found Tarek, grinning from ear to ear, wearing a riding helmet and mounted astride a tubby little pony almost as wide as it was high.

'Surprise!' He threw out his arms, bouncing in the saddle so Karim, holding the pony's leading rope, put out a hand to steady him.

'Easy, Tarek. What have I said about sitting still and not frightening Amin?'

The pony didn't look perturbed—merely shook its head and stood patiently.

Safiyah stopped in her tracks, torn between shock and delight. Tarek looked so enthusiastic, his smile like a beacon. She grinned back at him. He really was coming out of the shell of reserve that had so worried her.

But at the same time she forced down a sliver of something less positive—the feeling that she'd been excluded. *She'd* wanted to teach Tarek to ride, had looked forward to it.

Yet she couldn't be selfish enough to begrudge him his excitement. This was a positive change from Abbas, who'd never made time to be with Tarek, much less encouraged him to learn anything other than court etiquette.

'You're riding? Karim has been teaching you?'

Maybe that explained Tarek's recent willingness to have a nap in the afternoon. Before coming here he'd been adamant he no longer needed a rest. Had he and Karim secretly spent nap time in the stables?

Tarek nodded. 'Brushing Amin and feeding him and learning how to sit.' He chewed his lip. 'But not really *riding*...' He looked up wistfully at Karim.

Karim's eyes met hers. 'We thought you'd like to teach him that.'

His voice was suede brushing across her skin and Safiyah shivered in response.

'You're the expert rider in the family. I've told Tarek how you used to compete.'

Silly how much his words affected her. She drank them in like desert earth sucking in life-giving water. Because it was so long since she'd received praise? Or because it was for something she'd once excelled at?

But even after years of being denied access to the animals she loved she wasn't that needy. This warm feeling came from the way Tarek and Karim looked at her. Tarek with excitement and admiration and Karim with...

Safiyah wrenched her gaze away. Karim was doing what he'd promised—building a bond with Tarek, creating a sense of family so her boy could thrive. So they could present the image of a solid family unit. Karim was pragmatic, that was all. It would be crazy to read more into his actions.

She focused on Tarek. 'You're sitting up nice and straight. I'm impressed. Are you ready to ride out?'

'Can I? Can I really?' He jumped up and down in the saddle, then almost immediately subsided, leaning forward to pat the pony reassuringly. 'Sorry, Amin. I didn't mean to scare you.'

The pony flicked its ear at the sound of his name but otherwise didn't budge.

Safiyah suppressed a smile. 'You found a very calm pony, Karim. I only hope he moves as well as he stands.'

Karim passed her the leading rope. 'Time to find out.'

Amin did, indeed, move. In fact he turned out to be an ideal learner's mount—placid, but not obstinate, content to circle the courtyard again and again while Tarek learned the basics.

'I had no idea what you two were up to,' Safiyah said as they stopped before Karim. Despite her stern self-talk, she found herself smiling into those glinting eyes. 'You kept the secret well.'

He shrugged. 'We kept Amin at the far end of the stable, away from the other horses, so you wouldn't see him. He's only been here a couple of days. I don't think Tarek could have kept the secret any longer.'

Tarek piped up. 'I wanted to tell you, Mama, but I wanted to surprise you with how much I know.' He rattled off information about grooming his pony and even caring for his tack.

Safiyah raised her eyebrows.

'I told Tarek that if he had a pony he had to learn how to look after it.' Karim caught her eye.

'I agree.' She turned to her son. 'You've learned so much. I'm proud of you.'

He grinned. 'Can we go now? Can we?'

'Go?' Safiyah looked from Tarek to Karim.

'Our picnic, remember?' He turned and went into the

stable, emerging with her horse, already saddled. 'Up you get.' When Safiyah hesitated he continued. 'You and Tarek will ride. I'll lead the pony.'

Karim would walk, leaving her and Tarek to ride? She couldn't imagine many men of her acquaintance doing that—especially Abbas, even if he *had* been able to ride. Usually women and children tagged along while the man took precedence.

'Hurry up, Safiyah. I don't know about you, but I'm hungry.'

There was no impatience in Karim's expression, just a twinkle of amusement that she found far too attractive. With one last look at Tarek she took the reins and swung up into the saddle.

They didn't ride far, and not down to the beach—for which she was grateful. Even with Karim holding the leading rope, the track there was steep and would challenge a first-time rider. Instead they went to a sheltered grove a little way along the headland.

The view across the sea was spectacular, but what held Safiyah's eye was the tent erected for their convenience. It was tall enough to stand up in. The floor was covered with carpets and cushions. And she caught the glint of silver from platters, jugs and intricately decorated goblets. Cool boxes stood in one corner, no doubt packed with their picnic meal.

The place looked inviting and, she realised, deserted. The servants who'd set up this temporary camp had clearly returned to the palace. Maybe that accounted for the sense of intimacy here. There was silence but for the snort of the horses, Tarek's chatter and the whisper of the sea below.

She caught Karim's gaze on her. Warmth swarmed through her, climbing to her cheeks. Suddenly the tent with all its rich furnishings looked like the setting for seduction.

She remembered that morning, when Karim had persuaded her to stay in bed, ostensibly by reaching out one hand to stroke her bare body. But it had been the searing hunger in his expression that had held her there. For she'd been consumed by a matching hunger.

How dangerous it was, trying to keep her heart whole while sharing her husband's bed. This wasn't like her marriage to Abbas. Then there'd been no difficulty in maintaining an emotional distance. But with Karim—

'What are you thinking?'

His voice hit that baritone note that never failed to make Safiyah feel weak and wanton.

'I...' Her gaze shifted and she noticed for the first time that one end of the tent was a cosy bower, where a couple of Tarek's toys were propped against fluffy pillows. A kite lay beside them.

Safiyah swallowed, her throat closing convulsively as emotion see-sawed. This looked...felt...like the action of more than a man taking a pragmatic approach. It felt like the action of a man who cared.

'Safiyah?'

Suddenly he was before her, looking down from under sombre brows.

'What's wrong?'

She shook her head, swallowing the reckless words that crammed her mouth. Pushing away the almost overwhelming urge to pretend this was real. Once she'd yearned for love, had believed in it with all her heart. To her dismay it seemed even the hard lessons of the last years hadn't banished that craving.

'Mama! Karim! I'm starving. Aren't you?' Tarek raced into the tent, lifting the lid on one of the cool boxes.

'Nothing's wrong.' She aimed a vague smile in Karim's direction. 'You seem to have thought of everything. Thank you.'

Before he could question further, she hurried after her son. 'Wait, Tarek. You need to wash your hands first.'

Again Karim felt he'd missed his opportunity with Safiyah. In the rare moments when it seemed they were on the brink of something more than sex, or a purely dynastic marriage, the possibility shimmered for an instant and then shattered.

Was it weakness to want more?

He'd told himself he wanted to secure their future. If he and Safiyah knew and trusted each other they'd create a unit that would underpin his new role.

Or did his need for more from Safiyah have another explanation?

Personal experience made him particularly sympathetic to Tarek's situation. A childhood devoid of love had made Karim determined to do better for the boy than his own parents had done.

His mouth twisted in distaste. *His parents*. He didn't know who his father was. His mother had died when he was young and her lover had never lifted a finger to contact Karim.

Maybe that was it. Apart from Ashraf, Karim was alone. Maybe his determination to build a family unit wasn't just for Tarek's sake, but his own.

He scowled. The notion was absurd. He had a plan and he was determined to make it work. That was all. The throb of anticipation now, as he joined Safiyah and Tarek, simply meant he was pleased at his progress so far. No more than that.

Yet a couple of hours later Karim had ceased to think in terms of plans and progress. Relaxed and replete, he found himself enjoying Tarek's amusing chatter and Safiyah's company. Their easy conversation seemed the most natural thing in the world.

How long since he'd done something as simple and fine as enjoying a picnic?

The answer was easy. Never.

His early life had been filled with royal responsibilities. There'd been no lazy afternoons. And since he'd left Za'daq he'd thrown himself into his investment business, needing to fill the huge gap in his world where duty had once been.

Now he stood in the centre of the clearing, one hand on Tarek's shoulder as the boy leaned into him, his head flung back to watch the red kite bobbing above them.

'Look, Karim! Look, Mama! It's flying.'

'I'm looking, sweetie. It's wonderful.'

'Karim can teach you too.' The boy twisted to look up at Karim. 'Can't you?'

'Of course.'

The boy relinquished the kite's string and scampered across to his mother, dragging her back to Karim. 'Here.'

Ignoring Safiyah's rueful smile, Karim stepped closer. Immediately the light perfume of her skin teased him. So instead of merely handing the kite to her he moved behind her, wrapping his arm around her waist. He felt her sudden intake of breath and the silk of her hair against his mouth as he brought his hand to hers, offering her the kite.

For a moment she stood stiffly. Then the wind jerked the kite and she gave an exclamation of surprise and delight.

'Careful. Watch it doesn't dip too low,' he warned.

She tugged, and together they moved to catch the up-draught. It took some manoeuvring, and a near miss, but soon they had it flying high again.

'Thanks. I've never done this before. I didn't know it was so thrilling.'

She smiled up at him over her shoulder and the glow of her pleasure drenched him like sunlight banishing the night's shadows. Gone was the reserve she usually maintained when they weren't having sex.

Karim's chest expanded as pleasure filled him. 'I haven't either. That makes us all novices.'

'You haven't?' She looked astonished. 'I thought you must have learned as a boy.'

Karim shook his head. He was about to explain that there'd been little time for childish pursuits in the Za'daqi royal court when someone entered the clearing. His secretary—looking grim.

'Your Majesty... Madam.'

He bowed deep and Karim saw his shoulders rise as if he were catching his breath. Karim's smile froze. Such an interruption could only mean serious news.

'Sir, may we speak in private?'

Karim felt Safiyah tense and tightened his hold on her. 'You may speak in front of the Sheikha.'

This was more than some scheduling problem. With his staring eyes, the man looked to be in shock. Karim braced himself. *Not Ashraf. Not his brother...*

'Very well, Your Majesty.' He hesitated, then abruptly blurted out, 'There's a report in the media about your... background. Claiming that your father was—'

He stopped, and Karim came to his rescue. 'Not my father?' Weariness mingled with relief that there hadn't been a tragedy. But clearly there was no escaping some secrets.

'Yes, Your Majesty.' The man stepped forward and proffered a tablet.

Karim took it, reading swiftly. The news piece was carefully worded, but it noted that if Karim's father hadn't been the Sheikh of Zad'aq Karim had no claim to the title of Prince. The implication being that without that the Assaran Royal Council wouldn't have considered him a contender for its throne.

Regret surfaced that today's pleasure should be blighted by an old scandal that he'd thought dead and buried. But then Karim squared his shoulders and concentrated on what needed to be done.

* * *

Safiyah read the headline and froze. When Karim dropped his arm from her waist, moving away with his secretary, Safiyah took the tablet from him with numb fingers.

She felt blank inside…except for a creeping chill where Karim's body warmth had been.

'Mama! Look out!'

Safiyah's head jerked up. The line of the kite was slipping and she tightened her grip on it. With an effort she conjured a smile for Tarek, even as her mind whirled at the news story and Karim's matter-of-fact response to it.

It couldn't be true. The very idea was preposterous.

'Here.' She passed Tarek the kite. 'You can have it, but you must stay here where I can see you.'

A glance revealed Karim and his secretary deep in discussion. Karim was showing none of the outrage she'd have expected if the story were false. Her husband looked stern but calm.

Her husband.

But who was he if he wasn't the son of the Sheikh of Za'daq?

It felt as if the ground beneath her feet had buckled.

Slowly she moved into the shade of one of the trees fringing the clearing. Intent on answers, yet excluded from the terse conversation going on metres away, she turned back to the article. Reaching the end, she went back to the beginning and read it again, astounded.

It was an outrageous allegation, and no definitive proof was provided, though there was mention of a medical technician willing to swear to it. The story claimed Karim's mother had been unfaithful to her husband before deserting him and that the old Sheikh had only learned Karim wasn't his just before his death.

The report insinuated that Karim had then been banished by his younger half-brother, Ashraf, who'd threat-

ened to proclaim the truth if he didn't renounce his claim
to the Za'daqi throne. Yet when Safiyah had seen Karim
and Ashraf together at the coronation they'd seemed on the
best of terms. And Karim had been full of smiles for his
sister-in-law, Tori.

'Seen enough?'

Karim stood before her, eyes narrowed to gleaming slits,
hands clenched at his sides, in a wide stance that was pure
male challenge. Out of the corner of her eye she saw the
secretary hurry back towards the palace. Tarek scampered
around, ignoring them all, watching the kite.

'Is it true?' Her voice sounded unfamiliar.

Karim's mouth tightened, his jaw jutting aggressively.
'Don't play games, Safiyah. You know it is.'

'How could I?' She frowned up at him. 'You're saying
this...' she gestured to the article '...isn't a hoax?'

Karim surveyed his wife, his annoyance giving way to
dawning disbelief. Her skin had paled as if she'd received
a shock. That, surely, wasn't something she could feign.

Gently he took the tablet and put it down.

'Karim? What's going on? Why would anyone print
such a story?'

He watched the throb of Safiyah's pulse in her throat.
Surely only a consummate actress could pretend to be so
stunned? Yet this *couldn't* be a surprise to her.

'You know it's the truth. You heard it five years ago.'

'Five years ago?' She frowned.

'When you came to meet me in the palace courtyard
that night.'

The night he'd been torn between lust and the determination to do no more than kiss her lest he take advantage
of an innocent under his roof.

She blinked, her eyes round. 'I didn't go to the courtyard. That was the evening we heard Rana was sick. Father

and I packed up and went home that same night. He left a formal apology and I wrote you a note.'

Karim's lips curled. 'A note that said only that you were sorry you'd had to leave so quickly. That something urgent had come up.' A brush-off, in fact.

Safiyah shook her head like someone surfacing from deep water. 'I thought I'd have a chance to explain the details later, in person.'

When he didn't respond, she switched back to the news story. 'You're saying your father wasn't the Sheikh of Za'daq? *Really?*'

Karim stared into those velvet-brown eyes he knew so well and felt the earth tilt off its axis.

She hadn't known. She really hadn't known.

All this time he'd believed Safiyah had snubbed him when she'd discovered the truth of his birth. For one golden illuminated second joy rose. She hadn't spurned him after all.

But she would now. Nothing surer. She'd be horrified at the scandal. And then there was the way he'd treated her. Believing she'd dumped him, he'd refused to take her calls, deleted her messages. And, more recently, he'd forced her into marriage.

Karim reeled as the truth sank in.

He'd thought she'd understood who she was marrying.

This news threatened both his crown and the relationship he and Safiyah were building. It could yank both from his grasp.

He looked at his wife and a wave of regret crashed through him.

Suddenly Karim knew fear. Bonedeep fear.

CHAPTER ELEVEN

'WHO WAS YOUR FATHER, then?' Safiyah could barely take it in.

Karim shrugged wide shoulders. 'I don't know.'

'Don't *know*?'

Karim wasn't a man to live with doubt.

'Presumably the man my mother ran off with.' His voice was bitter. 'Though that's pure assumption. Maybe she had several lovers.'

'You didn't ask her?' It didn't seem possible that he hadn't pressed to find out.

'She died of pneumonia when I was a child. There was no one else to ask.'

Except her lover—the man who might be his father.

What must it be like, not knowing who your parent was?

She frowned. It would be worse for Karim, since his mother hadn't been around for much of his childhood. The only parent he'd had was the irascible old Sheikh—a man she'd found daunting and her father had described as arrogant with a mean streak.

'I'm sorry, Karim.'

Another tiny lift of the shoulders but his expression didn't lighten. Instead his gaze drilled into her.

'Surely the rest isn't true? You and your brother seem to be good friends. He didn't really banish you?'

Karim snorted. 'That's nonsense. I decided to step

aside from the crown. I actually had to persuade Ashraf to take it.'

'So,' she said slowly, 'it was your decision to leave Za'daq?'

He nodded. 'The last thing my brother needs is me hanging around. He's a good man—a fine leader. But there are conservative elements in Za'daq who'd prefer me to be on the throne because I'm the elder.' He laughed, but the sound was devoid of amusement. 'Though they won't feel that way now the truth is out.'

Safiyah disagreed. From what she could tell, most of the support for Karim had been because, while supporting his father, he'd proved himself an able statesman, fair and honest. He'd worked hard and achieved respect. The truth of his birth would be a shock, but it didn't change his record.

Safiyah wrapped her arms around her middle, torn between sympathy for Karim and hurt that he hadn't trusted her enough to tell her this before. But why would he? They didn't have that kind of relationship. Their closeness was only in bed.

She looked up to find his gaze fixed on her so intently she almost felt it scrape past her flesh to her innermost self. She looked away. That was nonsense—a product of sexual intimacy. But more and more she found herself stunned by how *close* she felt to Karim. As if with a little effort all those romantic dreams she'd once held could come true.

Except when reality intervened, reminding her they didn't have that sort of relationship.

'You thought I knew all this?'

Karim's expression was hard to read, yet she could have sworn he looked uncomfortable.

'That evening we were supposed to meet…'

He paused, giving her time to recall her excitement and trepidation at the plan to meet him alone. She'd been so in love, so sure of his affection—though he'd never come right out and said the words—that she'd been persuaded to break every rule.

She'd thought the night would end in his bed. Instead it had ended with her romantic daydreams smashed.

'Yes?'

'I was waiting for you when Ashraf arrived instead. He had the results of some medical tests. We'd been looking for bone marrow donors to extend the Sheikh's life.' Karim's mouth twisted. 'The old man had always believed Ashraf wasn't his son, but Ashraf was tested anyway—out of sheer bravado, I think. One test led to another and the results proved just the opposite. I was the illegitimate one—not Ashraf.'

Safiyah wondered how she'd been so blithely unaware of the undercurrents at the Za'daqi court. But then she'd been lost in the romance of first love—only love.

'I still don't see how—'

'Later I discovered you and your father had disappeared in the night with an excuse about a family problem. I assumed you'd overheard our conversation since it took place where we were supposed to meet.' His chin lifted as if challenging her to deny it.

Reading the pride in that harshly beautiful face, Safiyah guessed what a blow the news of his birth had been to a man raised as a royal, with every expectation of inheriting a throne. She breathed deep, imagining what it was like to have your world turned on its head.

She didn't have to imagine too hard. She'd had her life snatched off course not once but twice, her own hopes and goals destroyed when she'd been forced into marriages she didn't want.

'I see,' she said, when she finally found her voice. 'You thought I hid in the shadows and eavesdropped.' Safiyah felt something heavy in her chest—pressure building behind her ribs and rising up towards her throat. 'Then persuaded my father to make up some excuse to leave? As if he wasn't a man who prided himself on his honesty?'

She'd hated the subsequent marriage her father had pushed her into but he'd done it for what he'd believed to be good reasons. He'd been a proud, decent man.

'As if *I*...'

The stifling sensation intensified, threatening to choke her breathing. She forced herself to continue, her chin hiking higher so she could fix Karim with a laser stare.

'You thought I abandoned you when I discovered you weren't going to be Sheikh. That all I cared about was marrying a king? That I didn't have the decency to meet you and tell you to your face?'

Safiyah choked on a tangle of emotions. Disappointment, pain, distress. How could he have believed it of her? He knew nothing about her at all! She'd been in love, willing to risk everything for a night alone with him, and he'd believed *that* of her.

She swung away, fighting for breath. Through a haze she saw Tarek, running in circles, trailing his precious kite.

'You have to admit the timing fitted,' said Karim.

Yes, the timing fitted. Drearily, Safiyah thought of how fate had yanked happiness away from her. But Karim hadn't loved her. If he had, he'd have at least stopped to question his awful assumptions.

She turned to him, seeing not the man she'd once adored, nor the passionate lover who'd introduced her to a world of pleasure. Instead she viewed the man who'd thought the worst of her—and her family. Who'd refused to give them the benefit of the doubt, treated them with contempt.

No wonder he hadn't returned any of the increasingly desperate messages she'd left all those years ago. He'd excised her from his life with ruthless precision.

The choking sensation evaporated and Safiyah dragged in lungsful of clean sea air. They felt like the first full breaths she'd taken in years. For too long she'd lived with regret over the past. She'd hidden it away, pretended the pain wasn't there while she tried to make the best of life. Now, like glass shattering, regret fell away. With clear eyes she faced the man who'd overshadowed her emotions for too long.

'Yes, it was a coincidence. But, believe it or not, the world doesn't revolve solely around you and the Za'daqi royal family.'

'Safiyah, I—'

She raised her hand and, remarkably, he stopped. It was as if he sensed the change in her. The tide not of regret and hurt, but of cold, cleansing disdain. For the first time she could remember Safiyah looked at Karim and felt no yearning, felt nothing except profound disappointment.

'The night you heard you were illegitimate my father and I discovered Rana needed us.' A quiver of ancient emotion coursed through her, that dreadful fear that had stalked her too long. 'She'd tried to kill herself.'

'Safiyah!'

Karim stepped closer, as if to put his arms around her, but she moved back and he halted. Deep grooves bracketed his mouth and furrowed his brow and Safiyah read genuine concern.

'I had no idea.'

'No—because you never gave me a chance to explain.'

He recoiled as if slapped, his face leached of colour. Strange that Safiyah felt no satisfaction.

'Tell me?' he said eventually.

'Rana was living in the city, studying to become a vet. But university life didn't suit her, and she found the city challenging after being brought up in the country. Plus, although we didn't know at the time, she was being stalked by another student. There had been harassment and she felt isolated, afraid to go out. She became anxious and depressed. I knew something wasn't right, but on the phone she sounded…' Safiyah swallowed. 'She overdosed on tablets.'

'I'm sorry, Safiyah. Truly sorry.'

Karim's face was sombre, and she knew he wasn't just referring to her sister, but to all his assumptions about Safiyah's character and actions.

It was easier to focus on Rana. She didn't want to talk about herself. 'I think the shock hastened my father's death. He went downhill fast after that.'

The speed of his illness and his desperation to see at least one of his daughters settled had broken down her resistance to marrying Abbas.

'My husband arranged for Rana to have excellent support. She's doing well now. She enjoys working on a horse stud and she's even talking about doing part-time study.'

Karim was reeling. His feet were planted on the ground but he felt as stable as Tarek's kite, swooping too low towards a bush. All this time…

What must it have been like for Safiyah, watching her father die, worrying about her sister and facing the blank wall he'd erected to prevent any contact between them?

He swallowed hard and it felt as if rusty nails lined his throat. He'd failed her when she'd most needed him.

He winced, remembering how she'd said her husband had arranged support for Rana. Her husband Abbas. Karim had felt jealous of Abbas, and at the same time triumphant that Safiyah's passionate nature hadn't been awoken till he, Karim, married her. But there was more to being a husband than orgasms. Whatever his faults, Abbas had been there for her. She still thought of him as her husband.

How did she think of him?

As the man who'd shunned her? The man who'd blackmailed her into a marriage she didn't want?

He could argue that he was protecting her son, but should her body and her life be forfeit because of that?

Karim considered himself honourable.

Today he realised how far short he fell of that ideal.

'What now?'

Karim dragged his gaze back to Safiyah. Suddenly she looked so small. Minutes ago, as she'd sparked with indignation, she hadn't seemed so diminutive. Now her arms were wrapped tight around her slender body as if she were holding out the world. Or holding in hurt.

Guilt scored pain through his belly.

Most of the time her presence, her vitality, made Safiyah seem larger than life. Now he saw her vulnerability, her hurt. He wanted to protect her, to haul her close and repeat his apology till she forgave him and looked at him again with stars in her eyes.

Fat chance of that.

She hated him.

He'd abused her trust and, because he'd grown up in a world where distrust and double-dealing were the norm, he'd believed the worst of her.

Yet, despite his mistakes, the idea of letting her go was impossible.

'Karim? What are you going to do now the story is out?'

He raised his eyebrows. Did she think he might cower here?

'Go back to the capital. Consult with the Council. Write a press release, then get on with the job of ruling.'

Except it might not be his job for long. Now that he was Sheikh the Council couldn't oust him. Yet Karim didn't want to rule a country that didn't want him. That bitter truth, like the knowledge of how he'd failed Safiyah in the past, curdled his gut. He'd offer the Council his abdication if that were the case.

When he'd been offered the role of Sheikh he'd been

assured it was because of his character and his record as a statesman, not his supposedly royal lineage. What if it wasn't true? What if the stain of his birth was too much for his new country to stomach?

Karim inhaled slowly, deliberately filling his lungs. He'd suffered the fallout of his illegitimacy once, with devastating effect. If he had to do it again, no matter. He had a full and interesting life to return to.

Except that was a lie. Even after a mere couple of weeks Karim knew that *this* was the life he craved. He thrived on the challenges and rewards of his new role. Including his newfound family. Would Safiyah stick with him if he left Assara? Could he ask it of her?

'You're not concerned about a swing of support away from you?'

Had she read his mind?

'To Shakroun, you mean?'

Karim guessed Shakroun was behind this press story. His rival hadn't had the numbers to mount a public challenge, but trying to tarnish Karim's reputation by backhand methods seemed like the man's style.

'Don't worry, Safiyah, whatever happens I'll protect you and Tarek from him.' Shakroun would get his hands on them only over Karim's dead body.

Safiyah surveyed him sombrely, her expression drawn and her eyes dark with shadows.

Reading that look, Karim felt a fist lodge in his ribs and his lungs heaved. 'What do *you* think about it?'

'I think you need to see the Council as soon as possible. Lobby key people and sound them out—'

'I meant what do you think about my birth? About the fact I wasn't really a prince of Za'daq?'

She'd thought him an aristocrat. In reality he was nothing of the sort. Karim swallowed and pain ground through him. His station in life would have an obvious impact on his wife. Pity he hadn't thought of that before.

Safiyah's features drew in on themselves. Her eyes narrowed, her skin tightened across her cheekbones and her generous mouth tucked in at the corners. Her nostrils flared in an expression of disdain.

'You do it so well, Karim. I have to wonder if it's a natural talent or whether you have to work at it.'

'At what?' Karim drew himself up, ready to fight however he must to hold on to what was his.

'At insulting me.'

The words smashed against him, making him blink.

'You didn't have a high opinion of me all those years ago and it seems nothing has changed.'

Safiyah pushed her shoulders back and lifted her chin, and abruptly she seemed to grow in stature. Less crumpled and disillusioned lover and more imperious queen. Despite the fire flashing in her glare, Karim felt relief eddy deep inside him. He preferred her fiery to defeated and hurt.

'It was a simple question. I have a right to know what you think.'

Her fine eyebrows arched. 'Do you, indeed? When the only reason I know the truth is because someone else broke the story? When *you* didn't trust me with it!' She prodded his chest with her hand then quickly withdrew, as if she couldn't even bear to touch him.

'I apologise. I thought you already knew.'

Safiyah sighed. 'What I think doesn't matter, does it? We're stuck with each other.' She lifted her hand to her forehead as if trying to rub away an ache.

'Safiyah…' He stepped closer. He had to know.

For years he hadn't cared what others might think if they knew the truth of his birth. But he cared what Safiyah thought. More than he'd believed possible.

Her hand dropped and her eyes flashed. 'Yes, it's a surprise, but I don't care if your father was a sheikh or a vagrant. What I care about is whether I can trust the man I married. Right now I have my doubts.'

She spun away and gathered up Tarek. Her actions were decisive and distancing. They made Karim feel the way he had as a kid, when he'd tried and failed to please the Sheikh, who had expected nothing short of perfection.

Karim set his jaw. He mightn't be perfect. He might be as flawed as the next man. But he'd be damned if he'd allow anyone to wrench away what was his.

And that included his wife and child.

CHAPTER TWELVE

'IT'S ALMOST TIME, Your Majesty. Just a few minutes.' The technician nodded encouragingly, as if Karim were a stranger to microphones and cameras.

Karim glanced at the notes before him on the vast desk and pushed them aside, ignoring a stifled protest from one of his secretaries. He preferred to speak direct to the camera since the broadcast would be live to the people of Assara. He had no need of prompts.

What he needed, or at least wanted, was to know where Safiyah was. Since they'd returned to the capital he'd barely seen her. Every time he went to talk to her she was missing. 'Out', the staff said.

Because she couldn't bear to be with him?

The idea fed the hollow sensation inside him. His wife found him wanting not due to his birth, but because of the way he'd treated her.

To a man who prided himself on doing the right thing, the knowledge ate like acid, eviscerating him.

The door opened to whispered urgent voices. Then he caught a flash of red and a high, childish voice. He pushed back his chair and stood. 'Let them in.' It was Safiyah—and Tarek too.

Karim's heart hammered his ribs, climbing to his throat as he took her in. She sailed towards him, ignoring the minders who would have kept her out. She looked magnificent and beautiful in a dress of glowing crimson. Her hair was piled high and she wore no jewellery apart from her ruby and diamond wedding ring and matching earrings that swayed against her neck as she walked, emphasising the purity of her slender throat.

Their gazes meshed. She was here for him. To offer her support despite the chasm between them.

Karim's chest tightened, filled with a swelling bundle of sensations. He swallowed roughly.

His wife. His Queen.

She was regal, and stunning—and, he realised, the only woman ever to have power over him.

Just watching her approach battered him with competing emotions. Desire, pride and fear that he'd irrevocably destroyed any softer feelings she might once have harboured. For those eyes locked on him were coolly guarded, giving nothing away.

He'd given up pretending that it didn't matter. The news that he'd been wrong about her all this time had stripped all pretence away. He wanted his wife in every way. Not just her sexy body but her admiration, her kindness and her gentle humour.

Beside her marched Tarek, wearing fine clothes and a slight frown, as if he were concentrating hard. Karim felt a pang at the sight of him, remembering how it had felt as a young child, trying to be the perfect little Prince everyone expected.

'Safiyah.'

Karim started forward. But instead of taking his outstretched hand she sank into a curtsey, clearly for the benefit of their audience. Beside her Tarek bowed—a deep, formal, courtly bow.

Karim saw the Councillors on the other side of the room note the gestures of respect and nod to each other, as if approving this confirmation of the Sheikha's loyalty.

When she straightened Karim took her hand and pulled her to him, Tarek too. 'Where have you been?' His tone was sharper than he'd intended, but he'd felt stymied, not being able to find her.

Safiyah's eyes flashed, but she said evenly, 'In the city.' As if that explained everything.

The technician approached, hovering uncertainly. Safiyah nodded to the man and smiled, then turned to Karim. Her voice was low, for his ears alone. 'I thought it might help if we were beside you, Tarek and me, when you do your broadcast.'

'As a show of solidarity?' Karim felt his eyebrows rise. It wasn't a bad idea, politically speaking. Beyond her he saw senior government ministers, nodding in approval at the family group they made.

Before she could answer he shook his head. 'I appreciate your support, Safiyah, and yours too, Tarek.' He smiled at the boy, who was looking far too solemn, and ruffled his hair. The kid relaxed a little then and smiled back, leaning towards his mother. 'But this is something I need to do alone. I won't have anyone accuse me of hiding behind my wife's skirts, beautiful as they are.'

Safiyah stared up into stunning eyes and felt a flurry of emotion ripple through her. She saw pride there, and determination.

He took her hand, raised it slowly and kissed it.

Safiyah's knees almost buckled.

This was the man she'd fallen in love with all those years ago. The man she'd given her heart to. Who, if he only knew, still held that floundering organ in his keeping.

Fear settled in her bones. For though he smiled there was no softness in his expression. He was focused beyond her, on the challenge ahead. On the sheikhdom.

That was what mattered to Karim.

She, as a convenient wife, came a poor second.

Nothing had changed.

Except she'd discovered, faced with this crisis, that she *did* care for him. Had never given up caring. It was a burden she must learn to bear. A secret she'd have to live with.

She moved closer, leaning up to whisper in his ear. 'You haven't changed your mind, have you? You're not going to abdicate?'

'No.' He paused, then added, 'I want this too much to throw in the towel. But, no matter what happens, believe that I'll keep you and Tarek safe.'

She believed him. He would keep his word.

Karim looked past her, then to the technician. 'You and Tarek had better take a seat over there.' He gestured to some chairs clustered on the far side of the room.

And so it came to be that Safiyah was there for Karim's momentous broadcast. She ignored the questioning glances of politicians unused to having a woman present when government matters were being discussed. She hung on every word, and as she did so her respect for Karim grew.

His readiness to misjudge her in the past still rankled, but with time to cool down she'd acknowledged that the stress he had been under must have contributed to his actions.

Now, hearing him talk with simple honesty about his birth and his vision for Assara, Safiyah felt again a once familiar respect and pride.

He acknowledged the truth of the story about his heritage, and said that he'd told the Royal Council he would abdicate if the circumstances of his birth were considered an insurmountable problem. He also took time to sketch his plans for the nation if he were to stay as Sheikh, and ended by promising a final announcement in the near future.

When the broadcast ended Karim looked around the silent room at the powerful men, regarding him solemnly.

It was clear they hadn't yet made a decision on whether to support their new Sheikh. Thinking of the alternative, of Shakroun taking the throne, Safiyah shivered. How could they even consider letting that man into the palace?

Holding Tarek's hand, she made for the door, leaving Karim to deal with the politicians. She had her own priorities. Women might not have an overt role in Assaran politics, but that didn't mean they didn't have their own networks, or that they didn't have any influence at all. Safiyah had already been busy accessing those networks on Karim's behalf.

He was the best man for the position. More, he was the man she loved.

She would stand by him no matter what.

In the days after the public broadcast Karim followed his schedule of regional visits just as if there wasn't an axe poised to fall on his neck if the Council decided his illegitimacy overrode his merits.

Another man—Shakroun, for instance—would have clung to his position, since constitutionally the Sheikh, once crowned, had absolute power. Karim wasn't that sort of man. Call it humility, or perhaps excessive pride, but he needed his new country to *want* him.

Meanwhile he got on with the job he was there to do. Listening to the people, solving problems and planning new directions. And at his side, day and evening, was Safiyah.

She was a revelation. He'd seen her performing her part at the wedding celebrations, and the way she'd stood up for him on the day of his broadcast had filled him with pride and gratitude. But his wife was far more than a beautiful face to adorn a royal event.

Safiyah charmed both the public and VIPs alike, her manner almost unobtrusive but incredibly effective at helping people relax in the royal presence. Time and again

Karim found her leading people forward so their concerns could be heard or their achievements noted. Nor did he miss the way she drew apart from the official entourage on site visits to listen to knots of women who gathered on the fringes of the VIP parties.

Had she supported Abbas in this way?

Karim's mind slewed away from the thought. She was *his* now, through thick and thin. He had no intention of letting her go.

Since returning to the palace he'd slept alone—partly because of the crazy hours he worked, but mainly because of the hurt in her eyes when she'd discovered how he'd mistrusted her. The bitterness in her voice as she'd recommended they keep their distance.

Tonight, surely, they could put all that behind them.

He grinned and knocked on her door, anticipation humming in his veins.

'Karim!' Her velvet eyes widened in surprise and he vowed that tonight he'd smash through the barriers that separated them.

'Aren't you going to let me in?'

She clutched her pale blue robe closed with one hand as she pulled the door wider. He stepped in and watched as she took her time closing the door. Her robe was plain, but on her it looked incredible. Karim devoured the sight of those bounteous curves, the spill of lustrous dark hair. Arousal stirred, thickening his veins and drawing his body tight.

She turned towards him, automatically raising her chin.

Safiyah might be soft and feminine but she was no pushover. He liked that, he realised.

'You've had news? From the Council?'

'Just now. The vote was unanimous. They want me to stay.'

For a second she shut her eyes and he saw a shudder run

through her. It was a reminder that it wasn't just Karim whose future had hung in the balance. Safiyah's had—and Tarek's.

'It's all over now,' he reassured her. 'I'll make a public announcement in the morning.'

She nodded and he watched her swallow convulsively. She'd hidden her fear well but clearly she'd been worried.

Karim smiled. 'I have to thank you, Safiyah. Not every woman would have stood by me the way you have. And you've done more than that. I appreciate the way you've worked to help me, both in public and behind the scenes.'

Her eyebrows lifted. Had she thought he hadn't been aware of her networking on his behalf? His staff had informed him of much he hadn't seen personally. It was one of the reasons he knew he could bridge the gap between himself and his wife.

He moved closer, but then she spoke. 'What choice did I have? You're my husband. My son's fate rests with you.'

It wasn't the words alone that stopped him. It was her tone—flat and bitter. As if she regretted being married to him. As if she had no personal interest in his fate.

For a second, and he didn't know why, he thought of his mother. Had she been bitter about marrying the man her family had approved for her? Had she wished from the beginning that she could escape?

But Safiyah wasn't like his mother, running away and leaving her children. Safiyah had done everything she could for Tarek—even accepting a marriage she didn't want.

Karim's pulse dipped at the thought. Things would be better between them now. He'd make sure of it.

He watched her wrap her arms around her slender waist, her mouth a flat line. Her body sent an unmistakable message of rejection, but he persisted.

'I know I hurt you, Safiyah, and I'm sorry for it. But I also know there was more to your actions than necessity.'

There had to be. Once he'd taken for granted that she cared for him. Lately, learning that she'd never betrayed him as he'd believed, Karim had found himself yearning again for that devotion. Strange to realise how empty his world had felt without it. He'd told himself during those years in exile that he'd been like a rudderless ship, because he'd been cut off from the life he knew. Now he realised it was this woman he'd missed—Safiyah he'd wanted as his anchor.

Her arms tightened, pulling the fabric over luscious breasts. Karim felt a kick of masculine response in his belly.

'What more could there be?' Her eyes were dull with denial.

Karim rocked back on his feet. He'd thought it would be simple. He'd apologised for hurting her and now, with this news, they could start afresh.

But Safiyah wasn't ready to move on. His chest clogged. Pain circled his ribs. She hadn't forgiven him. The tenderness she'd once felt had drained away. She had just helped him because they were legally tied.

He felt a fool. He'd imagined she'd worked tirelessly on his behalf, *their* behalf, because she cared about him— about them. Now it turned out there was nothing personal about what she'd done.

Hurt vied with anger. And with a dawning sense of loss so vast it threatened to engulf him.

'Safiyah. Don't talk like that. You know you want—'

'There's nothing I want, Karim. Not now I know your position is secure and Tarek is safe.' She hefted a deep breath. 'I'll see you in the morning.'

As if he were a servant to be dismissed!

Karim's jaw clenched, his body stiffening.

And yet Safiyah's body betrayed her. Karim saw her

nipples peak against tight fabric, the out-of-control flutter of her pulse.

A hint of musky feminine arousal tantalised his nostrils. His body quivered in response.

She might be trying to hurry him out through the door, but still she wanted him. He lifted his hand to stroke one finger down her cheek. Her eyelids fluttered, then she jerked her face away, staring back with dislike.

Yet she couldn't disguise the glow of amber heat in her eyes—a sure sign, he'd learned, of sexual arousal.

Heat punched his belly. Triumph surged. Safiyah might not want to want him, but in this at least they were still partners, each caught in the same tangle of desire.

'Don't lie, *wife*. You want me.' A heartbeat pounded through him, a second, a third. Her expression gave the confirmation he needed. 'And I'll happily take what's on offer.'

Even if his soul craved far more.

He wrapped his fingers around the back of her skull and stepped in close, lowering his mouth to hers with a slow deliberation that, since it gave her time to pull away, proved his point.

She was his, and she wanted to be his, at least in this.

Wife, he'd snarled at her, reminding her that she was his possession. His words held no tenderness and anguish arced through her from where his fingers cradled her head down to the very soles of her feet.

She longed for so much more—which was why she'd cut him off abruptly when he'd pressed her, almost as if he knew her secret weakness.

When he'd *thanked* her for her help everything inside her had rebelled. She didn't want Karim's gratitude. She wanted so much more. She craved his love.

Which illustrated how mismatched they were. She

couldn't afford to let him know how she felt. He already had too much power in this relationship. She had to stand strong against him.

Except when his lips met hers shock jolted through her. His mouth wasn't harshly impatient. It coaxed gently...a slow brush that tempted then moved on to her cheek, her throat, then back to linger and tease. Strong teeth nipped at her lower lip and fire shafted to her nipples then drove low into her body. Her knees trembled and she found herself grasping his upper arms.

With a muffled sound of approval he wrapped those strong arms around her, enfolding her in searing heat. Hard muscle bound her, and despite her intention to resist Safiyah melted closer.

A sob rose in her throat that she should be so weak. But the pleasure Karim offered was too much, even though she knew it was purely physical. This sense of rare connection was illusory, the product of wishful thinking.

He deepened the kiss, drawing her up against him and delving into her mouth as if he couldn't get enough of the taste of her. As if his need matched hers.

This didn't feel heartless. It felt like everything she craved. And, with a sigh that shuddered right to her heart, Safiyah gave herself up to him.

When he swept her high in his arms she didn't protest. Instead she leaned against his chest, her hand pressed to the place where his heart pounded like a jackhammer.

When he laid her on the bed and stripped her, his eyes glittering like priceless gems from the royal treasury, Safiyah arched her body to help him peel off her clothes.

When he came to her, naked, proud and virile, she closed her eyes rather than search for tenderness in his gaze. She could pretend for this short time that the brush of his hands across her bare flesh was loving.

And when finally Karim stroked into her, deep and

strong, and she shattered convulsively, she steadfastly refused to think or yearn or hope. She took the pleasure he gave and told herself it was enough.

It had to be. For it was all he could give.

CHAPTER THIRTEEN

SAFIYAH OPENED THE window and leaned out, inhaling the fresh morning air, trying to dispel her anxiety.

She reminded herself of how much she had to be thankful for.

Tarek was safe. Not only that, but after only a few months living with Karim he was thriving. The nervous little boy who had expected only brusque orders from Abbas was learning to relax under his adoptive father's encouragement.

Rana was well and happy, actually excited at the prospect of studying again.

Meanwhile, Hassan Shakroun, the man she'd so feared, was on trial with a number of his associates for kidnap, bribing officials and conspiring to murder. Safiyah shuddered.

It truly had been a lucky day when Karim had agreed to take the sheikhdom. Everything was working out so well.

And yet…

Her heart beat high in her throat as she turned to look at the pregnancy test on the bathroom's marble counter. She didn't want to see the result.

The chances of a baby were slim. She'd begun taking contraception as soon as she'd realised theirs wasn't going to be a paper marriage. Yet since then Safiyah hadn't had a normal period. She'd ascribed that to stress, upsetting her cycle. Until yesterday, when she'd folded her arms and noticed her breasts were tender.

Safiyah bit her lip and breathed deep, chastising herself for her fear. Forcing herself closer, she picked up the stick and read the result.

Pregnant.

The indicator blurred before her eyes as her hand shook. She was having Karim's child.

Safiyah groped for the counter-top, grabbed it as she swayed.

She shook her head. Why was she shocked? Hadn't she known in her heart of hearts that there was a child? There'd been mornings where she hadn't been able to face breakfast, and that underlying sense that something was different.

She opened her eyes and stared into the mirror, taking in the too pale features of the woman peering back.

The fact was she'd made herself pretend pregnancy wasn't possible even though she knew no contraceptive was foolproof. Even though she and Karim had a highly charged sex-life. He spent every night with her, and she couldn't remember a night when one or the other hadn't instituted sex.

Her mouth twisted grimly. At least she had the terminology right. It wasn't making love as far as Karim was concerned. It was just sex. Convenient, explosive and satisfying. And she was so weak, so needy when it came to Karim, that far from repulsing him she was greedy for his touch.

Her hand smoothed over her flat belly.

There was nothing convenient about this child. Yet, despite the circumstances, she wanted this baby. Warmth spread through her as she contemplated this new, precious life. She'd do everything in her power to protect and nurture it. No doubt Karim, too, already so good with his adopted son, would love his own child to bits.

Her fears weren't for the baby, who would grow up cared for by both parents. Her concern was for herself.

She sucked in a breath that was half a sob.

Bringing another child into this world, even knowing it would be loved and cared for, revealed the stark contrast with her own situation. Unloved. Unwanted except as a convenience. As a means of propping up Karim's claim to the throne and to breed him heirs.

Pain sheared through her as the ugly truth hit her full force.

She was pregnant *again* by a man who didn't love her. Who'd *never* love her.

Her place in his life was cemented fast—sex object, for as long as his passion lasted, royal hostess and brood mare.

And what would she do about it? What *could* she do? *Demand* he love her?

A bitter laugh escaped, scoring her throat as if with gravel shards. That would only reveal her feelings for him, when the one thing she had left was her pride. She intended to salvage that, at least.

There was no question of her deserting him. She had Tarek to consider, and this new child. She *had* to stay for their sakes.

She drew a slow, fortifying breath, feeling the accustomed weight of responsibility and duty cloak her shoulders. This time it seemed harder than ever to push those shoulders back and stand tall.

It didn't matter that she'd once had romantic dreams, or that she still yearned with all her secret inner self for Karim's love. She had his respect and his gratitude. For the moment she had his passion too.

Time to do what she'd had so much practice at doing— bundle up unwanted yearnings and bury them deep, in a dark recess where they'd no longer tease her.

'Safiyah?'

She spun round. Karim filled the doorway with his broad shoulders and loose-hipped stance. Instantly her insides plunged. The sight of him reinforced her fatal weakness.

Who was she kidding? It wasn't just duty that kept her in this marriage. She didn't have the strength to walk away from the man she loved.

'What is it?' He crossed the room in a couple of strides, grabbing her hands in his. 'You look pale as milk.'

'I'm fine.' Practice allowed her to stiffen her drooping spine. 'What are you doing here?'

He frowned down at her, clearly not convinced by her words. 'I knew you'd planned to ride this morning and I rearranged a meeting so I could ride with you. But you didn't show.'

Bittersweet regret filled her. She'd have enjoyed riding with him. Enjoyed even more the fact that he'd changed his diary to make time for her.

Because you'll take any crumbs you can get from him and be grateful, won't you?

The snarky inner voice hit low and hard, making her press a hand to her churning belly.

Karim looked down. 'What's that?'

Safiyah fought the impulse to whip her hand behind her back. She'd barely had time to take in the test result herself. But what was the point? Karim had to know at some point.

Silently she lifted her hand so he could read the result.

'Pregnant?'

His voice was stretched out of all recognition.

Pregnant!

Karim's head jerked back as emotion punched him. So much emotion. A jumble of feelings such as he'd never known. Pride. Excitement. Tenderness. Fear.

'You're having our child?' His voice wasn't his own.

He'd wondered about the possibility, then set the idea

aside. But now… Safiyah carried his flesh and blood inside her.

Karim dragged in a rough breath, trying and failing to fill his lungs. He didn't know how he felt about passing on genes from his unknown father to another generation. About creating a new life. Far better to concentrate on Safiyah.

'Are you sick?' His hold tightened on her wrists. She looked pale. No, not just pale. Drawn. 'Come on. You need to sit down and rest.'

His heart pounded at double speed as he watched her draw a slow breath. But instead of assenting she drew back, pulling out of his hold, putting her hands behind her as if afraid he'd touch her again.

Karim's stomach dropped. The way she stood there—shoulders back, eyes focussed on a point near his ear—returned him to the early days of their marriage. To a time when Safiyah had been unhappy.

Karim had begun to hope they'd got past that. She'd seemed more content, more at ease with him since the crisis when his illegitimacy had been broadcast. Increasingly he'd basked in Safiyah's gentle smiles, revelled in her ease with him—not just in bed, but at other times. He'd told himself the marriage was working.

He was taking things slowly, not pushing, content to let her set the pace, knowing that after his earlier mistakes he needed to move cautiously in building their relationship. Even if he chafed for more.

He didn't expect miracles, and knew he had a lot to make up for, but surely he hadn't been mistaken? He *knew* she enjoyed being with him. Surely her tenderness hadn't been a lie.

'Safiyah?'

The sound of her name seemed to jerk her out of her thoughts and she turned away, preceding him silently from the bathroom. She didn't stop in their bedroom but kept going to the sitting room, choosing an armchair rather than sitting on the comfortable sofa.

Karim told himself not to read too much into that, even though he wanted to hold her close. He poured a glass of sparkling water and handed it to her, noting that her fingers felt cool to the touch.

Shock?

'You don't seem happy about the news.'

Whereas he, after that initial blast of surprise, felt a glow of satisfaction he had to work hard to contain. Safiyah... pregnant with their child. His whole body seemed to throb with a new vibrancy at the prospect. Even those lingering doubts about his ability to be a decent father were scattered in the face of triumphant excitement.

He watched her swallow a sip of water and then turn to put the glass down, her movements slow and deliberate as if she feared she'd drop it.

He tried again. 'I know we didn't discuss another child, but—'

'It's all right, Karim.'

Her eyes lifted to his and he was stunned to read the blankness there. A terrible nothingness that settled like a shroud over his excitement, instantly suffocating his burgeoning joy.

'I know my duty. That's why you married me, after all. I knew you'd want a child. I just hadn't expected it so soon.'

'Safiyah...?' His flesh prickled at the eerie coolness of her voice. Where was the passionate woman he knew? The caring mother, the warm-hearted Queen, the seductive red-blooded wife? 'Do you mean you don't want our child?'

Karim heard the unsteadiness in his voice and didn't care. He felt as if an unseen fist had lodged in his gut. Hunkering before her, he took her hand.

She blinked and shook her head. 'Of course I want it.'

But she sounded choked, her voice husky as if she fought back tears. 'I just...'

Safiyah looked away.

Karim had had enough of barriers and distance. He lifted his other hand to her chin, turning her to face him.

'Tell me.' His voice was soft but commanding.

For a second her eyes glowed bright, then she looked down. 'I just need time, Karim. Bringing a child into a marriage like ours...' She shrugged and looked up again, her mouth twisting wryly. 'Ignore me. It's just pregnancy hormones.'

'No.' He leaned closer, into her space, sensing for the first time that they teetered on the brink of the indefinable problem that still lingered between them. 'What were you going to say?'

Safiyah's lips thinned as if she was holding back the words by physical force, but eventually they slipped out. 'It's what women do in arranged marriages—breed heirs. It's just that sometimes it feels...lacking.'

Lacking! Karim sank back on his heels, his heart racing and a dreadful queasy sensation rolling through his gut. His hand tightened on hers, as if to reinforce their connection. His other hand cupped her cheek, his thumb brushing across her mouth till it lost its prim flatness and softened against the pad of his finger. He felt the warm humidity of her breath against his flesh and awareness rippled all the way up his arm to his shoulders and neck.

Yet his stomach hollowed. He felt gutted, and a dreadful tight ache seared through his belly as her words penetrated.

He'd felt bereft the night he'd learned of his parentage. But this was worse. This was Safiyah—*his* Safiyah—saying that what they had wasn't enough.

The edges of his vision blackened. This time it was Safiyah who grabbed his hand, steadying him. So much for his careful plan to give her time to grow accustomed to them as a couple.

'Don't talk like that!'

'Why not? It's the truth.' She breathed deeply, as if marshalling her thoughts. 'You're a good man, Karim. A fine ruler. And you've been wonderful with Tarek. Better than I dared hope for. Don't worry. I'll accustom myself in time.'

Accustom herself! As if it were a state of affairs she couldn't avoid. A royal obligation.

Which it was.

Safiyah had married him for Tarek's sake and to save her nation. She'd married dutifully and at first that had suited Karim completely.

But not now.

Karim exploded to his feet on a surge of restive energy. He marched the length of the room, spun on his heel and marched back.

Initially he'd told himself that Safiyah deserved no better. Then, later, when he'd understood the truth about her, he'd believed that if he worked hard enough he could make her care for him again as she once had, despite his mistakes. Yet it was only now, as he looked into her wan face and set features, that the full realisation of her sacrifice slammed into him.

Karim couldn't bear that she saw what they had as a necessity rather than a gift. Not when to him it was so much more.

He skidded to his knees before her, gathering her hands and drawing them against his thudding heart. He couldn't simply ignore her words about an arranged marriage, let them hang as if they meant nothing. Even if the alternative meant risking everything.

It would be the biggest gamble of his life, but he refused to imagine failing. Besides, he'd only held back because he hadn't wanted to put pressure on her.

'Our marriage is much more than that, Safiyah.'

She nodded, firming her mouth. Yet still she didn't meet his gaze. 'Yes, it's for the best. For Tarek and—'

'Much as I care for Tarek,' he murmured, 'this isn't about him. Or even about the little one you're carrying now.'

Karim felt a fillip of excitement, just speaking of their unborn baby, yet he couldn't allow himself to be distracted.

'Yes, there's also Assara. You're doing a wonderful job—'

'Not Assara, either.'

At his words her head jerked up, wide eyes catching his. How often he'd watched those velvety eyes haze with delight as he took her to rapture. How often he'd watched them dance with pleasure as they rode, or when they played with Tarek.

Karim turned her hands, pressing her palms to his chest where his heart thundered, letting her feel how she affected him.

'I want this marriage, Safiyah. I want *you*. I always have. Even when I pretended I didn't.'

Now the moment of truth was here Karim found it easier than he'd believed possible. He'd been taught to avoid discussing emotions, as if the mere mention of them would weaken his masculinity. What a crock that was. He'd never felt stronger or more determined.

Clamping her palms with one hand, he lifted the other to her face, feeling the dewy softness of her delicate flesh. 'I love you, Safiyah. I love you with every fibre of my being, with every thought and every breath I take.'

He paused and hefted air into his overworked lungs, watching emotions flicker across her features.

'Don't! Please don't!'

Safiyah tried to free her hands but he held them fast. She looked up at him with over-bright eyes. 'I'd rather you were honest with me than have you say what you think I want to hear.'

Her mouth crumpled, and with it something inside Karim's chest. He couldn't bear to see her hurting so.

It took a moment only for him to slide his arms around her and lift her high against his chest as he rose to his feet. From this angle he could see the wild throb of her pulse in her throat and her convulsive swallow.

Because he'd hurt her. Not just today but over years.

'I *am* being honest, Safiyah. For the first time ever I'm sharing how I really feel.' He paused, willing her to believe him. 'I don't know if I can ever make up for the mess I've made of things. When I believed the worst of you. When I never even followed up to make sure you were okay all those years ago.'

He strode to the long sofa and sank there, cradling her on his lap. It felt right, holding her like this, soft and warm in his arms. He never wanted to let her go. Surely it was a good sign that she didn't struggle to get away?

'I was hurting so much, Safiyah, because I loved you even though I hadn't admitted it to myself. But that's no excuse. You needed me and I turned my back on you.'

His voice cracked as he thought of her, scared for her sister, grieving for her father, faced with the prospect of marrying a stranger.

Dark eyes locked on his as she tipped her head back, and for once Karim didn't try to mask his feelings as he'd been trained to. His love for her swelled and filled him till he thought he might burst.

'Karim…?'

Her eyes, pansy-dark yet flecked with amber, held his so intently he felt raw inside, with everything he felt, every secret, laid bare. It was like facing his conscience.

'It's true, my love.'

He lifted her palm and pressed his mouth to it, scattering fervent kisses there. But not for long. This had to be said.

He held her wondering eyes. 'I was a proud, arrogant prince, used to attracting women, used to people pandering to my whims. I saw that you cared for me and I took that as my due, never bothering to question my own feelings. If I had I'd have realised that what I felt for you was unique. I'd never cared for any other woman the way I cared for you, Safiyah. After you'd gone I felt like I'd been torn in two, but I blamed that on my changed circumstances.'

He shook his head, amazed at his obtuseness.

'I couldn't bear to think of you—especially when I heard you were to marry Abbas. Because it hurt too much. I pretended it was fury I felt, hurt pride that you'd duped me into believing you cared.'

'I *did* care, Karim.'

Her hand curled around his, the first tiny positive sign from her. It made his heart contract. She'd cared for him once. But now…?

'When you came to me in Switzerland I behaved like a spoiled brat, trying to hurt you.'

'You succeeded.' Her mouth twisted, but her voice was stronger and her eyes shone. Hope rose.

'I've been so blind, my love.' He shook his head. 'So slow to realise *you* were the reason I came to Assara. Not because I wanted the crown but because I wanted to be with you. Become your husband.'

His words ran out and Karim was left listening to the sound of his heart throbbing out a frenetic pulse, looking for some sign he wasn't alone in this.

'You came here because of *me*?'

He nodded. The words had poured out of him—a torrent smashed free from a dam wall. Now he was spent. The rest was up to her. Would she believe him?

'Because you loved me?'

'*Love.* I love you.'

As Karim watched, her eyes filled with tears that spilled down pale cheeks.

'Ah, *habibti.* Please don't. I can't bear to see you so sad.'

He wiped her tears with his thumb but they kept falling. The sight broke him. Was it possible he'd destroyed all the feelings she'd once had for him?

A soft hand cupped his jaw. 'Silly man. I'm crying because I'm happy.'

'Happy?' Karim stared into her lovely face and saw that crooked mouth curve up in a smile that made his heart lift.

'Yes, happy.' Her smile widened. 'You really do have a lot to learn about women.'

Karim didn't argue. He was the first to admit his previous experience had been limited to casual encounters. Nothing that compared to this.

'Tell me,' he demanded, capturing her hand and kissing it.

'That I'm happy?'

Mischief danced in Safiyah's eyes, and for the first time the band constricting Karim's chest eased. He grazed his teeth along the fleshy part of her palm and she jumped, then leaned closer.

Her expression grew serious. 'I loved you all those years ago, Karim, and I never stopped.'

She swallowed hard and he felt the shadow of her pain.

'And now?' He didn't deserve her love, but he needed it. He'd never needed anything more. 'I can live without a crown, Safiyah. Without courtiers and honours. But I can't live without you.'

'Hush.' Her fingers pressed his lips. 'You don't need to. We have each other now.' She leaned close, wrapping her arms around his neck. 'I love you. Always have and always will.'

Karim opened his mouth to reply. To say something

meaningful and memorable. But for the first time ever words failed him. He drew his beloved wife up into his arms and kissed her with a tender ardour that told her better than words how he felt.

He vowed he'd show her every day of their lives together exactly how much she meant to him.

EPILOGUE

SAFIYAH STEPPED INTO the room and pulled up abruptly, seeing Karim alone by the window. It had been a risk, arranging this meeting, but one she'd believed worth taking.

Karim was a changed man—happy and positive and oh-so-loving, unafraid to express his emotions. Especially since their daughter Amira's birth. He doted on their little girl, while his relationship with Tarek grew stronger by the day. And with Safiyah he was everything she'd ever longed for.

But she knew the past cast long shadows. She couldn't change Karim's loveless childhood, but she hoped at least to ease the pain of his not knowing his parents. Which was why she'd tracked down the man Karim's mother had run away to. The man who might be Karim's father.

Seeing her husband's preternatural stillness, the air of barely contained energy vibrating from those broad shoulders, she guessed the meeting hadn't gone well.

Her hopes nosedived.

'You're alone?'

He swung to face her and her heart rocked against her ribcage when she read his expression. In a rush she closed in on him, wrapping her arms tight around his powerful frame.

'I'm sorry, Karim. I thought—'

'I know what you thought, *habibti*.' His mouth crooked

up at one corner in a tight smile. 'That it was time I made peace with the man who might be my father. And you were right.'

He gathered her in, then turned to look out the window. There, just emerging from the palace, was a rangy figure, shoulders straight and gait familiar. He paused, as if sensing their regard, and looked over his shoulder. Karim inclined his head and the man reciprocated, then walked away.

'Yet he's leaving?'

Was it crazy to have hoped the two might begin to build a tenuous relationship?

'No, just stretching his legs. We both need a little time to process things. He's accepted my offer to stay in the palace for a visit. To meet the family.'

No mistaking the pride in Karim's voice.

'He has?' Safiyah stared up at her husband, stunned.

His half-smile broadened into a grin that made her heart flutter. 'What you mean is you're stunned I invited him to stay. But then he *is* my father.'

'Oh, I *knew* it! You have the same walk…and the angle of your jaw…' She paused, searching his face. 'And you're all right with that?'

Karim raked a hand through his hair. 'They didn't know about me.'

'Sorry?'

Safiyah looked up at him with those lustrous eyes and he pulled her even closer. It had been a morning of revelations and powerful emotion. He found he needed the concrete reality of his darling wife to anchor him.

'When my mother ran away with him she had no idea that I was his son. He swears that if they'd realised she'd never have left me with the Sheikh.'

Karim believed him. His father wasn't what he'd expected. A proud yet gentle man, he was a schoolteacher in a remote mountain valley, devoted to the children he looked on as his own, never knowing till recently he had a son.

'He and my mother were deeply in love, but her family ignored that and arranged her marriage with the Sheikh. A lowly trainee schoolteacher wasn't considered good enough for her. They were only together once before the wedding— one night of secret passion before a loveless marriage.'

Karim's thoughts strayed inevitably to Safiyah's dutiful marriage to Abbas. How desperate must she have felt, knowing there was no escape, giving herself as a convenient wife?

Safiyah had given him a whole new perspective on his mother. A new sympathy for a woman caught in an unwanted, unhappy marriage.

'When I was born my mother believed I was the Sheikh's son.' Karim drew a slow breath. 'According to my father...' He paused on the word, testing its newness but liking it. 'She finally left the Sheikh because her marriage broke down. Emotional abuse turned into physical abuse and she feared for her safety. But she always believed he wouldn't lay a hand on me or Ashraf as his precious heirs.'

'Oh, Karim...' Safiyah gripped him tight.

'My father didn't even know she'd run away from the palace till she came to him and they fled together over the border. They only had a year together before she died.'

'That's so sad.'

He looked down into her soft eyes. 'At least they had that.'

'You're turning into a romantic, Karim.'

He smiled, and looked at Safiyah as the shadows inside eased. 'How could I not be when I have you, *habibti*? It's all your influence.'

'And in all those years he never took another wife?'

Karim shook his head. 'Another thing my father and I have in common. It appears we're one-woman men.'

'Sweet talker.'

He pulled his beloved close and stroked his hands over the gossamer-fine silk of her dress. It shimmered, indigo blue, over her delectable curves. Inevitably he felt the familiar tug of desire and satisfaction. This woman was his life, his home—everything he wanted.

'Just stating the truth.' He moved his hands more purposefully and heard Safiyah's breath snare. Anticipation quickened his pulse. 'But they say actions speak louder than words. Perhaps I should demonstrate my feelings.'

He backed her towards the long divan by the window.

'We've got an official lunch in half an hour and—'

'Some things are more important than royal duty, my love.'

Safiyah shook her head, but she was laughing as he lowered her onto the cushions. 'You're right, Karim. Some things are.'

Then she reached for him, using those supple, clever hands so effectively that Karim forgot everything but the need to show his wife just how he felt about her.

* * * * *

COMING SOON!

We really hope you enjoyed reading this book. If you're looking for more romance, be sure to head to the shops when new books are available on

Thursday 31st October

To see which titles are coming soon, please visit

millsandboon.co.uk/nextmonth

MILLS & BOON

Coming next month

HIS CONTRACT CHRISTMAS BRIDE
Sharon Kendrick

He remembered seeing her swimming in his pool, her strong arms arcing through the turquoise water in a graceful display of strength and power. Length after length he had watched her swim and when she'd eventually surfaced and blinked droplets of water from her eyes, she had looked genuinely surprised—and pleased—to see him. He shouldn't have been turned on by her plain and practical swimsuit but he had been, though maybe because he'd never seen someone of her age wearing something so old-fashioned. Just as he shouldn't have been unexpectedly charmed by the way she made him laugh—which was rare enough to be noteworthy. He'd found himself staying on for dinner, even though he hadn't planned to—and even though he'd told himself that her dress was cheap, that hadn't stopped him from being unable to tear his eyes away from the way the dark material had clung to her fleshy curves, had it?

Maybe it was inevitable that they had started kissing—and just as inevitable that they'd ended up having sex. The unexpected and unwanted factor had been encountering her intact hymen and realising he was the first man she'd ever been intimate with. At the time he'd been irritated by the fact she hadn't told him because, according to friends who knew about such things, taking a woman's virginity brought with it all kinds of problems—not least the kind of mindless devotion which was the last thing he needed. In fact, he despised it, for reasons which still made him shudder. His mouth hardened. He had enough difficulty keeping women at arm's length as it was, without some idealistic innocent longing for rose petals and wedding bells.

But his irritation had lasted no longer than it took to resume his powerful rhythm inside her. And she had surprised him. Not just because she had proved to be an energetic and enthusiastic lover who had kissed more sweetly than any other woman he'd ever known. No. Because she seemed to have realised herself the limitations of their brief affair and to have accepted the fact that he had ghosted her from his life afterwards. She hadn't made any awkward phone calls or sent texts carefully constructed in order to appear 'casual'. And if his abundantly healthy ego had been fleetingly dented by her apparent eagerness to put what had happened behind her, the feeling had soon left him, because it was entirely mutual. But it made him realise that in many ways Lucy Phillips was exceptional. Emotionally independent, a trained midwife and, thus, the perfect candidate for what he needed…

He felt his mouth dry as he studied her earnest face and the clothes which failed to flatter her curvy shape. It was hard now to believe that she had choked out her fulfilment as he had driven into her firm body or to imagine the way he had fingered her nipples in the blazing Greek sunshine so that they had puckered into tight little nubs just ripe for sucking. But when you stopped to think about it, *all* of this was hard to believe and he needed to present his case so that she would receive it sympathetically. Rising to his feet, he addressed her stumbled question as he slowly approached her fireside chair. 'I'm telling you because I need your help, Lucy.'

'*My* help?' she echoed, her bright eyes looking up at him in surprise as his shadow enveloped her in darkness. 'Are you kidding? How on earth can I help someone like you when you're one of the richest men in the world and I have practically nothing?'

'No, I'm not kidding,' he negated firmly. 'And, far from having nothing, you have something I need very badly. Niko's baby needs security and continuity. He needs a home and I'm in a position to offer him one. But not on my own. Not as a single man whose work takes him to opposite sides of the world and who has no experience of babies, or children. And that's why I'm asking you to marry me, Lucy. To be my wife and the mother of my orphaned nephew.'

Continue reading
HIS CONTRACT CHRISTMAS BRIDE
Sharon Kendrick

Available next month
www.millsandboon.co.uk

LET'S TALK

Romance

For exclusive extracts, competitions and special offers, find us online:

- facebook.com/millsandboon
- @MillsandBoon
- @MillsandBoonUK

Get in touch on 01413 063232

For all the latest titles coming soon, visit
millsandboon.co.uk/nextmonth

MILLS & BOON

THE HEART OF ROMANCE

A ROMANCE FOR EVERY KIND OF READER

MODERN

Prepare to be swept off your feet by sophisticated, sexy and seductive heroes, in some of the world's most glamourous and romantic locations, where power and passion collide.
8 stories per month.

HISTORICAL

Escape with historical heroes from time gone by. Whether your passion is for wicked Regency Rakes, muscled Vikings or rugged Highlanders, awaken the romance of the past.
6 stories per month.

MEDICAL

Set your pulse racing with dedicated, delectable doctors in the high-pressure world of medicine, where emotions run high and passion, comfort and love are the best medicine.
6 stories per month.

True Love

Celebrate true love with tender stories of heartfelt romance, from the rush of falling in love to the joy a new baby can bring, and a focus on the emotional heart of a relationship.
8 stories per month.

Desire

Indulge in secrets and scandal, intense drama and plenty of sizzling hot action with powerful and passionate heroes who have it all: wealth, status, good looks…everything but the right woman.
6 stories per month.

HEROES

Experience all the excitement of a gripping thriller, with an intense romance at its heart. Resourceful, true-to-life women and strong, fearless men face danger and desire - a killer combination!
8 stories per month.

DARE

Sensual love stories featuring smart, sassy heroines you'd want as a best friend, and compelling intense heroes who are worthy of them.
4 stories per month.

To see which titles are coming soon, please visit

millsandboon.co.uk/nextmonth